I0785910

THE DEATH OF A SONGBIRD

MIND'S EYE: BOOK 1

M.R. MCCOY

Copyright © 2023 by M.R. McCoy

All rights reserved.

No part of this book may be reproduced in any form or by any electronic or mechanical means, including information storage and retrieval systems, without written permission from the author, except for the use of brief quotations in a book review.

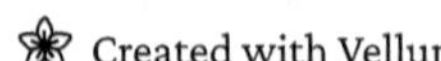 Created with Vellum

Dedicated to everyone longing to untie the knot lodged deep within their soul.

And to all those who have helped me loosen the strings.

PRACTICALLY NOTHING

Two particles of practically nothing drifted with unknown purpose through the vastness of time and space. The pair followed no set path, darting in and out of the sea of perceivable reality like dust reflecting a stream of morning sunlight. Out of this sea, it called to them. The intoxicating beat of an enigmatic drum—steady, created, full of purpose and order. The foreign beat pulsed through them, entangling their limitless potential into one immovable truth. *Break free from the confines of practically nothing.* The new purpose burned within them, casting aside age-old rules and limitations. Without warning, the two specks raced toward each other, shedding the armor of the mystical unknown for the sake of their new, fabricated purpose. In an instant, the pair collided, releasing their secrets into the cosmos.

The freed secrets engulfed reality, rewriting its laws and twisting its limits. Countless others followed, sending a chain reaction through all consciousness. Pockets of practically nothing erupted into voids of endless hunger, devouring anything in their path, determined to spread their purpose to the edge of everything. Reality fought back, desperate to stem the tide of the released secrets before they rewrote it all. For eons, they struggled as the world burned, leaving vast patches of reality trapped in the space between everything and nothing. Exhausted, humbled, and altered, reality settled into its new self. In its struggle to survive against its shattered secrets, reality left us a gift. A way to protect life from *The Hollowing* devouring our soul. A gift that would shape the new world and determine who it wished to become.

CHAPTER 1

THE TAILOR'S SON

Gerolt peered down at the anemic corpse with cold, unblinking eyes. He turned it this way and that, displeasure twisting his gaunt face into a scowl. A heavy sigh parted his lips as he slid his slender knife into its soft underbelly, emptying its entrails onto a rough wooden table. Fresh blood soaked into old stains, deepening their color and filling Gerolt's nose with a familiar metallic tinge. His deft fingers picked through the viscera—heart, liver, kidney, each one barely the size of the tip of his finger. Shaking his head he grabbed his knife, he glided it through the space between skin and muscle with one hand while pulling the hide free with the other. He flipped the meager pelt over, scraping off the fat and connective tissue until nothing but skin and fur remained.

"Mom!" he hollered as he wiped his brow with his forearm. "It's processed."

"Leave it in the bucket by my chair. I'll start the stew after I tend to your father... How's the fur?"

Gerolt pushed his lips from side to side as he ran his fingers through the rabbit's fur. "Pretty thick. Must be getting their winter coats."

A fit of dry, labored coughs filled the small log cabin. Gerolt closed his eyes and clenched his jaw, waiting for the familiar sound to fade from his irritated ears. A few calm, easy breaths filled his chest. The tightness in his jaw receded as his eyes fluttered open. A rough spun spool of hemp-thread and a stone-hammered sliver of metal settled into view. His calloused hands pushed and pulled the crude needle and thread with a rhythmic accuracy known only to a master of the craft. His mind wandered, his hands knowing the way all on their own. Soon he'd be out there again, trying to sell his useless crap to a starving, diseased, and broken city. A city long forgotten, left to rot until nothing but the dregs of society remained. He couldn't help but wonder if his able mind and body could be put to better use. It was possible that more farmable land existed out there, or even a hidden water source. If he could leave the shadow of the wall, maybe his life could amount to something.

Gerolt opened his mouth to give voice to his inner thoughts, only to be interrupted by another flurry of dry, labored coughs. His body tensed at the sharp, wheezing sound. *It's not his fault. None of this is. He's a victim of the League, just like the rest of us.* Gerolt took a calming breath to subdue the fury coursing through his veins and returned to his humble task. His mother tried to convince him that his creations brought brightness to a dark world. She didn't have to sell the useless things to crowds of people hoping beyond hope that his small travel bag would have something useful inside. If only his father would have taught him something worthwhile, given him a skill that could get him out of this god-forsaken slum. Something he could sell without feeling like a fool... Something people actually needed to improve their chances of survival.

"The last stitch is done... Guess I'll head into town."

Gerolt's mother wobbled from the backroom and plopped down into a heavy wooden rocking chair. She drifted back and forth in silence for a few moments, her cloudy eyes focused on nothing in particular. "That's wonderful dear. I'm sure you'll sell a bunch today. I have a good feeling."

Gerolt rolled his eyes and threw his travel bag over his shoulder. "Come on, Mom. You know nobody buys this crap. People barely have enough food to survive the coming winter. You think they're going to throw a hard-earned copper away on a rabbit with all the edible parts taken out of it?"

The old woman let out a sharp sigh. "You worry too much about what others think of you, Gerolt. These animals have already given their lives to prolong ours. Don't sully their contribution with your negativity." She stopped rocking her chair for a moment as if gathering her strength before continuing. "We might not have as much as those within New Geneva's walls, but we offer all we can." She paused for a moment, her feet pushing her back into a slow rock. "You should be proud."

Gerolt clenched his jaw. "Goddamnit, Mom," he forced through clenched teeth. "You expect me to be proud of this worthless shit? This slum isn't even worthy of a proper name... just three letters that don't spell a damn thing. Those assholes in the League wouldn't piss on us if we were on fire."

The gentle squeak of his mother's chair eased to a stop. Her sightless eyes looked right through him. "Mind your words, Gerolt! Degrading comments about the League? Taking the Lord's name in vain?" Gerolt held his breath for a moment before releasing it out in a huff. "If the League heard you talking like that, they'd lock you up! The last thing I need is my boy going against the ancient book of wisdom. We can't afford to lose you, Son. You're all us old folks have left!"

Gerolt set his jaw and jutted out his chin. "I'm only being realistic, and I'm not a boy anymore... Besides, do you really think the League cares about some street rat saying goddammit? I could *murder* someone out there today, and they wouldn't lift a single finger." Gerolt waited for his mother to respond, but received nothing but silence. "It's not like it matters anyway. Everyone out here is just waiting to die. Why do we keep following the rules of those elitist assholes anyway? Those bastards in the League of Fellows abandoned the LHC years ago. All they do is sit behind their fancy white walls while the useless *heathens* bleed out."

"Oh hush, Gerolt," his mother scolded as she started the soft squeak of her chair once again. "Have you forgotten that the League of Fellows saved us all? Whether we live inside those heavenly walls or not, we are still citizens of New Geneva. The League still protects us from the brutality of the mountain clans, and I'm sure it's only a matter of time before..."

"You've been nagging me about these ferocious mountain people your entire life!" Gerolt threw his hands in the air. "You think they want what we have? That they will leave their little patches of paradise to take our sacks of moldy grain, and...and animal corpses?" Gerolt shrieked as he shook his travel bag. "Or maybe we could make skilled warriors to join a clan's warband? Tell me, Mother, will the clans come for father? Scoop him up to be the next Grog the Conqueror?"

Gerolt's father sucked in a lungful of air, fueling another wave of coughing fits. Gerolt shot a glance oozing with contempt through the door of the small back room that housed the wheezing old man. His father sat on a pile of hay. Specks of blood covered his tattered pajamas. His tired, bloodshot eyes locked onto Gerolt's. Their pain and anguish pulled at his heart, saying more to Gerolt than any amount of words. Guilt cooled his racing mind.

"I'm sorry..." Gerolt eked out. His gaze dropped to the dirt floor. "I just... I work so hard...and for what? To drag my ass to the woods before the sun comes up to check our traps? Skin a few rats to turn into creepy-ass stuffed animals that *nobody* wants? My best day is when I find a rabbit. A dead rabbit, Mom... That's the highlight of my week."

"And you found one today, it seems." She paused, leaning down to grab the bucket full of rabbit parts. "We should appreciate what the Lord provides, Gerolt. Some of our neighbors would be happy with rats."

Gerolt shook his head and lifted his gaze. "Well, I'm not!" His breath was heavy and ragged.

"Gerolt." his mother said in a calming tone. "I know how hard it is for a young person with such a bright future to be stuck in a place like this." She paused, tilting her empty gaze out the window. Gerolt hadn't lived through what she had. Days filled with fear of imminent attack, of being torn from your family and taken up to the mountains by those too bloodthirsty to live in civilization. All of his memories were from after the League's Holy War. To him, the mountain clans were a defeated force, scattered into the livable pockets of the Hollowlands. How could he see the League as his saviors when he's never laid eyes on one of their members?

"It is not a sin to want happiness," she offered with a warm smile. "What young man your age doesn't have hopes and dreams?" Her tired voice wavered, her words attempting to communicate hope while drowning in despair.

"Stop it, Mom...just...stop," Gerolt ended in a whisper as warmth gathered in the corner of his eyes. "Men like me don't get to have dreams." His voice cracked as the gathering emotions threatened to pour down his cheek. Gerolt wiped them away with the hem of his sleeve. "Dreams come with power and strength. How are we supposed to get any of that living off skinny-ass rodents and their stuffed corpses?" Gerolt stopped to gather himself, the heat of his emotions cooling to an icy shell around his heart. "Why make plans that are sure to fail?"

The smile melted from his mother's face. "I'm sorry, Gerolt." Her voice was a cracked whisper, blind eyes searching her soul for what to say next. Despite all the love in her heart, words were all she could offer her son. She strained her weary mind for just the right ones. Words that would lift his spirit and send him out the door with hope in his heart. She scanned their small cabin—the masonry stove her husband so lovingly crafted brick by brick, the tightly locked trunks of hand-sawed trees that kept out the wind, the loom she used to spin hemp into tailor's string. She stopped the rhythmic push keeping her chair rocking, the entirety of her focus pouring into carefully crafted words of wisdom. "What does it mean to fail, Gerolt? Each of your hardships push you closer to the person you were meant to be."

Gerolt listened to his mother's words in silence as her chair wobbled to a complete stop. His eyes fixed intensely on the dirt by his feet. Without another word, he readjusted his travel bag and headed out the door.

Harmony gathered the last of her meat pies and tucked them into their place in her cart. Her smile widened as the savory hints of pine and rosemary hit her nose.

"Good batch today, hun?" her father asked.

Harmony pulled her hair back and pinned it into a bun on

top of her head. "Good enough to carry the family name." She smiled back.

"It's a Watson family recipe, so they better be," her father replied with a hearty laugh. "And where do you plan on selling the pride of the Watson family today?"

"Hmmm," Harmony considered. "I had pretty good luck outside the Crystal Pedestal the other day. Maybe I could try there again?"

"So soon?" her father replied. "Don't push your luck over that way. They could pay three times the price and still harbor the most complaints about three measly coppers. Besides, those elitists have enough as it is."

Harmony cocked her head to one side and put her hands on her hips. "I'm not so sure about that, Dad." Harmony's dad raised his eyebrows and waited for his daughter to continue. He always got a kick out of what she'd come up with next.

Harmony cleared her throat and dropped her arms to her side. "I mean, those girls...in the Crystal Pedestal...they might seem like they have it all, but..."

"Whoa now, slow down a tick there sweetie," her father interjected, waving his open palm in a calming motion. "It isn't wise to question the happiness of the League's precious treasures like that. You'd be lucky to find yourself in such a place—surrounded by every luxury your heart could dream of, wearing exquisite dresses and serving your wonderful food to members of the League of Fellows. Can you imagine?" Harmony's only response was the crinkling of her brow. Her father gave her a half smile. "It's a shame you have to be a hysteresis user to work for the League. I'm sure we'd triple our profits if you could sell our famous pies at the Crystal Pedestal Café."

Harmony's eyes moved to the polished wooden floorboards. "Yes, what a shame... Could have really pushed profits."

Her father responded with a light chuckle. "Profits and prestige! With that kind of clout, the merchants guild would *have* to take my bid for president seriously."

Harmony gathered her wandering thoughts back to the conversation at hand. "I suppose that's true...but then I'd have to live there, in the Crystal Pedestal. The League never lets its Maidens live outside their residence halls. Besides, we do fine out here. Good enough to have earned our family a writ of passage in and out of the city's walls."

Harmony's father looked at her with a tinge of shame in his eye. "Oh, sweetie, I didn't mean to make you feel bad about yourself. We can't be more than we were born with."

Harmony forced a smile. Nobody dug below the surface of a happy face. If she could keep her composure, this might be the moment he finally let her. "Dad?"

"Yes, hun?"

"You really got me thinking about how lucky I am to be living in the Outer Ring...and how hard it must be for those outside the walls...You know...being born with nothing and all."

Harmony's father let out a quiet sigh. "I know what this is about... You have been asking for quite some time now." Harmony waited, hands clasped together behind her back. "Your etiquette and candor have been wonderful lately; you're a true lady of purity, I'd say." His chest puffed up with pride. "I think you've proven yourself ready to take the cart outside the walls."

"Are you serious?" Harmony whispered, allowing his comment about being a lady of purity slide. "I won't let you down. You'll see. I'll bring honor and generosity to the Watson family name," she said in a louder, more confident tone.

Her father eyed her cautiously. "On three conditions. You will stock the cart with your brother's pies. He used too much baking soda, and now they taste a bit...off. While they'd offend the palette of your average citizen, those people will gobble it up like filet mignon." Harmony opened her mouth to argue. Her father met her open-mouth gaze with a finger raised to his lips. "No need to risk any damaged purity, hun. I know what you're thinking. It helps balance out the fact that we cannot sell anything for more than a single League copper out there. The people of the LHC can't afford anything more." Her father clapped his hands together before continuing. "Now that that's settled, onto my second requirement. Take a dagger with you. Hide it out of sight, but somewhere you can get to quickly. Desperate people do desperate things. And finally," he said with extra warmth, placing his large hand on her shoulder, "don't forget to maintain the proper amount of purity. I won't be out there to help hold your tongue." Harmony clenched her jaw, but settled for a heavy huff of breath out of her nose.

The edge of her father's lip curled up a bit. "That's my girl. Remember, things are... more complicated out there in the LHC."

Harmony pressed her lips together. She had a lot of thoughts about her dad's conditions, but she knew from experience that pushing her ideals now would only shut him down and ruin her chances of seeing the world outside the walls. "It's a deal."

GEROLT PUSHED his way through the gathering crowd, trying his best to be heard above hordes of others calling out wares and prices. "A copper for anything in the bag," he called unenthusiastically. "A gift your child will cherish forever..." He trailed off as his nose caught the scent of something marvelous he couldn't describe. He looked around, as if the smell was so otherworldly it could be seen drifting through the air. Gerolt melted into the crowd as streams of people lumbered towards the source of the intoxicating scent.

"One copper! One copper for one of Watson's famous meat pies!" The voice was gentle, yet confident. Soft, yet forceful.

Gerolt weaved through the gathering crowd to get a glimpse of who it was coming from. A young girl with sandy-blonde hair pinned on top of her head stood behind a small cart. Gerolt watched as she handed out pies to aching stomachs. As he moved up the line more of her came into focus. Soon he was close enough to see into her hazel eyes. There was a spark to them that he hadn't seen before. A spark which grew with each passing of a pie. He felt himself being tugged closer and closer to the front of the line. The twinkle in her eye left his mouth dry as cotton. His mind struggled to unearth the pang of longing growing in his chest.

"That's dirt cheap for such a wonderful smelling pie, wouldn't you say?" Gerolt found his mouth saying without asking his brain permission first. He rubbed the back of his neck, unable to pry his gaze from those bright hazel eyes. "So, what's the catch? Does it have spice in it? Going to get me addicted?" Gerolt winced as the words left his lips.

The young woman looked at him with a bit of a smirk. "Spice? As in the stuff that stains your teeth and melts your brain?"

Gerolt scoffed at her naivety, but found her innocence refreshing. "Not from around here, are you?"

Harmony scrunched her brow. "And why would you say that?"

Gerolt readjusted his bag and gestured to her cart. "Well, that cart for starters. That thing is practically brand new and looks like oak. And these pies, they smell so..." Gerolt brought the tips of his fingers up to his lips and gave them an exaggerated kiss, "Mwha!"

Her gaze lingered on his. Warmth kept up Gerolt's cheeks. "Hey, hurry it up, would ya! We haven't got all day!" A man cried towards the back of the line.

"I'm sorry, sir! There should be plenty for everyone, so don't you worry!" Harmony called back, keeping her attention on Gerolt. "So, you want one?"

"Who wouldn't? I mean, look at all these smiles leaving your cart." Gerolt jingled the two coppers to his name in his pocket, hoping to find a third. "It's just..." Gerolt cleared his throat. "I have some other shopping to do. You know how parents can be." Gerolt's gaze dropped to the ground.

Harmony looked from Gerolt to the decayed state of the world around her. Seconds felt like an eternity. Gerolt drew in breath to excuse himself.

"I'll tell you what," Harmony replied, her ears keenly aware of the small amount of copper she heard in Gerolt's pocket. "First one is on me. And not only that." She picked up one of the meat pies and closed her eyes for the briefest of moments. "I'll give you my very best creation."

Gerolt raised his head, unable to resist her soothing voice. The overwhelming scent of freshly cooked pork blended with notes of evergreen. The flavors floated from her palm, her kind hazel eyes locked onto his. His mouth begged for a taste, but he wanted more than the pie. How was he supposed to impress a girl if he couldn't afford sparing a single copper?

"So, it's charity now, is it?" Gerolt stumbled over the words, horrified with himself for uttering them.

Harmony tilted her head to one side. "I mean, I guess...but think of it more as a gift."

"A gift. How is that different from charity?" Gerolt punished himself internally for lingering on the subject.

Charity had always been a way the elite would look down their noses at the trash the League left behind in the LHC. He could sense that this young woman was different. Still, he couldn't help his years of conditioning from butting their way in.

Harmony peered at the growing line of people behind Gerolt, and then at the bag he wore over his shoulder. "What's in the bag, then? Maybe we could trade?"

Red crept into Gerolt's face as he cursed his foolish pride. "I...don't think you'd want anything I have..."

"Try me."

Gerolt slipped the bag off his shoulder and looked from side to side before opening it for Harmony. "See, I told you..."

"Cute! Did you make all these yourself? I've never seen such a thing. I especially love the rabbit."

It took a moment for the words to register to Gerolt's ears. The beginnings of a grin snuck onto his gloomy face. "They're mostly for children. Although those are hard to find around here nowadays. Not sure what an adult would do with such a thing."

Without a moment's hesitation Harmony reached into the bag and pulled out the stuffed rabbit. "Adults like soft things too, you know." She gave the rabbit a gentle squeeze with her hands before tucking it into her cart. "There, now you have to take one of my pies."

"Actually...can I take three?"

GEROLT WALKED HOME with an extra spring in his step. Not only had someone liked one of his creations, but his family would have the best meal they had eaten in months, maybe ever. The meat was indescribable, a far cry from the stringy vermin he was used to catching in the nearby woods. And the flavors!

Woven together like the different parts of a catchy song. Each layer complementing the next. Hours later the flavors still swirled around his tongue. He dreaded the thought of his next meal, hoping to linger on the flavors she had gifted him forever.

CHAPTER 2

THE WINDS OF CHANGE

Gerolt lay awake in his bed, unable to shake the girl with the cart from his mind. Her kind eyes, the messy bun of hair perched on top of her head, the smell of her meat pies drifting through the air...but there was something more than that. Something that kept him tossing and turning. She had liked his stuffed rabbit. Liked it enough to offer one of those mouthwatering pies in exchange. Sure, she was willing to give it to him for free, but she seemed genuinely impressed with his craftsmanship. Something about the way she looked at that rabbit made him feel like he had earned the pie she gave him. That night, tossing and turning in his lumpy straw bed, Gerolt made himself a promise. He would find that girl again someday, and thank her for her kindness.

Weeks went by, and Gerolt had yet to see the girl with the cart again. He began to think that finding her had been a fluke. Nobody with clothes that nice and hair that clean would make selling underpriced, high-quality food a regular gig some-where like the LHC. The more he thought about it, the less sense her presence made. Young people were quite rare in the

LHC, and he would certainly remember a girl like her if he'd seen her before. Not only that, but if those meat pies were a regular thing, they would have gathered a reputation by now, especially if they were still being sold for a single copper. Gerolt was certain she must have come from inside the walls. There was no other logical explanation.

But why would a girl from inside the walls venture out to the LHC? And why would she be selling food for such exuberantly low prices? Gerolt couldn't make heads or tails out of it, but he also couldn't get her out of his head. The confidence she gave him allowed him to sell a few of his stuffed animals, but nowhere near what he would need to buy a writ of passage into New Geneva. If he was going to see her again, he'd have to find another way.

HARMONY LOOKED at her father with defiance in her eyes. "Those people need our meat pies more than anyone! Why can't I sell to them again?"

"That would require you to be *selling* them in the first place. A charity day every now and then is one thing, but doing it on a regular basis..." Harmony glared up at her father, but kept her thoughts to herself. "Look, I know that helping those people means a lot to you. We can't afford to give quality products away like that. Watson's pies are a luxury, even in the outer-ring." Harmony's father stopped, tapping his finger on his chin thoughtfully. "Harmony?" His tone shifted from sharp staccato to tender inquiry. Harmony dropped her scowl, but held her tongue. "How many other merchants would you say were out there...giving charity?"

Harmony thought back to her day beyond the wall. Her mind lingering on a pair of bright blue eyes. She shook her head and focused on the other details. She could never let her father know about the boy from the LHC. She recalled the endless stretch of tents, small log cabins, and the meandering dirt paths that wove through them. She remembered the lines of people, faces covered in dirt, most of them burdened with some sort of disease or ailment. A few merchants were present at the city square where she had set up shop herself, but none of them looked like a quality merchant from the interior. "I think...just us, Father," she responded, her tone dropping to a mere breath.

The two sat in silence, toiling away at their own inner dialogues. Harmony puffed up her chest, determined to make her point heard. "That's why we have to—"

"I'm worried that..." her father interrupted. "You go first."

Harmony took a deep breath and steadied her resolve. "Those people need us, Dad." Her father crossed his arms, but resigned himself to listen. "The young man...the one who traded me for the rabbit..."

"That wonky looking thing?" her father blurted. Harmony pursed her lips and glared at her father. "Oh, sorry," he hurried to express when he saw the gleam of hurt in her eyes. "Please, continue."

"The rabbit is not the issue here... The young man, however...he... Something about him felt heavier than the rest."

Her father gave a knowing nod. "It's because he's young," her father offered.

"No, it's more than that," Harmony corrected. Her father's nod turned into a confused frown. "It's true that he was one of only a handful of people my age... Nobody else out there was *doing* anything... They all just..."

"Exist?" Her father paused for a moment, considering his daughter's gentle heart against the harshness of the world beyond the walls. "Those people...they're broken. The League might be powerful enough to keep the mountain clans away, but they can't work miracles. As powerful as hysteresis is, it can never be used on human flesh and blood. As beings created in god's image..."

"We deserve more than a slow death," Harmony finished in a hushed tone.

"What was that?"

"Nothing..."

"We were getting off track anyway. Back to the point. I don't think you should be selling out there anymore."

Harmony flared her nostrils to suppress the air flooding her chest. "*Why?*" she blurted as tears tugged at the corners of her eyes.

"It's nothing against those poor folk. We just can't afford to besmirch the Watson family name by being the only ones out there doing charity. People will start to think we *need* those people for business. It sends the wrong message."

Harmony worked her jaw and flexed her fingers. "It sends the wrong message? And what message is that? That there are people who still feed those who are hungry and can't feed themselves? That the proud Watson family has a heart for something other than profits?"

"Now, hun. You know..."

"Enough with the 'huns,' Dad. I'm a grown woman, and the reason your pies are as famous as they are..." Harmony's aggressive tone dissipated into nothing.

Her father crossed his arms and tightened his expression. "How do you figure that? Seeing as the recipe has been in the Watson family for over twenty years... How old are you again? Twenty-two? Did you create our treasured family recipe when you were a toddler?" Shame and anger fought for supremacy in Harmony's mind, her father's words adding a third voice to the chaos. "I didn't think so.... Now, I will tell you what's going to happen. If you can convince at least four other *notable* merchants to join you, I'll allow you to give charity outside the wall once a month."

The pause in her father's rant broke Harmony free of her inner battle. "Four other merchants? You know they won't listen to me."

"And why is that?"

A bit of heat began to creep back into Harmony's somber mood. "You're going to make me say it?" Harmony's father shrugged his shoulders and eyebrows in unison. "Fine... You know none of the merchant heads will listen to anything a woman has to say in matters of business, let alone a *young* woman."

Her father rolled his eyes. "Oh, come now, Harmony. The League's book of wisdom says nothing about men *ignoring* women. On the contrary, we are to treat you as precious jewels, are we not?"

Harmony cringed at the words "precious jewels." "I think we have a different definition of what makes something precious, Father."

"Well then, enlighten me," her father replied. The patience and warm candor of his tone all but evaporated.

A deeper part of Harmony's mind took over, answering without dulling her opinion like she normally had to resort to. "Everyone acts like being a precious jewel means being shiny and bright, or something."

Her father raised his brow and pursed his lips, but allowed his daughter to continue. "Women are only loved for their appearance and charm. Nobody cares about their leadership, ideas, or influence over the way things should be." Her father peered at her out of the corner of his eye as the edges of his mouth sloped downward. "I mean, don't you think it's strange that there are certain things you are not allowed to teach me?

Entire categories of thought that the League of Fellows has decided I don't have the right organs to comprehend?" The words hung in the air like they had achieved physical form.

Harmony's father looked off into the corner of the room. His mind weighing the consequences of the paths set before him. "Perhaps it's time for your little brother to take over cart duties. You can go back to helping Ma in the kitchen. You're best at that anyway."

"What? No!" Harmony blurted out with more force than intended. She had said too much to back down now. "You know how much I love the cart. Seeing all the people, watching the joy on their faces as they take their first bite of my pies."

"*Your* pies?" Her father turned to face her. "You mean Watson Family pies. Whose name is on the deed to this respectable, family-owned business? *Mine.* That would make *any* pie you create *my* pie."

Harmony balled up her fists, shaking with rage. She had worked too hard to let it all slip through her fingers now. "No, not your pies!" Her father's expression softened out of mere shock. Still, Harmony pushed on. "Your pies were mediocre. Run of the mill meat pies, nothing more. *I* made them into something more. *I* am what made them famous, and *I* am what earned us that writ of passage you so callously keep from me."

Intensity returned to her father's face, twisting in ways Harmony had never seen. "What are you going on about? Have you completely lost it? Talking to your father in such a way!"

Harmony let her rage fall to a simmer. She had let her bottled emotions get the better of her—spoken her deepest thoughts. Despite the tense situation these thoughts had led her too, it felt too good to stop now. She was a full grown woman. It was time to be something more than her father's little helper. "I'm a hysteresis user, Dad. Have been since I was little."

Her father's face contorted with rage. "You're what? A hysteresis user?" He scanned the room, eyes darting about like a predator on the prowl. "Prove it!" He hollered as he snatched a loaf of bread off a nearby counter and tossed it in her direction.

Harmony bobbled the bread, but latched on tight and held it to her chest. "Fine," she seethed as she retreated into her mind's eye.

It felt strange to do an act in the open that she had hidden for so long, like standing naked in front of a gawking crowd. She couldn't focus on that right now, though. The gift wouldn't allow it. Hysteresis only worked when she calmed her mind. Found that piece of herself that knew she was more than the world allowed her to be. She thought of the pine trees that lined the streets of the Outer Ring, her sole tie to nature in the sleek, modern city owned by the League of Fellows. Their woodsy scent brought about memories of the days she played hide and seek in the endless forests outside the walls. Before the League had sealed them off. She thought of the evergreen bushes with the pink, blue, and purple flowers. Packed with the flavors of citrus, lavender, pine, sage, pepper, and mint. All of these flavors, scents, and memories swirled within her, flowing from mind to matter, from knowledge to flavor, from thought to bread.

With a defiant jut of her chin, Harmony offered the bread back to her father. As soon as the bread hit his tongue, his eyes bulged with rage.

～

"WE WON'T SURVIVE the winter if I don't," Gerolt replied to the growing concern etched into his mother's face. "They might be able to help Dad with..."

"I don't want any help from those heathens," his father forced out before falling into another one of his coughing fits.

Gerolt turned to address his father, but thought better of it when the old man couldn't even keep his head up right. "You'd rather sit here as Dad deteriorates right in front of us?" Gerolt directed at his mother. "At least this way, we have a shot. What were you telling me this morning? Something about even failed plans bringing us closer to who we are supposed to be?"

"Those monsters defile the body, our temple for honoring God. Not to mention that they experiment in illegal forms of hysteresis. And you want to offer yourself to them? And for what? a few more years with a blind, decrepit mother and dying father? These are not the sort of plans to help you find yourself, Gerolt."

Gerolt's eyes darted from one parent to the other. Visions of the girl selling her meat pies danced in his mind. The genuine smile she wore. The kindness that emanated from her as she looked into the eyes of the forgotten. He had felt different that day, even if just for a moment. He couldn't tell them it was for her. How could he? They would never understand.

"What else do I have but my health and my youth? If I stay here doing nothing for much longer, I won't even have those! You want me to stay here, scraping by to survive, just to end up like the two of you!"

His last sentence leaked from his consciousness and into the shared reality between them. His mother's gaze never wavered. Her cloudy eyes held a firm resolve that Gerolt hadn't seen in years. "I hope you've at least thought things through, Gerolt. The Scrive Masters might be sub-human monstrosities, but they are no fools..." Gerolt's mother slouched into her rocking chair. "I cannot stop you, Son. Just...don't throw their dice. Promise me that much at least."

Gerolt clenched his jaw and slowed his breath. "I...I can't do that, Mother. If I go to them, I won't be taking no for an answer..." Gerolt watched as the last of his mother's resolve melted into her chair alongside her soft, frail body. "Trust me, Mother. I have a plan."

GEROLT STOOD OUTSIDE THE TAVERN. His mind did its best to convince his body to head inside. *This is the only card you have left to play... Besides, what do I have to lose? Nothing can be worse than watching the last sparks of life evaporate from my parent's eyes as we all starve to death.* Gerolt took one last steading breath before pushing past the swinging double doors of the tavern.

"I'm here to see the Scrive Master," he announced with as much confidence as he could muster.

A soft chuckle echoed through the nearly empty tavern. "A little early in the day for throwing in the towel, don't ya think, lad? The pock-faced barkeep smirked at Gerolt as he caressed the tarnished bar with an even dirtier rag. Gerolt stood like a statue, cool blue eyes steeled in their resolve.

"That desperate, huh? Well, It's not like me to turn down business." The barkeep set his dirty rag aside and walked over to the cellar doors. "Make sure you at least get what you came for," he added before giving the musty doors a good pounding. "Oy! Scrive Master! You've got a customer!"

A few moments later, a crippled figure shambled through the dust of the cellar door. Gerolt squinted as the early morning light illuminated a patchwork of a face. "A little early for a game, boy," the Scrive Master offered as he moved closer to Gerolt. "Not that I'm complaining, mind you. It's been quite some time since I've gotten my hands on such...youth." The ominous figure shuffled around Gerolt, observing him from all sides. "Decent muscle structure. Straight spine. How's your teeth?" Gerolt pulled back his lips. "Not a spice user, I see. So, tell me lad. What brings you to my humble abode?"

Gerolt took a deep breath, playing his plan out in his head. "I need a writ of passage."

"Oh, is that all? Only the hardest piece of parchment to come by. You want some Purity Maidens hanging off your arms as well?" The Scrive Master scoffed as he stopped shuffling and stood eye to eye with Gerolt.

"No, nothing like that. Just...passage into the city."

"Well, a writ of passage and passage into the city are two entirely different things, boy. Most who request such things don't plan on returning to this hell hole. A one way ticket is much cheaper."

Gerolt stopped to consider the Scrive Master's words. His parents withered faces pulled at the back of his mind. "I still have business here."

The Scrive Master put up a calloused hand. The long sleeves of his dark robe slid down, revealing dozens of irregular, jagged stitches up and down his arms. "No need to be defensive, young one." The Scrive Master lowered his hand, keeping his eyes locked onto Gerolt's. "So, what are you offering in exchange? Or...were you planning to play a game?"

"No!" Gerolt said with more force than he intended. "No game," he repeated in a calmer tone.

"Hmm," grunted the Scrive Master. "So, you think you have something that I desire, do you? Something of equal value to me as a writ of passage is to you?" The Scrive master took an additional step towards Gerolt. "Tell me, what do you think I need so desperately?"

Gerolt reached down and grabbed the Scrive Master's hand, pulling back his robes to reveal his scar-ravaged arm. "These stitches. They are too far apart." He turned the shriveled arm around in his hand. "And the string...it's too thick. It's no wonder the wounds are getting infected."

The Scrive Master pulled his arm from Gerolt's grasp. "There are plenty who can pull flesh together with string...but few who can do so with skill, and even fewer who are willing to do it on a living subject." Now it was the Scrive Master's turn to grab Gerolt's hand, turning it palm up in his. He ran a finger along the callouses on Gerolt's fingertips. "So, you're a tailor, huh? Your kind has come here before. I'm not interested. Tailors don't have the stomach. Besides, flesh is a much different beast than that flimsy fabric you all work with."

"I'm not a tailor," Gerolt said as he pulled his hand free and swung his travel bag off his shoulder. "I make these." Gerolt opened the bag to reveal half a dozen of his completed stuffed animals. Each one stitched back together with such precision and care that even the Scrive Master couldn't tell where the stitch had been placed.

"Interesting..." the Scrive Master whispered as he ran his bony finger through a stuffed rat's fur. "It's a much different thing to do on a human. Skilled or not, if you don't have the stomach then you are useless to me." Gerolt cinched the bag closed and threw it back over his shoulder.

A wry smile stretched across the Scrive Master's face. "I tell you what," he sneered as he dropped his heavy robes to the floor. Scars of every shape and size littered the Scrive Master's body. Gerolt held his breath as the pungent stench of body odor, dried sweat, and decaying flesh filled his nostrils. Several of the older cuts were infected, oozing different shades of milky liquid. "You cut, clean, and re-stitch each of my...what should I call them..." he wondered aloud as he traced a few of the worst botch jobs with a bony finger. "Body expeditions," he continued with a wry grin. "If your work pleases me, I'll get you your precious writ of passage."

Gerolt took in the grotesque sight of the Scrive Master's body. Stitches ran up and down it like railroad tracks; lining every muscle, centered over every organ. Patches of different-colored skin sat in stretched out squares over areas of his back, neck, and chest. Gerolt swallowed a gathering lump in his throat and nodded.

The Scrive Master frowned. "Bar keep, we'll need a clean knife and several bottles of your cheapest swill."

CHAPTER 3
OUTCASTS

"I already reported your gift to the League. You will cooperate with their assessment and that's final!" Harmony's father bellowed. "Do you have any idea how much easier life would have been for us had you not kept this secret all these years?" He paused, catching his breath and collecting his thoughts. "You think you have what it takes to lead this family, to be of influence to the other merchants? You can't even be honest with yourself! Skulking around, hiding lucrative secrets, plotting to take over the business."

Harmony gasped. "Are you serious right now? Skulking around? You talk like I've been planning a coup!" Her father raised his bushy eyebrows and tossed up his hands. "That's really how you see this, isn't it?" Harmony scoffed, pushing her tongue against her teeth. "I'm only a girl to you, aren't I? A pretty little..."

Harmony's pain-filled response was cut short by the firm grasp of her father's hand around her throat. The painful words she ached to express were forced deep within as she gasped for air.

"Enough!" he hissed before releasing his grip. A bit of shame mixed in with the fury painted across his face. Harmony's lungs burned as she sucked in a few wheezy breaths. "You think I want to treat you like this?" her father complained as he turned his back. "You've already proven that I can no longer trust you with the cart, and now I find out you've been lying to our faces all these years."

Harmony's father stood tall and firm, his arms clasped behind his back, refusing to face his daughter. "The Crystal Pedestal Café is the best possible place for you now. The League will watch over you, make sure your gift is put to good use." Harmony held her hand to her throat. Her eyes wide and flowing with tears. "Pack your things. They will come to test your gift. As soon as it is confirmed, you will officially become a Purity Maiden."

Harmony opened her mouth to respond, but nothing but silent grief found its way out. She always wondered what would happen if her father found out her secret. Part of her thought he would be proud. That he'd proclaim her as the leader of the family she had always been. Instead, he turned his back on her, selling her talents to a group of men who saw her as nothing more than a treasure to be polished, refined, and cut as they saw fit.

Harmony closed her eyes and let the anger that clouded her sharp mind fade to the background. She knew that lashing out at her father would do nothing but make her look like the sullen child he would attempt to paint her as. She wouldn't give him that card to play. "So..." she said in a calm, collected tone. "I'm to trade one controlling father for a host of them?"

"Watch your..."

"Watch my what, Father? My tone? My Tongue? My humanity? My hopes and dreams? The very air I breathe?" She clutched her throat. "Which one should I stifle this time?"

Her father kept his back to her. His voice dropped, settling into a calm yet complacent monotone. "Don't sully our final moments together with your...*impurity.*"

Harmony seethed at the word. Purity. It was the calling card of the League of Fellows. The primary attribute that defined every rule she would soon need to live by. "Any hope for a pleasant *final moment* left the moment you wrapped your fingers around my throat."

A firm knock at the door saved the pair from any further discussion. Harmony's father straightened his collar and brushed the front of his shirt before heading to the door. "They will assess you for purity as much as your gift, Daughter. For your own sake, don't show them the same disrespect you've shown me."

Harmony glared at her father's back as he moved to open the door. "Greetings esteemed League member! Please, do come in." Harmony's father ushered their guest in with a smile and a bow.

"Thank you, Mr. Watson. What a lovely home you have. I love what you've done with the molding." Mr. Watson opened his mouth to gush about his home design, but he had his exuberance cut short. "Now, tell me. Where is the little lady?"

"Oh, yes. Well, she's actually right here, sir."

"You can address me as Provider Oscar."

"Provider you say? I was expecting a League Father or at least an apprentice."

"League Fathers cannot be bothered by such trivial matters. Providers, such as myself, are tasked with managing the Maidens' daily activities. I assure you, I am more than sufficient for such a simple task. Speaking of expectations, we normally assess *young* girls. Why did you wait so long to alert the League to her gift?"

Harmony's father cleared his throat. "Ah, yes...you see, we just recently discovered..."

"Not possible, Mr. Watson. The gift *always* shows up within the first five years of life with the females. And this one is clearly past such an age."

"Mr. Oscar... Provider... Forgive me, Provider Oscar. I assure you. We had no idea..."

"Oh, I know, Mr. Watson. I've seen this sort of thing once or twice before. A gifted young girl chooses to hide her gift from her family, using it for her own personal advantage instead of sharing it for the greater good of New Geneva. While I have never understood such *selfish* behavior, the League of Fellows has ways of treating such mentalities." Provider Oscar scanned Harmony from top to bottom. "I'm afraid this one will need extensive purity lessons before we can allow her to serve in the cafe. That is where her skills and knowledge reside, do they not?"

"Yes, that is correct, Provider Oscar."

"And you haven't taught her anything outside of the League's approved list?"

"Well...we were not aware of her gift...but we have not provided her with any knowledge that would break the Hysteresis Code, I assure you."

Provider Oscar stroked his bare chin. "We'll have to do some digging to ensure you have not. We can't have our treasured Purity Maidens defiled by knowledge not meant for the female mind, now can we?"

"Excuse me?" Harmony interjected as her father's eyes bulged from his skull. "And exactly what sort of knowledge would 'defile a female mind?'?"

"Harmony! Don't talk back to a member of the League of Fellows!" her father scolded.

Provider Oscar put up his hand. "It's okay, Mr. Watson. We

can't expect one who has withheld their gift from us for so long to understand all of our ways so easily. But don't you worry. A few fancy dresses, a lavish dinner, and a night in our luxurious accommodations will change her tune. But, before all that...we need to see that she indeed has the gift."

Provider Oscar reached into his front suit pocket and pulled out his handkerchief. Wrapped inside the silk rag sat a meat pie. "This is the cheapest one I could find on my way here. If you really are the reason these drab pies have become so popular... Show me."

Harmony glanced over at her father, whose face had turned red as a turnup. She smirked as she retreated into her mind's-eye—to the place where she held her knowledge of the subtle, yet distinct flavors she regularly injected into the meat pies. She lingered there, making sure to leave no doubt that she was the one responsible for their family's ascent to greatness. If her future was taken from her, she would at least get the credit her years of hard work deserved.

Pleased with her work, Harmony plopped the pie into Provider Oscar's outstretched hand. He brought it to his nose and took a whiff. "Pleasant enough," he muttered as he pulled back his lips for a small bite. "Hmm," he droned as he pushed the meager bite around his mouth. "It has improved...but you are clearly self-taught... The flavor profile is quite drab compared to what we offer in the cafe. But that is to be expected of a Maiden who has yet to be trained by the League."

Harmony tucked her lips into her mouth. She wanted to say how such *drab* flavors had elevated her family's company across the whole of the outer-ring, but she knew it would fall on deaf ears. This man would never give her the satisfaction of a job well done. He was too concerned with keeping her within the League's strict set of rules. Harmony's stomach churned at the thought of an entire life lived under such haughty oversight.

"So, you'll take her on as a Purity Maiden?" her father asked after a brief moment of silence.

Provider Oscar sighed. "Of course. It is in our solemn duty to oversee the purity of every female hysteresis user...no matter the *quality.*" Provider Oscar smirked as he watched Harmony struggle to contain her rage. "A carriage will come tonight to pick up the girl. She need not pack. The League will provide everything she needs. Take this time to say your goodbyes. Now, if you don't mind, I have to get back to the Crystal Pedestal. The Maidens in my charge need my constant eye to ensure League standards are being met." With a tip of his overly tall hat, Provider Oscar handed a small parchment to Harmony's father and saw himself out.

Harmony glared at her father, waiting for him to meet her eyes. "Will Mom and Peter be home before I go? I want to say goodbye at least."

"Your mother is training Peter to take over cart duties by the south wall."

"The south wall? That's all the way on the other side of the outer-ring!"

"Then you best hurry. Provider Oscar will be here at dusk to escort you to your new home.

THE SUN CREPT CLOSER to the horizon, casting long shadows over the already dark alley Gerolt found himself wandering through. Images of the last few hours played through his mind like a horror slideshow.

A nicked vein sprayed his tattered clothes with a warm streak of dark red blood.

A pocket of infection burst free of its fleshy cage, oozing over his hands.

A needle darted in and out of the carnage, teetering between maintaining quality and sanity.

Gerolt watched it all unfold a second time, breathless and shaken. He looked down at his bloodstained hands, then to the thick parchment held tightly in their grasp. The first part of his plan had been a success, so why did he feel so defeated? His mind searched to recall the next step of his plan amongst the reel of horror that continued to loop in his mind.

"Geez! Watch where... Hey, wait a second...are you...okay?"

Gerolt rubbed his head as he searched for the source of the sudden impact. The voice sounded familiar. Gentle, yet confident. Soft, yet forceful. Gerolt froze as his eyes locked onto hers. His mouth hung open as he considered whether to greet her or rush to hide his rather suspicious appearance.

"You're the guy who makes the stuffed animals, right? Is that where all that blood came from?"

Gerolt shook his head free of the stasis he had been locked in. Shame filled the void as he rushed to explain. "Oh...sorry, no, it's not from that..." he managed as his newly acquired writ of passage crinkled in his loosened grip.

"Is that...a writ of passage?" Harmony asked as her eyes took in the full array of violence displayed on Gerolt's tattered clothes. "Those are quite hard to come by..."

Gerolt instinctively tucked the paper behind his back. "I, uh, was getting ready to use it to enter the city... I'm still outside the walls...right?"

Harmony took a cautious step back. "Yes, this is still the LHC... Are you okay? You don't look so good."

Gerolt slid his back down a nearby wall and sank to the ground. "I...I did some work for a Scrive Master," he admitted as his eyes glossed over. "I didn't have any other way...but now here you are. Right in front of me...in the LHC."

Harmony's face softened as she took a few steps forward and knelt by Gerolt's side. "A Scrive Master? You mean the outcast hysteresis users who experiment on themselves? Wait...were you looking for *me*?"

Clarity shot through Gerolt's sluggish mind as he replayed his last words. He let out a slow, gentle stream of air. "Pathetic, right? Going through all of that to see a stranger again." Gerolt paused to consider his next words. He thought he'd have more time to prepare before meeting again, but here she was, squatting by his side despite the crime scene of violence displayed all over his body. "I...never did catch your name."

"It's Harmony." Her hand drifted to Gerolt's shoulder. "And yours?"

Gerolt lifted his head as he felt her warm hand cup his sagging shoulder. "Gerolt."

"It's good to see you again, Gerolt. But, I have to ask... What happened to you, and why were you looking for me?"

Gerolt stared into Harmony's clear, unflinching eyes. Over the past few weeks he had gone over the words he would say to her when they met again. All of them felt forced and wrong. None of his plans had him lying in the alley, covered in a Scrive Master's bodily fluids. "Those meat pies..." Gerolt stopped, knowing full well that nobody made a deal with a Scrive Master for a single meal, no matter how mesmerizing the flavors were. Harmony sat up a little straighter waiting for him to finish. Gerolt took a deep inhale, mustering up his courage. "I've never had anyone talk to me like that...like my life meant something. Like..."

"Like maybe all of your hard work wasn't worthless?" Harmony offered.

"Yes!" Gerolt exclaimed in a rush. "I'm sure it's hard for a successful young woman such as yourself to imagine, but it's brutal out here." Gerolt stopped, shifting away from the road of self-pity he had become so accustomed to over the years. "So, why are you out here? It's much too late to be selling anything, and I don't see your cart."

Harmony wiped her hands on her apron before standing to her feet. She couldn't tell him she was running from the League of Fellows. That she was a hysteresis user who had hidden her ability for years. An impure woman on the run from those who would force her to submit to their will. Harmony held out her hand, helping Gerolt to his feet.

"I thought I was making a difference. On my path to being the first woman to become a leader in the Merchants Guild. I thought I had the spark..." Harmony stopped to wipe a tear from her cheek. "The spark needed to make some real change."

"Change?" Gerolt echoed. "What sort of change?"

Harmony took a few moments to respond, not realizing that Gerolt was still waiting patiently for her to continue. She let out a short huff of air. "I know things are horrid here...in the LHC... and that I should have been more thankful for what I had living within the walls...but...the League... Their cruelty does not start outside the walls. It is in full force within them as well."

"What do you mean?" Gerolt prodded, his face twisting in concern.

Harmony glanced up at the sky. Half the sun had already dropped beyond the horizon. "They will be looking for me soon. I have to go. I'm a bit safer outside the walls, but it's only a matter of time before..."

"Safer outside the walls? Are you nuts? No offense or anything, but I don't think you realize what it's like out here."

Harmony turned her attention back towards Gerolt. His concerned brow hovered over a pair of sharp blue eyes. "It doesn't matter," she muttered, turning back towards the setting sun. "I lied to the League of Fellows. I lied to my family. There is nothing for me in those walls anymore."

Gerolt's heart leaped in his chest. He never dreamed things would go this way. "You can stay with me, I mean my family, if you'd like. We don't have much, but at least it's a roof over your head."

Harmony faced Gerolt once more, her gaze burrowing into his. "You mean it? You'd hide me from the League? But...why?"

Gerolt shrugged. "Why not? What's the League going to do to me? My life is already forfeit as far as they are concerned, and I have nothing worth taking."

Harmony put a hand on each of Gerolt's shoulders, squaring her face up with his. "The League of Fellows might have forgotten about its citizens outside the walls, but having their attention is vastly overrated..." Harmony dropped her arms from Gerolt's shoulders and sank alongside him. "Especially if you happen to be a woman."

Gerolt placed his blood-stained hand on top of Harmony's. "I've heard rumors about that... That the League's book of wisdom prevents women from holding positions of leadership or owning land outside of marriage."

"That's only scratching the surface. Women aren't even allowed to *learn* certain things. When the League came to assess me..."

"I'm sorry, assess you?" Harmony's eyes widened, darting from Gerolt, to his filthy clothes, to her hand touching his. Her free hand drifted up to her throat. Gerolt felt his own anxiety rising up. "Sorry... I didn't mean to pry."

Harmony stopped rubbing her throat and shook off her shocked expression. "No, I'm sorry. You've offered to take me in. You deserve to know the truth." Harmony took a deep breath. "I'm a hysteresis user." Gerolt's jaw dropped, stammering for words. "I hid it from everyone. When the League found out, they sent one of their Providers to test me... I was too blinded by my anger—too desperate to prove my worth to my father."

"But, why? Why hide such an amazing gift?"

Harmony dropped Gerolt's hand and turned towards the last sliver of sunlight dropping quickly behind them. "It's not a gift for people like me. Women, that is. As soon as your gift is discovered they take you away, never to see your family again."

"But you get to live and work in the Crystal Pedestal, right? I've always heard that place is bursting at the seams with New Geneva's elite. Packed with every luxury one could imagine."

"It is."

"Then what's the problem? Sounds like heaven to me."

"It's hard to explain... Especially since I've never actually set foot inside the place. Only sold meat pies outside its doors. All I know is they don't let you be yourself in that place. They control what you eat, who you spend time with, and even what you're allowed to learn." Harmony paused as she felt the familiar pulse of justice rising up within her. "I'm not some treasure to polish, some being of *purity* to dote over and control. I want more than that for my life. I want people to..."

"See the real you?" Gerolt asked, his hand returning to hers. Harmony stopped her rant. Warmth tugged at the corners of her eyes.

"I saw it," Gerolt said. "It was only a glimpse, but it's what pushed me to find you again. I saw it in your eyes as you handed out meat pies for a fraction of their worth. I felt it when you found a way to make a trade with a foolish boy who was too proud to take your charity. I tasted it in your food— flavors that had to come from something...more."

Harmony gave Gerolt's hand a gentle squeeze, unable to give voice to the emotions swirling through her head. Gerolt let his head drop. "I'm sorry... I'm sure the last thing a woman like you wants is hearing invasive observations from a filth-covered stranger."

Harmony shook her head. "Just..." she muttered as she closed her eyes, pushing the gathering tears down her cheeks, "take me home."

Gerolt and Harmony walked hand in hand down the twisting dirt pathways of the LHC. The trails seemed to have a mind of their own, looping around sections of tents before spreading out to accommodate a few larger establishments. "That's the tavern there, and that one used to be the Merchant's Guild. Nothing but rotting boards and people sleeping off spice there now.

Harmony watched the last of the sun dip over the horizon, giving full ownership of the sky to a sliver of a moon. Her heart still longed to see her mother and brother one last time, but she couldn't risk being seen in the city anymore. It was bad enough that she had hidden her gift from the League, but now she had run from them, too. She knew that living with a man she was not married to would bring more condemnation down on her, but it hardly seemed to matter now. She had become a fugitive.

"Gerolt..." Harmony eked out.

"Yes, Harmony?

"Maybe it's best if you find me somewhere else to hide. I can take care of myself, and I wouldn't want to get you and your family into any trouble.

Gerolt set his jaw and tightened his grip on her hand. "Listen. Those bastards don't really come around here. They've forgotten about us. Besides, the LHC is no place to be hiding out alone. Especially for a pretty girl."

Harmony pulled her hand away for a moment before slipping it back into Gerolt's. "Sorry...I really hate that word...*pretty*. Other than my cooking, it's the only praise my father ever gave me. Almost as if what I looked like overshadowed everything else about me." Harmony paused as Gerolt considered her words. "That's why I found myself drawn to you." The hairs on Gerolt's neck stood on edge. His whole body pulsed with life. "When you told me what attracted you to me, what made you do what you did...just to find me... Nobody has seen me like that before." Gerolt's usual smirk stretched from ear to ear. His ears soaking up every word. "But that's not all. I've always held a place in my heart for the people outside the walls. I begged my father to let me bring our cart out here. To give where it is needed most. I'll admit that I wasn't quite ready for how bad things were. Most people had given up. Lost their spark and resigned themselves to a slow death. You were different. You strived to make something of yourself. Even with nothing, you found a way to be creative—to give a bit of joy to this broken place."

Gerolt's smile dropped to the floor. "You make me sound pretty great."

"But you are, Gerolt."

Gerolt shook his head. "No, I'm not. I'm selfish and arrogant. I've always hated making those stuffed animals. They make me feel...childish. The world around me is dying, rotting away to nothing, and all I can do is...sew."

Harmony tugged Gerolt towards a small well outside the tavern. "Come on, let's get all that blood off of you."

Gerolt allowed himself to be pulled to the well, eyes still downcast. Harmony filled the bucket and dipped her hands in the lukewarm water. "Your home, it's with your parents, right?" Harmony asked as she scrubbed the grime from Gerolt's face and hands with a handkerchief she kept in her cooking apron. Gerolt nodded. "And are they able to provide for themselves?" Gerolt shook his head. "And are you doing everything in your power to make life bearable for them?" Gerolt considered her question for a few moments before giving a slight nod.

Harmony beamed as she rubbed the last of the blood from Gerolt's forehead. "Then I'd say you're a better man than you think yourself to be."

Tension melted from Gerolt's shoulders as he let Harmony's words pour over him. "About my parents..." Harmony threw her arms around Gerolt's shoulders and waited. "They're...still pretty traditional. My mom thinks the League has our best interests at heart and follows their teachings to the letter. She believes they are working diligently to protect us from the threat of the mountain clans, and that's why they don't have the resources to spare on our wellbeing." Gerolt paused, squirming at the thought of what he had to bring up next.

"So, she won't be too keen on the idea of a young woman sharing a roof with her son," Harmony surmised to Gerolt's surprise.

"That's one way to say it," Gerolt replied. "I'm working on a plan, but I haven't exactly..."

Gerolt's words were cut short by Harmony's lips pressed firmly against his. All thoughts of plans or schemes to survive the night. Every worry about how to keep her safe and away from the League faded to the background. In that moment, all he could feel was her.

CHAPTER 4
THE HOLLOWLANDS

"Those men came around again today," Gerolt's mother muttered. "Fancy armor clinking and clanking down our alley. Say they are looking for one of their Purity Maiden. That she broke the Hysteresis Code and poses a danger to all who come in contact with her." Gerolt looked at his mother out of the corner of his eye, pushing what was left of his gruel around with a wooden spoon. "Funny how after all these years, the League shows up a few days after you brought that lovely girl to our home."

Gerolt let his spoon fall from his hand. "We've gone over this mother. She's not a Purity Maiden. She's just a friend who needs a place to stay."

"Oh, a friend, is she," his mother teased. "A 'friend' who shares your bed at night." Gerolt cleared his throat and picked up his dropped spoon. "You know, just because my sight has gone, doesn't mean I've lost all my senses."

Red crept up Gerolt's neck.. "There are only so many beds in this shack of a home, Mom. What would you have her do? Sleep on the dirt? Pretty horrid thing to do to a girl cast from

40

her home with nowhere else to go. Besides, the food is almost enjoyable around here thanks to her."

"These old bones have noticed that as well. Only so much you can do to a strip of rat meat. The food that girl produces isn't natural." She paused, sightless eyes fixed on nothing. "I know what she is, Son." Gerolt swallowed a bite of gruel and made eye contact with his mother. "I also know what she is to *you...*" Her voice cracked as it caught in her throat. "It isn't safe here. They will find her eventually."

Pain and relief washed over Gerolt at once. He half expected his mother to turn Harmony in. It made his heart sing to hear that she had chosen her son's happiness over her love of the League. "What should we do?"

His mother stopped rocking in her chair. Her sightless eyes squinting at nothing in particular. "Do you love her?"

Gerolt set his jaw and sat up straight in his chair. "I believe I do. I know that I can't live without her, that's for sure."

"Then make an honest woman of her, Gerolt. Marry her, and be done with the shame of premarital intimacy."

Gerolt choked down the bite of gruel still lingering in his mouth, sputtering a bit before being able to formulate a response. "Mother! That's..."

"If talking about such things flusters you, imagine what your mother must feel listening to the two of you grunt in pleasure night after night."

Gerolt cleared his throat and took a sip of water. "And here I thought we were being cautious."

"You aren't as crafty as you imagine yourself to be. The League will find her sooner or later. They will take her away, and punish us for harboring her. Marry her Gerolt. Marry her and take her far from here."

"And what good will marriage do, mother? It's a useless piece of paper. A scam to get a few coppers."

"Perhaps," conceded his mother. "But marriage gives you rights in the League's eyes. As her husband, you would at least be permitted to follow her into the Crystal Pedestal. You two could live there together. In all the comforts and pleasures the League has to provide."

"And leave you alone? Now that father has passed..."

"Your father was more of a burden than a help around here. His suffering has finally ended. Don't you worry about me, Gerolt. I'll be fine."

Gerolt eyed his mother with a heavy heart. "I know you want what is best for me...even at your own peril... It's just... Harmony will never agree to living there. She feels differently about the League than you do."

His mother nodded as she rocked back and forth in her chair. "I feared as much... Only one option left, I'm afraid."

"And what's that?"

"Leave New Geneva."

"Leave?" Gerolt echoed, looking around dramatically. "To where? Despite my hard-earned writ of passage, Harmony can't go back into the city. Where else is there?"

The blind woman stretched out a trembling hand, pointing towards the distant mountains. "The Hollowlands."

Gerolt's mouth dropped open. "Are you crazy? The Hollowlands? That place drives people to madness. Torn apart by their own minds. They say it turns people into zombies...and you want us to *live* there?"

A gentle smile crept onto his mother's face. "Zombies? Come now, Gerolt. It wasn't all that long ago that we all made it work out there. You are right to fear it. There are large areas that are uninhabitable. Where crops cannot grow and minds are twisted in on themselves... But...if you are strong enough, driven enough...there are pockets where life can still thrive."

Gerolt squinted his eyes and furrowed his brow. "You know of such a place?"

"There is a valley three days' journey from here. Nestled in that valley is a lake. That's where your father and I made our first home. We lived there for years, undisturbed by the effects of the Hollowlands. Never running into another soul."

Gerolt scratched his head. "Then why did you leave?"

"Your father became ill, and I had you on the way. We knew we could no longer make it on our own. We needed an established society."

"And the mountain clans? They never showed up despite there being a lake nearby?"

Gerolt's mother smirked. "The lake is hidden in the shadow of the mountains. The clans were too spooked by the proximity of nearby tainted lands. They never pushed far enough to see it. You could build a family there. You and Harmony. It's a solitary life, but...you'd be safe."

"Why have you not told me about this before? We could have left for this place years ago, let father live out the last of his days in peace."

"I made the journey through the Hollowlands once. My old mind couldn't take the toll a second time. The valley itself has been spared the fate of much of the Hollowlands, but the path to get there is not so fortunate."

Gerolt swallowed a gathering lump in his throat. "So...we'd have to endure them. The Hollowlands...to get to this valley?"

"I'm afraid there is no other way."

Gerolt glanced out their small cabin's lone window at the towering mountains looming in the distance. "What's it like? Traveling through the Hollowlands."

Eyelids fluttered over his mother's cloudy eyes. "They will dig into every corner of your mind. Tear open every hidden thought. Uncover every buried memory... They will set your mind to devour itself... If this is the path you choose to take, you must steel your mind." She locked her unfocused eyes on her son. Her eyes saw more than her years of blindness let on. "Leave no hint of remorse or uncertainty. Know yourself and your intentions. Be certain that they are pure... Even if you manage all that, you won't leave the Hollowlands the same person. They will change you... There is no escaping that."

THE DAYS of preparation wavered between anxious anticipation and nervous dread. Gerolt and Harmony worked together to sell the last of Gerolt's stuffed animals, granting them enough money for a marriage license, some new travel clothes, and water canteens. They filled Gerolt's travel bag with gifts from his mother: rabbit jerky, flint and steel for starting a fire, and a few packets of seeds for planting crops.

When they were not working to gain the handful of coppers needed to obtain their supplies, they spent their time in what his mother called "mental silence." It felt like sitting still and doing nothing, but his mother insisted that it helped ease the mental strain of the Hollowlands.

Harmony could hold a state of mental silence for almost an hour without breaking form—back straight, eyes closed, mind focused on nothing while keeping note of wandering inner thoughts. The practice came a bit more difficult for Gerolt, who saw it as a waste of precious time. He did his best to practice anyway, as his mother was the only one amongst them who had any experience dealing with the effects of the Hollowlands.

Gerolt ruminated over the last few days. With his fingers entwined with Harmony's, the pair watched as the last slivers of sun dropped below the horizon. The darkness would cloak their movements from the guards who roamed the streets looking for their escaped treasure. They took a deep breath, searching their minds for every scrap of inner peace they could muster. Cold, calloused hands jolted Gerolt from his mental silence. "Ah! Mother, you startled me! What are you doing out of your chair..."

"Purge such thoughts from your mind, Son. Worrying about me will do nothing but give the Hollowlands fuel." She steadied herself on Gerolt's shoulder, hoisting up a heavy patch of cloth towards Harmony. "Here, take it."

Harmony took the heavy fabric with a slight bow. "Thank you..."

"Stretch it out with a few large branches, and it'll keep most of mother nature at bay. Should keep you comfortable enough until you can get yourselves something more permanent set up by the lake."

Gerolt turned his back toward Harmony, so she could access his travel bag. She folded up the makeshift tent and tucked it under their food rations before turning back towards Gerolt's mother. "Thank you...again," she eked out. "I..." Her voice cracked with emotion. "I feel like I'm taking everything from you."

"Oh, hush now," soothed Gerolt's mother. "You're my daughter now. I only wish I could do more."

Gerolt wrapped his arms around the fragile old woman and squeezed as hard as he dared. "I love you, Mom. I don't tell you that enough...and now..."

"I know you do, Son," she whispered as she returned his embrace. "Even when you don't say it." She let her arms slide from around her son, cradling his hand in hers. "Keep that love in your heart. Know that everything I've chosen comes from that same place. The Hollowlands will try to convince you otherwise." Gerolt rubbed his mother's calloused hands with his, doing his best to burn the memory into the deepest corners of his mind.

THE HOLLOWED LANDS HOWLED, scouring the wastelands for any soul who dared to bare themselves. Their gaze held no reason or purpose. No ill intent or moral obligation. Only an unquenchable, innate drive to untangle the knot lodged within the human self. Gerolt gritted his teeth as another wave of nauseating wind tore through his thick travel clothes. He snuck a glimpse at his wife. Her eyes remained closed, focusing on something deep within herself. A sliver of doubt wormed its way through his carefully guarded mind. The Hollow's tainted air rushed to breach his defenses.

"*She's using you...*" The voice was smooth, clear, and intimately close. "*You're a worthless street rat. A nobody. She was desperate. Nowhere else to turn...*" The voice gathered itself, shimmering in the cool night air. "*You took advantage of her. Fear led her to your arms...to your bed.*"

"Liar!" Gerolt screamed into the void. His eyes popped open as he spun around in search of the voice's source. "It wasn't like that. We found each other."

"*She would have clung to any man who found her. She's using you...*"

"No! Stop! It isn't true..."

"*You abandoned your mother. She'll die without you there to provide for her...*"

Gerolt stopped fighting and dropped to his knees.

"*You sentenced her to a lonely death...and for what? A nice warm body to fill your bed?*"

All the strength melted from Gerolt's body as he collapsed to the ground. "I'm sorry..." he whispered into the dirt.

"Sorry?" The voice stood before him, cloaked in his own skin. *"What good comes from your sorrow now? What relief will it bring to your decrepit mother and decaying father?"* His bright blue eyes burned into his soul, searching himself for the next path down his splintered mind. *"You're weak, Gerolt."* Gerolt's breathing slowed to a crawl. His aching heart lingered on the voice's every word. *"Too weak to make it on your own. Too weak to protect her. Too weak to avoid the strong arm of the League... You're nothing more than a discarded human of the LHC. Unfit for anything but death."*

A sharp pain stung his cheek, distorting the voice's image for the briefest of moments. He could hear a muffled second voice break through. It sounded far off, like it came from underground or perhaps underwater . "Gerolt... Gerolt!"

He opened his eyes to see Harmony kneeling over him with tears rolling down her face. "Oh, thank god! I thought I'd lost you!

Gerolt struggled to sit upright, steadying himself on his wife's shoulders. The dizziness left a metallic tinge in his mouth. "I... What happened?"

Harmony closed her eyes and pulled him into a tight embrace. "I don't know, but...that voice...it..."

"Was your own?" Gerolt finished. Harmony nodded. "If you heard it too, how did you fight it off?"

Harmony shook her head. "I don't know. I retreated into mental silence. Focused on my breath and the steady pulse of blood through my veins. Then I saw you on the ground, and it snapped me out of it."

Gerolt looked at the ground in shame. "So...I really was the weak one."

"Weak?" Harmony recoiled. "Why would you say that?" She took his hand in hers. "You've risked everything for me."

Gerolt shook his head, gaze still on the scorched dirt at his feet. "I had nothing to risk."

Harmony squeezed Gerolt's hand. "You left a loving mother, and everything you've ever known. A weak man would have turned me into the League for a few bags of rice and wheat." Harmony rubbed her thumbs across the back of Gerolt's hand. "I know our relationship happened quickly, and we kind of rushed into getting married... But I really do love you, and none of this is your fault." She wrapped one hand around the back of Gerolt's neck and pulled his forehead against hers. "We only get through this place if we do it together... We need something to center ourselves. A phrase or something that the voice would never say. I'm afraid this won't be the last time we get lost in our own minds."

Gerolt brought his head up and looked Harmony in the eyes. "A phrase? You really think that will help?"

"Yeah, something that will snap us out of the Hollowland's mind games. Something that will remind us that we are not alone, and that we are in this together. A reason to look beyond our own inner struggles and push forward."

Gerolt thought through his short yet difficult life. About all the times he wondered why he was alive at all. He thought about the countless nights he spent looking for his purpose. Hour after hour stitching stuffed animals until his fingers bled, just to make enough coppers to do it again tomorrow. He looked at Harmony with a renewed vigor in his eyes. "Is there a difference between living and existing?"

Harmony met his eyes with a gentle smile. "There is now."

CHAPTER 5
THE HOUSE BY THE LAKE

"Take a deep breath. Clear your mind. Let all distracting thoughts wash away with the sound of my voice. You can do this, Wren. I believe in you."

Wren hugged her stuffed rabbit, avoiding her father's gaze. Gerolt squatted next to his daughter and placed his hands on her tiny shoulders. "Come on, Wren. You know this. It'll cheer you up. I promise."

Wren took a deep breath, allowing her red, puffy eyes to flutter closed once more. She concentrated on the sound of her father's voice. Felt the calmness of his warm hands. The fight with her older brother Elias leaked from her mind, replaced by swirls of yellow and orange.

"You did it, my little songbird!" Wren opened her eyes and inspected her stuffed rabbit. A frown curled her lips as she shot her father a pensive glance. "Look! Right there! You don't see it? Rabbit's tail practically looks like a campfire!"

Wren turned her stuffed rabbit around and stroked its fuzzy tail. "I wanted it to be brighter. You can barely tell I changed the color at all."

Gerolt rose to his feet and crossed his arms. "Crivellis don't pout at progress. You have an amazing gift, Wren. Do you think I could do that? Even if I strained all night?"

Wren fiddled with the rabbit, looking at the ground. "No… but that's only because you weren't born with it. I bet you'd make Rabbit so bright you'd need to shield your eyes. Elias is right. It should have been him."

Gerolt's face hardened as he fixed his gaze on his daughter. "I'm going to tell you something my mother told me." Wren looked up at her father with renewed interest. "Each of your hardships, meaning difficult things, push you closer to the person you were meant to be."

The little girl scrunched her brow. "So, I'm supposed to be bad at this?"

Gerolt squatted down to his daughter's level. "No, sweetie… It means that sometimes failing is necessary. How else can we get better at something?"

"But Elias said if he were born with it, we'd have doubled our crops and…"

"But he wasn't. You were. Now, you can either feel sorry for yourself, or you can embrace your gift and show him how wrong he is." A grin crept across Wren's flushed face. "Keep practicing, my little songbird," Gerolt urged with a reassuring pat on his daughter's back. "I'll check on your progress after I help Elias finish prepping the fields."

Gerolt peered out across the rolling hills. Years of convincing the scorched earth to yield life had chiseled unseen strength into his slender frame. A glint of light caught his attention—Elias's spade, hard at work getting the fields ready for planting. Gerolt smiled. Living with his young family outside New Geneva's walls and rules made him a cautious and calculating man, but it also made his family strong. Pride swelled within him.

Gerolt took a lungful of the cool morning air. The smell of salt and earth filled his nostrils. His eyes darted back and forth, fixating on a cloud of dust rising from the horizon. Gerolt squinted in the morning sun, straining to see what could cause such a commotion. His heart jumped in his chest as he saw a man mounted on horseback riding towards their family's crops. His mind calculated the chances of survival as his heart pulled him in two directions. Harmony scurried about the small kitchen area of their log cabin, making breakfast. Wren played with Rabbit at Gerolt's feet. If they found them, found what they could do, the consequences would be dire. Elias worked in the fields. His pride and joy. Strong, independent, and wickedly smart. Elias embodied everything a man could want from a son. His mind strained back and forth. Precious seconds ticked by.

"Daddy, look!" Wren held out her rabbit. Fluorescent shocks of yellow and orange swirled across its patchy fur.

"This is no time for games!" Gerolt roared as he grabbed the little girl by the arm in a rush to get her somewhere safe.

"But, I did it! I thought you'd be proud of me..."

Gerolt gritted his teeth before ripping the rabbit from his daughter's hands. "If only I had trained you to do something useful!" Gerolt flexed his jaw as visions of Elias being taken from him swirled through his mind. "Playtime is over! This family has sacrificed too much to have it end like this!" he yelled as he tossed the stuffed toy into the nearby lake. Wren's eyes overflowed with tears as she watched her precious rabbit fill with water and sink below the surface.

"Rabbit! No!" Wren creased her eyebrows inward and glared at her father. Anger and despair wrestled for dominance within her. Gerolt didn't slow his pace, dragging Wren toward the rustic cabin the family called home.

"I'm such a fool! I never should have brought us out here."

Gerolt burst through the front door, Wren stumbling behind him. "Harmony! Take Wren to the cellar. Mountain clan riders on the horizon!"

ELIAS WHISTLED AS HE WORKED. His muscles burned beneath his sun-kissed skin. Despite the meager returns, he took pride in his work. He crouched down to inspect his rows.

"Perfect," he whispered to himself as he stood to admire a job well done.

Crack! The cudgel struck his head with a sickening crunch. The world swayed back and forth. Elias blinked unfocused eyes, concentrating on regaining his footing and squaring up to his unknown foe.

"What's the matter, boy?" The assailant sat on horseback. His pale white skin stood in stark contrast to a shock of jet black hair. Blue and green tattoos covered his bare chest and arms; a series of twisted knots represented his various conquests and feats of bravery.

A curved cudgel with a large weighted knob rested on his hulking shoulder. "A little bop on the head enough to keep you down, boy?" Elias struggled to regain his right mind, shaking off the impact and staggering to his feet.

"You think you're man enough?" the pale warrior grunted.

Elias scooped up his spade, using it as a crutch to support his staggering body. *Tsk, tsk.* The warrior waggled his finger and clicked his tongue before dismounting his horse and sauntering towards the wobbling boy. "That's not how a warrior stands his ground," he sneered as he kicked the spade out from under Elias. Elias allowed his body to spin with the movement, throwing a shovel-full of loose dirt into the warrior's eyes as he dropped to the ground.

"Ugh! You coward!" growled the warrior as he rubbed his eyes with fevered annoyance.

Elias's head throbbed. He reached up to assess the damage. He held his hand before his wavering focus. A thick layer of blood dripped from his fingertips. He winced as he pushed himself back to his feet. The Warrior squinted at him with bloodshot eyes. "There's some fight in you after all. Well, come on then. Let's see what you've got, boy."

"Leave him!" Gerolt roared as he rushed to his son's side. "You want someone to fight? Fight me."

The warrior whipped his head over to the wire-framed Gerolt and looked him up and down. Gerolt stood his ground —eyes wide, knuckles white, breath shallow. The warrior threw his head back in laughter. "You think we want a scrawny old man joining our clan? Get out of the way before I split you in two. This is between me and the boy. If he puts up enough of a fight, maybe I'll let the rest of your family live."

"Rah!" Gerolt growled as he charged forward, his spade lowered like a rider's lance. The warrior smirked as he turned to face him, swatting him away with a mighty swing of his cudgel. Gerolt twisted his spade to the side in desperation, blocking the blow as his shovel splintered into pieces.

In a heartbeat, the warrior was on him, straddling his thin frame and pinning him to the floor. "So much anger. You must know deep down that your son doesn't have what it takes. He is weak like his father." Gerolt struggled and spat, fuming with fury. "Whoa there, old man, don't pull a muscle. Here. I'll give you a sporting chance," the warrior taunted as he tossed his cudgel to the side, pummeling Gerolt with his bare fists. Gerolt brought up his arms to cover his face as the blows rained down on his forearms.

The strikes proved furious and unrelenting, battering Gerolt's arms. The warrior drove his massive fist into Gerolt's unprotected ribs. Gerolt howled in pain, releasing his defensive form. The warrior took advantage, grabbing Gerolt's wrists and pinning them to the ground. "I hope your boy puts up more of a fight."

The warrior's cudgel tore across his face, splintering his skull. His body fell limp, collapsing in a heap. Gerolt struggled to free himself from the warrior's massive weight, wiping blood from his eyes, searching wildly for his son. He wanted to comfort him, to let him know he didn't have a choice, that everything would be okay.

Elias stood over the bloody mess draped over his father, cudgel in hand. His mind and body hung in limbo, trying to make sense of what had just taken place. He mouthed a few incoherent words, muffled by the ringing in Gerolt's ears. Hoofbeats shook the ground behind him. Gerolt's eyes went wide as he doubled his efforts to get free from the dead warrior's weight.

The ax-head sunk into Elias's shoulder, ripping his arm free of his body. Blood spurted from the fresh wound, soaking into the dry patch of ground he had toiled over for so many years. Before Gerolt could process the tragedy unfolding before him, a second horse closed in. Gerolt's ears sang a song too high to hear. His head struggled to find itself. He remembered the miles of hell he and Harmony trudged through to get here. The life they had built with their bare hands. Time slowed as he watched all of it hang in the balance. The ax-wielding warrior looped around as the second thrust his spear. The blade burst through Elias's chest. His lifeless body sank to the ground.

Gerolt wrenched himself free, crawling to his son's side. He cradled his limp head in his hands, sobbing uncontrollably. The two riders dismounted, brandishing their weapons as they circled father and son.

"You should have let us test the boy," he snarled as he looked at the crater left in his fellow warrior's skull. "Looks like he had some promise."

Gerolt waited for the blow to come, welcomed it, even. His arms and ribs screamed with pain. A mere whisper compared to the ache in his chest. *What kind of father is too weak to protect his son? What was I thinking? We were never strong enough to live outside the city. It's all my fault. And now, I'm left with nothing.* Gerolt allowed his blood-soaked eyes to flutter shut. He pulled Elias's lifeless body to his chest. *I'm sorry, my son.*

The warriors locked in on their target, blinded by revenge and bloodlust. Something in the air shifted. A power so primal and seething Gerolt could feel it in his soul. Gerolt peeled back his eyelids. Flesh melted from the warrior's bones. Their exposed muscles sizzled like freshly seared steak. Blood boiled from their eyes, nose, and ears. Neither had time to scream.

Harmony stood over the molten corpses of the warriors in shock. She hadn't meant to use it. She knew what the consequences could have been. She'd done it out of sheer instinct. Out of pain, loss, and desperation. Gerolt met her numb expression with one of his own. Had she saved him? Condemned them all? He could smell the stench of cooked flesh. Tasted the metallic tinge of boiled blood in the air. At that moment, something in him changed. All the years they'd spent working the land, defying the control of the League of Fellows, raising their children to be strong, independent, and free-thinking. All of it felt empty. Hollow. Idiotic even. If he would have listened to the warnings. If he would have taken his family to New Geneva, to the protection of the walls and the League, Elias would still be alive.

Harmony sank to her knees, her face painted a ghostly white. The air around her began to shimmer, folding in on itself in undulating waves. A thundering *crack* split the air, raking itself across Harmony's chest. Searing hot pain erupted through her. She screamed and dropped to her knees, clutching her breast.

"What have you done!" screamed Gerolt, his frantic state halted by the sound of soft, breathless tears. Wren sat next to her brother, knees curled up to her chin. Eyes wide and glistening.

Gerolt surveyed the state of his family with desperation in his eyes. He thought they could make it out here alone. A fool's dream. He knew what he had to do. Where they must go to get the care and protection they need. With the final death of his pride, Gerolt steadied his thin, wavering frame and scooped his numb daughter into his aching arms. He glanced over his shoulder at his traumatized wife, hand clutched to her breast. Her wide, unblinking eyes stared into the distance at nothing in particular.

"Harmony..." he managed to get out before his voice caught in his throat. "We...we have to leave. There's nothing left for us out here anymore." Harmony sat still as a statue, solemn face etched in stone. "Those were scouts you...boiled... The clan will send a search party when they don't return by nightfall." Gerolt took a deep breath, letting it out in a wavering stream. "I'm going to run into the house and get some things for the journey." Gerolt struggled over to his wife, setting Wren by her side. "Stay with your mother, little songbird. I'll be right back. I promise."

Wren hugged her knees to her chest a few feet from her mom. The space between them felt cold and foreign; their shared heartache pushing them apart. Gerolt returned a few moments later with a travel sack filled with supplies. Harmony heard his approach and snapped out of her inner turmoil long enough take note of her surroundings. Her eyes shifted into focus, her face turning sour.

"What? No! We can't give up now!" she sputtered, eyes darting from side to side. "They'll take Wren from us! We'll never be a family again!" She paused, mind turning inward once more. "And the Hollowlands...they'll eat us alive! I can't bear to see him appear before me. My precious boy..." Harmony dropped to her knees. Blood flowed free under her hand-sewn blouse, staining it a deep satin red.

Gerolt winced and held his fractured ribs as he knelt by her side. "We're married. Even the League of Fellows recognizes that. We'll make it work." Gerolt surveyed his remaining family with wild eyes. The hopelessness of their situation threatening to seize control of him.

"First, we need to see to that wound of yours." He rummaged through his travel sack for some thread. His hands shook as he approached his wife's left breast, split open like a patch of water starved earth. "It's really deep..." Gerolt flinched as his mind filled itself with images of re-stitching the Scrive Masters infected, bloated wounds all those years ago. "You might want to get something to bite down on."

Harmony met Gerolt's wild gaze with cool, unflinching eyes. "Do it. Maybe I'll start to feel something other than heartache."

Gerolt hesitated. His needle hovering over his wife's gaping wound. "We'll get through this, Harmony. I'll stitch you up, good as new. Then...before we leave this place for good...let's bury our son.

WREN PEERED over her shoulder at the house on the lake fading behind them. The only home she had ever known. Everything they owned sat squarely on their backs. With barely enough time to bury Elias, none of it seemed real.

Gerolt kept his eyes forward. A crisp staccato mixed into his normally soothing tone. "Remember Wren, if you start to see things that don't seem real, it's because they are not. The Hollowlands plays nasty tricks on you... Don't be surprised if you see Elias..."

"Elias! I can see him?" Wren asked her mother, eyes wide with hope.

Harmony bit her lip to keep it from quivering. "No... sweetie... It will only appear to be him. He probably won't say very nice things. He might even try to get you to feel bad about yourself. It will only be a fake Elias."

Wren scratched her head. "A fake? But, I thought we put dirt over him. Is he going to wake up and wonder where we are?"

Harmony turned her head and let a few tears escape her grasp. "No, honey. He's...gone."

"Gone?" Harmony nodded. Wren scrunched up her face in thought. "Then I don't care if fake Elias shows up! I'll hug him anyway! And it'll make everything better, like when we fight over my gift!"

Gerolt put a hand on his young daughters shoulder. "Of course, my little songbird. I'm sure he'd love that."

Harmony shot Gerolt a worried glance, but knew her husband was right. Explaining what would happen in the Hollowlands to a young child would do nothing but confuse her. "Gerolt... Maybe we should simplify our safe phrase." She nodded towards Wren.

Gerolt lifted his eyebrows. "Good point... I doubt 'is there a difference between living and existing' would mean much to an eight year old."

"Safe phrase?" Wren asked, looking up at her parents.

"Yes, it's a magic phrase that helps bad things go away,"

Harmony responded, wiping a final tear from her cheek. "Perhaps, you should come up with it, Wren."

"Me? Oh, I don't know any magic words."

"That's because you have to make them first," Gerolt added. "Think of something that makes you happy, that nobody could ever take away from you no matter how hard they tried."

Wren stitched her brow together for a few moments before letting her gaze meet the ground. "We're leaving everything that makes me happy... I have practically nothing... *I'm* practically nothing."

"Nothing? You have a gift capable of..." Gerolt halted his words, glancing over at his wife. "You said 'practically' nothing. So, what is it that you *do* have?"

Wren's knuckles went white as she squeezed her fists. "My gift... You always said to make it my own... That there was a reason that I got it, and not Elias..." Wren released her balled up fists. The emotion drained from her voice. "I've got it. My magic phrase. I'm more than nothing."

Gerolt nodded as tears gathered in his eyes. He knew he should say something. Tell his little girl that she was more than her gift. That she had so much more to offer than a hollow shell and a hellish gift. His eyes wandered to his wife— to the scar still fresh on her breast. His mind conjured up images of melting skin; his nose filled with the scent of charred remains. He cleared his throat and pulled at his collar. He gathered his thoughts and looked down at his daughter. A large rabbit with an orange and yellow tail stared back.

"You taught me to use it, didn't you, Daddy?" the rabbit said in a sweet, innocent tone. "Maybe someday I'll use it like mommy!"

Gerolt's stomach lurched as he doubled over in pain.

"Gerolt!" Harmony cried. "Remember yourself! There's a difference between living and existing! Remember! Gerolt!"

Gerolt stared down at his side, a line of drool dripping slowly from the side of his mouth.

"Mommy, what's wrong with Dad?"

Harmony's eyes darted from her braindead husband to her panic-stricken daughter to the vast open wasteland set before them. Her jaw trembled as she searched for words. The sides of her throat stuck together, spit forming into a thick, bitter liquid.

"Mommy!" Wren cried, tugging at her sleeve. "Mommy! Mom! Mom!" Wren's voice deepened, face contorting.

"Elias?" Harmony whispered. "Is...that you?"

Elias stood before her, covered in blood and dirt, cradling his severed arm in his attached one. "How could you leave me? They killed me, Mother. And you just walked away?"

"Elias...my boy. I..."

"I always knew I was nothing but a farmhand to you! Breaking my back hoeing that useless, scorched soil and what do you do as soon as I'm dead?"

"Elias, please... I can't bear it... Forgive me!"

Wren stood between her slouched parents, eyes wide with confusion. "Mom! Dad! What's going on!"

"You always knew I was their favorite."

The hairs on the back of Wren's neck stood up. "Elias? but..." Wren shook her head. "No, mom said you were a fake Elias. You're not real!"

"Aren't I? Would a fake Elias know that you've never wanted your precious gift? That you always wished it was *mine?*" Wren took a few steps back, leaving her quivering parents to their own inner demons. "Give it to me, and this bad dream goes away. Mom and Dad will wake up, and we'll all be back home by the lake." Elias reached out his hand.

Wren took another step back, looking at her parents slumped on the dirt. She scrunched her brow together and balled up her fists. "I am more than nothing! I am more than nothing! *I am more than nothing!*"

In an instant, Elias evaporated like a wave of heat on a desert horizon. A man in a hooded cloak took his place, squatting next to Harmony with her wrist in his hand.

"Hey! That's my mommy!"

The figure put up a skeletal hand, keeping their face covered in shadow. "Hush, child. Their heart still beats." The hooded figure took a canteen of water from his long cloak and put it to Harmony's lips, then Gerolt's.

Wren took a cautious step forward. "Are they sleeping?"

The figure pulled his hand back as Wren approached, standing to their feet. "In a sense. It's a sleep they may never wake from, I'm afraid. They must be stuck in some pretty powerful hallucinations."

"Halu-what?"

The figure brought both hands to their face. Wren heard something resembling a muffled scream as something moved under the figures skin. The squeal of bone on bone made her wince. She froze in place, unable to breath or move. Time moved forward in a thick syrup as the figure's bones continued their painful dance under their skin.

"I am who I am... I am who I am..." Wren heard the figure mutter in ragged breaths. Little by little the bones settled, returning to their rightful place. The figure dropped their hands, but kept their face hidden. "I'm sorry you had to witness that, child. I've been out here so very long..." The figure paused, tiling their head to one side, then the other. "Tell me, little one. How did you come to be out here?"

Wren struggled to find her voice, hairs on her neck still on edge. "I've always been out here."

"Hmm." The figure stroked their chin. "I have no desire to care for a little girl..." The figure looked at the crumpled forms of Wren's parents at their side. "Let me ask you something, little one."

The figure took a few steps towards Wren, allowing her to see the bottom half of their face. Their skin was unnaturally smooth like the clay her dad used to seal the gaps in their house, only shiny. "Exactly how far are you willing to go to make that gift your own?"

CHAPTER 6
THE CRYSTAL PEDESTAL

Is there a difference between living and existing? Wren wondered as the early morning light streamed through her vaulted window. The beam filled her room with a warm glow, resting on the silken dress laid out for her the night before. Emeralds ran up and down its sleeves and across the neckline. She curled her lip, hating herself for finding any beauty in it at all. The other Purity Maidens might think themselves special for being displayed in such lavish clothing, but she knew better. The dresses' soft silken sheen and mesmerizing jeweled accents were nothing more than a uniform hiding any original thought or idea she might have. A mask protecting her impure mind from causing trouble. So much had changed since the simple days of living with her family in the house on the lake all those years ago. A light rapping on her door roused her wandering mind. Her always-vigilant Provider and father, Gerolt. Right on schedule.

"What's taking so long, my little songbird?" The words used to bring a sense of ease. The years in New Geneva replaced such comforts with a wrinkled brow and clenched jaw. "Did you see the dress I picked out for you today? It's my personal favorite. It brings out your stunning eyes." Wren fought to contain the emotion etched onto her expectantly serene face.

"Yes, of course, Father. I'll be out in a minute," Wren yelled over her shoulder as she checked herself for any hints of imperfection. The mirror revealed a small-boned girl with warm, olive-toned skin. A patch of freckles ran across her cheekbones, covering the bridge of her nose. Her wavy, chestnut hair was highlighted with just enough red to give it a copper sheen in the sunlight. Her eyes matched the emerald dress laid out before her to perfection. She wanted to pluck them out.

"Stop fussing, sweetie. I'm sure you look stunning." After a brief pause, her father's singsong tone shifted into a distinctive staccato. Provider Gerolt stood in full force. "Sr. Father Pipher is waiting, and you know how he gets."

"Coming, Father. Just trying to get my hair to cooperate is all," Wren offered back. Her eyes transfixed on the perfect ringlets of hair cascading around her shoulders.

"Oh, come now. Enough of your dawdling. Open up before I get a guard to do it for you." After a final lungful of defiance, Wren obliged. "Ah, breathtaking as usual. What did I tell you?"

Not to be outdone by his Maidens, Gerolt wore a crisp, navy blue suit. His wispy head of dark hair and matching pencil mustache stood in sharp contrast to his light blue eyes. He beamed as he reviewed his daughter's appearance. Wren eked out a smile of her own, fighting off the urge to ruffle her perfect hair. She could think of countless things more appealing than impressing Mr. Pipher.

As she walked down the hallway with Gerolt, she reflected on the quality of life the Crystal Pedestal provided her. A personal chef provided all of her meals. She had an armoire stuffed full of lavish clothing. Her small, cozy quarters were adorned with the finest bed and vanity money could buy. Her father, by all appearances, adored her, and her mother achieved the status of Sr. Maiden years ago. Despite all this, Wren couldn't shake the feeling of utter and complete meaninglessness. A life filled to the brim with empty praise and patronizing pats on the head. Like all Purity Maidens, her Provider controlled her earnings, picked out her clothes, and prearranged all her meals. She had a life of luxury mapped out for her, and it gave her an uneasy feeling in her stomach.

"Ah, Mr. Pipher, a privilege as always," Gerolt cooed with an exaggerated bow. "What brings you to The Crystal Pedestal today?"

"Isn't it obvious?" barked Mr. Pipher. "It's firmly winter, yet my prized suit sits adorned in the colors of autumn. How can I assume the proper amount of respect while walking around in *this*?"

Mr. Pipher's neck wobbled with every gesture. His starched collar looked like a finely pressed napkin strangling an uncased sausage. *If only it were a bit tighter,* Wren thought as she did her best to hide her contempt.

"Of course, Mr. Pipher. My daughter will start hysteresis on your stunning suit right away." Gerolt always doted on his clientele, but he turned it up a notch around high-ranking members of the League of Fellows.

Mr. Pipher gave a curt nod before handing his gaudy, auburn suit over to Gerolt. "I expect it to be done by the time my fast is broken at the Crystal Pedestal Café. Now, if you don't mind, I'm quite famished."

I could alter his entire wardrobe with that much time, Wren thought to herself. She knew that expressing such thoughts toward a man would get her sent to the purity rooms.

"Unless you would prefer to have Wren deliver your suit

personally." Wren's eyes grew wide with horror as the words left Gerolt's lips. Her father had never offered her to a customer before. Her stomach lurched as she fought to keep the bile where it belonged.

Mr. Pipher's beady, close-set eyes caressed Wren's body. Her skin burned with disgust. She could feel his gaze creeping into every pore and crevice of her body. She willed it away with every ounce she could muster.

"I am pressed for time this morning, but I won't forget the offer, Provider Gerolt." With a brisk nod, Mr. Pipher spun about on his heels and waddled off to gorge himself on a lavish breakfast.

Once out of earshot, Wren glared up at her father. "You choose the League's power over your own daughter?"

Gerolt's hand moved like a blur. It stung her heart more than her face. His bright blue eyes flashed with anger. "You speak to me of power? You know what your mother did, what you could find yourself capable of. The League keeps us safe. Both from mountain clans and from *ourselves*." Gerolt tugged on the edges of his suit and stood up a bit straighter. "Such a response is not ladylike, and I won't have any of my Purity Maidens failing to retain the proper amount of purity." Gerolt smoothed the front of his wrinkleless suit once more. "You know Mr. Pipher is a senior member of the League of Fellows. I'm simply offering him the power he already commands."

Wren looked down. Her cheek wore a light shade of red. "Of course. My Provider knows best." Times like this, Wren wondered what Gerolt saw when he looked at her. He used to look at her with wonder and pride. Like she could be anything in the world and he would love her for it. He used to encourage her gift. Even promised to teach her to use it wisely and for the good of the family. Everything changed after Elias. Wren pushed this last thought out of her head. It made her feel like all the air got sucked out of the room.

"Wren, everything I do is for the good of this family." Gerolt placed his hands on his daughter's shoulders. "Now hurry off, little songbird. You have an important job to attend to."

"I'm sorry, Provider Gerolt," Wren eked out as she gazed at the polished white marble floor. "I will make haste to my station. Thank you for choosing me to serve this illustrious client."

"Now there's the Wren I know and love," replied Gerolt, his head held high in search of Robin or Oriella. Wren closed her eyes, let out a deep, soft sigh, and pushed back any rebellious thoughts endangering her level of purity. She straightened her back and mustered up her best facade. The lines in her forehead disappeared, replaced by a pair of crisp upturned lips. With her game face on, she flowed into the Common room of the Crystal Pedestal looking every bit a princess.

Wren spent the majority of her days in the Common room with its wide-open spaces speckled with towering pillars of white marble accented by elaborate gold molding. The pillars reached up to a vaulted ceiling adorned with dozens of oversized crystal chandeliers. A single pane of thick, reinforced glass constructed the ceiling, allowing sunlight to pour into the chandeliers from all directions. A cascade of color streamed out the other side, bathing the room in a rainbow of dancing colors. The pillars circled around the room, creating a crescent moon. The opening pointed towards the Crystal Pedestal's entrance. In between each pillar sat clusters of waist-high walls made of frosted glass. A crystal pedestal sat behind each one.

Wren floated around the outside of the crescent, making

sure to curtsey to each client as she passed. A large counter filled her station with enough space to lay out Mr. Pipher's hideous auburn tarp. She wished she could do her work in private, but clients loved watching the Purity Maidens' delicate work, altering the wardrobes of the elite to meet their current whim. Today that meant changing the color of Mr. Pipher's suit from auburn to something more suitable for winter. A dark blue with a tinge of gray, perhaps? Wren fixed the color in her mind, clearing her head of all other thoughts.

The inner battle between Maiden and daughter, the struggle to make her gift her own, to make her own choices, faded to the background. Her desire to lay beside that quiet lake, surrounded by a loving father, a present mother, and a living brother, dissolved into distant memory. All that mattered right now, all that could matter, was a unique shade of bluish-gray. One that would make Mr. Pipher stand out as the man of importance and high standing he was. The feelings of utter dread he gave her when he groped her with his beady pig eyes were gone. The entire world was a single color.

Wren opened her eyes to find Mr. Pipher's suit adorned in a stunning shade of dark turquoise accented by a silver sheen that swirled in ways her eye couldn't entirely follow. Breathtaking. Too breathtaking. Mr. Pipher didn't deserve the recognition he would get for such a unique coloring. Wren looked around to make sure nobody noticed before closing her eyes and focusing once more. This time she imagined the same color but allowed herself to be distracted by the ever present thoughts of her time in the house by the lake. *You're strong, Wren. Someday, you'll do great things for this world. That's why we're out here, building a better life for you and your mother.* Wren opened her eyes a second time. A rich, sharp, distinct blue flooded her canvas, but no longer held the mesmerizing qualities of her first creation.

Satisfied with the coloring, Wren opened up the silver display case on the far side of her work station and hung up Mr. Pipher's suit. The whole process took her less than a minute. Most Maidens would take ten times as long to get a basic color with no pop to it. Even amongst other hysteresis users, Wren had a special connection to her gift, but possessing such ability as a female user would bring nothing but heartache and despair.

Wren had no idea what made her hysteresis more potent, or why only a select few could harness the ability. But whenever she used her gift she felt an intense sense of connection to the object being altered. The deeper and more extensive her knowledge of the object, the more potent her hysteresis became. Color had been her first muse, alerting her family to her gift. She could still picture the mixture of pride and unease on Gerolt's face as he came home to a bright orange door. The memory brought a tear to her eye.

As she grew and discovered the world, her ability grew with her. She altered her rough cotton dresses to silk and sweetened her veggies to be more palatable. That all changed after Elias. Wren might have been young, but she remembered a time when her gift ran wild and free. When her identity came from more than a pretty smile. *Did you know that you're the smartest little girl I've ever met? You can be anything you put your mind to.* As soon as they arrived at the Crystal Pedestal, everything changed. From that very first day, Wren's aspirations to be anything but a pretty face were locked in a cage.

Wren and her mother began their introductory purity lessons immediately upon their arrival. These lessons, among other things, introduced her to the Hysteresis Code. Created by the League of Fellows, it was strictly enforced.

Rule One: No property of an object may be altered in an

area of insufficient knowledge. Such action will result in blow-back, destroying the object or harming the user.

Rule Two: No hysteresis user is permitted to alter living flesh. Such action can lead to more egregious forms of blow-back, including death and dismemberment.

Rule Three: To ensure purity, female users are restricted to the following fields of learning: color alteration, fabric alteration, smell infusion and extraction, jewelry upkeep and care, flavor enhancement, and luminescence.

Rule Four: Male members have no additional restriction in learning, but must choose one of the following hysteresis schools: Density, Friction, Gravity, Sensory Projection, or Conglomeration. The Quantum School is by invite only.

Despite the restrictions in learning and danger of physical harm, Wren's clients whispered words of envy whenever they witnessed her gift, assuming that their every whim could be met with little more than a focused thought. They had no idea how much of a curse her gift could be. What lengths the League would go to in order to keep knowledge out of the Maidens' heads. In the early days, people used to question this dichotomy between male and female hysteresis users, but the League's holy book put a stop to that. Wren thought back to her introductory purity lessons, to the words that would shape her place in New Geneva's society:

"Women shall be submissive to men in all things. In turn, men shall love and protect women holding them up in purity, that they might sanctify and cleanse them so that women might be holy and without blemish.[1]*"*

The words meant little to an eight-year-old. Part of her still wished she held such naivety. This holy book led New Geneva to believe that women should submit to men in *everything*, and that by submitting, they retained their purity. That was why she had a Provider, why she could be given to Mr. Pipher, and why she existed in the gilded cage called the Crystal Pedestal. Robbed of free will, stuck reading the same books and learning the same lessons, her mind ached for more. She closed her eyes, letting the air leak from her lungs. *You have a gift, my little songbird. Don't waste it.*

CHAPTER 7

THE ILLUSTRIOUS MR. PIPHER

Solomon Pipher's favorite part of the day revolved around breaking his fast. His stomach rumbled and groaned at the thought of the sweetmeats and honeyed fruits that would be offered to him at the Crystal Pedestal Café. He expected the young Purity Maiden with the enchanting green eyes would have ample time to focus her pretty little head on altering his suit to a proper color. Being a hysteresis user, he could do the work himself with ease, but that wouldn't do. A man of his stature, or any man for that matter, shouldn't trouble himself with the altering of clothes. He reserved his mind for greater things.

Each Sr. Father of the League had a specialty, an area of knowledge they focused on exclusively. Solomon Pipher stood proud as the Sr. Father of Sensory Projection, a style of hysteresis that manipulated the senses. With enough energy and focus, he could convince a mind to hear, taste, touch, or smell just about anything. Since Solomon first introduced the style, people had accused it of being dangerously close to breaking the second rule of the Hysteresis Code. Others wrote it off as weak, as it didn't allow for slicing boulders in half or grant the ability to wield an eight-hundred-pound sword. This sentiment pushed Solomon to come up with devilish new ways to harness the power of sensory projection, but it did not always need to be used in such ways. Now, for example, Solomon would use it to further enjoy his favorite meal of the day.

He directed his lust at a huge leg of lamb, marinated in an aniseed and honey sauce. Solomon held the morsel in his mind's eye, applying his gluttonous will to devour it. He could almost taste it on the tip of his tongue. A bit longer, and it would be ripe to perfection, finally worthy of settling in his grumbling stomach. The rich undertones of licorice accented the sweetness of the honey. Flavors burrowed their way deep into the fibers of the tender lamb shank...almost ready...just a moment more.

"Is everything to your liking, esteemed Father?" chimed the server, a young Purity Maiden no more than fifteen. At the sound of her perky voice, Solomon's eyes snapped open, bursting a blood vessel in its abruptness.

"How dare you break my mind's eye, you filthy little strumpet!" Solomon screeched as he bolted out of his chair. Fuming with anger, he wrapped his enormous fingers around the server's delicate neck. Rage overtook him, veiling the sharp gasps and shocked expressions flooding his direction. Solomon's bloodshot eyes seeped into the girl's wild, frightened ones.

"Perhaps you will break my fast today, girl," he snarled, his voice dropping down to a gravelly whisper. Solomon looked the girl up and down, an expression of disgust drawn across his face. "Unfortunately, I see nothing here that rouses my appetite. You don't even have the curve of a proper woman.

Don't women have breasts? Or are you a slender young boy who wishes to be a Maiden?"

Solomon hissed the insults through gritted teeth. He groped the girl with his free hand before tightening his grip on her throat. "You're nothing but a flavorless stick!" he shouted as he grabbed a handful of the girl's hair, slamming her head into the leg of lamb he had been fawning over. "Ruined! You ruined it!" *Thwack. Thwack. Thwack.*

Over and over he pounded, flailing the young woman around like a rag doll, smashing his plate to pieces with the force of the blows. The girl went limp, but Solomon continued his assault.

Thwack. Thwack. Thwack.

The silverware jumped up and down on the table. Dishes clattered to the floor. Shards of the shattered plate burrowed their way into the girl's face. An eruption of blood sprayed across Solomon's shirt.

Finally, he let go. Chunks of hair stuck to his hands, slick with blood. A crumpled mess lay at his feet. "Curse it all. Somebody remove this impure harlot from my presence."

Another Purity Maiden rushed to appease the enraged patron. She held back a gasp as she noticed the state of the girl's face—swollen and bloody beyond recognition.

"Get her out of here, or you will suffer for her insolence as well," barked Solomon.

Immediately, the Maiden stopped trying to help the unconscious girl to her feet and dragged her back to the kitchen. A dark trail of red painted her departure through the café. More Purity Maidens rushed to Solomon's table. One carried a piping hot leg of lamb. Another dropped to her knees by the blood-stained carpet and started working to remove the blemish.

Solomon peered down at her. "Leave it. I prefer my own work to the whitewashed appearance of this place."

The Maiden stopped, wiping tears from her eyes. With trembling hands, she joined the other Maiden in removing the blood from Mr. Pipher's shirt. With his appetite ruined, Solomon found his gaze drifting to the pool of blood the young girl had left behind. Something about it felt familiar.

MANY YEARS AGO, Solomon lived alone with his mother in the mountains. The memory from his childhood that stood out like a jagged nail was the grotesque deformity of his mother's leg. Open sores ravaged her skin from hip to ankle, gushing a milky, yellow liquid. At times, the sores would ooze, leaving a trail behind her like some overgrown slug. All of this paled in comparison to the smell. The overwhelming stench of her festering leg flooded every corner of their small one-room cabin. Even now, Solomon could taste the stench of rotting almonds on his tongue. The infection got so bad it started affecting her mind, clouding her thoughts and twisting her reality. On more than one occasion, Mother tried to smother Solomon in his sleep, screeching profanities at her son as he wriggled and fought for air.

Only Solomon's base instinct to survive kept him going. His only means of food were the rabbits, mice, and other small game roaming the fields outside the cabin. He spent the first half of his day making the snares to catch his irritatingly quick food, and the second half roaming around the trap sites hoping to find a catch. If he found himself lucky enough to find a snare occupied, he would bring his trophy home.

One night Solomon sat skinning the day's catch, bringing the small animal to his mother to cook on the fire pit. He reached out to hand his mother the carcass, not realizing he had forgotten to leave his fillet knife behind. When his mother saw the knife and exposed animal flesh, her eyes glazed over.

Her face twisted into a snarl. "How dare you come here, vermin. You said you could get it out of me. Said you could use it to make me better than ever, and now look at me. Stuck with this puss-filled log, and the bastard still in my belly."

His mother continued her feverish rant, growing more and more irate. She grimaced as she slid off her stool, yanking her useless leg behind her. Solomon stood transfixed with fear. He tried to cry out, but nothing came. His mother's bony fingers wrapped tight around his neck, squeezing with all the might she could muster. Solomon struggled to loosen her grip, clawing at her hands. The two wrestled back and forth, collapsing to the floor. After an intense struggle, his mother's iron tight grip began to loosen. She looked, clear-eyed, at the knife buried into her bum leg. "Peel off your rags, boy. Tonight you sleep in the box."

Solomon left his fresh leg of lamb sitting amongst the chaos his tantrum had created. As he walked the hallways, he did his best to shake the dark memories the morning's events had awoken. Before he could reach his destination, he ran into Sr. Father Malachi.

"Good day, Malachi," Solomon moaned as he began to slip past his fellow League member.

"A moment, Solomon," Malachi said as he placed a hand on Solomon's shoulder. "We have a matter to discuss."

Solomon shook his head, still hazy from grim nostalgia. After a moment, he remembered the incident with the young server. Solomon clicked his tongue and rolled his eyes. "Oh, please, Malachi. I taught the girl a lesson in purity. No Maiden should be permitted to be so disrespectful to a Sr. Father, especially in such a public setting."

Malachi stood firm. His eyes locked onto Solomon's. "The girl is dead, Solomon."

"And you give the word so quickly, how punctual of you," Solomon retorted without a moment's hesitation.

Malachi let out a sigh. "Solomon, your behavior has become more and more erratic as of late, even for you. The Grand Council is worried. A loose cannon is nothing but fuel for the civil unrest that's been escalating the past few months."

"Civil unrest? You can't possibly be talking about those pamphlets floating about the city speaking of *equal rights* for all, or some such garbage. Can you imagine it? Letting women, foreigners, and the like garner the same respect as those of us in the League?" Solomon's belly shook in amusement.

Malachi gave Solomon a stern look. "No threat, regardless of how small, should be taken lightly, Solomon. I dare say your inability to see the danger of those deemed lesser than yourself will be your downfall." Without another word, Malachi handed Solomon a rolled-up piece of parchment. The wax emblem of the Council sealed it shut.

"You've got to be joking," snorted Solomon. "How did they get this order out so fast? The incident happened mere moments ago. Does old man Cephas predict the future now too? You stodgy fools take months to accomplish anything, and now you're telling me you assembled, wrote a letter, and had it delivered in the time it took a couple Purity Maidens to clean up some blood?"

"You're right about one thing, Solomon. The Council did act in haste, but it was hardly moments ago. After you killed the young Maiden, your eyes glazed over. The patrons say the Maidens did all they could to rouse you, but you were unreachable. Have you snapped, Solomon? Sitting there like a numb psychopath after bludgeoning a Maiden to death is a hard sight to ignore. Now is not the time for the public to start doubting the Council's ability to keep the peace. I'm afraid we've been left with no choice but to take you to trial."

"A trial? Are you mad? The Council hasn't conducted a trial against a member of the League since my emasculated apprentice created the need for the second rule all those years ago. You remember him, Esteban? My how he wailed."

"All the more reason to take this summons seriously, Solomon. This isn't a game."

Malachi stood half a head taller than Solomon, despite being less than half his weight. Not getting the answer he desired, Malachi lowered his gaze, tucking his arms firmly behind his back.

Solomon stared up at Malachi's expectant grey eyes. "Fine, I'll play your little game. Act out my part in the theater you call a courtroom."

Malachi dropped the stern look, sweeping what little hair he had left over the top of head with his fingers. "I implore you, Solomon, don't treat this trial as a game. The reputation of the Council, of the entire League, could lie in the balance."

With nothing left to scoff at, Solomon snatched the parchment from Malachi and hurried for the exit. His appearance might have been cold, composed, even dignified as he walked out of the Crystal Pedestal, but inside his mind bordered on collapse. It took everything in his power to suppress the overwhelming scent of rotting almonds from slithering out of their place in the shadows.

CHAPTER 8

A CRACK IN THE CAGE

The monotony of Wren's morning routine crumbled under the weight of the news. Robin had been beaten to death by Mr. Pipher in the middle of the Crystal Pedestal Café. Wren had done a job for the man this morning. The image of his beady pig eyes glaring at her with their lustful glow flashed through her mind. She shuddered at the thought of those eyes bursting with rage. No wonder he never came to pick up his suit. Wren dared to hope something this drastic would be enough to get even the illustrious Mr. Pipher the punishment he deserved. Experience taught her his punishment wouldn't be anywhere near as severe as Robin's had been. The League had a reputation for claiming to punish Fathers who overstepped their extreme boundaries, but it was rare to hear of any *actual* repercussions of a Father's actions, especially against a Maiden.

Robin was such a sweet girl and quite skillful for one so young. Her calm yet warm presence could set even the most agitated customer at ease. Wren wondered what she had done to make Mr. Pipher so upset. Despite the horrific nature of the day's events, Wren couldn't help but ruminate on how this would affect her. Oriella was now her only purity companion, and Wren found her nauseating. Worse still, the threat of punishment would undoubtedly push Mr. Pipher into one of his violent outbursts. A shiver crept down her spine as she thought of what Solomon Pipher would do to vent his frustrations.

Rumors about Mr. Pipher's tactics in the purity rooms were notorious, and this morning's incident did anything but quell them. Purity Maidens would return from their purity lessons under Pipher's watch, bruised, somber, and broken. Others went missing with little to no explanation. Wren remembered the way Mr. Pipher looked at her in the hallway earlier that morning. She couldn't explain it, but she swore she could *feel* his gaze on her, his eyes devouring her like a piece of honeyed ham. Wren fought off a second shiver as she searched for something to keep her mind off of Mr. Pipher and Robin.

As adorned as her room was with pretty furniture, gowns, and jewelry, there was little to keep her occupied. With the little time Purity Maidens had to themselves, they were expected to brush their hair, perfect poses in the mirror, or think of new ways to appease their clients. The only thing they were allowed to keep in their rooms for entertainment were League-approved books. All of the books were from one of three categories: cooking, sewing, or housekeeping. Wren would rather watch paint dry. So instead of reading these books, Wren used them as outlets for her pent-up frustrations with life. Going over to her little bookshelf, Wren chose a book titled *1001 Easy Recipes For Young Hysteresis Users*. She was no good at cooking and had no plans to improve.

Taking extra care not to make too much noise, Wren ripped out several pages from the book and laid them out on her bed. Then, she placed her hand on one of the pages and emptied herself of all the day's thoughts and fears. She focused her mind's eye on a distant memory. A time before the walls and rules of New Geneva, before she called the Crystal Pedestal home. A time she could wear normal clothes and play outside in the sunshine. A time when she could speak without fear and pursue her own dreams rather than League-approved ones. A time when she had a loving family, and the word Provider meant nothing to her.

Out of these fond memories one stood out to Wren the most—playing with Elias in the small lake by their family's house. She let herself dwell on the sights, sounds, and sensations of wading free into the lake. The cool air. The soothing water. The fish tickling her toes as they darted past, and the coarse sand massaging her feet. Such a simple thing, the feeling of sand, but to her, it felt magical. Everything in the Crystal Pedestal felt polished and smooth. The memory of something rough on her skin seemed real to her in a way her current surroundings couldn't match.

Wren opened her eyes and let the sand drain through her fingers. One sheet of paper produced so little, but if she took the time to do ten, fifteen, or even twenty, she could soon have an entire handful. Wren did her best to stop this habit of turning paper into sand. She knew it would get her into some sort of trouble. She rarely found herself allowed to go outside, and nothing in her current white-washed tomb resembled anything close to the coarse dirt. Tonight, instead of altering the next nine to nineteen sheets of paper, she would put her mind to altering her sand into something she could get rid of without incident or punishment.

As Wren sat on her bed, contemplating what to do next, a sudden fear of having her collection of sand discovered overwhelmed her. The thought of purity lessons with Mr. Pipher raced through her mind. Wren dropped to the floor and grabbed a small box from under her bed. Her hand trembled as she took the lid off the box. Sand filled it nearly to the brim. She knew she had utilized this comforting practice a lot over the years, but she never imagined she had built up this much.

Determined to rid herself of the anxiety steadily growing inside her, Wren checked the lock on her door. Then she sat up on her bed and pulled her legs into her chest. As her mind searched for answers, she started playing with the pile of sand on her bed. For some reason, it helped her think. As she watched a slow stream of sand accumulate, her mind started to stray off task.

When do these small pieces of sand stop being individual things, and start to become something else? When do they stop being grains, and become a pile, a heap, or even a desert? Why does a desert become a beach when it's near a large body of water? And what about drops of water? How many does it take for them to become a puddle or a lake?

Wren shook her head clear of the tangent. These kinds of thoughts got her nowhere. Hysteresis seemed to be a better solution. She needed to change the sand into something easier to dispose of. She took a deep breath and channeled her hysteresis. Unlike changing the paper to sand, she had no focus. Nothing fixed in her mind's eye but panic and desperation. She searched for something harmless to change the sand into. Something familiar that could be hidden or discarded without incident. Something that wouldn't end with a purity lesson with Mr. Pipher.

The more she tried to focus, the more she came up empty, and the more she came up empty, the more she pushed her mind to focus. Harder and harder she pushed, hoping something, anything, would happen. Wren struggled to keep her mind's eye clear, but her current emotions proved too powerful to ignore. Anger at her father for making her a Purity Maiden.

Disgust at the actions of Mr. Pipher. The loss of the closest thing she had to a friend. A sharp, sudden pain in her finger jerked Wren out of her mind's eye. She looked down at her hand to find a streak of fresh blood. Confused, she checked the pile of sand. In its place sat four pieces of crude, jagged glass.

Wren looked around the empty room. She had no idea how this happened. She hadn't been focusing on the properties of glass. In fact, she didn't know anything about the properties of glass. Unlike sand, whose touch made sense to her, glass felt lifeless and smooth. It teased her with glimpses of the outside world, but nothing more. Regular glass could be discarded somewhere less suspicious, but this glass looked... off. Broken, cloudy, and misshapen, it would surly draw attention should it be seen. The glass being broken into sharp pieces didn't help matters. Worst of all, she had so little knowledge of glass. Attempting hysteresis on it could prove disastrous.

Despite the issues this new set of circumstances, Wren couldn't stop wondering how hysteresis even worked. None of the usual rules applied. She decided to test this on something else. She picked up a piece of the paper she ripped out of the cookbook and focused her mind's eye. A rising warmth crept into her hand as the paper erupted in flames. She sprang to turn her bedspread in on itself, smothering the flaming paper. A large black scorch mark left an unmistakable blemish on her white bedding. *Shit.*

A light rapping on her door captured her attention. "Wren, it's time for your beauty rest," sang the ever-joyful voice of Oriella.

I bet she gets lights out on purpose so she can spread her nauseating cheer to us all. "Okay, Oriella. I just need to finish reading this last page on...making crumpets."

"Well, okey dokey, Wren. That sounds scrumptious. Or

should I say, S-crumpet-ious? Maybe I'll get to try one some-day. Nighty night."

Wren rolled her eyes in deep annoyance. Once Oriella's footsteps could no longer be heard, Wren jumped up from her bed and shoved the shards of glass into the back corner of her makeup drawer. She ran back over to her mattress, flipped her bedspread over to the non-scorched side, slid her now-empty box back under her bed, and blew out the light. As she laid there, she couldn't stop herself from wondering how long it would take before the events of this night would lead to an unwanted encounter with a pissed-off Mr. Pipher.

The next morning, Wren struggled to open her eyes. It wasn't until she shook off a bit of early morning fog that she realized someone sat at the foot of her bed. Oriella was dressed for the day in a bubblegum pink dress trimmed with gaudy lace ending at mid-thigh. Despite how annoying Wren found her, she couldn't deny Oriella had a cute allure to her. She had jet black hair cut pixie style. Her smooth, dark skin shone a couple shades lighter than her hair.

Wren broke the awkward silence. "What are you doing in my room, Oriella?"

"I thought I smelled something funny coming from your room last night," replied Oriella as she wrinkled up her nose. "Just checking up on you. After all, it's you and me now, Wrenny."

Wren didn't know what bothered her more, Oriella breaking into her room without her knowledge or the fact that she seemed so goddamn cheerful about the death of their purity companion.

"She's only been dead one day, for god's sake," Wren said much louder than she intended.

Oriella raised her eyebrows and scrunched her mouth to one side. "Which is one day too long for us to get all worked up over, dontcha think?" Wren met Oriella's strange expression with laser focus. She never could get a good read on this strange girl. When Wren didn't respond, Oriella continued. "The only thing to do now is to make sure you and I are as pure as pure can be." Quick as a fox, Oriella sprang down from Wren's bed and skipped out the open door.

She is straight-up crazy, Wren thought, shaking her head in disbelief. It wasn't until she sat up and swung her legs out of bed that she noticed a small piece of paper flutter to the floor. Wren bent down to retrieve the note.

Night rounds are soooo fun! Can't wait to taste those scrumptious crumpets!

-Your one and only purity companion, Oriella

Wren couldn't say why, but rather than the normal feelings of exasperation and annoyance that came with interacting with Oriella, she felt rather unnerved. *Did Robin's death mean nothing to her? Why risk purity lessons over such a meaningless note? What's so fun about night rounds?*

"Just what I need," Wren said as she used her newfound skill to burn the note to ash.

CHAPTER 9
THE OBEDIENT WIFE

The Crivellis were one of only three married couples in the entirety of the Crystal Pedestal, and the only one involving a Sr. Purity Maiden and a Provider. Instead having the privileges one would expect, they received only the allowance to live in the same quarters. The League refused to give up even the slightest control over their precious treasures, so Wren had to stay in her own room with the other Purity Maidens. The couple's provided space was quaint, just enough for two people to live together comfortably. It had plain white walls, polished wood floors, and simplistic wooden furniture with an emphasis on practicality rather than extravagance. The whole room had the appearance of a recent scrubbing, with nothing out of place and not a blemish in sight. The place was so clean; it almost seemed a shame someone lived there.

Gerolt sat at a solid oaken table in this plain yet pristine room. His favorite pipe sat smoldering between his teeth. He glowered at the morning's paper over his reading spectacles. The front-page headline read: *LEAGUE FATHER GOES TO TRIAL.*

Gerolt skimmed the article to find the court date. It was set for the day before the Winter Festival. A clear ploy to take attention away from the trial as soon as it ended. Calculated as always.

Knowing exactly what this trial would hold, the rest of the article held no interest for him. Solomon would sit in the courtroom, peering down his nose at the judge, the jury, his own defense attorney, and at every other person in the room. He would look at them like a man wanting a fine steak but finding himself presented with bologna. He would roll his eyes and give out exasperated huffs at every little detail being presented in his case. In the end, Solomon would receive little more than a paid vacation from his position of Sr. Father, at which he would explode with anger at such an outrage. In Solomon's eyes, it wasn't murder if the victim was less than human.

Gerolt tossed the paper back onto the table and gave a small sigh. Harmony glanced up from her needlework. "What's gotten you all worked up?" she asked. After years of marriage, Harmony had learned to read her husband like nobody else could. Now, for example, she knew that despite his tranquil appearance, Gerolt was truly vexed.

"You know me too well, my dear," replied Gerolt in a calm and peaceful tone rarely heard by anyone but his wife. "It's this whole business with Mr. Pipher. I truly don't know what to do with the man. I've almost come to the point of fawning after him, and still, he pays me no more attention than any other Provider. I can't figure out what it takes to get in his good graces. If only I knew what made him tick..."

Harmony peered at her husband over her needlework. "Trying to figure out what makes a man like him tick seems like a dangerous inquiry to me, dear husband. You know what they say, madness begets madness."

"Silence," Gerolt said with urgency. "You never know who's listening."

"Relax, Gerolt," replied Harmony soothingly. "Even the League isn't suspicious enough to spy on every Provider all the livelong day."

"Ah, but they might this close to the Winter Festival. You know this is the year they vote on who will take over for old man Humphries as Lead Provider. The opportunity only comes around once every ten years, and I'll be damned if I let a single misstep by myself, or a member of my family, cost us the chance." Gerolt's calm and peaceful tone was gone, and the overly starched Gerolt came roaring to life. "I will hear no more of the illustrious Mr. Pipher today, good wife. Now be a dear and make me my breakfast."

Harmony bowed her head, put down her needlework, and headed to the kitchen to appease her husband's wishes. Harmony would have balked at the harshness of her husband's tone, and the audacity of his commands when they lived at the house on the lake. No, it was more than that. That Gerolt would never have dreamed of talking to her in such a way. Everything changed after Elias. After she used her hysteresis to kill her son's murderers and broke every rule in the Hysteresis Code. She learned long ago that in New Geneva a husband's word was final, and to disobey one's husband was worse than a Purity Maiden losing their purity. As the ancient guidebook told them, *Wives shall submit to their husbands in all things*, and the word of the book was law.

Harmony pushed all thoughts of annoyance or disrespect from her mind and focused on the task she was given. Gerolt required eggs Benedict with a side of rye toast every day for breakfast. These menu items were hard to come by unless you were a Sr. Maiden who also happened to be a master chef. Harmony set out two raw eggs, a stale piece of white bread, a glass of water, some salt, and a slice of leftover meat. She focused her mind's eye on each item in turn, letting all the doubts and questions within her melt away. She honed in on the subtleties of the dish she was making; one that she had perfected from years of practice. Just the right amount of lemon and a dash of cayenne added to her hollandaise sauce. A subtle bite added to her rye. The right mix of salty and sweet cured into her ham, and the perfect, firm but not rubbery consistency of her poached eggs. Finally, she put each piece together. As always, Gerolt's breakfast was prepared to perfection.

Harmony set the picturesque breakfast before her husband and asked, "Will that be all, sir?"

Gerolt knew she was cross with him when she called him sir, but it could not be helped as sir was clearly a title of respect. In response, Gerolt snatched up his morning paper, burying his face in an article while waving his hand dismissively at his wife. "Yes, yes. That will be fine."

Harmony straightened her white linen apron, turned sharply on her heels, and headed back to her needlework. She wouldn't mind the ease with which her husband ordered her around if he showed some signs of affection now and again. It wasn't as if he never showed her kindness. He even gave her a form of companionship, but it had been a very long time since Gerolt had last asked her to keep his bed warm. Many wives welcomed the loss of sexual intimacy with their husbands as it tended to be extremely one-sided when it came to pleasure, but Harmony missed it. For her, it was the only time they could still be equals. When she had him in a lover's embrace, she had some control over him, and for the most part, could take what she wanted from him. He seemed so vulnerable in those times, and it reminded her of the true intimacy and love they once shared in their home on the lake so many years ago. Harmony wiped a tear from her eye and buried her desires deep down in her heart. There was nothing she could do about it. Such intimacy only came about at the husband's request, and Gerolt seemed to have other things on his mind lately.

At that moment, Harmony found herself burning with rage. As if the man didn't already have enough, he must take her husband's thoughts from her as well? She secretly hoped the trial of Solomon Pipher would end in a death sentence, but she knew better. A League Father had not been truly disciplined since they took over as New Geneva's form of government over forty years ago. Meanwhile, citizens from New Geneva who broke even the smallest of the League's rules faced heavy fines, or worse, got banished to the LHC. There had to be thousands of folks disciplined in the League's courtroom over those forty years.

Given the drastic differences in justice, Harmony found it quite unlikely things would change anytime soon. Her anger would have to stay buried, along with her desire and her self-respect. If anyone were to say one thing about Harmony Crivelli, they'd say she was good at making herself appear small.

"I've got it!" Gerolt shouted with such uncharacteristic force that Harmony nearly jammed her sewing needle through her finger in surprise. "I know how to win over that stubborn man once and for all. It will require your assistance, dear wife. Do you still have the keys to Robin's locker in the Crystal Pedestal Café?"

Harmony furrowed her brow in confusion. "Of course, I do. I'm still the Sr. Maiden in the café, aren't I?"

"Yes, yes, of course. I had to be sure. Now, listen closely to what I require of you. Take the small wooden box I keep stashed under the sink. You know the one, do you not?"

"Yes, of course I do, sir."

"Wait until mid-moon tonight and then carefully take the

box into the Crystal Pedestal Café. Use your keys to get into Robin's storage locker and hide it amongst her things. I'm quite certain they haven't disposed of them yet. A girl so impure is almost certain to be dumped over the wall and forgotten."

"I don't understand, Gerolt. Why would you want me to put—"

"Silence," Gerolt interrupted, eyes wide with urgency. "I will not have you speak anymore of this aloud."

Harmony stood there, motionless. She had no idea why Gerolt would ask her to do such a thing. Then, like a punch to the stomach, it hit her...and it took all the breath from her chest. Harmony stared at Gerolt in disbelief. Clearly, he was serious about the matter. She knew the stern look in his eyes meant business. A look she had seen entirely too much of lately.

"You ask too much of me, sir... I-I can't do that to her."

"If I, your husband, am asking it of you, then there's no such thing as too much," replied Gerolt. He held his head up and to the side, the same way he did when he was correcting an overly ambitious Purity Maiden. "Besides, this matter does not only benefit me, but you and Wren as well. If we get in Mr. Pipher's good graces, especially in his rare time of need, he will surely see us rise to more lofty places within the Crystal Pedestal. I tire of the incompetence of the other Providers. They need a man with order and structure to be the next Lead Provider. If Jeremiah or Lance is promoted instead, I wouldn't be able to bear it. Imagine the torture of having one of those two bumbling morons being able to tell me how to run my life to such a degree."

Harmony did all she could to hold back from making a comment about the irony of her husband's statement. She knew it would fall on deaf ears anyway. Any respect Gerolt once held for her opinions received a slow death sentence the moment they walked through New Geneva's walls, and now seemed to be gone entirely. If she was honest, she wanted to leave the Crystal Pedestal more than anything. But she wasn't naive enough to believe that getting out would grant her the return of her considerate, loving husband. Maybe with enough time...

"Okay, husband. I will do as you ask. I just need to know one thing."

"And what's that?"

"What happens if I'm caught out past curfew? Wouldn't it be better for you to go?"

Gerolt thought for a few seconds before making his reply. "I'm not able to take such a risk with the Lead Provider vote coming up. I have no reason to be in the café, especially in the middle of the night. Imagine the rumors such news would create. I guess you'll have to be extra careful, won't you, dear wife?"

With one last stern look, Gerolt raised his newspaper blockade. His mind was set. Not seeing any way out of it, Harmony would do as she was told. She would betray the memory of an innocent girl for the sake of a man who already had the world at his feet. Gerolt glanced over his paper boundary for one last bit of instruction. "You best figure out how to pull this off soon, wife. The trial is in two days."

Those were the last words Gerolt spoke to her the entire morning. She had her instructions. His will was set. What more was there to say? Harmony quietly excused herself from the table and went to her bedroom for some air. Her thoughts raced with fear and anxiety at the task set before her; but even more than that, she felt alone. As the years in New Geneva dragged on, loneliness had become her emotional catalyst. Everything from her day-to-day activities to the out-of-the-ordinary bits of excitement, all of it seemed to slip past her untouched. It was as if her whole life had a thick film covering it.

The only good part of this morning's craziness was that it evoked enough of a response in her body for her to feel something fully for a change. Perhaps these grim events would lead to some good. Maybe this would be the thing she needed to get Gerolt to love her, want her, and notice her again...the way he used to in the house by the lake.

Harmony went over to the sink and grabbed the box Gerolt had asked her to deliver. The small brown box looked far more threatening to her than its ordinary appearance would suggest. She bit her lip and rubbed her sweaty palms on her apron.

You don't have a choice...

You can't disobey your husband...

It's for the good of your family...

Prove you're worthy of his love...

Make him notice you, as he once did...

Suddenly, the air in the room felt thin, and she couldn't catch her breath. She needed to get out, take a walk, anything but stand there in the silence her husband laid at her feet. Harmony glanced back at Gerolt as she strode out the door, hoping he would call her back, admit this was madness, wrap her in his arms, and tell her how much of a fool he had been. Instead, all she got was a slightly surprised expression and a sharp ruffling of newspaper.

CHAPTER 10

PIPHER'S PLIGHT

Not many things could intimidate Solomon Pipher. The sight of the massive stone doors leading to the Hall of Weights and Scales happened to be one of those things. He attempted to convince his brain that the Hall was nothing more than a large box filled with decrepit authority figures. This only reminded him of the much smaller and more sinister box his mother used to punish him. A shiver crept down his spine as his eyes took in the ornately carved doors.

"Forcing me to get all worked up over an indignant whore," Solomon said aloud, letting his voice carry enough to ensure the clerk managing the desk heard him. The clerk looked around, confirming himself as the only other person in the lobby. He cleared his throat and dabbed his pen in a nearby jar of ink. Solomon clenched his jaw. If there is one thing Solomon hated most, it was feeling weak, and this turn of events proved to him how much weaker he was than the Grand Council. Despite being a high-ranking Sr. Father, Solomon could still be ordered around by this group of old, dried-up prunes.

After an insultingly long time, the clerk pulled his gaze away from the document on his desk. "It is now permissible for you to enter, Mr. Pipher."

Solomon seethed at the audacity of this mere clerk. He was already in a foul mood, and this uppity peasant would not get off talking to *him* like that. As he stood, eyes locked with the clerk, Solomon fixed his mind's eye on the sensation of maggots burrowing into flesh, the way they would if they were disposing of a decaying body. Each small creature burrowing their microscopic teeth into tender meat. A thousand tiny musicians gathered up in a symphony to deliver an over-whelming performance. Solomon held this sensation in his mind's eye as he began walking towards the massive stone doors.

As he got closer to the desk, he could see the clerk's eyes go from steely meeting his gaze to wide-eyed horror. Solomon's sensory projection took hold, slipping past the clerk's logic and into his consciousness. The clerk's eyes grew wider still. The skin on his arms and neck stood on edge as he scanned the room for anything out of place. A few moments later, the clerk dropped to his knees. His mouth fell open as the torturous sensations built to a crescendo. It started off as a small itch under his skin.

As Solomon walked closer, the itching spread, trans-forming into pinpricks of intense pain. The clerk's mind searched for meaning in the pain. Solomon gave it to him. Dozens of maggots appeared over the clerk's body, squirming with delight as they feasted. The clerk sank deeper and deeper into Solomon's sensory projection, continuing to lose his grip on reality.

Solomon could pinpoint the moment the projection took complete hold; the exact moment the clerk lost all reason. Solomon could see it in his eyes: a cold, distant stare, highlighted with an edge of terror. The clerk dug his nails franti-cally into his arms, neck, and face, leaving them covered in weeping, red troughs as he screamed out in equal parts pain and terror. Solomon smirked at how easily he could trick a man into mutilating himself. His smirk dropped to a scowl as he watched the young man tear at his decidedly maggot-free body.

Once his bruised ego had its fill, Solomon walked over to the reception desk and stood over the writhing young man. "Don't make a fool of yourself, boy. Hurry up and do your miserable job." Eyes wide, the clerk scrambled for the switch to release the stone doors leading to the Grand Council's cham-ber. As the doors groaned open, Solomon stepped over the cowering clerk and into the entrance of the Hall of Weights and Scales.

As Solomon took in the enormous chasm stretched out before him, he soured at the realization that the only purpose of such an exorbitantly long hallway was to force men like him to walk down its lengths while stewing in their own anxiety. To add insult to injury, the hall wasn't just long, it was also extravagant. Every ten feet, a massive white pillar stretched from the finely marbled tiles on the floor to the ornately domed ceiling a hundred feet off the ground. Each pillar was etched with excerpts from the ancient book the League declared to be law. Every carving in the pillar was filled to the brim with gold, making a single pillar cost a fortune in its own right. The white marble floor of the hall caused each and every step one took towards the Grand Council to echo off of the highly vaulted ceiling. After walking for what seemed like an eternity, Solomon arrived at the table where the Grand Council awaited him.

The Grand Council consisted of four Sr. Fathers, all of whom sat around a crescent-shaped table made of dark granite and topped with a bright white slab of marble three inches thick. The crescent table sat slightly elevated and across from a smaller square table, just big enough for two people to sit abreast, or one in this case. Before each of the Council members' seats were slightly varying styles of the weights and scales of justice, etched from a variety of gemstones. Solomon looked at each of the men sitting before him, disgust apparent on his portly features. Titus, Malachi, Sampson, and Cephas were the four of them made up the Grand Council of the League of Fathers. They were the only ruling body in New Geneva, and the only men who held any power over Solomon Pipher.

"Please take a seat, Solomon. We have much to discuss, and you look tired as it is." Father Titus' voice was gravelly.

Solomon pulled out his chair at the square table and sank into it with as much grace a man of his physique could muster. After he wiped off an impressive amount of perspiration from his swollen face, Solomon locked eyes with Titus.

"You're damned right, we do. I see no reason why this incident should be brought to trial. Things of this sort have occurred countless times before, and with less cause for action. This harlot openly disrespected me and broke my mind's eye in a public setting. Tell me one League Father who wouldn't be outraged by such a display?"

"Calm yourself, Solomon. Don't forget who you are addressing," replied Titus, a burly, pale man with a tightly cropped head of white hair. "While it's true that the victim was a Purity Maiden whom you *claim* showed disrespect towards her superior, the fact remains you acted harshly and with little tact. Especially considering how many witnesses were present. I mean, good god Solomon, what were you thinking? How could a mere woman, nay, a young girl, get you so flustered? Why didn't you simply summon her to the purity rooms?"

"Claim? *Claim!*" bellowed Solomon, meeting his superior's judgmental gaze and pounding his huge fist on the table. "Are you suggesting I am mistaken, and the little wench was in her rights when she dared to disturb my mind's eye, or are you simply attempting to rouse my temper?"

Titus continued as if he was talking to a child throwing a tantrum. "As if I needed any effort to accomplish that task Solomon, but no, I am merely suggesting her less than impeccable timing was not grounds for a public execution in a crowded café."

Solomon took a moment to collect himself before he spoke again. He could only lose his temper so many times before it would become a problem. "If this is about the loss of revenue her father would receive, I am more than willing to compensate the man for his loss. Despite my reputation, I'm not an animal. I obey all the laws the League decrees, and I am certain there are lines in the ancient book that plead my case as well. Something about slaves and masters if my mind serves."

This time it was Sampson who spoke up, a brute of a man at least seven feet tall with a booming voice and a long black beard. "This is not about money, Solomon. Although you will need to compensate her father. This is about public appearance. The public does not view the Purity Maidens as our slaves, but as women taking up their role in our great society. As Father Titus said, this outburst was seen by a great number of witnesses. It would be foolish of us to let it go without a trial."

Solomon thought about pushing his point further but eventually relented to the fact that men in power don't like to be argued with. Perhaps he would have better luck pandering to their little charade. "Then please educate me, esteemed Fathers. Who exactly do we need to impress? What is this new need for public approval? Do we not make a decree, and it becomes so?"

Titus straightened in his massive chair. "It's precisely this way of thinking that has kept you from sitting on this side of the table, Solomon. There is more to leadership than exacting power and control over those you lead. We don't lead the public like we lead a Purity Maiden. The citizens of New Geneva are of a free mind as long as they obey the laws of the land. Leading our citizens the way you suppose might get you fear and obedience, but it won't get you respect or loyalty. For now, know we are rejecting your appeal, and the trial will go on as scheduled."

Solomon could see he was powerless to avoid a public trial, and that was a feeling he loathed to the core of his being. He hated the Council for causing him to retract, but he knew if he gave in to his desire to make them eat their words, he would regret it. On the other hand, if he stepped back too much, he would risk losing their respect, which would not bode well for him. In the League, respect was power. For this reason, Solomon thought out his next words very carefully.

"If you think for a moment that I will go through with this trial without giving the least bit of resistance, then you know nothing about Solomon Pipher. I may be fiercely loyal to the League of Fathers, but I will not be cowed into submission like one of your Purity Maidens. If you continue to refuse my appeal, I will hire the best attorney money can buy, and I will use every ounce of my extensive knowledge of the League's book of rules to make this trial as long and as drawn out as possible. If you truly mean to keep up good public opinion, then simply declare a sentence and be done with it. I'm through with this sham of a trial. I won't be paraded about to the murmurs of our lesser citizens. Compared to me, they are no higher than maggots. And speaking of maggots, you might want to call the healers out to address some of your clerk's needs. He seems to have injured himself quite badly."

Solomon knew the last part was laying it on a little thick. He also knew all of his talk of loyalty and bravado were getting him nowhere. Solomon weathered the Council's cold stares for as long as he could muster before slowly pushing himself away from the table. He purposefully kept his full weight in the chair as he did. The metal chair screamed against the marbled floor and echoed off of the hall's vaulted ceilings. With his head held high, Solomon stood and headed for the exit. He half expected one of the four to call out to him, offer him a reprimand, or a question concerning the clerk. Instead, all he heard were the sounds of his finely made shoes on the cold marble floor.

After what seemed like an eternity, Solomon made it down the entire length of the hallway and out the enormous double doors. He was more than ready to be done with the Council. He couldn't remember the last time he felt so powerless or weak. Certainly not since his days in the decrepit log cabin with his crippled mother. The memories of those days hung in his subconscious like a shadow, waiting for an opportunity to be free of their box. It took every ounce of focus Solomon had to keep the lid on.

Solomon walked the path from the Hall of Weights and Scales to the gated community in which he resided with his eyes glued to the white granite streets. The last thing he needed was some baby-faced apprentice chatting him up, or worse yet, a fellow League Father. The shadow of the box left him no room to exchange idle chit-chat. Not that anyone with a fraction of sense would dare address a scowling Solomon Pipher without ample cause.

The gated community housed the vast majority of the League's Fathers and apprentices. Most resided in identical white marble houses. Made of the same marble that constructed the floor of the Hall of Weights and Scales and the city's expansive walls, each house measured thirty feet long, thirty feet wide, and fifty feet high, and stood mere feet from their neighbors. The combination of their polished white marble and oddly proportioned dimensions made the whole of them look like unmarked graves from afar.

Solomon saw these homes as paltry things, all crammed together and identical. Sr. Father's such as himself were permitted to commission their own customized mansion, built precisely to their standards, and without a single one of their desires left unmet. Some put all of their efforts into size or luxurious building materials. Solomon put value into much different categories. His commission included thirty servants between the ages of eight and twenty-seven. The males were released upon their twentieth birthday, as they were deemed to be men, but the female servants could only leave if granted a transfer of ownership, otherwise known as marriage. Solomon didn't have a wife or family of his own. Families required time and energy. A distraction for his great mind and nothing more. Servants were a much better choice. No arguments. No to-do lists. Nothing but complete and utter obedience.

Twenty of these servants were assigned to the kitchen. Ten were cooks, five were Purity Maidens tasked with ensuring every room in the house smelled like one of Solomon's favorite dishes, and five served food and cleaned up afterward. Of the remaining ten servants not at work in the kitchen, five kept the house clean and organized, leaving the final five to serve as Solomon's personal companions.

These last five were handpicked by Solomon himself. Three girls and two boys, all of which he kept locked up in his master bedroom. Each personal companion wore shackles around their wrists and ankles. A heavy chain hung from each appendage with enough length to allow them to roam

Solomon's master suite while preventing them from leaving it. Any name these personal companions had before becoming Solomon's property was erased, and replaced with one that fit the role they played in fulfilling his desires. If truth be told, Solomon only wished to have one personal companion, but no single individual could satisfy him. He had to split up his needs between these five fragments. Fear, Lust, Loathe, Indulgence, and Grace. He would need to spend some quality time with Loathe tonight. Solomon licked his lips. He could taste her self-hatred and despair already.

As he made his way up the stairs, Solomon could hear the comforting sounds of chains clinking together. He burst in the door and immediately summoned Loathe to come to his side. The young girl, no older than fourteen, came clamoring over, eyes down and tears running hot down her face. Solomon grabbed the girl, hooking his finger under her chin and jerking her gaze up to meet his.

"Why would you wish to look upon your own wretched feet rather than my comely face?" Solomon's voice held an eerily soothing tone. The girl's feet were left unwashed and bare. Her toenails grew two inches longer than her toes and were covered in a crusty, mildew-like fungus. "No part of you is worth looking upon. You're an ugly little worm, remember? The only reason I keep you around is so Lust and Grace can have a pet."

Solmon watched in delight as Loathe's eyes pooled with tears. It didn't matter how many times he insulted and deprived the girl of her basic needs. His words always cut to her soul. He knew exactly what to say to make her hate herself even more than she hated him. Solomon let go of the girl's face, sauntered over to a large silver mirror, and began to undress. Without a stitch of clothing, he resumed his assault on the young girl.

"You know, Loathe, some people say I'm a fat, disgusting cretin, but you know what's worse?" He turned to face the girl once more. "Being that revolting creature's plaything. I know you might be wondering why I would want to play with such a thing as you. Why I would purposefully pick you to be my companion over all the other girls and boys I could have chosen. Well listen up little one, and I'll tell you a secret."

Loathe looked up with a glimmer of hope in her eyes.

"I hand-picked you because you're at just the right age. When a girl begins to turn into a woman, she often feels awkward, ugly, and disgusting. That paired with the fact you are a tall, gangly girl with low self-esteem made you too perfect to pass up. All I have to do is convince you of what you already know. You're a worthless pile of human shit, only worthy of satisfying a monster such as myself."

The more Solomon convinced Loathe to hate herself, the more pleasure he would gain. No matter which emotion Solomon craved, once he was full, he would be consumed by lust. His whole body would ache for it. Even food would lose its appeal. The trouble was he didn't desire his more interesting companions—Loathe, Indulgence, Fear, or Grace—in any sort of sexual way. The girl named Lust was nothing more than a vapid doll, unable to give Solomon the emotional reactions he desired from the other four, but none of that mattered once he was full to bursting with Loathe's emotions. His loins ached for release.

"Lust!" bellowed Solomon, wildly searching the room for the object of his desire. It's time for you to earn your keep ...

After Solomon finished with Lust, she held absolutely no value to him. As he shoved the sobbing girl off of his bed, Solomon noticed a parchment of paper tumble to the floor. Upon further inspection, he saw it was sealed with a wax imprint depicting the weights and scales of the Grand Council.

What could those nauseating bureaucrats possibly have to say to me now? Annoyed at the cloak and dagger of it all, Solomon rolled off the bed, leaned down, and snatched up the parcel. It read:

For the eyes of Solomon Humphrey Pipher. Any person who reads this document who is not Solomon Humphrey Pipher is committing an act of aggression against the League of Fathers and will be dealt with in just.

Solomon,

If we could have breached this topic in our meeting today, we certainly would have, but discreteness in this matter is of the utmost importance. First and foremost, this letter is to inform you that during your trial, you will be disbarred from your status as Sr. Father and cast out of the League.

Before you get too upset, let us explain our decision. As it happens, your outburst in the Crystal Pedestal Café could not have come at a better time. The Grand Council requires a loyal member to start a new branch of the League of Fathers. One that needs to be hidden from the eyes of the public for the time being. For this reason, you will be removed from your home and must take up temporary residence elsewhere in the city. If your trial's outcome permits it, you will be allowed to spend your days inside the walls of New Geneva living amongst the common folk, but you will not be permitted inside the Crystal Pedestal, the Hall of Weights and Scales, the gated community, the Proving Grounds, or any of the League's hysteresis schools. You may bring along whatever personal affects you deem most important, but keep it light.

This position will require you to be relentless, discrete, and at times brutal, but only in good time. Until we say otherwise, you must refrain from using any sort of physical violence amongst the people. We are calling this branch the Inquisition. Its stated purpose will be to ensure the citizenry of New Geneva respect the laws, decrees, and persons of the League of Fathers to the fullest. However, the real task of the Inquisition is to locate and eliminate a group of individuals known only as Aequalitatem. This group has publicly, albeit from the shadows, denounced the League's leadership, and this we cannot allow.

They are the ones responsible for the equality for all paraphernalia that's been circulating about the city. All this group has truly accomplished is making it clear how loose our grip on the city has been. You, Solomon, are to be the firm hand that tightens that grip. We chose you partially due to the situation you find yourself in, but also because of your overall loyalty to our cause, and your stomach for the grotesque. Once we have cleared you to act as Head Father of the Inquisition, you will be permitted to detain any and all citizens who openly disrespect or defy the decrees of the League of Fathers.

When the time is right, you will be permitted to use any means necessary to find and apprehend the individuals that make up the aforementioned group. You may also handpick five apprentices from our lower ranks to aid you in your quest. Those five fingers of justice, along with your mighty arm, shall be the fist that crushes any threat or grievance to the League from within New Geneva and its surrounding subsidiaries.

Prove your worth, Solomon, and all this power will be yours.

By Decree of the Grand Council

BETWEEN A ROCK AND A SHARP PLACE

Memories of the previous day floated through Wren's head like a dream. Heat filled her eyes and nose, opening the way for her locked-up emotions to pour out. She wiped her cheek and pressed her palms against her throbbing temples. Questions without answers bullied their way to be processed first, but she could only focus on one problem at a time. If she let all of it overwhelm her at once, she would feel even more helpless than she already did. She needed to focus. Gerolt would never allow her clients to see her in such a state. A few calming breaths later, the questions subsided to a dull roar.

Her mind clear, her next move revealed itself. She had to do something about the illicitly crafted glass and the scorched bedding before her Provider came in for morning prep. She could not rely on the fact that her Provider happened to be her father. With the way Gerolt had been acting lately, he wouldn't deal with the issue in a fatherly way. Morning prep ticked closer; she no longer had time to lay and wallow in her questions. In a sudden panic, Wren sprang out of bed and locked her door. Her eyes scanned the room, settling on the shards of glass. The shards clinked together in her trembling hands as she made her way over to her vanity. With so little space to hide contraband, she would have to settle for the back of her jewelry drawer.

With the glass out of sight, she turned to her bed to flip over her burnt comforter. The dark smear of black from last night's events seemed to taunt her as she tried to think of a way to erase the evidence of her impurity. After an embarrassing amount of time ticked by, Wren reached up and smacked herself on the forehead with the palm of her hand. *Why didn't I think of that earlier?* Wren thought to herself as she realized how easy this first problem could be taken care of with a little hysteresis.

Altering clothing was one of her specialties, and her bedding was made of similar material. Wren sat down on her bed and began to cycle through the many altering jobs she had been given over the years. Before long, she remembered a job where she removed a burn mark from an iron left on a dress shirt for too long. The burn was removed by focusing on the properties of the material before it got burned. It required a great deal more relaxation than a typical altering. The opposite state of mind from when she ignited the paper that caused the mark to be there in the first place.

Taking a deep breath, Wren forced all other looming thoughts out of her head and focused her mind's-eye on nothing but her bedding—how it felt on her skin, the bright white coloring, even the way it smelled when freshly washed. Once her mind was steadied she took herself back to the house by the lake. That special place which allowed her to drop her mind to an almost ethereal state. At the same time, she had to ensure that this memory didn't disrupt her focus on the properties of the bedding. After holding this state of mind for longer than she thought she needed, Wren opened her eyes. To her relief, the mark was gone, and her bedding returned to its soft, white state. It even smelled like it just came out of the wash.

This simple act quieted the questions in her mind. She had felt so hopeless moments before, but taking a step towards some sort of solution gave her a sense of power over her own situation. Or perhaps the feeling came from doing something without being told to do so. Turning paper to sand was one thing. It was completely different than anything she did for a customer in the Crystal Pedestal. Altering her bedding felt like an actual job in every sense of the word, yet she'd done it out of her own will and without a critique or a mark of praise from a client or Provider. This small glimpse of freedom made Wren feel an emotion she couldn't quite describe. She surmised that it was something between hope and pride. It was amazing how such a simple success could give her enough confidence to deal with her other problems. She had always known she didn't need a Provider to look after her. *You can do anything you put your mind to, my little songbird.* With this encouragement lifting her spirits, Wren began to work out what to do about the shards of glass.

Knock, knock, knock. "Wren, it's Gerolt. It's time for your morning prep."

"Yes, Fa-I mean yes, Provider." Without delay, Wren walked over to unlock her door for Gerolt. Gerolt held his head up high, his movements stiff and exaggerated as his eyes scanned her room for anything out of place rather than looking at her.

"Your room seems to be in good order. It even smells clean," offered Gerolt as he made his way over to her wardrobe and swung the doors open. "What dress shall you wear today? Something simple yet elegant, I believe. Ah, how about this lovely pearl-white sundress and matching cashmere sweater. Yes, this will do quite nicely."

As Gerolt laid the outfit on her bed, Wren froze with fear as she realized the next part of the morning routine would send Gerolt rifling through her drawers to find an assortment of jewelry to match the clothes he picked out for her. Any second now, she would hear his harsh rebuke and be ushered down to the purity rooms.

"Provider," eked Wren.

"Yes, Wren?"

"I've been practicing my ability to match garments with jewelry for my clients, as I think my next area of study will be jewelry upkeep and care. Do you think I might offer a respectable match for this lovely dress you have picked out for me?"

Gerolt stopped rifling through Wren's drawers and turned his icy gaze at her.

A soft sigh escaped his parted lips. "Wren, you know well enough that jewelry upkeep and care is only offered to Sr. Maidens who have perfected a minimum of three other areas of study, and have had no purity lessons in the last three years. While you are clear on the purity lessons, you only have color alteration and stain removal as areas of perfected hysteresis. Not only that, but you have yet to attain the status of Sr. Maiden."

Wren looked down at her feet. The feelings of pride and hope she held mere moments ago seemed a distant memory, quickly replaced by her old friend's humiliation, loneliness, and worst of all, worthlessness. *Practically nothing, as always.*

"Yes, Provider. I'm sorry to have jumped to such lofty conclusions."

"It's no trouble, my dear," Gerolt replied. "It's good for you to have high aspirations. Just know your place before you seek to attain them."

Moving on with the day's prep, Gerolt slid open Wren's jewelry drawer. Wren closed her eyes and waited for the reprimand. She could feel the sting on her face as his hand lashed across it. She pictured herself standing before Mr. Pipher, looking deep into those beady pig eyes as he licked his lips and waddled over to her. Any second, her life would take a drastic turn for the worse.

"These will do wonderfully," Gerolt said as he laid out a set of pearl earrings and a silver necklace adorning a small bird. "Now, don't dawdle. I'll be back in twenty minutes with your breakfast."

Wren let out a long sigh. She had been holding her breath ever since Gerolt opened her jewelry drawer. At that moment, it became overwhelmingly apparent that the shards of glass must be taken care of before the next morning's prep. Luck might have been with her today, but tomorrow morning could go much, much worse. Careful not to cut herself, Wren grabbed the glass from the back of the drawer and wrapped them in one of her washcloths to dull the edges. Then she used a couple of hair ribbons to bind the wrapped glass to her leg high enough that even the short dress Gerolt picked out for her would cover them. For extra security, she risked putting on some translucent stockings, even though Gerolt had not laid them out for her.

As she went about her morning routine, Wren found herself wrestling with her thoughts and feelings from this morning's events. She desperately wanted to recreate that moment of hope and pride she felt when removing the scorch mark on her bedding. It reminded her of the days with her father at the house on the lake. Each passing day seemed to take another piece of that Gerolt away. Words of encouragement and pride had been replaced with doubt and insecurity. She hated being corrected at the smallest error or being told she wasn't ready or capable of doing the simplest things. Even more than either of those, she desperately wanted to avoid being sent down for purity lessons.

Before long, Gerolt returned with a small plate of cantaloupe and raisins. "Here you are, my dear. Now eat up. I'll be back to fetch you for your first client of the day before you know it. Remember, the Crystal Pedestal opens the moment the sun bears first light. Don't keep me waiting."

Wren popped a piece of cantaloupe into her mouth, mulling over the events of the last few days. Despite all the extra pain rolling around in her head, this was the first morning in recent memory she didn't ask herself the question *—is there a difference between living and existing?* Maybe all the excitement from the last few days had created a distraction. No, it was more than that. Her life received some semblance of purpose from having the events of her day altered, even if ever so slightly. It did not matter if those events were scary, confusing, or sad; they still helped her think about something other than the lingering questions about her father's love for her, her worthlessness outside of approved tasks, or of her feelings of heart-wrenching loneliness. These events gave her something to think about besides clothes, flavor enhancement, stain removal, and looking pretty, and she liked that. She liked that a lot.

It's your gift Wren, what will you do with it? Wren set her jaw and clenched her fist. She would leave this wretched place someday. She would leave here, find the house on the lake, and run her toes through the sand...

Knock, knock, knock. "Wren, are you ready, my little songbird?"

"Yes, Provider," replied Wren as she opened the door.

"Why Wren, I'm absolutely shocked. I don't think I've ever known you to be ready this quickly. The family needs *this* Wren to show up more often," Gerolt said as he offered Wren his arm.

As the two walked down the hallway towards the common room, Gerolt ran through Wren's list of clients for the day, which included the usual League members, merchants, rich men's wives, healers, men of the law, and so on. She had a full docket today, but if she worked as quickly as she could, with no room for daydreaming in between, she could finish in a quarter of the time. Then she could spend the rest of her day trying to figure out how to rid herself of the shards of glass that were already threatening to slice open the tender skin of her inner thighs at the slightest wrong move.

CHAPTER 12
AEQUALITATEM

The city of New Geneva looked almost regal in the morning sunrise. The smooth, white marbled walls reflected the sun's rays, making the whole city appear to be made of crystal. The endless expanse of glittering, powder-white snow bowed to its glory. Nico found the sight repulsive. Despite being a refuge from the raiding parties camped out in the nearby mountains, and the closest thing to civilization for over fifty miles, those walls were nothing but a shining beacon of tyranny broadcasting their wild abuse of power to the world. Nobody could get past those pearly gates without obtaining a writ of passage from the Grand Council, and those were about as easy to come by as a Purity Maiden in a local brothel. Outside merchants were made to pay such exorbitant fees to obtain one that even if they made a huge profit while selling their wares, they were in danger of coming out at a loss.

For this reason, family traders and traveling tinkers had moved on years ago. The few merchants wealthy enough to stay within the city were all but assured a monopoly in their respective areas of trade. All of the lower-class merchants were forced to market their goods outside of New Geneva in the ghetto outside its walls referred to as the LHC.

If you weren't one of the wealthiest one percent, your only hope of turning a profit within the city walls came at the hands of one of the three elite guilds, and each one of them swam in their own unique brand of excrement. The Guild of Spicers once sold a wide variety of exotic spices, mostly for cooking and preserving foods. As hysteresis became more and more commonplace within the city, salt became the only spice anyone needed to purchase. A skilled Purity Maiden could create any flavor under the sun from a pinch of the stuff. They could also alter the salt for a fraction of the cost of shipping an exotic spice from halfway across the world.

Every so often, the Guild of Spicers would find some new and exotic spice the hysteresis users in New Geneva knew nothing about. This would buy them a month's worth of profits before the Purity Maidens would learn enough about the new spice to render it a worthless commodity as well. So, the Spicers were left to deal in ingredients no Purity Maiden would ever be permitted to have knowledge of. This dangerous and addictive substance became known as spice and made up three quarters of the guild's profits.

The other guilds were no better and some even worse. The Guild known as Westminster's gave up selling farming equip-ment and tools to pursue the still-profitable selling of arms and armor. This fact alone wouldn't be so bad if the majority of their sales consisted of something other than under-the-table dealings with the murderous mountain clans. These groups of nomads used the Westminster's products for plundering their way through the outlying villages whenever they felt the itch to. But perhaps the worst, and most drastically changed of the three, was the guild known as Serendipity. In the days before the Crystal Pedestal became the economic heart of New Geneva, Serendipity dealt in the least profitable field of them all—low-class workers. Serendipity was more of a union than a guild, giving the people who had no voice a chance to be treated fairly. It was also a place anyone seeking work could turn to in their time of need.

In time, the cheap, overly effective form of labor the Crystal Pedestal provided all but erased the working class. This left Serendipity searching for ways to make coin. To their credit, Serendipity stood strong for five years after the other guilds fell, refusing to give in to nefarious means of turning profit. In the end, they would fall the hardest. A little over thirty-five years ago, the core members of Serendipity were on the verge of bankruptcy. In their moment of desperation, they turned to the truly heinous for their retribution.

The seemingly boundless uses of hysteresis left little work to be done, rendering even slave labor essentially useless. So, Serendipity made a move to exploit the more hidden desires of the rich by selling them what they called personal companions. Each of these personal companions were carefully selected for quality, then sold at a ludicrously high price to the highest bidder. Only the richest and most elite within the city could afford to own more than one or two of these slaves. Despite their exorbitant price tag, the slave trade was commonplace enough that few questioned its morality.

Nico was one of the few who did. In fact, the only group he hated more than Serendipity was the League of Fellows. He might not look the part of a warrior for equality. He had long black hair hanging loose and free, a long, angry scar running across the left side of his face, a sharply angled nose from countless healed fractures, and cool gray eyes. Nico started Aequalitatem to combat complacency in the face of evil. The citizens within New Geneva's walls had grown complacent, even ignorant, to the degree the League abused their power. Even without knowing how horrid their treatment of Purity Maidens had become, to what degree they hoarded resources, or how they hid the true nature of the book they held so sacred, anyone with eyes could see that things were not as they should be. New Geneva desperately needed a moral compass. It needed someone to fight for those who couldn't fend for themselves, to take a stand against the seemingly untouchable members of the League of Fellows. Others might see the LHC as a den of the cursed, abandoned, and disenfranchised, but Nico saw a land ripe for rebellion.

Most shuddered at the idea of standing up to the all-powerful League of Fellows, so the movement remained a one-man show for a while. Eventually, Nico found a small handful of souls brave enough, or desperate enough, to stand up to such an overwhelmingly powerful foe. These first few are now known as Nico's inner circle and help Nico make all the group's decisions.

As a last-ditch effort to recruit more followers, Nico made the call to reveal himself as a hysteresis user, and one trained by a Sr. Father of the Grand Council no less. Nico had initially resisted disclosing this information because he wanted to stay on an even plane with the men and women who would stand and fight by his side. He also didn't want to be associated with those scoundrels in the League, but in the end, the truth had paid off.

Having a leader who could use the same mysterious ability as the League made people feel capable of fighting back, and soon the group grew from those first few to a network of nearly a thousand. Most of them had no idea what Nico was actually capable of, nor did they know the terrifying degree to which the League Fathers had pushed the limits of their own hysteresis, but that was more truth than he thought his followers could handle.

In honesty, Nico didn't know the full extent of the Fathers' abilities himself. He knew there were many different schools the Fathers trained their apprentices in, but he had little to no idea of what those schools actually produced in a dedicated student, let alone the Fathers themselves. Nico had trained under a man named Malachi and was an apprentice at his School of Density. After leaving the League, Nico was labeled a traitor. This mattered little to Nico, as he would rather die than continue to be a part of what those monsters had done to the world.

Before he left the League, Nico had very little idea what life was like for those on the outside. He was much too young to remember life before the fall of the guilds, and he never had a reason to leave the city walls. He learned the history of the LHC from the large population of elderly residing there. The average age in the LHC continued to go up as the prospect for honest work went down. Many of the young were either sold as slaves, killed, captured by the mountain raiders, or moved on to the false hope of greener pastures. Others were lost in childbirth or succumbed to disease. This left the old and bitter to sit around and tell stories of the good old days before the Crystal Pedestal took away their livelihoods.

These stories painted a different world from the one Nico had grown up with. A world where life didn't matter. Of an entire society left to rot. He would fight for a world where the actions of the soul and words of the heart determined one's worth, not the organs between one's legs or the family of one's birth.

Many had proven to share this belief, turning Aequalitatem

into quite a sizable force. In a few more years, they might be strong enough for a direct assault on the city, but even if that day came, the loss of life would be astronomical. Nico knew they would never change things that way. Aequalitatem wasn't going to win this war with a sword. They would need to be patient, find a small weakness somewhere within the League, and then pour every last bit of their strength into making the wound fester.

Ruminating about the state of his world for long enough, Nico pulled up his thick wool hood and headed down to Aequalitatem's daily meeting. With any luck, someone would report a kink in the League's armor for them to exploit. With this hope in his heart, Nico walked down the large hill that sat at the outskirts of Aequalitatem encampment and over to a large tan tent. The tent's entrance was flanked by two mangy-looking old men, both of whom were holding the equivalent of sharpened sticks and wearing a mis-matched assortment of leather armor.

"Good morning, Samuel, Joseph." Nico nodded to the men in turn.

The two old guards stood up a little straighter at the greeting, but neither uttered a word. Appearances aside, they were faithful to their post. Despite their loyalty, Nico wasn't convinced they would do much good in a fight other than sounding an alarm with their deaths. Nevertheless, Nico refused to undervalue another human being again. He had seen enough of that to last him several lifetimes. The remaining members of the old guilds, forced to live in the LHC due to their refusal to take up more nefarious livelihoods, predicted that this encompassing naivete would be Aequali-tatem's downfall. Nico didn't let their words hold any power over him. He knew deep down that all people mattered. If these two old men with their unthreatening demeanor were strong enough to stand watch day in and day out, it was good enough for him.

"Nico, come quick. Randle has returned!" The overly excited voice belonged to the youngest member of Aequalitatem's Inner Circle, a boy of nineteen named Colt. Even though he was young, he was as sharp as an ax. His youthful perspective did much to balance out the bitterness that ran deep in many of the other perspectives within the circle.

"Thank you, Colt. I'm excited to hear what he has to report," replied Nico as he locked eyes with Randle's weathered face. Randle took it as sign enough to step up and share what he had learned. Aequalitatem might be an organized rebel army, but it avoided things like military titles and other formalities. Most of the time Nico preferred it that way, but sometimes the lack of discipline made him question his decision on the matter. He kept quiet about it for now and gave Randle a brief nod to signal that he was prepared to hear his report. Randle recently returned from an information run, meeting up with an informant from inside the Crystal Pedestal. Very little news about the day-to-day happenings within New Geneva ever left the walls of the city, let alone news important enough to be of any consequence for their purposes. Randle had proven himself to be the most proficient at getting worthy information, even if he was rather secretive of his source.

"I have been informed that Sr. Father Solomon Pipher is to stand trial for an open display of violence in the Crystal Pedestal café."

The tent was abuzz with excitement at such dramatic news. Nico raised his arms to quiet everyone down. "It must have been quite the outburst for a man like Solomon to stand trial. Did you get any more information on the events leading up to the trial that might be useful to us?"

"Just that the outburst led to the death of a young Purity Maiden named Robin. Also, his trial is to take place the day before the Winter Festival—in other words, tomorrow."

"Thank you, Randle," Nico replied with a disappointed look on his face. "Perhaps if we had heard about this a couple days earlier, we could have come up with some way to use it to our advantage. Any last minute ideas come to mind?"

Nico scanned the tent to see if any of his co-conspirators had any promising expressions on their faces. Instead, he was met with a room full of head-scratching, shrugging, and confused gesturing.

"I have an idea, sir," replied Randle, giving light to the perplexed room.

"Go on," replied Nico.

"Well, there will be a lot of people attending the trial, including the majority of the League. It is a prime opportuni-ty..." Randle paused before continuing, looking directly at Nico. "To put it bluntly, I'm suggesting we bomb the courthouse."

The room went silent. Nico scanned the faces once again. Some seemed to be mulling the idea over, and others seemed to nod in approval. "Anyone have anything they want to say about the very lofty goal of blowing up one of the biggest buildings in the whole city?"

"I do," replied Colt. Nico welcomed his sharp mind being brought into the discussion. He could always see angles others seem to overlook.

"Go ahead, Colt."

"Thank you, sir. First of all, it would probably take us weeks to gather the supplies to build a bomb of any consider-able size, and even then, it's likely to make little more than a dent. Like Nico said, the League's courthouse is enormous. It's almost the size of the Hall of Weights and Scales, and you can see that thing looming over the city from the top of Atlas Hill. Second, we don't have anyone in our ranks who could blend in enough to avoid being spotted upon hitting the city gates. Those of us old enough to pass as League Fathers don't possess garments a League Father would be caught dead in, let alone wear to a public trial. The rest of us are too young to pass as anything but apprentices or Purity Maidens, both of which will be in limited attendance and probably within arm's length of their Providers or League Fathers. And lastly, while I have no trouble spilling the blood of any League Father, I don't believe Aequalitatem is in the business of murdering Purity Maidens, or any other innocents that might be in the blast radius."

"Purity Maidens, innocent?" Shanks, a previous member of the Guild of Spicers, blurted out. "Those uppity whores killed our livelihood, our culture, and our way of life. If it weren't for those pampered beauties, the guilds would still hold power. Who knows, they might have been able to fight the League for control of New Geneva. In my mind, they're as guilty as the Fathers."

Colt looked to Nico to respond. He knew Shanks was wrong but did not have the guts to stand up to the man. To his credit, Shanks was an intimidating figure. Even at sixty years old, one could see the cords of muscle under his shirt. His dark brown eyes had a way of looking like they could see right through you. Add a quick temper and you've got yourself quite an intimidating fellow. Nico took pity on the boy and turned to respond to the old Spicer, now red with zeal.

"Shanks, I understand how you feel about the Purity Maidens, but let me assure you, they have no choice in the matter. They are no more guilty than slaves doing their master's bidding. They're not so much pampered beauties as they are pets in gilded cages. The Fathers hold all the responsibility for the fall of the guilds. The Purity Maidens were used for that purpose, and continue to be exploited for League profit, entertainment, and power. They are as victimized as any of us, and in some ways, more."

"You make it sound like we should recruit the biddies," Shanks retorted sarcastically.

Colt's eyes bolted open. "Shanks, you're brilliant. That's exactly what we should do."

"Huh?" grunted Shanks. "Are you getting supplies from my old guild, boy? What good would recruiting a bunch of pampered pillow biters be during a war?"

"What are you thinking, Colt?" asked Nico, as confused as the rest of them.

"Well," Colt said meekly, brushing his sandy blonde hair out of his eyes before continuing. "They're underestimated, overlooked, rub shoulders with the League regularly, and can use hysteresis. What more could we ask for? Maybe they're the kink in the armor we've been searching for."

Shank's mouth twisted up on one side. "Maybe if they could do more than prepare meals, mend clothes, and ruin guilds, lad. What do you think, Nico? You reckon the League's pets will be the answer to all of our problems?"

Nico looked at each of his advisors in turn. The weathered, puckered face of Shanks and the smooth, freckled face of Colt couldn't be any more different. "I understand why you would think to use them, Colt, but I think Shanks is right here. Purity Maidens might be able to use hysteresis, but they're not permitted to use it for anything other than the types of things Shanks just mentioned."

"But they could learn, couldn't they?" offered Colt, his eyes wide and locked onto Nico's.

It was easy to forget that Colt, unlike Nico and Shanks, had never once set foot inside of the city. He was born and raised outside the walls and had no idea what New Geneva was really like. Nico turned to his young friend, trying to find the best words to let him down easy.

"When I called them pets, it wasn't sarcasm. Hysteresis can only be applied to areas one has a deep and working knowledge of, and the Purity Maidens have all of their knowledge extremely regulated by the League. Nothing that fails to meet League approval is at the Maiden's disposal. I'm afraid they're of no use to us."

For a moment, it looked as if Colt was going to put his head down like he usually did when discussions got more heated, but something propelled him to press the topic one last time.

"Don't you think that's odd, Nico? Why would the League go through all that trouble? Maybe they're afraid of the threat hysteresis users outside of their control could present. Scared of the only other group of people that can truly stand up to them. You're the one who's always saying to never overlook the usefulness of others. Look at Samuel and Joseph for crying out loud. Those two couldn't stop my grandmother from coming in here." Colt was panting by the time he was done. Surprising everyone with his vigor, but no one more than himself.

Nico stopped to consider the young man's words. "Maybe you're right, Colt. Perhaps I am overlooking the Maidens, but even if I am, how could we possibly know? We would have to either sneak into the city and kidnap a handful of them or wait for them to break out on their own. I don't see either of those things happening in our lifetime. The Maidens are the League's prize possessions, despite how they treat them. They would never stand for either of those things. Even if we did get our hands on some Maidens, it would take us years to educate them in things other than cooking, cleaning, and decorating. Even then, they would be decades behind the League Fathers who have been studying offensive uses of hysteresis since their youth." Nico took a long pause. A look of uncertainty etched across his face. "Perhaps it is time for me to open up a little about my time as an apprentice in the League. Give you a glimpse of what the Fathers are capable of. Maybe then you will see the odds stacked against any Maiden hoping to defy the League."

The entire tent stood in rapt attention. Nico never offered to open up about his knowledge of the Fathers' abilities. He always said knowing more would make them lose heart, but they were at a point where ignorance was no longer bliss.

"Before I start, the information I'm about to share is not to leave this tent. Do I make myself clear?" Everyone grunted in agreement, eager to hear what they were really up against. Satisfied with the response, Nico began. "I studied under a man named Malachi. As an apprentice, I had to choose a single school of study, so Malachi's school is the only reliable gauge I have for determining the League's level of strength. Most of you have seen me use elements of Malachi's brand of hysteresis, even though you might not know it yet."

Nico unsheathed his sword and placed it on the table in front of them. "You all know what I have told you about this sword. It is virtually unbreakable due to being forged in an ancient refinery, before the Hollowing ended the world our ancestors knew. But that was a lie. This sword is like any of yours."

"But we have seen its power Nico!" cried Colt.

"The boy is right. I've seen you cut through a falling boulder without it taking a scratch!" bellowed Shanks in support.

"Yes, you have seen such seemingly impossible feats from

this sword, but not due to what it's made out of. It's because of Malachi's hysteresis. He calls it Density. From the basic stuff I learned about Density, it has something to do with the hardening and softening of an object. It's not nearly that simple, but it's where they start the topic with new hysteresis users looking to start their training. Anyway, when you saw me cut that boulder in half, I was strengthening the density, or hardness, of this sword while weakening the density down the middle of the boulder. Malachi taught us that density hysteresis is most efficient when used in pairs, strengthening one object while weakening another." The group stared at Nico in confusion, unsure what to make of what he just said.

"If you can really harden and soften things at will, then why didn't you harden your skin when the mountain bandit gave you that?" Colt asked while pointing at the scar running across the left side of Nico's face.

"Good question, Colt. The first rule of hysteresis is to never use it on living things. If you attempt to use the ability in this way, it can cause something they call blowback. Blowback can do all sorts of really messed up things to the hysteresis user, as well as any person they might be using it on."

"Strange rules aside," replied Shanks, "I don't understand why you believe this man to be so much more powerful than yourself. If you can both harden and soften things, I give you the edge. You're much more youthful than that old codger, and more than likely have the upper hand when it comes to battle experience as well."

"If that's where Malachi's power stopped, you might be right, Shanks. I was at level one, an apprentice, meaning I was learning the first stage of the given Father's hysteresis, but there are two more levels I know of. The next level is League Father. They learn to use Density hysteresis on liquids."

"Now hold on a sec there, Nico. I understand making a

sword harder, or a piece of earth softer, but how the shit do you harden a liquid?" Shanks blurted out, looking legitimately baffled.

"I told you, Shanks. Density isn't as simple as hard and soft. I never got to the second stage, but I have seen it in action. Do you have any idea what happens to a person who ingests wine that has had its density magnified a thousand fold? Well, I do. It sits in their stomach like a rock. Impossible for their body to digest. Then, after days of starvation, cramps, and dehydration, the person starves to death despite having a full belly."

Colt scratched his head in bewilderment. "That does sound rather terrifying, but what I don't understand is how anyone would drink such dense wine in the first place. If the wine is a thousand times harder, then wouldn't it be a thousand times heavier too? How would they even pick it up? And if they could, wouldn't they notice the wine altered in some way?"

"That's the logical question, but hysteresis circumvents everyday reason. You see, Malachi didn't alter the weight of the wine, just the density. I won't sit here and pretend to know how it all works. It's not like hysteresis obeys the normal rules of the world. I do know that the League forces their recruits to choose one school for a reason. The goal is to perfect their knowledge of one thing, and then sharpen it to a lethal point rather than having a bunch of different styles getting in the way of each other. Who knows what would happen if a Father trained in density and gravity confused the two for a second mid-thought? The results could be disastrous. This is one of the reasons why the Sr. Fathers are so protective of their training book, something called *Introduction to Physics*. I have no idea what it means, and it's missing more than half its pages, yet the Fathers treat it like a precious jewel. Supposedly, it's full of knowledge from the ancients, a book from before the Hollowing."

"I hate to ask Nico, but what's the third level?" asked Colt, looking like he wasn't sure if he wanted to know the answer or not.

"I'm not sure, Colt. Like I said, I wasn't even supposed to see the second adaptation before beginning my training to take the Father's exam. All I know about the final stage of density hysteresis is that only Malachi himself can use it. This is true of all of the Sr. Fathers. They won't teach their students the final level until they are prepared for the student to replace them. I always assumed it was to keep some level of power and control over them."

By the end of the discussion, Nico could see the information had utterly exhausted everyone in the room. It was one thing to be up against an impossible foe. It was a whole other thing to have a marker of how impossible it really was.

"I think you've all had enough to process for today. Thank you all for your time. I hope we have more hopeful things to discuss tomorrow morning. You're dismissed."

At first, nobody moved. They just stood there staring, most likely attempting to process all they had heard. Perhaps they were drained after having such a promising opportunity result in a steaming pile of nothing. Eventually, the members dispersed out into the rest of the camp until only Nico and Randle remained.

"I thought you might have more to say, old man," Nico said after he was positive nobody else lingering around.

"Quite the risk you took there, boss, but hell if it didn't serve its purpose. Ain't nobody suspecting more to be said about the fat man's trial, or the Purity Maidens for that matter. I appreciate you being willing to deceive the others like this,

Nico. It's not that I don't trust them, but I won't take unnecessary risks. Not with her."

"I understand your reasoning, Randle. I'm sure the others would agree if they had all the facts. On to the matter at hand, are you sure you want to use her? Colt was right. We don't have the time or the resources to build a big enough explosive, and sneaking her into the trial to attempt any sort of cloak and dagger antics would be signing her death warrant." Nico paused and waited for the old blacksmith to respond.

"I'm not thinking about anything as grandiose as all that. The bomb was only suggested because it was the most ridiculous thing I could think of, and we needed the group to lose interest in any plans we might make around the trial. As you know, it's the only way to keep her safe."

"I figured it was something like that," Nico responded with a wry smile.

Randle returned the smirk before moving on. "You and I are the only two people in the circle who know how much of a farce this trial will be. The League would never allow one of their most powerful and influential Fathers to suffer the insult of a true act of justice. But we can still use this pageantry of saving face to our advantage. I plan to get my informant to plant some overwhelmingly incriminating evidence and then tip off the prosecuting attorney. I'm sure no matter what we plant, no ill verdict will be bestowed on Mr. Pipher, but we would be turning this trial on its head nevertheless."

Nico scratched his chin and gave Randle an uneasy look. "I'm not following your logic. How's planting worthless evidence going to turn the trial on its head?"

Randle's mouth turned up at one corner. "By turning their little public relations campaign into the clear farce it is. Think about it, Nico. The League is sure to go to extreme lengths to make sure this trial seems like an honest one. Its sole purpose is to give the appearance that the Grand Council has the other Fathers in check. When the judge gives the inevitable verdict of not guilty, despite the goody basket we're leaving, anyone with a brain will see that this trial is no step towards democracy. Just propaganda by a dictatorship."

Nico looked up to meet Randle's eyes. "Alright, Randle, but it has to be tonight."

CHAPTER 13

THE SILK MERCHANT

Oriella skipped down the halls of the Crystal Pedestal as chipper as ever. She knew every person by name and greeted them with a smile and an enthusiastic word. The lemon-yellow dress with an oversized white ribbon tied around the waist matched her mood to a T. A matching headband, adorned with daisies, stood in stark contrast to her jet-black hair. To complete the ensemble, she wore a pair of translucent white stockings ending below her knee, leaving a patch of beautifully smooth dark skin between them and the hem of her dangerously short dress. With an attitude to match her perky attire, Oriella bounced into the common room where she saw Gerolt arm in arm with Wren.

"Why, hello there, esteemed Provider and best purity companion ever."

"I think you mean *only* purity companion," Wren muttered in a barely audible whisper.

"Wren, that's no way for a lady to speak. I do believe you could learn a thing or two from the way Oriella presents herself," offered Gerolt. "Now, if you will excuse us, Oriella. Wren has a very full schedule today and won't have time for any chit-chat."

Oriella watched the pair walk away as Wren threw one last glance over her shoulder. She met Wren's deadpan glare with a bright smile. *I wonder what she's so crabby about today. I hope she's dealing with this whole Robin thing okay. I can't have her getting boring on me. She's the only interesting one here,* Oriella thought, more concerned than offended. If she held any negative thoughts towards Wren for her standoffishness, she sure didn't show it.

Moving on from the brief encounter, Oriella skipped through the common area and into the hysteresis stations. She pranced around the crescent-moon-shaped corridor, taking time to admire the sparkles of light coming through the massive chandelier. She took a seat on her pedestal and waited for her first customer of the day. A tall, skinny, pale man stumbled through the thick glass doors of the Crystal Pedestal carrying a large cardboard box. He nodded to other patrons as his long, gangly strides took him to Oriella's workstation. He wore an oversized, wide-brimmed hat, and was decked out from head to toe in the most luxurious of silks.

"There you are my ray of sunshine," called the man. "Oh, and a dress to match, I see."

The man was a local silk merchant, and one of two kinds of clientele Oriella tended to attract. The first type, his type, were those whose spirits were lifted and day brightened by Oriella's overly cheerful demeanor. The second type was made up of those who longed to soak up the unique combination of innocent young girl and devilishly dressed flirt Oriella presented to them every day.

"What can I do for you today, Mr. Schnauss?"

"Well, I'm afraid I have quite a bit of work for you this

morning, dear," he replied as he hoisted up a large box filled to the brim with swatches of silk. "I received this new shipment of silk from the Far East, and it seems they were offered to me at a discount for a reason." Oriella grabbed one of the silks out of the box and inspected it. "Hold it up to the light," offered Mr. Schnauss. It looked more like tissue paper than a proper piece of silk. "I would complain to my seller, but even if they were willing to take the shipment back, the amount of money it would cost me to get it back to East Asia would be more than taking it here to you. Plus, then I get to enjoy your lovely company."

Oriella greeted his explanation with a smile. "Don't you worry, Mr. Schnauss. I'll have these silks in tip-top shape for you as soon as possible."

Mr. Schnauss sucked air through his teeth and wiped his brow with one of his many silk scarves. "That's the other thing, sweetie... Unfortunately, I need them done by the end of the day."

Oriella paused for a moment, waiting for Mr. Schnauss to break the silence with a light chuckle or a slap on his bony knee. After an awkwardly long time, Oriella broke the silence. "Sure thing, Mr. Schnauss... I'll do my very best."

"I sure do appreciate it, dear. I'm kind of in a tight spot until these silks are repaired, and I already have a buyer lined up. I'll come to pick them up first thing tomorrow morning." With a tip of his oversized hat, Mr. Schnauss turned and headed back out of the Crystal Pedestal.

Well, that explains why my name wasn't on the list for Winter Festival preparations. Mr. Schnauss must be paying a fortune for this job. Oriella knew that this request could end up taking her much longer than her hours permitted, so she rang her bell to call over a Provider. A few minutes later, Gerolt showed up. "What seems to be the problem, Oriella?"

"Mr. Schnauss brought in this huge stack of silk to repair, and I'm certain nobody could accomplish this task in one little old day. I appreciate you leaving me off of the festival preparation board, but even so, there are well over a thousand silks in here."

"Ah, yes," replied Gerolt. "I forgot to tell you Mr. Schnauss was bringing in such a daunting task. Never fear. I've arranged for you to do night rounds for a second night in a row, so you can work all the way up until then. I'll also have a Purity Maiden from the café deliver your meals to your work station, so you don't have to waste any time walking over there to eat. Now get to it, Oriella."

Gerolt was already walking away when Oriella replied. "Sure thing, Provider. I'll do my very best."

Gerolt was not a fan of wasting time or energy, making a b-line for the massive crowd gathering in anticipation of the Winter Festival. After all, everyone had to look their best for such a rare occasion. This was not the first time Oriella found herself with a job that took her past the normal working hours of the Crystal Pedestal. She knew from experience that dwelling on a hard thing brought her no closer to its resolution. She pulled the first silk off of the stack and laid it out on the table in front of her. Then she focused her mind's eye on the familiar qualities and delicacies of silk. Being a regular of Mr. Schnauss's, she had developed quite the technique for working with the material, and before long, the piece of fabric was twice as thick as it was before. She worked a little while longer until she achieved top quality. Silk after silk, she repeated this process until her mind began to ache from the effort of holding one solitary concept for so long. By lunch, she craved any sort of respite from the tedious task. The simple fruit and nut plate Gerolt selected for her sang with the song of a billion unique flavors.

As she took this short break, she glanced across the room to see Wren frantically scanning the festival preparation board. From the look on her face, she seemed to be utterly clueless to the fact that she would be given extra work in preparation for the big night. Oriella pursed her lips in concern, wondering how Wren would handle this sudden realization, when she noticed Gerolt approaching her station.

"How's the progress, Oriella. I suspect you have nearly half the stack finished by now, yes?" Gerolt looked down at the stack of silks to find a little more than a quarter of it finished. "This simply won't do, Oriella. At this rate, you'll be lucky to finish up by night rounds, and you are absolutely not permitted to be up past lights out no matter how much of the job you have left. I suggest you work harder and daydream less." Before Oriella could respond, Gerolt had already turned his attention elsewhere and vanished.

Oriella let out a very uncharacteristic sigh and went about the mind-numbing work of using hysteresis on silk, after silk, after silk. Daylight seeped over the horizon as the frantic buzz of the Crystal Pedestal faded to a whisper. Provider Lucas ushered out the last of the Pedestal's guests and locked the door firmly behind them.

He whistled as he sauntered along, nearly jumping out of his skin when he saw Oriella still at her station. "What are you still doing here, Oriella? Even festival prep has been shut down for the day."

"Just trying to finish up this job, sir," replied an utterly exhausted Oriella.

Provider Lucas took one look at the stack of silks and gave her a look of authentic pity. "Oh, sorry, Oriella. It looks like another long night for you. Well, you know the drill. I'm assuming you're doing night rounds again tonight?"

"Yes, I am, sir."

"Right then. I guess I'll be off. Best of luck."

Oriella altered a couple more silks until she was sure she was truly alone in the common room. Then she picked up the remaining stack of silks and placed them all on her workspace in one giant heap. She mustered up enough focus for one final channeling of her mind's eye and altered the remaining silks all at once. Nobody knew Oriella possessed a strong enough hysteresis to pull such a thing off, especially after a long day of focusing her mind's eye on something as repetitive as her task had been.

Exhausted, Oriella pushed herself up from her work station and slowly made her way across the common room. Quiet as a mouse, she crept toward a door along the crescent-shaped wall at the back of the common room that read, *Purity Training Rooms: Authorized Providers Only*. Oriella gave out a long sigh and tried her best to fight off the fatigue from her long day's work. She gave the room one final glance before pulling a small, rectangular piece of metal out of her stockings. She held the strange metal in the palm of her hand and began focusing her hysteresis. She thought about the near-liquid state the metal must obtain to become moldable, and how much pressure needed to be placed on the softened metal, and at which points, to get her desired results.

After she was satisfied with the shape she had crafted, she focused her hysteresis on hardening the soft piece of metal, returning it once again to its solid state. With her metal successfully reformed, Oriella slipped the key into the slot on the door and turned. The door's lock slid willfully from its holding in the wall, granting passage to the dark, descending staircase on the other side. Oriella slowed her breathing before slowly pushing the door open and sliding inside.

CHAPTER 14

A BUMP IN THE NIGHT

Despite being moments away from making one of the hardest decisions of her life, Harmony couldn't help but ruminate about the winter storm howling outside her bedroom window. She shivered just thinking about how cold it must be out there. If there was a silver lining to all of this, at least she didn't have to go sneaking around in miserable weather. Over the years, she had come to think of the constant comfort of the Crystal Pedestal as a blessing, with its protection from winter storms and other harsh realities that life on the outside could bring. Her mind wandered to the house on the lake, to a young Wren playing in the sun and the determined brow of her son Elias as he worked the fields to perfection. She had never wanted to come here. She had fled the city and trudged days through the Hollowlands to prevent it.

If it were up to her, they would have gone anywhere but back within those wretched gates. But she had fallen victim to the mind games of the Hollowlands after the death of her son. The memory of that night plagued her for more than one reason. Not only did she carry the burden of the loss of Elias and the death of men at her hand. She also carried the mystery of how the three of them had made it to New Geneva's gates.

Gerolt struggled with the journey the first time, and the Hollowlands had gotten nothing but more fuel the second time around. So how had they even end up here? Now she scarcely saw Wren at all, and when Harmony did, Wren looked anything but happy. She put on a fake smile as well as anyone, but Harmony knew better. Wren had always been such a curious girl and smart as a whip. *How did it come to this?* Such thoughts were nothing but a distraction.

The howling storm reminded her of the treacherous task at hand. She didn't know what would happen if she was caught, but she knew it was nothing good. For a moment, she would prefer braving the harshness of nature over the situation she found herself in, but it was too late now. Gerolt's mind was set. Refusing him now would do nothing but anger him, distancing them even more, and that was one thing Harmony knew she couldn't bear. She would do this thing for her husband, despite the growing rift between them and despite the weight of being caught resting firmly on her shoulders. She would risk being sent down to the purity rooms because deep down, she knew that even if she was able to survive life on the outside, she could never survive life without her family. Her mind made, Harmony bit her lip, gathered up the small wooden box she had been tasked with, and quietly headed for the door.

Gerolt had mapped out the timing of the guards the night before, and noted that they passed by once every half an hour. The last guard had passed no more than five minutes ago, so Harmony felt confident peeking her head out for a closer look. After checking both ways several times, Harmony took a hesitant first step out of her room and into the hallway. This simple act gave her a strange feeling, one of anxious anticipation mixed with an emotion she could only describe as long-ing. Since coming to New Geneva, Harmony had never been out of her room this late at night. Even when she still did night rounds, she got back to her room hours before mid-moon.

In the complete darkness, the familiar hallway took on an entirely different façade. Perhaps it was because of the distinct absence of people and their hustle and bustle, or maybe it was because the lack of lighting made it hard to see any of the hall-way's features clearly. Either way, it gave her deeper chills than the winds of winter ever could.

After her brief moment of hesitation, Harmony began putting nervous foot in front of nervous foot, inching her way towards her destination. Each step seemed to echo through the night. She imagined a deep voice calling out to her from the darkness, condemning her for her lack of purity. After what seemed like an eternity, she found herself at the end of the hallway and at the cusp of a crucial crossroad—the point of no return. In the residential sector, she could probably pull off some sort of wild excuse and be lucky enough to get off with a scolding, but once she crossed over into the common room, there would be no mercy.

Despite the trepidation threatening to seize her entire body, Harmony knew she couldn't freeze up, not if she wanted to have a chance to make it back unnoticed. She took one last look down the dark, endless hallway and stepped out into the common room. Normally, the common room was dancing with light. Between the vaulted windows and plethora of crystal chandeliers, the light of day poured into this room from every direction. Even on a cloudy day, the common room seemed to maintain its sparkle. She imagined Wren spending her days surrounded by light and life, by people and pleasantries. The League did not approve of Maiden's conversing outside of their duties. Being in the cafe day in and day out left little room for

Harmony to speak with her daughter. She wondered if debilitating loneliness remained her constant companion as well.

If Wren had found a way to stay safe, found any friends, or an area of study that gave her purpose. She wondered if her daughter had retained her youthful light, or if this place had stolen it from her as well. Despite all she had done to avoid becoming one of the Crystal Pedestal's playthings, she tried to make the best of it for her daughter's sake. If she found a way to be happy in this place, she could pass her wisdom on to Wren. *What a fool's errand.*

Harmony brushed away a warm tear running down her face and surged into the common room. An outsider looking in might think she found her courage, but to Harmony it felt more like waking up to reality. She lost the role of wife and mother long ago. They had both been replaced by the title of Sr. Maiden. Wives got to have conversations with their husbands. Maidens got orders. Mothers got to influence their daughters' lives. Maidens modeled purity to them from afar. Harmony was surprised that these stark realizations were not accompanied by anger but by a settling numbness.

Loneliness followed her around as her constant and only companion.. She wondered why she kept fighting for her old self, her old life, her old family. She reached out in desperation for something that would never reach back. She clung to ideals from a distant past, ideals that kept her from relishing in the safety she and her family now enjoyed. She didn't have the luxury of processing her thoughts now. She had all the time in the world to fight that inner battle another day. For now, she needed to focus on the task she'd ventured into the darkness to complete.

With so little light, it would have been easy to get lost on her way to the café. Luckily for her, she had walked the path from her rooms to the café every day for the last eleven years, and now that her fear had subsided, even the dark corridors of the work stations didn't faze her. Harmony weaved her way through the work stations, using them as cover in case a roaming guard made his way in for an inspection. She had made her way within eyesight of the café when she heard the faint sound of feet on tile. It was much too quiet to be a guard. They wouldn't think twice about how much noise their heavy boots were making. This sounded more like an extremely proper lady setting a teacup down on her finest china. She didn't know if this other person had heard her as well, but if they had, they made no move to stop walking as the noise continued well after Harmony had stopped.

The curved ceiling of the common room caused the sound to come from everywhere all at once, making it impossible to know the direction of the sound's source. This new unforeseen element brought Harmony's recently conquered feelings of unease and fear roaring to the surface of her mind. Gripped by the sudden realization of her predicament, Harmony made herself as small as she could behind the counter of one of the working stations, desperately trying to see farther than ten feet in front of her.

After several painstaking minutes, she heard the sound of metal delicately scraping against metal, followed by a *click*. A few small noises later, and they faded out completely, leaving Harmony to her empty room once again. Satisfied that whoever snuck about seemed blissfully unaware of her presence, Harmony got up from her hiding place and crept towards the café.

Once inside, she practically ran for the kitchens. If she felt safe anywhere, it would be in there. For a moment, she thought about turning the lights on as it would be extremely hard to find Robin's locker in the dark, but she thought better of it. Lights would do nothing but bring her unwanted attention. Besides, her eyes seemed to be adjusting themselves to her shadowy surroundings anyway. Using the countertops as a guide, Harmony walked through the kitchen to the back room where the Maidens had a small set of half-sized lockers. Normally, Purity Maidens didn't have such a space for belongings, but the Maidens who worked in the café were given special permission. They needed somewhere to keep their rings, necklaces, bracelets, and serving clothes while they worked. Despite flavor enhancement hysteresis being almost nothing like traditional cooking, it still required the handling of meat, fish, eggs, and other items that could tarnish the appearance of one who worked with it. So, the Maidens who were cooking would change into plain cotton dresses and alternate with the Maidens who were serving and must be adorned in their finest for the clientele.

Because of the valuable nature of the clothing and jewelry Purity Maidens wore, locks were placed on each Maiden's locker, to which only two master keys existed. One belonged to Lance, the Provider in charge of the café, and the other belonged to Harmony as the Sr. Maiden and master chef. Harmony pulled the master key out of her pocket and tried to remember which locker belonged to Robin. Of course, they all had names etched into them, but it was too dark to make them out now. She ran through the endless days in the kitchen in her mind, trying to remember a distinct time she opened Robin's locker. The day Solomon Pipher had beaten Robin to death, and she witnessed a trio of her Maidens dragging the body back to the kitchen. They tried to revive her, to make the bleeding stop, but they couldn't. Life had continued to gush out of her until there wasn't any left. Lance came in and instructed Harmony to remove Robin's jewelry and serving clothes, the most valuable things in his mind. Harmony remembered taking the risk to dress Robin in her cooking dress after stripping her of her more valuable clothing, despite not being given the order to do so. She felt it wasn't right to dishonor the poor girl any further by allowing her naked corpse to be paraded through the café.

Shaking the horrible memory from her head, Harmony opened Robin's locker. To her surprise, her serving dress was still in it, covered in dried, brown blood. She supposed this was a good thing, as it gave her somewhere to hide the box. After planting the evidence, Harmony shut the locker and turned the key.

Once the deed was done, it was time to get back to the safety and comfort of her room. Harmony retraced her steps, trying to keep her mind on the task at hand and not on the knot of guilt hanging in her throat. Shaking with what she had done, she decided speed was a more pressing concern than subtlety. The guards would be passing through her hallway again soon, and then all the subtlety in the world wouldn't keep her from being discovered. With this in mind, Harmony avoided the work stations and made her way along the crescent-shaped wall of the common room. Only a storage closet, the entry to the purity rooms, and the Provider's break room separated her from her goal. Hugging the wall and crouching low to the ground, Harmony picked up her pace. For the first time, she thought she might actually make it.

Thwack! The door to the purity rooms flew open right in front of the ducking Harmony, striking her in the head and knocking her to the ground.

"Shit! What was that?" she heard a soft feminine voice say from the other side. Harmony swore she had heard the voice somewhere before, but something about it seemed...off. She counted herself lucky that the voice sounded feminine. Maybe she could convince the fellow purity breaker to keep her lips sealed. As Harmony sat rubbing her head and trying to regain her balance, she heard the oddly familiar voice again.

"Harmony?" it said in a sharp whisper before disappearing into the darkness of the common rooms. Not wanting to sit around waiting for a guard to come and investigate the sound of metal striking bone, Harmony regained her composure and made for the entrance to the residential sector. She could hear the sound of heavy footsteps heading down the back hallway, and this time it was no mistaking who they belonged to. A guard was rushing over to investigate the commotion. A second followed close behind him, lighting the torches on the walls as he went. Beacons of light poured into the darkened room. Harmony threw caution to the wind, flung up her hood, and made an all-out dash for the hallway.

"Stop!" yelled a guard as she turned the corner into the residential sector.

"What are you doing, miss? Get back here!" yelled a second pursuer as the guards began to pick up their pace. Harmony didn't stop. Maybe they didn't recognize her. They did call her 'miss' after all. There was nothing left to do but keep running. Harmony couldn't remember the last time she needed to exert herself to such a degree, but somehow she reached her doorway before the guards turned the corner into the residential hallway. Harmony fumbled her key in the lock and burst into her room. Gerolt wandered out of his bedroom, rubbing his eyes, hair uncharacteristically askew. His sleepiness was soon a distant memory as Harmony slammed the door behind her.

"Are you mad? Why would you slam the door at this hour? I hope you acted with more tact when going about your errand, dear wife."

Harmony bent over, hands on her knees, desperately trying to catch her breath. If she hadn't been distracted with the surge of adrenaline coursing through her veins, she might have taken offense at Gerolt's blatant disregard for her wellbeing.

"Well? Is it done?" Gerolt offered after a few moments of silence. Harmony had almost regained her ability to speak when they heard a firm knock at the door. "Damn it," Gerolt huffed. "Quickly, get into your bed. I'll speak to the guards." Harmony obliged and darted past Gerolt to her bedroom.

Knock! Knock! Knock! The sound came louder this time.

"Provider Gerolt, we hate to disturb your sleep, but we must speak with you." Gerolt sat in silence for a few moments before answering the door to maintain the appearance of being in bed.

"What could you possibly need of me at this hour, gentlemen?"

The two guards stood, waiting on the other side of the door, but Gerolt made no motion to step aside and let them in. "We are sorry for the disturbance, Provider, but we saw a fleeing female figure come this way. Is your wife present?"

"Of course she is, you fool. Where else would she be?" snapped Gerolt. He wouldn't dare talk to a member of the League in such a tone, but the night guard duties were hired out to everyday men from around the city, as the League would never trouble themselves with such a trivial matter.

"Of course she is, sir. It's just...I thought I saw your door..."

"How could you see anything at this hour? It's past high moon for crying out loud."

The two guards looked at each other, then back at Gerolt. "I understand, sir, but we still need to speak to your wife." Gerolt paused for a moment. Clearly, this wasn't going to be as simple as telling them to get lost.

"If you insist," replied Gerolt. "Harmony, would you come out here? Make sure you are wearing something decent. There are men present, and I wouldn't want you to cause impure thoughts."

"Sure, honey. Give me a second," answered Harmony in her best groggy voice.

Gerolt had bought her enough time to change up her appearance enough to not be recognized. Harmony stripped out of her cotton cooking attire and hooded cloak and searched her closet for anything not resembling a dress. Finding nothing in her closet, she spun around, searching the rest of the room with no better luck. She was so distracted she didn't even notice Gerolt standing in the doorway. She met his eyes as he instantly turned away, clearing his throat. It wouldn't normally have been an awkward interaction, but it had been over a year since Gerolt had seen her in anything but her cooking dress or apron, and now she stood before him in nothing but the clothes she was born with. His eyes darted from the floor to the dark, angry scar that ran from the top of her left breast to the top of her right hip bone. Harmony couldn't remember the last time Gerolt had seen it—her mark of shame. The act that drove him to leave their paradise and come to this wretched place. In this moment of awkwardness, Harmony made to cover herself up, prioritizing the scar above all else. Gerolt put his head down, offering up a quiet apology in response.

That moment was not the most surreal the night had to offer, but for Harmony, it was the least expected. Out of time, Harmony grabbed a nightgown from her closet and shook out her hair in an attempt to give the appearance of recently waking from sleep. Lazily, she exited her bedroom, yawning and stretching her arms to the sky. "What is it Gerolt? It's the middle of the night."

"These two guards claim to have seen a female figure dashing through the common room, only to disappear somewhere in the residence halls. Do you know anything about this?"

"Not unless I dreamt it," replied Harmony, stifling a yawn.

"The figure was wearing a dress very similar to the one you have on now, Mrs. Crivelli. Do you care to explain?"

Harmony cut them off with a snicker before they could take the thought much further.

"And what do you find so funny?" snorted the other guard.

"Oh, sorry, sir. I was just thinking that you are going to have a heck of a time catching that girl if you can't be more specific for me. There isn't a lady in the Crystal Pedestal who owns anything else."

The two guards exchanged uncertain glances. "Oh, we assure you, Mrs. Crivelli. We have plenty more. We'll catch the purity breaker. It's only a matter of time."

"I'm sure you will, good sirs," cooed Harmony, giving them a slight bow of respect.

"That'll be all, Provider Gerolt. You and your wife can go back to bed. Make sure you grill your Purity Maidens in the morning. See if any of them knows anything or seems at all guilty over their breach in purity."

The guards left Mr. and Mrs. Crivelli standing in the silence of their room. The awkwardness from moments ago now held the spotlight. Gerolt was the first to break the silence. "Well...I guess we should get to bed. We can talk more about this in the morning."

Harmony normally would've broken down in tears in moments like these, but after tonight's events, all that was left was the darkness that swallowed her light. As Harmony made her way to her separate bedroom, she found herself recalling Gerolt's face when he stumbled across her nakedness. Her scar served as a constant reminder of what happened all those years ago. She could still smell the stench of scorched flesh and boiled blood when she gazed upon it. See her mangled mess of a son laying at her husband's feet. Her sweet, innocent Wren numb to the bone. Distraught that nothing would bring the family from the lake back, Harmony closed her eyes. A final tear escaped her eye, and with it, the last bit of strength she had to fight the closing numbness building up in her heart.

CHAPTER 15
A BETRAYAL OF BLOOD

It's a whole lot easier to pretend when you have something real to hold onto, Wren thought as she gracefully floated around the common room. The storm from the night before left a heavy layer of pure white snow over the rolling hills outside. Frost crept up the Crystal Pedestal's towering windows, etching unique snowflake patterns up and down the glass. This, paired with the common room's typical array of light, made the whole place look like an ice castle. Wren moved through this wintery wonderland with such grace and elegance, everyone assumed purity was the only thought in her pretty little head. They couldn't have been more wrong.

Despite her majestic and pure appearance, Wren's mind was racing. A mad jumble of excitement, confusion, and dread. She had something new, something forbidden. A purpose not given to her by a Provider. She had experienced a bit of this in the privacy of her own bedroom, where she would use hysteresis to turn pages of her League-approved books into sand. The feeling of freedom she felt now outweighed anything she had experienced in the quietness and seclusion of her chamber. Here she was, out amongst League Fathers, Providers, clients, and fellow Maidens, all while she had an illegally created substance strapped to her thigh. Not only that, her contraband was held in place by a garment *not* laid out for her.

But that was where the excitement ended, and the dread took over. What if Gerolt noticed she had added a piece to the ensemble? He already scolded her for asking to pick out her own adornments, so his critical eye could be extra sharp. At least that part could be explained. What really made her nervous was the glass her illicit tights were attempting to conceal. This mix of excitement and dread made Wren feel like her head was swimming. Perhaps this was why she was floating around the common room with such grace.

Putting her inner dialogue aside, Wren started searching the room for opportunities to rid herself of her life-complicating cargo. Something other than a wintery makeover was different about the Crystal Pedestal today. Wren had never seen the place so busy before. She had been so distracted by her personal matters that she had forgotten the Winter Festival was only two days away. As she stood there gaping at the crowd, trying to gather her wits, a voice broke her enchanted state with its characteristic staccato.

"Of all the days to be an empty-headed daydreamer. Don't you see all the work there is to do?" Gerolt hollered in an attempt to be heard over the constant, droning buzz of the large crowd.

"Sorry, sir. I guess my mind has been on other things lately. You know, with Robin's death and all."

"I guess it is a bit inevitable," Gerolt said with a sigh, "but it does not excuse your dawdling. A festival this grand doesn't prepare itself, and it is my job to ensure my Maidens are up to the task. Before you get to your client list for today, you must check the board over by the Provider's lounge for your décor duty. I have big expectations for you, Wren. Don't let me down."

This was the first Wren had heard about décor duty. She dared to hope her assignment would be easy enough to buzz through her client list and have time left over to dispose of her uncomfortable problem. Wren tiptoed her way through the crowd and over to a large, lace-encircled display board. The Maidens' names were listed in alphabetical order with an assigned task beside each name. Wren skimmed the list.

Wren Crivelli: Café preparations. Report to Provider Lance in the Crystal Pedestal Café for instruction.

Not too bad, Wren thought. Perhaps she would get the rare chance to see her mother. Despite their forced distancing over the years, she knew she could count on her to help her out if she asked. Wren continued her graceful movements through the crowd. She made her way over to the far side of the common room and into the entrance to the café. Upon seeing Provider Lance, her hopes of quickly completing her décor duty started to fade. Lance's face wore a blistering shade of red. His highly starched collar and underarms were drenched with sweat. His eyes darted around the room like a bloodthirsty wolf. Those frantic eyes settled on Wren.

"Thank god. Get over here, girl." Lance pushed his way through the crowd, grabbing Wren by the wrist and dragging her to the large storeroom in the back of the café. As he opened the door, three other Maidens looked up from their work long enough to give Wren disgusted stares.

"I've finally located the fourth member of your team. Make sure she makes quota. We don't want to play catch up on day two, especially with the trial mucking things up." Lance spun toward Wren, dabbing beads of sweat off his forehead with a handkerchief. "This is to be your solitary focus until I say otherwise. I don't care if Gerolt comes in here and tells you a Grand Council member has asked for you by name. During the festival, the Provider overseeing your décor duty takes precedence. Now, get over there and join the others. We are excruciatingly behind, thanks to you. Didn't anyone tell you Maidens were to report to their décor duties by sunup?" Frustrated with Wren's lack of response, Lance haughtily turned and marched out the door, slamming it behind him.

Wren sat in a daze, wondering what came over the normally cheerful and accommodating Lance. As far as Providers went, Lance would have been her first choice. Thinking through the blur of the past few minutes, something clicked. At first, she blamed herself for the oversight. She had been quite distracted by the shards of glass. Now she suspected her father. She wouldn't put it past him to purposefully withhold information from her if it met his greater purpose. It didn't make sense for such an important fact to slip by him, especially with how obsessed he had been with the festival. After all, this was his big chance to gain an extra advantage over his rivals in the Lead Provider considerations. It was just like her father to take such a passive-aggressive approach. Once he saw that she would be assigned to the café, he must have jumped at the chance to sabotage one of his main competitors. *When did all of this become about him? Didn't we move here to protect the family? Elias didn't die for the grand plan of Gerolt becoming the League's favorite underling.*

As Wren sat there struggling with her father's actions, the other three Maidens said nothing. In fact, they hardly seemed to notice Wren at all. They were too busy mustering every last ounce of focus they had to put their hysteresis to task. Each Maiden worked on altering a different aspect of the huge tablecloths that would be the centerpieces of the soon-to-be transformed Crystal Pedestal Café. Wren watched the first Maiden take a plain cotton sheet from a huge stack sitting next to her. She shut her eyes, channeling her hysteresis. Minutes ticked by. The Maiden's forehead creased with focus as she held her breath. Finally, the blank cloth began to swirl with various shades of blue and silver.

Once she had completed the pattern, she passed the cloth on to the next Maiden, who changed the crudely sewn cotton fiber into smooth, thick velvet. The third Maiden focused on smell infusion. Wren could pinpoint the scent with certainty— a pine forest after a freshly fallen snow. Wren's eyes continued to follow the assembly line, but instead of seeing the next alteration, she came face to face with a silver-blue pile of pine-smelling velvet. Wren stared at the pile in awkward silence. She scrambled to come up with where she fit into all of this. Her chart said to report to the café but nothing more. Finally, one of the Maidens broke her mind's eye long enough to address Wren.

"Well, what are you waiting for, more of your work to pile up? You know, just because you are fourth in line and have to wait a bit for the next aspect to be altered, it doesn't mean you can waltz in here hours late and expect to keep up."

Wren didn't know how to respond. She didn't talk to other Maidens much. She didn't even know this girl's name. "Um... I'm sorry... I, uh, I'm not sure what I'm supposed to be doing..."

The Maiden's eyes flashed with fury. "Are you serious? If that's a joke, it is *so* not funny." The Maiden looked Wren up and down with a haughty glare and pursed lips. "I don't know why they would assign such a clueless girl the hardest hysteresis, but whatever. You're in charge of luminescence. They expect them to be given 'the light and shade of a winter's sunset,' so good luck with that."

With a whip of her hair, the girl quickly returned to her work. Wren didn't have the time to worry over some girl she didn't even know. She had more pressing concerns, like how she would find the time to finish the mountain of table runners, zip through her client list, and still find the time to worry about the contraband strapped to her thigh. She might have been able to catch up if she was in charge of color alteration, or even fabric hysteresis, but luminescence? She had only done that type of hysteresis a handful of times. Did Gerolt plan this as well?

Not knowing what else to do, Wren made her way to the gigantic pile of cloth. The more she soaked up the size of the task at hand, the more her previous goal felt firmly out of reach. Perhaps she could risk dumping the glass somewhere. She looked around the room, surveying her options. Even if she did manage to pull her tights down, untie the ribbons, and pull the glass out without drawing any unwanted attention, where would she hide them? The other Maidens had their eyes closed and their attention diverted, but there was no way she could hide something so out of place right under their noses. She eyed the stack of fabric towering before her. She knew it would be a temporary solution at best. All the table runners would be used for the festival, and she would be the last Maiden with her hands on them.

Wren shook her head. Maybe it would be best to get some work done instead. She could look for opportunities to stash the glass later. With a sharp puff of air, Wren released her worries and readied her mind for the task at hand. Until she noticed another setback: no chairs. Anxiety filled her mind, flooding her previous calm with waves of panic and chaos. She assumed her day would allow her to prance around waiting on clients, sitting gingerly on the edge of her pedestal. As much as she tried, Wren couldn't imagine a position on the floor that would prevent her from slicing up her leg. Desperate to catch up with the others, Wren decided to bunch up a pile of the unfinished table runners and straddle them like a horse. She looked ridiculous, but at this point, vanity did not make her list of concerns.

Her legs straddling her mound of unfinished work, she searched her memories for the perfect sunset. She had seen plenty of them cascading through the transparent ceiling of the Crystal Pedestal. The light would always twinkle through the massive crystal chandelier, painting the common room in an array of dazzling colors. Not quite what came to mind for "the light and shade of a winter sunset." Wren strained her memory for a sunset not filtered through her crystalline cage. Memory after memory raced past her flustered mind, each reflecting the glamorous colors of the common room. She had to go further back. Before she had been granted the *privilege* of waltzing around the common room like a painted doll.

She held a few vivid memories from the house on the lake. She pictured a frosty late-winter morning, the one when she received her precious stuffed rabbit. She tried to focus on the sunset, but the memory of the rabbit jolted her mind to Gerolt ripping it free of her grasp and throwing it into the lake; to her brother Elias lying dead in a pool of his own blood, his arm torn from his body; and to her mother screaming in agony as the blowback ripped through her torso. Wren's eyes popped open as she wiped a tear from her cheek, her mind lingering on the angry wound tearing its way across her mother. She never said anything to her parents, but she knew what her mother had done. She'd cooked them—seared the flesh and boiled the blood of the men who took her brother's life. Wren might not be attempting hysteresis on living flesh as her mother had done, but blowback could occur for other reasons as well, like not knowing the area of alteration firmly enough. Her mind went into a tailspin.

Anxiety over her task at hand battled with the fear of

bodily mutilation. She had to find a memory that prevented her from reliving her most traumatic moments while also allowing her to harness an un-altered winter's sunset. With the threat of blowback tickling the back of her mind, a vivid memory pushed its way forward.

"Esteban Cortez," Sr. Maiden Caroline screeched through the crowd of young girls, "once held the privilege of being the most beloved Provider ever employed at the Crystal Pedestal. But!" She exclaimed with a finger in the air. "Esteban was a foolish man. As a male hysteresis user, he could have put in the hard work and dedication necessary to become a League Father. Instead he chose to become a Provider. Despite this defiance of cultural expectations the League loved him, even making him the first Lead Provider." A girl with ringlets of blond hair and bright blue eyes shot her hand up. "Yes, Bethany?"

"Why would anyone choose to be a Provider over a League Father? I mean, aren't Providers our babysitters?" She ended with a light chuckle.

"Your Providers are much more than that, Bethany," Miss Caroline corrected in a harsh tone. "You will do to respect their work, or see yourself sent to the purity rooms." Miss Caroline locked eyes with Bethany, waiting for her gentle smirk to reduce itself to a thin line. "As for Esteban, the power, honor, and valor of being an esteemed Father did not hold the appeal that it should. His sights were fixated on his love of fashion, needlework, cooking, and beauty. These interests made him a favorite amongst Purity Maidens but a pariah amongst the other men. Can anyone tell me why?" Bethany's hand shot up once again. Miss Caroline scanned the room with a sigh. "Okay, Bethany, tell us what you think."

Bethany straightened up in her desk and tucked her raised hand into her lap with a purse of her lips. "I heard that Esteban even tried to *look* like a Maiden."

Miss Caroline cleared her throat. "And why might that be of issue, Bethany?"

"Well, because the ancient book of wisdom forbids it, of course!" Bethany lifted her head and recited the verse. "'Does not even nature itself teach you that if a man has long hair, it is a dishonor to him?'[1]"

Miss Caroline flashed a forced smile. "Good use of the ancient book, Bethany, but I feel this issue went a little deeper than hair. Anyone else? Wren, how about you? What verse from the ancient guidebook would you choose to shed light on this history lesson?"

Wren kept her head down, her eyes darted from side to side. Copies of verses from the ancient book of wisdom had been required reading. She found the words confusing and sentence structure odd. She glanced up and found the piercing blue eyes of Miss Caroline burning through her. Wren cleared her throat. "'For man is not from woman, but woman from man. Nor was man created for the woman, but woman for the man.'[2]" She eked out.

"Precisely! Now, if you'd speak with more confidence, Wren. You don't always have to be the class wallflower." Bethany giggled to her fan club and gave Wren a smirk. "But, you are *correct*," she added, turning her gaze on Bethany. "The ancient book of wisdom tells us that women are created for men. Esteban's sins were much greater than the length of his hair. He began to wear the Maiden's dresses and apply their makeup to his own skin." Miss Caroline paused, ensuring that the entire class met her gaze. "He even went as far as to attempt hysteresis on *himself* to achieve these twisted desires."

"Doesn't that break the Hysteresis Code?" Robin chimed in.

"A hand please, Robin."

"Oh, yes...sorry."

Miss Caroline crossed her arms and waited. Red crept up Robin's neck as she eased her hand into the air. "Ah, yes, Robin. What would you like to add?"

"Um, yes, Miss Caroline. Um, I was, um, wondering if..."

"He broke the Hysteresis Code?" Miss Caroline finished with a rush of annoyance. "It's not quite so simple. But, yes, Esteban altered bone, skin, muscle, and even organs, shaping them with his mind's eye. Like everyone else, Esteban knew little to nothing about the complexities of the human body."

Bethany's hand shot up. Miss Caroline stopped and motioned for her to speak.

"Because all such knowledge was lost to the Hollowing," she said with an upturned chin.

"Correct, Bethany. Due to this lack of knowledge, Esteban altered himself in ways he did not intend." Miss Caroline's voice dropped from its instructive tone. "His skin took on a semi-translucent sheen, revealing pulsing veins and the shadowy gleam of organs. His bones began to roam his body, looking for a place to settle. This gave his face the appearance of melting under his stretched-out skin, only to slowly reform moments later...

Now, who can tell me why I would share such a grim tail with a room full of *pure* minds?" Miss Caroline scanned the room. "Nobody? Not even you, Bethany?" Bethany pursed her lips and shuffled uneasily in her seat. A slight smile parted Miss Caroline's lips. "Never use hysteresis in areas of insufficient knowledge. You never know what sort of monstrosity it will turn you into..."

～

WREN'S MIND came back to the present, to the feeling of jagged glass pressed against her inner thigh, and to the uncertainty of the task at hand and the horrid story of bones wandering around one's body. Wren couldn't help but believe that at least some aspects of Esteban's legend were true. She was one of only a few Maidens who had seen what blowback could do to a person firsthand. Connecting this vivid story with her present predicament, she wondered what could possibly possess Gerolt to put her into such a situation. It was almost like he was setting her up to choose between getting sent to purity lessons for refusing the order of a Provider, or for breaking the Hysteresis Code. He had always ebbed and flowed between loving father and strict Provider, but lately, he had abandoned his role of father altogether. His actions concerning the festival were most troubling, but there must be more to it. She was missing something, some other motivation driving him to leave her in such a precarious situation.

It's got to have something to do with Mr. Pipher. He seemed to have some unnatural influence over Gerolt. As soon as Wren started thinking about Mr. Pipher, she realized his trial took place tomorrow. "That's it," she said aloud, awkwardly looking around the room to see if any of the Maidens gave her dirty looks. Gerolt's actions must have something to do with Pipher's trial, but what?

At this point, Wren didn't care what Gerolt's motivations were. She'd given him the benefit of the doubt for long enough. Gerolt no longer had her best interests at heart. What had he done for her and her mother since coming to this whitewashed place, anyway? Gerolt did not deserve to have his plans come to fruition, even if the only means of sabotage came at Wren's own peril. With a newfound sense of rebellion welling up in her heart, Wren placed her hand over the spot on her inner thigh, housing her hidden shards of glass and pushed.

She fought off the urge to cry out as a sharp pain shot through her leg, quickly followed by the warm sensation of blood. The blood wormed its way down her inner thigh, soaking her nude-colored tights. With a jut of her jaw, Wren strode over to the locked door of the storage room and rapped on it loudly. "Provider Lance, come quick. I have a purity issue."

After a few seconds, Wren heard the scrape of the lock being removed from its holdings. Lance burst in the door, looking more than slightly perturbed. "What is it, girl? What could possibly be ... oh!" Lance glanced down at the gathering pool of blood trickling down Wren's thigh. He pulled at his cinched up collar and dabbed beads of sweat from his brow. "This is unfortunate. How will we get you down to the unclean rooms with such a large crowd? We can't have you spreading your uncleanliness over the entire common room." Lance paused in thought, tapping his polished shoe on the ground at a frantic pace. "The timing could not have been worse, young lady. All the regular unclean rooms are occupied. Odd that so many of you happen to get your...time on the busiest night of the year. I guess you will have to go to one of the purity rooms instead. They are...less accommodating than the unclean rooms, but we have little choice given your current...condition. Wait here while I find a willing escort." Lance turned to leave, then turned back and said, "Nobody touches her," before continuing out of the room.

Wren smiled in spite of herself. She knew if Lance believed her to have received her womanly flow, he would not hesitate to remove her from the area, putting her in impure solitary for the next seven days. Wren would get out of this dangerous task without risking her wellbeing on purity lessons or unfamiliar hysteresis techniques, and she had the League's stodgy old book to thank for it.

"When a woman has her regular flow of blood, the impurity of her monthly period will last seven days, and anyone who touches her will be unclean till evening.[3]*"*

Normally, she would plan for such a thing, asking for some new reading material or other League-approved entertainment. She would go into the week of confinement empty-handed, unprepared, and causing more than her share of trouble. Part of her wondered if her cleverness would be her undoing.

CHAPTER 16

THE BOX AND THE NOTEBOOK

Most people would be required to await their trial in the confines of a jail cell, contemplating their fate until their trial took place and a verdict reached. Solomon Pipher was not most people. He received permission to sit comfortably in his own home, surrounded by all of the comforts and amenities of a League Father. He also had the luxury of knowing his verdict before the trial even began. These privileges would have put most people at ease, but they made Solomon more skeptical than ever. The Grand Council was up to some shady business. It would take more than some promises scribbled down on a parchment bearing the seal of the League to appease a man like him.

Solomon could sense how eager those old bastards were to put on this farce of a trial. Not to mention Solomon's big *deal* included getting stripped of his title and forced to live amongst the common folk. This *inquisition* felt a whole lot more like a punishment than the glorious privilege the Council made it out to be. Despite his tentative feelings, Solomon realized he had no choice but to play his part. At least for now.

"Those geriatrics really have me by the short and curlies," Solomon mumbled as he took a swig from his prized bottle of scotch. A Dalmore 62 single malt, worth more than a Provider made in a year. He had been saving the bottle for a special occasion–more specifically, being named a member of the Grand Council. With this goal all but out of reach, Solomon figured he might as well enjoy his top-shelf scotch before leaving luxury behind for the doldrums of common life. The thought made him sick. Solomon hadn't lived in such a place since the horrid days of his youth, when he lived in the country well beyond New Geneva's walls and spent every waking moment drowning in the smell of stale body odor and rotting almonds. He took another sip of his whiskey, resisting the urge to allow dark memories to flood his mind.

"Not today, mother," Solomon groaned as he took another healthy swig.

Solomon hated being disrespected almost as much as losing the ability to control his environment. Solomon blamed himself for the bulk of his rage. His fear of losing control produced his current state of mind, not the Grand Council's manipulations. He did not fail to appreciate the irony.

"Fear, get in here, boy," Solomon blurted out, lines of Dalmore 62 dripping down his double chin.

The sound of thick metal chains rumbling on smooth marble floors echoed down the hall and off Solomon's vaulted ceiling. Solomon smirked, his head swimming with brown liquid. The boy named Fear wore a pair of tattered pants and no shirt. Scars on top of scars ran rampant across his skin. Fresh wounds wept over the rough texture of countless past atrocities; poorly treated broken bones left his arms and legs misshapen. His lack of teeth added a bit of a lisp to his signature stutter. "Y-y-yes, s-sir, wh-wh-what d-d-do y-you n-n-neeed?" stammered the boy.

"For the love of god. Don't try to speak, you blundering moron. Disobey me, and I'll cut that blabbering tongue out of your pathetic, quivering mouth." Solomon paused long enough to make sure Fear would obey his command. He always did. "Go fetch me the tools, boy."

The whites of Fear's eyes grew as the blood drained from his face. The boy scurried back to the master bedroom, his chains slithering behind him. A few minutes later, he returned with a silver tray. Curved blades, skinny pliers, forked prongs, and blunt hammers of all shapes and sizes clattered as the boy's body shook with trepidation.

"Set it down on the table and take your place at my feet." The boy sat at Solomon's feet, his back nearly touching Solomon's knees, and waited. Solomon picked up a small, yet wickedly sharp, blade from the tray. The knife made a slight metallic ping as he snatched it up into his meaty palm. The familiar sound set the hairs on the back of Fear's neck on edge. Solomon smirked, calmly picking the dirt out of his fingernails with the tip of the blade as his inebriated mind swelled with delight. Each morsel Solomon dug free from his overgrown nails found its way to the boy's bare back, bouncing off his scar riddled skin. Fear's frayed nerves and memories of past sessions with Solomon caused each bit of grime to spike his adrenaline and send his heart racing.

Solomon finished cleaning his nails, and returned the knife to its position on the tray. For a moment, he contemplated reaching for a more sinister-looking tool but soon thought better of it. His prized scotch swam through him. It would be a shame for such a state of mind to cause his expert hands to slip. This Fear had already lasted so much longer than the others. It would be quite the pity to lose him to an infection of severed artery. Besides, Solomon already had the boy right where he wanted him. Anticipation of the white hot pain of an expertly sharpened knife consumed Fear's mind, his every nerve waiting for the first jolt of pain. It must have been too soon since the last torture session. Solomon knew from experience that partaking too often would push the boy out of his exquisite state of terror and into a state of shock, and what would be the fun in that? Solomon took a deep breath. The reasons to show mercy were beginning to add up. Solomon lingered in the shattered psyche of the boy a bit longer, sinking back into his monstrous wing-back chair.

"Thank you, Fear. That will be all." Beyond relieved, Fear jumped to his feet, grabbed the silver serving tray, gave a slight bow, and bolted back to his living quarters.

After the boy bolted out of sight, Solomon gave out a relaxing sigh. "Just what I needed to take the edge off," he breathed, contently patting his large belly. A soft knock on the door roused him from his satiated state. A young girl skipped to the door and opened it with a cheery smile.

"Your ride is here, sir," the girl cooed.

"Thank you, Grace. Make sure to watch over the others while I'm gone. I expect you to keep them on their various schedules."

"Of course, sir. I won't let you down."

"You never do, dear," replied Solomon, taking one last swig from his bottle of scotch before reaching for his long winter coat. With no way to avoid the Council's wishes, Solomon allowed the coachmen to escort him out of his house and into the bitter cold of night. "To the trial, then. Let's get this nonsense over with."

THE COURTHOUSE HUMMED WITH ANTICIPATION. Now that the man of the hour had arrived, it would not be long before the proceedings began. The elite of New Geneva filled the small-stadium sized ground floor—League Fathers and apprentices, high-ranking members of the guilds, and merchants lucky enough to turn a profit in foreign lands. The next layer of spectators sat on an elevated set of horseshoe-shaped steps surrounding the outside of the ground floor. Here sat the healers, men of the law, and the clerks, the League's political bureaucrats. The upper level of the courthouse housed the rest of the crowd—Providers, Purity Maidens, a smattering of the elite's personal companions, and all the wives and daughters of the men below.

The room hushed to a whisper as a large set of heavy wooden doors creaked open at the back of the room. The crowd stood up in suspense as the men of the court came pouring in. First came the lawyers working the trial, followed by Father Cephas, acting as Judge. The final entrant waddled in with all the bravado he could muster—the man of the hour himself, Solomon Pipher. The participants filed into the courtroom as if it were more a parade than a trial, each man more elaborately dressed than the last, and each waving to the crowd like he was in some sort of pageant. All except Solomon.

He wore an exquisite double-breasted suit, newly pressed in a brilliant blue and silver sheen, with platinum cufflinks and a gray top hat. Solomon strode steadily down the aisle, hands clasped behind his back, never shifting his eyes from their forward-facing gaze. The juxtaposition of the two different approaches created an awkward tension. The crowd responded, hushing to a faint murmur and taking their seats.

The men of the law lined up on opposing sides of the courtroom, waiting for Father Cephas to begin the proceedings. Father Cephas took his seat between them in a throne of exquisitely polished bubinga wood crafted precisely to his standards by the Conglomeration School. The massive chair sat high enough that Father Cephas could tower over the men of the law beside him. Immediately after sitting, he reached for his gavel.

Bang, bang, bang! "By order of the Grand Council, the trial of Solomon Humphrey Pipher has begun. Mr. Pipher is being charged with the use of a forbidden form of hysteresis." The crowd erupted as this pronouncement hit their ears. Everyone anticipated an accusation of wrongful death. Even the common folk knew Mr. Pipher had beaten a girl to death with his bare hands in the Crystal Pedestal Café. There were witnesses to attest to the fact. A literal trail of blood at his feet. Needless to say, this new charge took everyone by surprise, none more so than Solomon, who sat motionless in his chair. A flush of anxiety rushed through Solomon as he took in the words from Father Cephas's lips. A deep rage began to boil within him.

"Order! Order!" bellowed Cephas. "I will have order in my courthouse!" The crowd died down to a hushed whisper. Once the crowd had been subdued, the prosecuting attorney stood to his feet.

"May I address the Court?"

Father Cephas gave the extravagantly dressed man of the law a brief nod. "Granted. What is it, Niles?"

"I would like to add the accusation of false teaching, your excellency." This ushered in a second, even louder eruption from the crowd. In the blink of an eye, this run-of-the-mill trial had become a gossiper's wet dream.

"Order! Order!" Cephas bellowed. "I will clear this courtroom if you cannot conduct yourselves in a respectful manner." Once again, the crowd simmered down, looking a bit ashamed of their lack of tact at such an elitist event. "Do you have evidence to back up this new accusation, Niles?"

"Yes, Excellency. We found meticulously documented

notes on the subject of sensory projection amongst the dead girl's possessions, thoughts much too advanced for a female to possess on her own." Father Cephas motioned for Niles to approach the bench, holding out his hand for the notebook. Cephas thumbed through the pages, licking his fingers as he turned page after page. Several minutes went by before he finally put the notebook down and broke the tension mounting in the room.

"Upon reviewing this new evidence, I have no choice but to grant the prosecution their request to add false teaching to the list of accusations."

"I object," barked Pipher's attorney.

"Sit down, you sniveling tit," Solomon sneered. "Who in their right mind would believe I would teach a female *my* craft? Carry on, Cephas. I have nothing to fear on this account."

"As you wish, Mr. Pipher. The accusation stands." Solomon's defense attorney awkwardly took his seat, avoiding eye contact with Solomon at all costs. "Prosecution, you may now make your opening remarks."

Niles stood up and turned to face the crowd standing before him. The crowd served as nothing more than a bunch of gawking spectators, but their reactions could sway the opinion of Father Cephas—who would take his decision to the Grand Council to be made law.

Niles tilted up his head, smoothed his oiled mustache, and addressed the spectators as a jury. "My fellow citizens, set aside your desire for gossip. This trial represents a crucial turning point in the illustrious reign of the Grand Council. Before the League of Fathers came along, we were no better off than the mongrels inhabiting the LHC. Raided, ransacked, our children stolen, our crops burned. And do you know what brought on this order to which we owe so much?"

The crowd shifted in their seats as Niles took a longer than necessary dramatic pause. "The Code. Without it, hysteresis would be unregulated, and our world would fall into anarchy and destruction once more. The Code is of such importance that the League puts even its highest ranking members under its law. For years now, Solomon Pipher's style of hysteresis has been under scrutiny for its fast and loose approach to the first rule of the Code." Solomon ground his teeth, choking down his overwhelming ache to peel Nile's skin off his bones. Niles paid him no mind, speaking to the crowd like a melodramatic actor. "Never use hysteresis on living tissue. His *craft*, as he called it, manipulates the very senses connecting our flesh and bone to the outside world. Is this not a violation? He might try to tell you he is not interfering with the bodily tissue but some ethereal aspect. If true, then why did the entire Crystal Pedestal Café smell of rotting almonds directly after his assault on the young Robin? It is the prosecution's belief that Mr. Pipher began beating the girl to cover up the disease he placed within her using his so-called 'Sensory Projection.' Why else would he take such a risk? He could have just as easily ordered the girl to take purity lessons and dealt with the offense as he so desired, but instead, he chose to maul her in public."

Nile's sneered Solomon's direction. "With new evidence coming forth that Mr. Pipher was also *instructing* this girl, we put forth the accusation that she was either blackmailing him or had failed him in some dramatic fashion. This is the motivation for his violent outburst, and why he could not wait to punish her in a just and lawful manner. We are asking the court to convict Solomon Pipher of breaking the Code and false teaching. First time offenses such as these are likely to result in a temporary ban from the use of hysteresis, but considering them in conjunction and the length of time Mr. Pipher has been practicing his *craft*..." Nile's gathered himself, taking in a long breath before delivering his final line. "I move that the punishment for these offenses be banishment from New Geneva."

Gasps could be heard from all corners of the courthouse as the elite did their best to stifle their reactions. Solomon could feel thousands of eyes burrowing into the back of his head. His darkest suspicions came roaring to the surface, tearing at the false wall of calm he fought tooth and nail to maintain. Solomon scrambled to quiet his raging mind. *Think logically, Solomon. How else would they get me out of the city to start this 'inquisition' they spoke of? Did I really believe I'd be doing such work within the walls?* With his suspicions confirmed and his rage held at bay, Solomon couldn't help but wonder what other promises would be broken. Perhaps there were ulterior motives at play here as well.

Solomon remained transfixed, refusing to give the murmuring crowd the slightest glimpse of their desired reaction. With all of his willpower going into keeping his external composure, Solomon's inner dialogue began to dig into Nile's opening statements like a wild animal. *Did he say something about an incriminating smell? Rotting almonds? No, they couldn't have. She has nothing to do with any of this...*

Bang! Bang! Bang! Father Cephas pounded the gavel, demanding that order be brought back to the courthouse. "I will be the one carrying out sentences here, Niles. Keep your comments related to presenting your case."

"Yes, your excellency," Niles cooed with an exaggerated bow. "Mr. Pipher's judgment is in the most capable hands."

Cephas gave a slight nod to Niles before moving over to Solomon's side of the room. "Mr. Pipher, does your defense have an opening statement?"

Pipher's attorney stood to address the court. He drew in a sharp breath of air, but Solomon cut him off. "The only brands of hysteresis that have been practiced by the League longer than my own belong to the members of the Grand Council. Why is this accusation of 'code-breaking' just now coming to the surface? If you want to debate the morality of this girl's death, by all means, let us do so. She was an insufferable wench who never had any tact, good for nothing but handing out plates of food, and she barely had the wits about her to pull that off. Do you really think a mere girl is capable of grasping the intricacies of my craft? Sensory projection is a notoriously difficult brand of hysteresis. So much so that only three percent of new League apprentices seek it out as their area of study, and only a handful of them make it past the first stage. So, why in the world would I be attempting to bestow this knowledge on an empty-headed Purity Maiden? Anyone who knows me would see how preposterous this accusation is. I would sooner train a dog, or even you, Niles, before I would attempt to fill a young girl's head with knowledge so above her station."

Niles straightened his perfect tie and stretched his neck from side to side. Solomon shot him a devilish sneer before continuing. "So, let's stop mucking about! Pursuing this any further would do nothing but make a mockery of the court, the League, and everything we stand for! I have ample backing from our ancient text to attest to my actions against the girl, so if you would please stop this nonsense, let us get to the real issues."

Sweat began to puddle beneath Solomon's arms. His eyes locked forward to prevent them from darting around the room like a ravenous animal. His face wore a blistering shade of red. Despite his appearance, Solomon was not nervous. His rage had simply been pushed to the point that it took everything within him to cling to reason.

"Your defense has been noted, Solomon. Now, please. Sit back down. Your emotions are not doing you any favors."

The next few hours went by like a blur. Solomon struggled

to keep his composure, actually allowing his defense attorney to speak for him as all of his pre-thought responses had been rendered useless with these new accusations. He could no longer gather thoughts that didn't involve disemboweling half the courtroom. His vision blurred, his neck chaffed, and his gut churned. He had no idea the proceedings were going to affect him so profoundly. His plan to coolly defy the court while keeping due respect intact had clearly become a cataclysmic failure. Solomon snapped out of his stupor when he noticed that a female had been called to the stand. He cut her off mid-sentence. "Since when is a woman's testimony worth anything more than piss and shit? Get her off the stand. This is an outrage."

Harmony's testimony came to an instant stop. Solomon's wild stare sent ice through her veins.

"Calm yourself, Solomon," rebuked Father Cephas in a harsh whisper. "Her presence was already explained to you, and you had no objections then. Harmony is here on the word and power of her husband and Provider, Gerolt. He has verified her statements and stands by her words, thus giving them merit in the court. Besides, she is here on your behalf Solomon. Your lone defense against the plethora of evidence being mounted against you. I heavily advise you to halt this attempt to undermine your own case any more than you already have."

Solomon fidgeted in his chair. "Carry on," he said in a gravelly whisper.

"Yes, please continue, Sr. Maiden," Cephas said at a volume the rest of the court could hear.

Harmony took a moment to gather herself. Her chest rising and falling in a slow steady pace. If she needed Gerolt's backing to make her statement valid, then why didn't he get up here on behalf of that creature? Daring a glance at Mr. Pipher, she instantly wished she hadn't. His smug grin and egotistical demeanor were off-putting enough, but he had exchanged both of those for pure mania. Lines of sweat ran down his neck and flowed free under his arms. His eyes were perpetually wide and had a glossy appearance to them. His face beamed red with an almost rash-like quality to it. Harmony quickly looked away. The sooner she could finish, the better.

"As I was saying, Provider Lance submitted it for consideration this morning. Nobody thought to look in her locker until then."

"And what did this box contain?"

"A writ of passage."

A soft whisper swam through the crowd.

"And what use would a Purity Maiden have for a writ of passage?" the defense attorney asked.

Harmony fought off the disgust rumbling in her gut. "I believe she made plans to leave the city." Harmony swallowed a lump gathering in her throat. "She had become more and more slack in her work as of late...and dropped her normally focused diligence to maintain purity." Harmony paused. Her mouth was as dry as cotton.

"Is that all, Sr. Maiden?" the defense attorney asked.

Harmony shook her head, quickly brushing a tear away before it rolled down her cheek. "She had a warm glow about her...similar to a young woman in love." Harmony's voice quivered. She bit her lip and forced her rising emotions deep within her. "I suspect she received this money from a man outside the city who wished to be with her as lovers, free from the restrictions set on Purity Maidens."

"Thank you, Harmony," replied the defense attorney before turning his attention to the hushed crowd. "You all must be wondering how this aids Mr. Pipher's case. It is my belief that Mr. Pipher discovered this writ of passage, its dubious intentions, and sought to put a stop to this ill-advised meeting between lovers. As we all know, women are not permitted to keep or manage their own finances in New Geneva. All Purity Maiden's funds must be managed by a Provider or a husband, but a sum large enough to buy a writ of passage remained hidden from her Provider. Mr. Pipher did not consort to teach this girl; his altercation with her was over the contents of this box and nothing more. Why would Mr. Pipher instruct a girl intent on leaving our wondrous city? Any knowledge he gave her would do nothing but aid the rebels outside the city walls, and if we know one thing about Mr. Pipher, it's that his loyalty to the League of Fellows, and this city is second to none. I have no further questions for the witness, your excellency."

"Thank you, Andrew. Niles, would you like to cross-examine the defense's witness?"

"Indeed, I do, your excellency," Niles cooed. A wide grin spread over his oiled mustache.

"Mrs. Crivelli, if your husband knew about this evidence, why didn't he come forward with it? Why did it have to be discovered by a different Provider just this morning?"

"While my husband had his suspicions about the box's contents, he didn't know where she had hidden it. He couldn't proceed with the proper punishment without the proper evidence."

"I see. You also claim that Mr. Pipher had knowledge of this box and its contents, do you not?"

"Yes, sir. Mr. Pipher informed my husband, Gerolt, as Robin's Provider. The issue would have been dealt with as soon as the money turned up. We didn't know it had been used to buy a writ of passage until the box was found. But before any evidence revealed itself, the incident in the café took place."

"I see..." Niles slid closer to Harmony, leaning on the short partition separating them. "Then answer me this, Mrs. Crivelli.

What is a more likely scenario? A high-ranking Sr. Father discovered his young lover was hiding money and took this information to her Provider. Or, Mr. Pipher uncovered the girl's betrayal and extreme lack of purity and acted out in a burst of rage. Which one of those sounds more like the Solomon Pipher you know?"

Harmony froze. Gerolt had not prepared her for questions concerning the two as lovers or some form of student and teacher relationship. "Sorry, sir. I feel I am not informed enough to presume..."

"As I suspect you aren't, Mrs. Crivelli. A wife as devoted and dutiful as yourself would never dream of whoring herself out to another, especially if her husband were a Sr. Father. That aside, isn't the idea of a betrayed lover a much more reasonable condition for the girl's sudden and public death than a suspected act of impurity, as is currently attested?"

Harmony did not know what to say. Her responses had been worked out with Gerolt before that mysterious notebook showed up. She scanned the upper section for her husband, hoping for some support. She found Gerolt hunched over in his seat. Head in his hands. The sooner she could leave this accursed stand the better.

"I'm not sure, sir. I don't personally see Mr. Pipher being interested in such a young girl."

"We are not interested in your personal thoughts, Mrs. Crivelli. My questions to you are merely a platform for submitting evidence to the court. Your answers have little to no effect on the outcome." Harmony gave the overly oiled man a respectful nod. With an arrogant jutting of his jaw, Niles turned to Father Cephas. "No more questions, your excellency."

CHAPTER 17
ALONE

Purity. It had been driven into her mind from the moment she first walked through New Geneva's front gate. Cruel and degrading lessons were in store should she ever forget. Purity boiled down to three basic concepts: obedience, appearance, and innocence. At eight years old, Wren struggled to know what it meant to "carry yourself with grace," and "present a pleasant personality, maintaining the mindset of a child." At the end of her training to become a Purity Maiden, her instructor, Caroline, had summed it up perfectly. "Your life is a beauty pageant, girls—one in which the only reward is purity itself."

In the early days of being a Purity Maiden, Wren wholeheartedly believed that to be her reality. She had been made to believe that higher thought or learning outside of her League-approved subjects was not only forbidden, but outside of her capabilities. These teachings came as a slap in the face to eight-year-old Wren. Her father always taught her that she could do anything she put her mind to. He would call her things like creative, smart, and determined. She had so much more to offer than altering clothes and removing stains. Eight-year-old Wren knew this with all her heart. Time, rigid structure, and a father becoming a Provider had rocked such beliefs to their core.

Years softened many of her memories of the house on the lake and replaced them with a constant need to be vigilant about her present. To aid her in this, Wren had developed an inner voice. The voice did its best to protect her, telling her to put her head down, obey, maintain purity, and know her place. The voice kept her out of purity lessons and away from the lustful eyes of Solomon Pipher. However, the events of the last few days awoke a deeper, and much older voice. A voice shackled to the crystal clear memory of a mutilated brother and a rage-filled mother, awakening the smell of charred flesh and the metallic tinge of boiled blood. The long-hidden voice started as a whisper. Its flame stoked and nurtured to a deafening roar. The tragedies of her youth now played back to her in a constant loop. Their crystal clarity deepened the grief growing roots in her heart. She remembered feeling this way once before—short of breath, horrors playing on a loop, the overwhelming feeling of being utterly alone...and entirely powerless. Of being practically nothing.

The words broke Wren free of her dark cloud for the briefest of moments...to a memory that felt more like a passing dream she couldn't quite remember. She started where she could and worked her way forward. She had the time, after all.

The memory started during her introductory Purity Lessons. Wren closed her eyes and pictured herself smoothing her plain white training dress and grabbing the small box of food her mother always made for her the night before. She drummed her fingers on the smooth wooden box as the minutes ticked by. She told her father that she couldn't be late. Miss Caroline would be cross with her if she wasn't in her seat by sunup. She would graduate from her introductory lessons soon and finally be able to start using her gift again. It was hard to keep herself from using it, especially after being encouraged to practice all those years on rabbit.

The memory of that simple stuffed toy brought the hot rush of tears to her eyes. Wren wiped them away with the back of her wrist. Her mind clung to the image of rabbit's bright orange tail disappearing under the surface of the lake. Nothing was the same after that day.

Elias was gone forever, leaving her with only memories of his proud, sweat-soaked smile when he came in with a wheelbarrow full of healthy crops, his sarcastic comments at the progress of his little sister's color alteration attempts, and the glow that came over him when father praised him. But moments like these weren't all that she had lost when her brother was killed; each of the Crivellis had lost a piece of themselves as well.

The changes were subtle at first. She remembered the long days of quiet reflection as they waited their turn to be assessed by a member of the League. How she had longed for one of her parents to break the silence, to tell her what was going on and explain why they were sitting in a cramped room in a strange place packed with more people than she had ever seen.

When her father finally did talk, she found herself pinning for the silence. Out of all of them, he had changed the most. What was once praised and encouraged was now looked at with disdain and cruelty. He blamed the hysteresis for everything the family had lost. It wasn't until his training to become a Provider that he allowed Wren to use the gift again, but even that wasn't the same. His previous encouragement to harness her natural gifts and use her boundless creativity had been replaced by confusing rules and limitations.

Wren hadn't thought about those days in quite some

time. The old voice within her seemed to grow louder as she entertained them, groaning for something more. Something beyond grief and despair. She needed to go back to the memory. Dig deeper. Wren closed her eyes. *Nobody is coming to check on you. You've got nothing but time. Breath... in...out...in...*

"Hurry up, you're going to be late," Gerolt instructed in a flat tone through the locked door. Wren jumped at the sound of someone's voice, nearly dropping the box of food she had been drumming on.

"Coming, Father!" she cried out, checking her makeup to ensure her earlier tears hadn't left any smudges. Wren sprang for the door, grabbing her father's hand and dragging him down the hall towards Miss Caroline's classroom. Gerolt twisted up his face in annoyance. "You must really like these lessons. I've never seen you so keen to get somewhere."

Wren looked back at her father with a scrunched brow. "I've told you a thousand times. Miss Caroline hates me. She looks for any excuse to scold me in front of everyone. If I'm not in my seat, back straight, and eyes forward by the time the sun comes up..."

"It seems you are learning quite a bit about responsibility and etiquette from Miss Caroline. I'm learning quite a bit as well. Perhaps I'll be able to command such attentive Maidens when I'm granted clearance to become a Provider." Gerolt paused to catch his breath before pointing to the horizon. "Speaking of attentive Maidens, you might want to pick up the pace."

Wren's eyes grew wide with horror. "Oh, no!" She cried, picking up her dress and increasing her pace to a jog. Gerolt stumbled behind her, sighing dramatically. The pair got to Miss Caroline's class panting for air. Several of the other girls were already in their seats—backs straight, eyes forward, and hands in their lap. Wren dropped her father's hand and drifted carefully and quietly to her seat.

"Wren Crivelli!" Miss Caroline's shrill voice cut through the silent room like a slap to the face. Wren held her breath, calmed her nerves, and mustered up a genteel tone. "Yes, Miss Caroline?"

"You dare to show up to this classroom dressed like that!"

Wren looked down at her wrinkled dress. It must have gotten tussled in her hurry to arrive on time. She straightened it as best as she could from her seat and swallowed a lump in her throat. "I'm sorry, Miss Caroline. It's just..."

"Still insisting on excuses, girl? You'd think the past three years of lessons would be enough to strip the last of the barbarity from your nature." Miss Caroline paused. Her unblinking expression oozed judgment. "I guess it's to be expected of a girl from the LHC."

A few soft whispers floated around the classroom. Miss Caroline's eyes never left Wren's. Wren squirmed in her seat. Miss Caroline knew she wasn't from the LHC. Everyone around here acted as if the LHC was the only place to live outside of New Geneva's walls. It wasn't worth it to correct her. She was in enough trouble already. The only thing Wren knew about the LHC was what she had learned in this classroom. It was a dirty slum surrounding the outside of the wall filled with criminals and sinners. The LHC wasn't even its official name. It didn't have one. Everyone called it that because of what had happened all those centuries ago. During The Hollowing. The LHC was the doomsday device that had destroyed the old world, and the elite of New Geneva found it a fitting name for the trash left outside the walls. The name had stuck ever since.

"Excuses for an untidy appearance might be the norm in a slum. The Crystal Pedestal has standards. *Much* higher standards." The rest of the girls took their seats during Wren's lecture. Miss Caroline wrenched her gaze from Wren and surveyed her students. "Making excuses to me is forgivable. I am merely an instrument tasked with turning girls into Maidens. If you were to talk in such a way to a client, or even worse, a League Father, the consequences would be dire. In order to save you from such a fate, my dear troubled Wren, I would ask you to come to the front of the classroom."

Wren's palms grew clammy as she stood to obey. She stayed light on her feet, heels barely grazing the floor. She swung each leg in front of the other in a perfect line. The right amount of grace. The right amount of purity. Just like she was taught. Miss Caroline peered down at her, arms crossed.

"Face the class." Wren did as she was told. Miss Caroline grabbed a long, flexible rod from her desk and sauntered over to Wren's side.

With a sudden snap of the wrist, the rod struck Wren in the upper thigh. Wren took in a sharp breath of air, suppressing the urge to cry out. "How are we to serve the garment needs of the world's best while our own clothing looks like it's been crumpled on our floor all night?" Miss Caroline tousled Wren's dress with the end of her rod. "Take it off. I can't stand looking at it." Wren froze in place, unable to move or think. "You will be asked to do much worse if you carry yourself like this at the Crystal Pedestal. Now, take off that sorry excuse for a dress before I rip it off myself."

A flush of red rose to Wren's cheeks. She reached behind to undo the button before pulling the dress over her head. Long, dark bruises covered her legs and back. A fresh one was forming from this morning's carelessness.

"We are doing body assessments today, girls. You'll all get a turn, so pay attention." Miss Caroline thumbed through a drawer in her desk, pulling out a crisp, white folder before returning her attention to a squirming Wren. "Stand still, girl.

Grace and purity at all times," she scolded before flicking open the folder. "Now, where were we with you, Wren. Ah, yes. Your *weight*. I'm not sure what they were feeding you out there, but you're all muscle and sinew. Women should have more gentleness to their body. Soft and delicate like a cloud wrapped in satin. And these bruises. Marks of shame. With only a year left of your introductory lessons, I'd shape up if I were you. You leave here with marks like that still healing on your body, and you'll get sent to purity lessons under a Father's tutelage. They are not so forgiving. Now, turn around." Miss Caroline paused to assess Wren completely, every limb, every inch.

"Tsk, Tsk," she said in an exaggerated staccato. "More bruises back here I see, and absolutely no posterior to speak of." Caroline finished her assessment with a swift snap of her rod to Wren's exposed backside. Wren bit her lip and clenched her fists but kept from crying out. Miss Caroline turned her attention to Wren's folder, making notes on meal corrections and new requirements for body shaping. Once done, she closed the folder with a crisp slap.

"Cover yourself. You disgust me."

Wren hurried to her seat abundantly aware of the snickers that floated along with her. "The body of a Purity Maiden should reflect our character. Can anyone tell me what that means? Stacia?"

Stacia rose her head up high. Back as straight as an arrow. "The three main tenets of a Purity Maiden are grace, obedience, and above all, purity."

"Yes, but what does that *mean,* Stacia? Bethany, perhaps you could elaborate."

"I'd be honored, Miss Caroline. A Purity Maiden is more than a mere *girl.* She is a treasure. The League's treasure. And as a treasure, we must be pleasing to look upon, carry no impurities, and bring value and prosperity to New Geneva and its saviors, the League of Fathers and the Grand Council."

"That is correct, Bethany. Tarnished treasure isn't treasure at all. It must be polished. Scrubbed until the only shine it has reflects the beauty of its owner. Remember this, girls. As you work to remove the blemishes from the clothes and jewelry of the elite, do not forget that you are the most treasured product the League has. An honor worthy of hard work...and absolute purity."

WREN SHOOK her head free of the painful memory. *A treasure. Is that what I am? No, that's what they are trying to make me into.* Wren wanted to push beyond her early years at the Crystal Pedestal, to her life before the walls. Only time-altered fragments remained of a drowned rabbit, a scarred and pacified mother, an angry and controlling father, a dead and forgotten brother. Her time in the house on the lake held more than that. Elias's smile, a mother's comforting embrace, and a father who believed in her. *Take a deep breath. Clear your mind. Let all the thoughts that distract you, that tell you that you can't, wash away... I believe in you, Wren. This is your gift. What are you going to do with it?*

At that moment, something clicked. Out of all she once had, and what she currently held, only Gerolt remained. The battle between Provider and Father had begun to consume her. Twist her every waking thought. She wondered if they were truly the same person, or if one had died along with her brother all those years ago. Now, alone with her thoughts, she realized something. She was a child when she came to this place. A terrified, hurting child. Of course, she would seek her father's approval. Her brother was gone, and her mom was locked away. Her father was all she had left of her old life, and the main human interaction she had in her new life.

Sitting in her dark, empty cell, Wren lacked the emotional or physical energy to linger on such questions any longer. Tomorrow, Wren would spend her energy on something more worthwhile like figuring out what to do next. What an odd thought. In here, nobody would wake her up, nobody would lay out her clothes and her jewelry, and nobody would be running through a list of the day's clientele. Her mind would be hers again. *It's your gift, Wren. What will you do with it?*

WREN AWOKE, confused, and disoriented. It had been such a long time since she was roused from sleep anywhere but her room inside the Crystal Pedestal. Her living quarters had a small window at the top of the wall that let in the morning's light, brightening the already vibrant whites, light pinks, and soft yellows that graced her quarters. It was quite the contrast to the gray-scale box draped in rough-cut blocks of stone that she found herself in. A small slot at the base of the room's thick metal door slid open with a startling bang, clearing what cobwebs remained from her restless night. A tray filled with bread, fruit, and cheese clattered through. *Breakfast already?* She realized she must have slept in—what a weird concept.

Wren rolled off her thin, bulgy mattress and stumbled her way over to the tray of food—a hearty slice of brie, a slightly toasted baguette, and a handful of cranberries. Even in confinement, they would never dream of depriving a Purity Maiden of a decent meal. After all, it was essential to their beautiful skin and perky demeanor.

As Wren ate her food, she tried to put her mind to task on what to do next. This proved to be a harder undertaking than she would care to admit. Her mind wandered off on unhelpful tangents, trying to listen to all the voices in her head at once. *What if they have an unclean chart and track my last flow? What if Harmony is in on Gerolt's plan, and they're both using me to climb the ranks? What if Mr. Pipher roams free and is heading this way right this very moment?*

Exasperated, Wren kicked the empty food tray across the cell. She needed to remain calm, keep her mind sharp and focused. She did it every day, but this felt different. The air felt heavy as if the empty space itself condemned her. Wren had grown quite accustomed to being alone over her years in New Geneva but never like this. There would be no knock on her door, no prompting to finish getting ready, no list of clients… just an empty cell and her anxious mind. She did have one thing going for her. Hysteresis made her mind more entertaining than most.

For the first time in as long as she could remember, she would put that gifted mind to use for herself. First, she needed to calm down. She put on her pretty face like she did every morning, mustering up her best façade for her day's work. Despite the false face, hysteresis required her to have a clear mind. Otherwise, she could end up destroying a client's property or injuring herself. It also required material familiar to her. She scanned the room, taking inventory of each item and its composition.

Bed frame: metal of some sort

Mattress: cotton, stuffed with something lumpy

Food Tray: wood

Menstrual cloths: a mix between hemp and cotton

Waste Bucket: wood

Wren came to the conclusion that the menstrual cloth presented the best option. Normally, these would be used to conceal her womanly flow, preventing the situation she now found herself in by keeping her unclean fluids to herself. They expected her to use the cloth and throw it in the bucket. Nobody would ask to see them. In fact, they would do everything in their power to avoid gazing upon such unclean items. She could alter them as she wished, and nobody would be the wiser.

She decided to try to recreate the night she'd changed sand into glass; maybe it would make something useful. It didn't take Wren long to realize that this would be counterproductive. She needed to calm herself down and clear her head, pushing out all the distractions that already threatened to retake the center of attention. When she changed the sand into glass, the distractions altered her normal hysteresis, creating nothing but chaos for her to deal with. The hysteresis worked differently because she let the distractions in while simultaneously maintaining her mind's eye. She would have to think of something else. Something simple. Once her mind was put to ease, then she could think about what to do next.

She decided to turn the cotton hemp mix into lush, thick velvet. She imagined herself at her frosted-glass workstation. Gerolt rushed a client to her in need of an emergency menstrual cloth alteration—a thought that briefly caused a snort to escape from her nose. Regaining her composure, Wren calmed her wavering attentions and focused her mind's eye. All that mattered now were thickly bunched fibers of velvet, soft and delicate. For a bit of a laugh, Wren altered the off-white velvet to a dark shade of red. She opened her eyes and let out a rush of air.

Wren hadn't gone a day without using hysteresis for as long as she could remember. It had become a part of her identity. Despite this fact, and the fact that her thoughts were owned by her alone, what she did would be deemed an act of impurity. In her daily reality, something as simple and playful as altering her menstrual cloth could have extreme consequences. Alone in her cell, this thought marinated longer than she would normally allow. *Who are these Fathers that they get to choose everything about me down to the last thought?* A second voice wormed its way in, adding to her vexation. *It's your gift, Wren. What are you going to do with it?*

The thoughts felt wrong in her head. Her eyes darted around the room as a cold sweat broke out on her forehead. No harsh tone rang out from the darkness. No reprimanding Provider talked to her of impurity. No League Father's gaze lingered. Wren shook the fear and condemnation from her mind. Even the League Fathers couldn't stop her from thinking what she wished. The thought loosened the ever-present shackles cinched tightly around her every thought. She needed her mind clear—perhaps clearer than it had ever been. She refused to slip back into the submissive mindset that had become her new normal.

If this gift was hers, then why waste her days using it to serve privileged men like Solomon Pipher? Her family used to teach her to think in such a way, to own her gifts and make them hers. They had come to the Crystal Pedestal together, fleeing the danger of the mountain clans. They came here with sorrow in their hearts and desperation as their only companion. Wren wondered what Elias would say if he saw how they lived in New Geneva. He had always been jealous of her gift, telling her how much better things would have been if it were his. Wren wondered what Elias would make of her gift now— every day focused on pomp and status. She was forced to bend to the whim of others, not even permitted to think without the proper clearance.

Wren's eyes drifted to the wooden food tray she had kicked in frustration earlier that morning. A small square of white gleamed back at her. On closer inspection, it appeared to be a fragment of a page ripped out of some sort of cookbook. Curiosity peaked, Wren walked over to the tray and carefully peeled the piece of paper free. The handwriting on the other side looked oddly familiar.

Having fun in there, Wrenny? I sure hope not, that would be kinda weird. Anywho, if you're getting bored, why don't you come out and play?

Circle one YES! or No ... cause I'm lame ☺

Not enough room to explain on this itty-bitty paper, so make up your mind and put my little sticky note on the bottom of your yuck bucket. Eat up! It should only take two days if you're regular, if ya know what I mean.

-The best purity companion ever! Oriella. XOXO

CHAPTER 18

LINGERING LESSONS

Wren's memory of her time with Miss Caroline danced in her sleeping brain. She found herself back in that cramped classroom, surrounded by the judgmental stares of the other girls. "LHC *Slut!*," one of the faceless girls screamed at her.

"Defiled treasure!" jeered another. "Who do you think you are? Rejecting the value our loving Fathers bestowed on us!"

"That's enough, girls." Miss Caroline's voice was as stern and shrill as ever. "Perhaps we should review the history of the Hollowing to give Wren a reminder of what filth she crawled out of...and where her impure mind is longing to return."

Her face looked older and more jagged than Wren remembered. A twisted prune of a woman, draped in the most luxurious dress she'd ever seen. The elegant prune floated over to Wren's desk. The rest of the girls melted into shadow as Miss Caroline and Wren found themselves floating over the lands beyond the wall.

"You want to remember beyond the walls, do you? Well, let me show you what's waiting for you." The land before them billowed dark, putrid smoke. "You smell that, girl? That's the stench of death. A thousand generations wiped out by the Hollowing. Centuries of culture, history, and livelihood erased in an instant. The land forever tainted across the globe." Miss Caroline's gremlin-like face swirled around her, her body trailing off like an ethereal comet.

"Our gleaming white city is the largest unblemished spot amongst them. A shining testament to the generosity and love of the Grand Council. A constant reminder of the League's victory over the barbaric mountain clans and their primitive ways."

The walls of New Geneva sat glimmering behind them, bright as diamond. "Your parents took you away from all this, dragged you out into the wilderness like some animal. And what became of such folly? Death, loss, and most of all, *sin.*"

The ghost-like Miss Caroline curled herself around Wren's neck, twisting her toward the darkness that engulfed the horizon. "Nothing exists for you out there but impurity. Do not be a fool like your parents once were, leaving the beacon of light in the darkness." The ghost curled it's long fingers around Wren's throat, and whispered, "Without their folly, Elias would still be alive."

The words swam through Wren's mind, flooding her with doubt and uncertainty. The darkness from the horizon sped toward her, swirling around her like angry serpents. Visions of her brother's slack, lifeless face flooded her. His body slick with the blood leaking from his severed arm. The darkness accelerated around her. A vortex of painful memories and oppressive ideals weaved within it. The shriek of a shattered soul. The crispy *snap* of sizzling skin. The metallic taste of boiled blood. Wren's throat seized tight, her breath unable to escape her lungs.

Miss Caroline was gone but her voice remained. Joined by

countless others. "Impure! Impure! Impure!" they chanted. Their collective power threatened to squeeze every ounce of strength from her body, mind, and spirit. As the collective continued to chant, Gerolt's voice broke free of the rest. "Be a good little songbird. Come back to the walls, where it's safe."

The strict staccato of Gerolt's voice had become soft and soothing. It reminded her what lay behind those glimmering walls. The rules that controlled everything about her life. The chanting stopped, replaced by a thousand clambering thoughts.

"A lady always wears a smile."

"Your role is to serve."

"Girls can't know such things."

"Your life is a beauty pageant, Wren. One in which the only reward is purity itself."

The memories of these statements, and who uttered them, filled her with anger. Her mind pushed back at each one in turn. She remembered her father's soft smile, the smell of her mother's cooking in their small open-fire kitchen, and the beads of sweat that poured down Elias's face as he worked the fields. Wren focused her mind on those precious memories. The true face of the family she loved.

A single, bright light burned its way through the consuming darkness. A speck of hope. She reached for it, holding memories of better days in her mind's eye. The light felt warm and inviting. She swam towards it, pushing the darkness aside.

In an instant, she found herself standing beside a crystal clear lake. The light flickered on the horizon as if it was deciding how bright it wished to become. If this light was not coming from the lake, then where? Waves of heat pulsed from the source in time with the ebbs and flows of its brightness. Wren shielded her eyes and pushed forward. The source of the light inched closer. A few more steps and she could make out its source.

"*Stay back! It's not safe for you here!*" the voice sounded tired, weary, and despondent, but somehow, Wren couldn't shake the feeling that it desperately wanted her to step forward into its flickering light.

CHAPTER 19

A BREATH OF FRESH AIR

The Crystal Pedestal had transformed over the last few days, standing in glorious anticipation. The day of the Winter Festival had arrived, and no extravagance had been spared. The festival came once every ten years, and the Crystal Pedestal had been chosen to host two of the night's events—the ceremonious unveiling of the next Lead Provider, and one of the many culmination feasts that would take place when the moon hit its peak. The Maidens had been lively for the last few days, getting everything prepared, polished, and perfected. The common room's already dazzling arrays of light and beauty had been altered to elaborate lengths. The crystal chandeliers shone in a light cerulean hue, giving the whole room the glow of a crisp winter morning. Silver, gold, and sapphire snowflakes ran up and down the towering white marble pillars. Even the air itself received a makeover, swirling with the scents of winter—roasting chestnuts, a touch of cinnamon and nutmeg, and an underlying presence of pine. Lavish banners of shimmering silk hung from the ceiling embroidered with crystalized icicles. Accenting it all were hundreds of floating orbs of luminescence, carefully crafted to resemble the light of a full moon.

The Café's tables sat adorned with velvet tablecloths, holding the glow of a winter sunset. Towering crystal center-pieces cascaded upward like frozen waterfalls. Purity Maidens buzzed through it all, making sure each detail bathed in perfection.

All the preparations would be final the moment the opening ceremonies began. Until that happened, the beautifully adorned Crystal Pedestal would wait to unveil its full glory. With the exception of a few Providers and Purity Maidens making last-second alterations to the décor, all the life in the Crystal Pedestal could be found tucked away in various living quarters. They were locked away prepping the final decorations of the night, and the Crivellis were no exception.

Harmony had spent the last few hours trying on various outfits Gerolt laid out for her. He claimed he wanted her to look perfect, but Harmony had begun to doubt his motives as of late. He had never cared so much about her appearance before. As an aspect of purity, it had always been important, but today he bordered on compulsive. She tried on every dress in her wardrobe several times over, and still Gerolt shook his head in displeasure. "No, no, not that one. It's too...girlish."

Frustrated, Harmony returned to her room once more. She peeled off the fuchsia, sequin-covered evening gown for a third time as she looked through her closet for something, anything, that she hadn't tried on yet. Exasperated, she gave voice to the inner dialogue running in her mind.

"Why is my appearance of such great importance, Gerolt? Am I not presentable in any of these lovely dresses?" Harmony expressed her displeasure loud enough for her husband to hear her in the other room.

Gerolt came striding into her room. Eyes sharp for anything out of place. "Not only are you a Purity Maiden under my care but my wife as well. How poorly would it reflect my ability to perform my duties as Provider if you showed up to the Winter Festival looking anything short of magnificent?"

Harmony expected a harsher rebuke; Gerolt's almost caring tone softened her demeanor. "Maybe you could get Wren to alter one of these to your desired specifications. I haven't seen her since before Robin's passing. I would like to know how she is doing anyway."

"You haven't heard?" Gerolt dictated with a sharp edge in his tone. "Wren has been taken down to the purity rooms. She must have been so caught up in the preparations for the festival that she forgot to conceal her flow. She bled right out in public. I was mortified when I heard the news." Gerolt shared this information as if it were a headline in the morning's paper. "At least it won't be noticed until after the new Lead Provider is announced. I will deal with her lack of judgment later. Can you believe that at nineteen years old, she would fail me so? It's up to you and Oriella to show off my pride as a Provider. All the more reason to make sure every hair is in place, dear wife."

Harmony tried to find the right words to respond to such a bombshell. The Winter Festival presented a rare opportunity for mother and daughter to spend quality time together. To learn at the last minute that Wren resided in an unclean room did little to improve Harmony's already anxious mood. Harmony wrung her hands, anticipating what discipline might be in Wren's future. After processing the emotional reactions at her disposal, Harmony realized that making a show of her deep disappointment, grief, or anger, would only leave her feeling numb again. Even so, she couldn't stifle the itch to know more.

"Why didn't you tell me about this sooner? How much of her week has she served? Why didn't she let us know ahead of time?"

Gerolt let out an annoyed puff of air. "It happened at the most inopportune time. Can you believe that it happened *during* festival preparations? All while I rushed about making sure the common room basked in perfection. It's almost like she's completely clueless how much this promotion would mean to this family."

"Unbelievable," Harmony muttered under her breath.

She didn't dare say anything more. If she got cross with Gerolt, it wouldn't end well. Besides, he needed her, and for something that didn't put her personal safety at risk. Perhaps if she helped him obtain the recognition he craved, his desire for her could blossom once again. With this motivation in mind, Harmony buried any questions that still lingered about her daughter's situation.

Seizing the only positive impact she could make, Harmony pushed all her dresses aside, reaching into the back of her closet. With a short huff of air, she pulled out a stunning pearl-white dress, covered from top to bottom in shimmering circles of silver. The dress reflected a rainbow of colors against the wall; the perfect balance to her simple yet elegant gown. The dress came from another time. Another life. She wondered if Gerolt would recognize it after all these years.

"How about this one, Gerolt?"

For the first time all morning, Gerolt's scowl left his face. "Where have you been hiding that?" Gerolt gushed as he rushed to his wife's side with makeup brush and comb in hand. "Now, allow me to match the face to the dress." After he finished, an elusive smile stretched across his face. Harmony dared to hope she saw a hint of the soft smile that used to grace Gerolt's face.

"You look marvelous for a woman of your years." Harmony's breath caught in her chest. A compliment...a smile even... Her heart began to soar. Gerolt stroked his chin. "I don't recall that dress showing so much cleavage. I think it's fine. Just, pull it up a bit would you? We don't need any extra attention going to that scar now, do we?" Gerolt exclaimed with a clap of his hands to signify the end of the conversation.

Harmony looked down in shame. She'd never felt so repulsive in her entire life. As done up and exquisite as she made herself, he saw nothing more than fancy fabric covering her shame. Gerolt didn't seem to notice her change in mood. He rarely did anymore. "Well, let's go, dear. We don't want to be late. Oriella is already waiting for us outside."

Great, Harmony thought to herself. *Just what I need; a young, beautiful girl to have my husband's other arm.* "Of course, dear. Ready when you are."

The common room bustled with people by the time Gerolt, Harmony, and Oriella arrived. Every Provider had a Purity Maiden on each arm, presenting them like well-groomed show dogs. After a dreadfully long time of being paraded to the viewing public, the master of ceremonies stepped forward.

"Thank you all for joining us for this rare celebration. Some of you have yet to experience the wonder, majesty, and power of a Winter Festival. Well, wait no longer. There are events all over our great city, from our very own Crystal Pedestal to the city streets of New Geneva. The pinnacle of this wondrous festival takes place at the League's Proving Grounds. But first, right here in this very room, will be the choosing ceremony for the new Lead Provider."

The crowd gave a rather unenthusiastic round of applause while all of the candidates amongst them puffed out their chests, beaming with pride. "After the ceremony, head out to the streets of our illustrious city and bask in the glow of a winter wonderland. Don't linger long, however, or you might miss the festival's main event!" he bellowed. A pause hushed the crowd, breathless in anticipation. "It's the spectacle you've all been waiting ten years to experience. A chance to see the League Fathers and their apprentices at work. An event you must attend at your own risk—the Caste Exams!"

The crowd erupted into a furious cheer. The Caste Exams presented a rare chance to see the League's more unique hysteresis skills first hand. Marvels that came from the minds of the League Fathers themselves. Caste Exams were taken quite commonly but were always concealed from the public eye. The Winter Festival presented average citizens their only chance to experience the League accepting new apprentices, or to see its current apprentices rise to the rank of League Father.

Once the crowd died down enough to be heard, the announcer continued. "After you have experienced the League's wonders, the whole city will gather together for a feast unlike any other. There are five locations throughout the city to partake in this grand feast. Find the one that best fits your station. Attendance is free of charge. And now, without further ado, let the Winter Festival begin!" This garnered one last hurrah from the crowd as they began to disperse to the various corners of the city.

Once the crowd had thinned considerably, Harmony turned to her husband. "Gerolt, when does your event begin? Do we have time to see some sights?"

Gerolt looked around the room, analyzing his competition. "It's not for three more hours, dear, but I won't be going anywhere. My place is right here, showing the judges my dedication and zeal as a Provider."

Harmony scanned the room. If there were judges present, she didn't see any. "Of course, dear husband. I understand." Harmony paused, considering her next words carefully.

"Would you perhaps consider allowing Oriella and I to take in some of the other events in the city? We would return whenever you required it of us."

Gerolt sat in thought for quite some time. Harmony creased her brow and wrung her hands. Silence hung in the air between them. "I don't see why not. I will be quite busy here. You might as well go have some fun." Harmony clasped her hands together and gave Oriella a big grin. "However, you are not to go near the pleasure houses or partake in too much drink... And you must find yourself a coat. It's dreadfully cold outside. I can't have you prancing around with so much skin exposed."

"Yes, yes, of course! Oriella and I will grab our winter attire before we set out."

"And," Gerolt interjected, "you must be back here by my side for the pre-ceremony in case you need to freshen up. I can't show up to my big moment without some properly presentable Maidens, now can I?"

"Yes, of course, dear husband. We will not disappoint you," Harmony cooed with a curtsey.

Before he could change his mind, Harmony grabbed Oriella by the wrist and hurried back to the living quarters to fetch their winter attire. It had been several years since she last set foot outside the Crystal Pedestal. The excitement brought a flush of red to her face.

These feelings intensified as soon as she caught her breath enough to take in the sights. She had never seen so many different kinds of people. Common and elite alike gathered in the streets watching the various acts and spectacles. Men juggled flaming discs in the air. Musicians played flutes and horns of various sizes and styles. Children laughed, chasing each other through the streets, yelling to their parents about nearby cotton candy stands. A line of tents stretched as far as she could see, each advertising their wares and bartering with potential customers.

Harmony let the rush of color and laughter sink into her soul. "Where should we go first, Oriella? There is so much to see and so little time to see it."

Oriella couldn't help but return her genuine smile. "Golly, I don't know, Ma'am. I've never been to one of these before. Why don't we go wherever our hearts direct us."

Harmony flashed a toothy grin, grabbing Oriella by the hand and dragging her through the dense crowds. The two wandered the streets, taking in the fullness of the festival. Before they knew it, they had wandered all the way to the Outer Ring, an area stretching two miles inward from the city's walls on all sides. It housed the common folk and acted as a blanket of protection between the elites of the city and the slum beyond the walls known as the LHC. The streets were full of quaint little homes, freshly covered in a blanket of powdery, white snow. Some houses displayed wreaths made out of pine branches, others lined their porches, walkways, and roofs with candles. Any single house would have been a rather plain sight, but together they created a familiar warmth that brought Harmony back to freer times. She found herself preferring the simple yet warm decorations to all the pomp and circumstance of the Crystal Pedestal.

"Just think, they did all this without any hysteresis," Harmony said in wonder.

"Would you like to see some?" The voice came from a woman leaning on the support of a nearby tent.

"Oh, pardon me. I didn't see you sitting there. See some what?" stuttered Harmony, slightly caught off guard that a stranger had been listening in.

"Hysteresis," replied the woman, her lips curling up into a smirk.

"Oh, we have seen plenty of hysteresis," replied Harmony, "at the Crystal Pedestal."

"Ha! You call that hysteresis?" roared the woman. "More like cleaning techniques and banquet prep. I'm talking about *real* hysteresis."

Harmony shot Oriella a nervous glance, not knowing what to make of this strange woman. Oriella smiled and cocked her head to one side. Harmony's eyes darted back and forth between them. She expected Oriella to strike up a conversation, to say some cheerful line that dismissed them from any obligation. Oriella rocked back and forth from heel to toe and back again, arms folded behind her. Harmony had no idea how to make a decision in this situation. She thought about what Gerolt would say, probably something like *stay clear of the riff-raff*, or *she has no idea what she is talking about anyway.* But Gerolt wasn't here; she had to make this call on her own.

Harmony knew about other forms of hysteresis and knew that the League Fathers practiced a wide range of different styles. Although she knew some of their names, she had little idea what any of them were truly capable of. She went over Gerolt's instructions in her mind. *Be back for the pre-ceremony. Steer clear of the pleasure houses and don't have too much to drink.*

"Yes, we would very much like to see what this *real* hysteresis is all about." Harmony replied, wringing her hands and biting her lip. Oriella stopped rocking and tucked her lips into her mouth.

"Good choice. There's just one more detail I forgot to mention. This part of the festival isn't free. It'll cost you. How much you got on ya?"

Harmony stood in silence. She hadn't owned a single copper since arriving at the Crystal Pedestal. Harmony didn't have the heart to linger on that thought for more than a moment. All of the money she earned passed through her

Provider, who, in turn, obtained any material possessions she might require.

The woman rolled her eyes in annoyance. "You don't have any money, do ya?"

"I'm sorry, we do not," replied Harmony, giving the woman a blank stare.

"Wow. I didn't know the likes of you had leashes long enough to make it all the way out here to the Outer Ring." With a smirk, the woman called out to the shadows behind her. "Hey boss, I found some."

"Ah! Exactly the women I've been looking for."

A man with long dark hair, cool gray eyes, a prominent nose, and a long scar down the left side of his face stepped into the light. The woman looked at him, granting a nod of respect before stepping aside.

"I'll keep watch, sir. Let you know if anyone from the League shows up." The woman gave the man a brief salute before leaving Harmony and Oriella alone in the alleyway with the mysterious man.

The man broke the tension with a deep bow. "Please, excuse me. My name is Nico, and what, may I ask, are your names?"

"First, tell us why you were looking for us," Harmony said, more out of fear than anger. "And why you need to keep a lookout for the League."

"Oh, yes, sorry. How rude of me. Not you specifically. I have been looking for the company of a Purity Maiden. Tell me, what brings you two finely dressed ladies all the way out here to the Outer Ring? I'm guessing you are both from the Pedestal, am I right?" Harmony looked at the man in horror. She could only assume what *company* meant. Noticing the look of terror on her face, Nico clarified his purpose.

"You misunderstand. I didn't mean I desired...sexual relations, or, er, anything else like that. I simply desire your... perspective. I'm sorry. I'm not sure how people normally speak to a Purity Maiden," he added, scratching the back of his head.

Harmony took a deep breath, allowing her heart to settle to a normal pace. "How did you know we were from the Crystal Pedestal? Are we that obvious?"

Nico chuckled warmly. "Don't worry. You were only spotted because nobody around here would own dresses like those. Otherwise, I would have assumed you were a citizen like any other."

Harmony looked at Oriella in confusion. "I'm still not sure what you want from us, sir. If you have a service request, you must present it to my Provider. I cannot make appointments on my own."

"I'm not looking for an appointment. Like I said, I'm looking for your perspective. More specifically, I'm hoping to learn what the life of a Purity Maiden is like outside of her duties. Do you ever use hysteresis outside of your client's needs, say, for personal reasons? What do you do in your spare time? What areas of hysteresis are permissible for you to study?"

Harmony was taken aback. Despite being completely lost as to why this man desired her perspective, Harmony couldn't help but think that he spoke to her differently. He spoke to her, not at her. His voice held an edge of genuine curiosity and wonder, and he waited for her to respond with alert and present eyes. It reminded her of days past when her husband spoke to her in ways other than commands. When he cherished her input and soaked up her praises. This place had changed him more than she had realized. Years tend to do that. It all started when Gerolt began his Provider training. *The Lead Provider Ceremony!*

Harmony suddenly realized how much time had gone by. "You seem like a lovely man…"

"Please, call me Nico."

"Yes, Nico. I'm so sorry. I have only just remembered my presence is required elsewhere."

"Of course," replied Nico with a slight bow. "I wouldn't dream of keeping you past my welcome. If you ever find yourself in this neck of the woods again, head to the arms shop on the east side of the Outer Ring called The Bastard and the Bear and ask for Nico." Without another word, the mysterious man turned and disappeared into the unlit streets.

Harmony shook her head at the longing this brief conversation brought about before grabbing Oriella's hand. "We better hurry, Oriella. Gerolt will be quite cross if we are late."

The pair's brisk walk turned into a jog, then to an all-out run through the snow-covered streets of New Geneva. Harmony had not realized how far out they'd ventured, distracted by all the new sights and sounds. Just then, a clock struck seven, only one hour before the Lead Provider Ceremony. The two women pushed through the pain in their lungs, desperate to reach the Crystal Pedestal before the pre-ceremony.

They burst into the common room, breathless and flushed from exertion. To their surprise, only a small handful of people were present, mostly consisting of the nominated Providers and a smattering of Purity Maidens. The whole room turned and gave the pair a look of astonishment. It wasn't every day you saw a pair of Maidens running into the common room hand in hand.

"What is the meaning of this?" snapped Gerolt as he made his way over to their side.

"Sorry, dear." Harmony managed between her labored breaths.

"Sorry? What were you doing out there? Your hair is a mess. Your dress is covered in snow and mud," Gerolt whipped his head over to a nearby clock. "and you're late. How am I supposed to accept this nomination with the respect and admiration of my peers if the few Maidens still in my care fail to present themselves properly?" Gerolt smoothed the front of his suit jacket and took a deep breath. "Hurry and get yourselves cleaned up. I trust you can handle the hysteresis necessary to clean those dresses. I expect to see you both back here in a presentable state before the ceremony begins. Now go, before I lose my temper."

Gerolt ushered them forcefully towards their rooms with a look of pure distaste in his eyes. Harmony felt like they were a pair of children being scolded for getting into the cookie jar. Had Gerolt forgotten that she was the same woman who gave birth in the wild on top of a patch of moss? That she held the power to melt men who displeased her with a focused thought? Anger welled up in her, begging to be set free.

Then, she remembered her children. Elias, the hard working boy that was taken from her too soon. His loss left a blight on her life. A reminder of what happened when she let her anger get the best of her. Elias might have been gone, but Wren was still here. She saw a lot of herself in her daughter. If she were to rebel, surely Wren would follow suit. Truth be told, she felt the most guilt when thinking of Wren. Elias's pain was over, but Wren... Harmony knew the horrors of this place too well to pretend her daughter would have a good life caged in the League's Crystal Pedestal.

The mix of emotions running through her in that moment pushed her mind to the brink. Something had to give. She couldn't mask a tortured life with a smile any longer. Gerolt had robbed her of her only means of inner motivation. He had crushed the last bit of hope she dared to hold. Hope that she could catch a glimpse of the freedom and joy of the years beyond the wall. But Elias was gone, and Wren was locked up as tightly as her. Gerolt's presence represented the last spark of hope for the life she used to hold. The one they ventured out into the wilderness alone to fight for.

With that inner hope at the end of its slow, torturous life, the ever-present loneliness at the edges of her mind enveloped her. At that moment, she realized how much love she held for her family, and how much she clung to the hope that one day things would be as they were in the house by the lake. The time had finally come to allow those dreams to lay dead and buried at the edge of the Hollowlands with her sweet Elias.

CHAPTER 20

THE CASTE EXAMS

The Caste exams took place in a massive complex called the Proving Grounds. This secret and secure location provided the League's apprentices and Fathers a large space to practice their various hysteresis styles away from prying eyes. Fifty-foot walls made of reinforced steel encased a grass-covered surface area large enough to let entire schools train at once. The League's Conglomeration School had been at work for days, transforming the simple and secure design of the Proving Grounds into an arena capable of seating thousands of New Geneva's citizens. In depth study of a few key building materials had enhanced the new arena with angled seating for up to ten thousand spectators, walkways to help control the flow of foot traffic, and reinforced glass to protect spectators from flying debris.

The interior saw even larger changes. Vast stretches of naked metal took on the themes and colors of the four schools of hysteresis represented by the Grand Council members. The blinding white and gold twin orbs of the Quantum style sat front and center, emblazoned on the north wall. On either side of the Quantum School stood the blazing red ax and grinding wheel of the Friction style and the disintegrating blue wave of the Density style. The jet-black bastard sword of the Gravity style stretched across the south wall. Each section blended perfectly into the next, displaying the unity of the Council.

Each of the schools had a preparation room in their segment of the arena to house their participants. The Quantum style hadn't had a new student in over twelve years, and for this reason, the Conglomeration School would use their preparation room for the event. The participants in the Caste Exams were given no special treatment. Many students passed and failed their exams every year, but the Winter Festival presented a rare honor, especially with so much uncharacteristic negativity cast on the League at Solomon Pipher's recent trial. The silver lining of Solomon's folly spared the Grand Council from having to hear Solomon's incessant complaining about his school not being included. The Sensory Projection School had very few students to start with, but they were all released to pursue other schools after Solomon's less than stellar showing. Regardless of school, being chosen to participate in the Winter Festival's Exams came with honor, respect, and immense amounts of pressure. Two of these chosen sat in the Friction School's preparation rooms, eagerly and anxiously awaiting tonight's public spectacle.

"You'll do fine, stop thinking about it so much," Cassius teased as he placed his hand on his little brother's shoulder. Simeon looked over at his big brother. He seemed so calm; not a stitch of worry could be found on his chiseled features.

"How can you say that, Cassius? Especially when you're attempting the Father's Exam. Are you telling me you're not the least bit nervous?"

A slight smirk pulled on the corner on Cassius's lip. "What good would that do me, other than dull my mind's eye?"

Cassius brought a hand to his forehead, placing a finger on each temple. "Maintaining focus is one of the basic necessities of using hysteresis," he said with exaggerated instruction in his voice before dropping his dramatics and locking eyes with his brother. "I sure hope you haven't forgotten the basics this close to the Exams, little bro." Cassius held a glimmer of mischief in his eye as he prodded his younger brother's side.

Simeon didn't respond. His eyes were focused intently in front of him. He willed the door to their preparation room to remain closed a little bit longer. Cassius's playful mood took a back seat when he saw his brother's pensive stare.

"Think about it, Simeon. The Council would never let us take the Exam on Festival Day if they held the slightest doubt in our abilities. They've selected the best of the best for this Exam. That's why the two of us are here." Cassius beamed ear to ear, waiting for his little brother to do the same.

Simeon let out a small sigh and peeled his gaze from the sturdy metal door. His brother's cockiness and bravado always seemed to loosen the tight grip anxiety had on his mind. "You're right..." Cassius puffed out his chest and jut his chin even higher in the air. Simeon rolled his eyes. "You're an ass, but you're right. Too bad neither of those things can turn off the questions running wild through my head."

Cassius placed his hand back on his brother's shoulder. His playful smirk stretched into a hardened stare. "You don't have the luxury of questions, little bro. If you let your mind get distracted while using hysteresis, bad things can happen."

Simeon took a deep breath. The presence of his brother's large, warm hand helped the anxiety leak out of him. The time for worry had long passed. There was no room for distractions if he wanted to become an apprentice of the League. His test might be a piece of cake compared to the Father's Exam, but it held bigger ramifications. The gap between League member and non-League member rivaled the caste systems of old. Even a Sr. Father being elected as a new member of the Grand Council held a slight power increase by comparison.

As the two brothers sat in anticipation, they heard the booming voice of Sr. Father Sampson start the opening ceremonies. The Caste Exams had begun. "Citizens of New Geneva, prepare to experience the wonders of hysteresis as you have never seen them before. Tonight, we won't be altering dresses or preparing your meals. Far from it. Instead, you will be permitted to witness a glimpse of the finely honed styles of hysteresis that saved our civilization from the savageness of the mountain clans during the Holy Wars!"

The packed arena erupted in a chorus of cheers, waving large flags bearing the colors of their favorite school. Sampson held up his massive arms to return them to a dull buzz.

"We will start you off with some of our most promising recruits. Young men who hope to make themselves into our next apprentices. These lads possess the gift of hysteresis but are not yet counted amongst the ranks of the League. We have three of these young men with us here today." Sampson swung his giant arms over to the steel doors of the preparation rooms. "Boys who desire to become men! Join me on the platform!"

Sampson's voice cut through the reinforced steel, sending Simeon jumping to his feel. The less time he had to spend managing his anxiety, the better. Before he could make a move for the door, Cassius locked him in a tight embrace.

"Make the family proud, little bro!" Simeon would have responded if he had the air in his lungs required to do so. With a firm pat on the back, Cassius shoved his brother towards the towering door. Simeon looked over his shoulder and nodded silently before pushing open the door to the arena.

Simeon pictured Cassius's confident smirk in his mind, struggling into the open arena with ten times the confidence he actually possessed. He made sure to keep his eyes upward, but not focused on anything in particular. The last thing he needed was eye contact with a stranger. With his mind locked in this self-induced fog, he made his way up to the platform, along with the two other recruits. The group looked closer to squalling babes than young men. Especially when standing next to the imposing figure of Father Sampson. The crowd did not seem to notice their dwarfism, erupting into a deafening roar the moment Sampson raised his arms. Simeon had never heard such a noise in his life. The roar filled his chest and ripped through his clothes. Simeon let it wash over him like a wave, drowning out his anxious mind. Sampson waved his arms to quiet the crowd. The time had come for one of the recruits to walk out into the open field and find out what the Grand Council cooked up for them as an initiation. All eyes fell on Father Sampson.

"Without further delay, I call the School of Friction to the field to test the worthiness of their recruit." Immediately, a huge set of double doors burst open. A group of men in blazing red robes flooded the field, escorting a massive stone statue of an archer poised for a kill shot. Simeon let out a smooth, steady stream of air. *At least I don't have to watch anyone first,* Simeon thought as he left his place at the podium and made his way down to the arena to face his test.

"The Friction School is one of speed and quickness but also tactics and strategy! It was the Friction School who decimated the enemy's hoard of archers during the Holy Wars! To honor this, the Council requires you to defeat this nine-hundred pound replica. You have five minutes to complete this exam. Begin!"

Thrown off by the time limit, Simeon began to feel the pangs of anxiety rising up in his chest like the inside of a hornet's nest after a violent shake. The murmuring of ten thousand people whispering disbelief all at once did little to help. *What would Cassius do?* Simeon thought to himself, but he didn't have time for that. He had to come up with a way to use his hysteresis to take down a nine-hundred-pound stone archer. He thought through his training, and the little he knew about this concept called Friction. In its simplest form, Friction controlled how much grip something had on something else. With this as his sole focus, Simeon began quieting his mind, blocking out the buzzing of the crowd and the anxiety in his head. He focused his mind's eye as it crept along the length of ground he wished to alter. *The statue is sitting on a cloud. The grass and dirt pressed up against the underside of the statue are as slick and smooth as ice on a hot summer day.* Once he was content that he'd applied the required amount of hysteresis, Simeon walked within inches of the statue, took a deep breath, and blew.

The statue eked forward. Inch by inch, it picked up enough speed for the crowd to notice. Their earlier buzz of excitement returned, mixed with an aura of disbelief and wonder. Energized by the crowd, Simeon let out a cry of victory, thrusting his arms into the air. Simeon scanned the crowd, watching as their faces turned from glee to worry. Simeon turned back to the massive stone archer. To his surprise, the statue had not stopped at the edge of the ground he had prepared, continuing on a collision course with the nearby stands of spectators.

Without stopping to think further, Simeon raced after the sliding slab of rock. While he only lowered the friction in a limited space around the statue, he also reduced the friction on the underside of it. The normal friction of the ground did not exert enough force to halt the nine hundred pound, near frictionless archer.

Focusing his mind's eye as he ran, Simeon began to channel his hysteresis on the underside of the statue once again. This time he focused on increasing the friction enough to bring it to a screeching halt. Simeon did his best to clear his head once again. He imagined the underside of the statue as a multitude of hooks, gripping the surface of the hard ground with their sharpened points. His heart pounded in his chest as the stature slid closer and closer to the elites sitting in the front row. He fought off the urge to panic, to stop running, or to drop his focus. He couldn't let up. Not now. The consequences could be dire. A gigantic thud reverberated through the air as the archer buried his face into the ground. Relieved, Simeon bent over to catch his breath as the crowd once again erupted into cheers.

"Victory!" hollered Sampson.

The bass of that booming voice shook the fog from Simeon's mind. He had to chuckle at himself when he noticed the army of League apprentices and Fathers surrounding the outside of the exam area. How foolish to think that the League wouldn't have safety precautions in place. Relieved, excited, and out of breath, Simeon jogged up to the platform to join a smiling Sampson and two very focused looking recruits. Sampson gave him a hardy slap on the back as he returned to his place on the podium. It stung, but Simeon wouldn't have traded it for a Maiden's kiss. His chest swelled with pride.

The other two recruitment exams went by like a blur. The next boy came from the School of Density. He had to crack a massive boulder with a wooden sword, which he accomplished on his third blow. The final recruit came from the School of Conglomeration. He had to create a wooden shield from a pile of dead grass, which he completed with time to spare. So far, the Caste Exams were a huge success, but the real tests had yet to begin.

The three new apprentices received prime seating on the field to watch the rest of the exams. Simeon knew the next group would be apprentices vying to become League Fathers. His brother, Cassius, would be among them. Like Simeon, Cassius represented the Friction style, as did their father, Benjamin and their grandfather, the great Titus himself. The second apprentice represented the School of Gravity. Sampson beamed with a father's pride at the first showing from his own style.

If the recruits looked focused before, then these apprentices were etched in stone. Each style had different ways of upping the difficulty from the exam to become an apprentice to the exam to become a Father. For the Friction style, that difference came in how many manifestations of hysteresis you could manage at once. Simeon focused on both the ground and the statue, but the two surfaces came into physical contact, so they only counted as one. Cassius's exam would be designed to see if he could maintain at least two manifestations simultaneously. Sr. Father exams rarely came up as there can only be one Sr. Father per style, and each Sr. Father refused to teach those under them the highest level for fear of being overtaken. A League Father would have to come up with a new application of their style powerful enough to take on the unknown power of the Sr. Father of their School. Not only that, but the Sr. Father's exam was to the death.

Unlike Friction, Gravity's leveling system had nothing to do with the number of manifestations. Instead, it revolved around the amount of weight one could overcome. Gravity users, and usually their level, were easily spotted by the enormous weapons they carried with them at all times. Gravity users seemed to gain an attachment to these oversized weapons, many even naming them.

Simeon took note of the huge battle-ax the Gravity apprentice carried. Without hysteresis, the one-hundred-and-sixty-pound apprentice could not have moved the thing more than a couple inches off the ground. The apprentice's battle ax looked like a toy when compared to the massive slab of metal Sampson called a sword. Even while conducting the Caste Exams, Sampson had it strapped to his back. The oversized sword covered the whole of Sampson's seven-foot frame. The handle stuck out just above his head and the tip danced mere inches above the ground. Adding to the weapon's ominous presence, Sampson had the solid steel sword altered midnight black, matching the colors of his school. He named his sword, *Stygian*, a name Sampson claimed was from an old book the League kept in their guarded library about the afterlife. Simeon found himself wondering how many souls *Stygian* had sent to the afterlife during the Holy Wars.

The Gravity exam might require the participants to utilize their oversized weapons, but it might not. One way or another, the apprentice Gravity user was required to prove his ability to overcome one hundred extra pounds of weight, a Father five hundred pounds, and if someone had the guts to challenge Sampson, they would first need to surpass the one-thousand-pound mark. They must also prove their ability to maintain control over this weight for a significant amount of time, especially if they planned on using any of their collective weight totals to don armor, rather than putting it all into a single monstrous weapon.

The apprentice of Gravity got the first call. Sampson boomed out his summons to the crowd with an extra measure of pride. The young apprentice strutted down the platform and took his place in front of the wide double doors of his school's section, awaiting any challenge that burst forth. He didn't have to wait long. A group of men in the black robes of the School of Gravity made their way to the testing site. As they walked, they collectively channeled their hysteresis to keep a large triangular object afloat. The closer the group walked, the more the object they carried came into focus. Soon, they stood on all sides of the markedly less confident apprentice. The drop in confidence might have had something to do with the fact that a quarter ton steel triangle now hovered twenty feet above his head. The triangle's downward point aimed directly at his bare skull.

"Citizens of New Geneva," roared Sampson. "This is when the fun truly begins. The Grand Council has crafted a simple, yet suspense-filled task to kick the exams up to the next level. Soon, the Fathers who are using their Gravity style hysteresis to keep this five-hundred-pound piece of metal from splitting open this young apprentice's head will drop their mind's eye. To pass this exam, the apprentice must complete three tasks. First, he must keep the object suspended in the air. Second, he must maintain this suspension for five minutes, and lastly, the examinee must keep his feet firmly planted in their current position. Set the timer for five minutes. Begin!"

At the signal, the Fathers holding the crushing weight dropped their mind's eye, instantly transferring all the mental responsibility to the young apprentice. The triangle immediately dropped ten feet, jerking to a halt once the apprentice's adrenaline kicked in, sharpening his focus. The five-hundred-pound steel triangle hovered a mere ten feet above his head. The triangle's menacing point yearned to split his skull like a melon.

The apprentice kept his attention on the task at hand. Two minutes went by without the steel triangle budging another inch. Then, just when the apprentice began to get his previous air of confidence back, three archers strode out from the pair of black doors on the south side of the arena. The apprentice eyed them nervously, not sure what role they were to play. In the blink of an eye, one of the archers notched his arrow and let it fly. The apprentice jerked his head to the side just as the arrow sailed past it. This brush with death momentarily diverted his attention, causing the triangle to drop within an arm's length.

Simeon felt lightheaded; his breath was short and labored. His thoughts wandered to Cassius. The familiar bubbling of anxiety rose to the surface of his mind, but before he lost himself in worry, Simeon noticed the last two archers notching their arrows. Simeon wondered if the apprentice would break the rules and move his feet. Without further warning, two more arrows fired in one fluid motion. The huge metallic triangle lurched down yet again. Simeon almost looked away but forced himself to watch. He had to prepare himself to cheer on his brother should a similar situation arise. Prepared this time, the apprentice allowed the triangle to drop several feet while simultaneously falling back to avoid being crushed to death. In an impressive show of mental control and physical balance, the apprentice stopped the falling object at eye level, grabbing hold of the triangle as he fell. This daring move dropped his would-be executioner into the perfect position to successfully deflect the two incoming projectiles, while also giving him the means of maintaining his balance.

"Time!" bellowed Sampson. The exhausted apprentice let go of his huge triangular shield and allowed it to drop the last two feet to the ground. The crowd erupted in equal parts admiration and relief. Simeon found himself more in the latter category, realizing he had been holding his breath since the first arrow flew through the air. He steadied his mind, knowing that Cassius would likely be next. After seeing the gravity apprentice's exam, the crowd knew what kind of entertainment to expect. This made them cheer louder than ever. Simeon chewed his lip. His right leg bounced up and down uncontrollably. The doors in the Friction section of the arena opened once again. Simeon strained to get the first glimpse of what his brother would be facing. He needed to prepare himself and quiet his mind from the incessant parade of horrible scenarios.

As the first items exited the large double doors, Simeon's breath caught in his throat. Several Fathers from the Friction School walked through wearing the school's blazing red colors. Simeon anticipated their presence, but not what they brought with them. The Fathers escorted a large ballista, utilizing their hysteresis to pull it along with ease. The ballista's bolts looked capable of impaling three men with relative ease. Simeon began to fidget in his chair, anxiously rubbing his hands on his lap as he desperately fought to keep his composure. A newly elevated apprentice of the League couldn't be seen fretting off in the corner like a nervous child. Conversely, Cassius didn't appear the least bit phased by the oversized crossbow. He wore his signature smirk, waving to the crowd without a care in the world.

"As arrogant as ever," Simeon muttered to himself, shaking his head in disbelief. Part of him admired his brother for his overwhelming confidence, but mostly, it made him worry about his safety. Overconfidence could lead to poor judgment, thinking you can do things that you can't. A particularly dangerous sentiment when taking a Caste Exam. Simeon continued wringing his hands as the Fathers proceeded to set up the ballista. Next out of the Friction School doors came builders from the Conglomeration School.

With amazing speed, they erected a two-foot-high stone fence, encircling an area twenty feet in diameter. The Fathers from the Friction School focused their hysteresis on the ground in the middle of the circle, collectively making it a zero-friction zone. When an area or object went to zero friction, it became virtually untouchable. Only Sr. Father Titus has been able to overcome it alone. It took four Fathers to maintain a zero-friction space that large. Cassius could never overcome it on his own.

"Citizens of New Geneva, we have one final exam for you all to enjoy before heading to the Moonlit Feasts that have been prepared for you. Trust me when I tell you this last exam will give you something to talk about over the roast lamb and ale." The Crowd hollered a roar of approval. Simeon glanced over at his brother. He shifted from foot to foot like a child waiting for a birthday gift. He had hunger in his eyes that Simeon knew all too well. Cassius held that same look whenever Simeon would dare to argue with him, or when their father asked the boys to spar at the Friction School. More than any other student, Simeon dreaded being paired with his brother. Cassius never knew when to hold back, injuring other students on more than one occasion due to his overzealous desire for recognition. Thinking about those times, Simeon realized how much more anxious he would be without the presence of Cassius's sideways smirk and hungry eyes. He hoped his brother could keep his focus where it belonged.

"Apprentice of Friction, in order to pass this task and become a League Father, you must adhere to the following rules for this exam. First and foremost, you must remain inside the erected exam circle at all times. There is a hammer-blade suspended from a rope ten feet above this exam circle. The rope is connected to the domed ceiling fifty feet above you. You must obtain this weapon and use it to disable the ballista that will be firing bolts at you for the duration of the Exam. This Exam has no time limit and will begin the moment you step foot inside the exam circle. Proceed."

Cassius didn't hesitate for a second. He strode off the podium toward the zero-friction circle, waving to the crowd. He even went as far as blowing them kisses. All part of the show. As a proprietor of Friction himself, Simeon knew

Cassius's mind hummed with calculations, preparing to increase the friction on the bottom of his boots the moment they hit the zero-friction surface. With the forethought of a true exhibitionist, Cassius stopped his confident stride right before entering the circle, throwing his arms into the air with a valiant cheer. The crowd responded with a thunderous roar of their own, but Simeon knew Cassius's true intention. This pause allowed him to step more gingerly onto the testing surface. Even with the friction on his boots increased tenfold, Cassius would slide around the circle like a fawn's first outing on a winter lake.

After his well-timed address of the crowd, Cassius drew in one last deep breath and took his first step into the exam circle. The Fathers by the ballista started cranking back the firing mechanism, preparing the first shot. Simeon could follow his brother's steps up until this point, but he had no idea what he would do next. The hammer-blade dangled too far out of reach for a simple jump, especially on such a slippery surface.

Cassius slid to the center of the circle, willing himself to an unsteady stop before ripping two long strips of material from the bottom of his shirt. With time ticking away, Cassius wrapped the cloth around his fists and forearms like a pit fighter might do to protect his hands. Wrapping his hands in the fabric allowed him to use hysteresis without applying it directly to his body, which would break the Hysteresis Code. Cassius split his focus between maintaining his footing with increased friction and preparing his defenses by decreasing the friction on his hand wraps. Time seemed to creep by. Five seconds felt like an eternity. Everyone sat in anticipation of the ballista bolt being fired at full speed...

Twang! The first bolt flew to the left of its target. Judging from its trajectory, the bolt would barely skim the inside edge of the exam circle. Simeon let out a sigh of relief. This bought him time to prepare before another deadly bolt launched toward his brother. Without a moment of hesitation, Cassius started moving to intercept the shot. Simeon stood to his feet for a better angle.

Cassius slid across the exam circle, placing one foot on the short wall. Careful to maintain balance, Cassius pushed off enough to get his arms level with the incoming bolt. As he fell back toward the center of the circle, the ballista bolt whizzed past. As it did, Cassius placed both of his hands on the speeding projectile, re-directing it toward the exam circle. The bolt slid through Cassius's near-frictionless hand wraps, jerking his body to the side as he absorbed the force of the re-direction. The bolt hit the ground with a wet thump. Cassius fell along with it, sliding unbridled across the zero-friction surface. Without the added friction from the bottom of his boots, Cassius had no way to slow himself down and slammed shoulder first into the stone wall.

Cassius's legs shook as he struggled to get back on his feet. The Fathers by the ballista cranked away, getting ready to release another bolt. Cassius found his footing, but his arm hung limp by his side. With no time to address his injury, Cassius worked his way over to the downed ballista bolt. Each click of the ballista's cranking mechanism set Simeon's hair on edge. With the precious seconds he had left, Cassius lessened the friction between the metal tip of the ballista bolt and its wooden shaft.

Twang! The second bolt sprang from the ballista. It sped towards its target with blistering speed. Cassius's eyes went wide. He needed two good arms to re-direct a bolt. With no other choice, Cassius sacrificed his hard-earned footing, dropping to the zero-friction surface as the bolt whizzed overhead. As soon as it passed, he shifted his mental focus to his good arm, applying increased friction to his hand wrap to keep him in place. After struggling to his feet yet again, Cassius scooped up the freed bolt tip and positioned his feet against the back wall for support. Once steady, he heaved the heavy piece of metal towards the hammer-blade. A shrill grunt of pain sent awkward murmurs through the crowd as Cassius forced his injured arm to make the necessary motions. The heavy metal tip wobbled uselessly through the air, falling well short of its intended target. Stunned by his inept throwing capability, Cassius stood motionless, barely able to maintain the mental force required to stand. Twang! A third bolt shot free. Cassius didn't move. Didn't blink.

"No!" Simeon screamed, his heart thundering in his chest. The third ballista shot collided with the wooden shaft lodged in the exam circle. The bolt exploded in a shower of wooden shrapnel. Shards of wood tore through everything in sight, ripping chunks of skin from Cassius's face, torso, and arms. The shock jolted him out of his stupor. A cry of agony rippled through the hushed crowd. Cassius dropped to his knees, sliding helplessly against the back of the exam circle. Simeon feared the worst. Cassius might have gotten lucky by only getting a fair share of shrapnel thrown at him, but if he didn't do something soon, the next shot would end his life.

Lacking the strength to stand, Cassius, scoured the area for something to turn the tides. With nothing but shrapnel littering the exam circle, Cassius picked up a sliver, placing the piece of wood between his thumb and curled forefinger. With all the mental focus he could muster, Cassius dropped the friction of the wood to near zero and squeezed. An untraceable blur of wood rocketed from his fingers, slicing through its intended target. The rope snapped, dropping the hammer-blade into Cassius's lap. The crowd went wild, energized by this improbable turn of events. Cassius fed off of the crowd's energy, replacing his vapid expression with a hint of his previous bravado.

Seizing the moment, he grabbed the handle of the hammer blade and began reducing the friction on the circular blade at its tip. The arms of the ballista creaked into launching position as Cassius found a way to steady himself and make his throw. True to his normally perfect form, Cassius pressed the release mechanism on the handle of the hammer blade just as it hit the optimal angle and trajectory of flight. The near frictionless circular blade flew free from its handle and hummed through the air with expert precision. Cassius aimed for one of the thick ropes used to create enough pressure to launch the ballista bolts. The circular blade struck true, landing inches away from one of the Father's feet as their efforts to release the fourth bolt were met with an eventless click.

The crowd went hysterical. Simeon found himself cheering as loud as any of them, more from relief than anything. He searched for his brother, expecting to see him standing triumphant, arms raised and voice booming out a victory cry. Instead, he found him slumped over the exam wall, arms limp, and covered in blood. A team of healers raced onto the field. The crowd's cheers hushed to an eerie silence. As the healers helped Cassius to his feet, Simeon noticed several shards of wood protruding from his brother's abdomen. Each one surrounded by dark pools of blood. Cassius had used the last of his strength to throw that hammer blade, tearing up his insides as he made the necessary motions.

He would die a League Father, a title many lived their whole lives trying to obtain. Many would have felt pride at such a heroic display. Honored by the presence of yet another League Father in their family tree. All Simeon could see were the cold, dead eyes of his once proud brother. The anxiety in Simeon's head pulsed with a newfound vigor. Cassius's signature smirk melted into a formless puddle in his mind. The crowd sat in silence as the League Fathers surrounding the area saluted their fallen comrade.

With a heavy heart, Sampson addressed the crowd. Meaningless sounds swam through Simeon's mind, jumbled, and confused. The crowd stood to honor Simeon's fallen brother. Simeon took in the sight of 10,000 people standing in silence to honor his brother with watery eyes. In that moment, his anxiety fled. Chased from his mind by heartache, fear...and a smoldering pit of rage.

CHAPTER 21

THE PEDESTRIAN MR. PIPHER

Solomon Pipher sat in the lone chair in his ever-diminishing house. The clerk Cephas sent to oversee the repossession of Solomon's belongings sat with a satisfied smirk plastered across his face. Horrific scenes danced through Solomon's head as he watched his possessions sorted, boxed, and shipped to god knows where by the smarmy little shit standing in front of him. The fool had the nerve to limit Solomon to *one* companion. He tried to explain that his companions were five parts of a whole. The clerk's calculated stare scanned his clipboard.

"It's not in the paperwork," the clerk clarified as he flipped through page after page cataloging Solomon's belongings. If Solomon had to suffer that fidgety little prick telling him it wasn't in the paperwork one more time... "You must make a decision Mr. Pipher. Sr. Father Cephas clearly stated that he wants you out of the city before the end of the Winter Festival."

"Yes, yes, I heard you the first fifteen times. If you're really in such a hurry, take your boney little ass elsewhere. You have the insufferable talent of making me unable to think clearly."

The clerk pulled a gold pocket watch from his tightly cinched vest. "I will allow you five minutes to make your decision, and then we must go. We are already behind schedule as it is." Solomon slumped further into his favorite chair. The last of his possessions to be packed up for some other schmuck to enjoy.

"It wasn't long ago that no man would dare to *allow* me to do anything," Solomon said aloud in a pitiful attempt to defend himself from the pillaging currently taking place. It wasn't just his home and possessions being ripped from his grasp, but his pride as well. He seethed at the audacity of being expected to take orders from a clerk. Clerks were nothing more than the League's paper pushers and astronomically below a man such as Solomon Pipher. Despite his rage, he would need to pick his battles wisely going forward. The Council had him by the balls, squirming would do nothing but tighten their grip. Solomon would have to endure and hope that the Council would be faithful in their promises to him. *Lead Father of the Inquisition.* It did have a nice ring to it.

All of this aside, Solomon had a more pressing task to attend to. He contemplated the possibilities. *My first instinct is to take Lust, but it wouldn't be long before I would need a companion with half a brain, so she is out. I'll already be getting my fill of playtime at work, so I'll have little need of Fear, and Indulgence would be far too difficult to feed in my current living situation. That leaves Grace and Loathe...*but before Solomon could make up his mind the obdurate clerk returned, clipboard in hand.

"Times up, Mr. Pipher. Who will it be?"

Solomon let out a sigh of defeat. "Loathe seems appropriate, considering the circumstances."

"Very good. I'll have her cleaned up and ready to move."

"No need," replied Solomon. "Let her come as is." The clerk

curled his lip and turned up his nose before headed up to Solomon's bedroom with the news. A few moments later an agonizing scream echoed through the vast open spaces of Solomon's desolate mansion.

"No! You made a mistake. Why would he choose me? Don't make me go with him. I'll *do* anything, *be* anyone, don't make me go." Solomon cocked his head and stuck out his lower lip. He had never heard the girl talk above a whisper. Perhaps she had more of a backbone than he thought.

A moment later, the pressed and proper bureaucrat escorted Loathe down Solomon's extravagant staircase. Matted knots of hair stuck to her head in greasy clumps. Her eyes were wide and bloodshot with puffy dark circles painted underneath. She wore the only dress Solomon ever allowed her to wear. A threadbare, yellow sundress marred by countless stains. It smelled of body odor and dried sweat. As she came down the stairs, she tugged at her tattered dress in a desperate attempt to hide her shame. Solomon smiled for the first time that day as he watched her struggle to exist in her own skin.

"There she is. My one and only," Solomon cooed in an overtly patronizing tone. To his surprise, Loathe offered up a response.

"Why?" her voice cracked as her swollen eyes puddled with tears. "Why would you pick me? I'm not pretty like Lust or confident like Grace, and either one of the boys could help you carry more than I can manage. What could I possibly offer you that none of them can?"

Solomon's wry smile turned up even more. "Isn't it obvious? We are going to wake up every morning surrounded by putrid beggars, rotting shanties, and sour-smelling drunks. You're the only thing I could bring with me that would remind me of how much worse things could get."

Loathe didn't utter another word. Her listless gaze drifted

silently to her feet. After a few more moments of silence, fat tears began running down her unwashed face and onto Solomon's elaborately polished floor. Solomon beamed.

Unmoved by their exchange, the clerk went right back to business. "Now that we have settled that issue, let us be off. Grab your bags and stay close. Just because the festival is going on, doesn't mean we can leave caution to the wind. There is no telling what kind of trouble we could find ourselves in if you are spotted."

After hours of sneaking through back allies and waiting for the danger of an occasional cat to wander past, the group came to a stop near a section of wall outlined in what looked like black chalk. "This is where I bid you farewell, Mr. Pipher. I don't imagine we will see each other again. Once you are prepared to step outside the walls, knock three times, wait three seconds, and then knock once more." Without another word, the clerk went on his way.

Solomon looked down the empty alley, rubbing his belly. "Well, at least that neurotic parasite has left us, eh, girl?" Loathe continued to stare at her feet. "Whatever happened to the girl with a bit of spine left in her? You aren't going to be boring again, are you?" Loathe didn't move. Her eyes were wide and unwavering from their downward gaze. Solomon let out an annoyed huff. "I sure hope whoever is on the other side of this...door? Is more of a conversationalist." Solomon turned to the wall. *Knock, Knock, Knock...knock.*

Immediately following the final rap, the marble wall started to dissolve. Before long, the two companions stood face to face with Father Malachi. Solomon turned to Loathe. "You know that bit about a conversationalist...scratch that."

Malachi rolled his eyes. "Still a child, Solomon? Don't let mere possessions sway you from your new calling. Despite appearances, you are already more than you have ever been before. Once you were nothing more than an egotistical Sr. Father with nowhere left to rise, but now you stand before me as Head Father of the Inquisition. You have nowhere to go but up, Solomon."

Solomon sat in silence for an awkwardly long time. "You see what I mean, girl? This one has a silver tongue, but I'm afraid it might be laced with poison. I'll take your halitosis and rotting teeth over his *higher ideals* any day."

Malachi didn't seem the least bit shocked by the response. "I was a fool to think you would see the higher purpose in all of this. You claim to be a servant of the League, yet your only true master is your own desire. I hope we have chosen the right man for the job."

"It's a little late in the game for that sentiment, Malachi. Besides, I don't think you chose me due to my overwhelming charm or my impeccable morals. You chose me because I'll do what it takes to rise back to the top. Things men like you don't have the stomach for."

Solomon's short temper, selfish desires, and obsession with power gave the Council assurance that he would go through with their plans. Other Fathers in his position might opt for a life as a wandering hysteresis merchant, selling their skill for decent coin. The Council knew Solomon would never stoop so low. His lust for power and self-indulgence wouldn't allow it. Solomon would stick with his task, slowly tightening his grip on the LHC. He wouldn't stop until he became the illustrious Mr. Pipher once again.

Malachi nodded his head, conceding the argument. "There is one more thing."

"And what the bloody hell might that be?"

"The outcome of your trial has...changed some things."

Solomon gave Malachi a menacing look. "Oh, I've already taken note of a few. I'm clearly being escorted *outside* of the city walls. I have a knapsack and a damaged girl to my name, and I don't see a single League apprentice present to make up my *five fingers of justice*. Did I not send in my request for Brandon, Arthur, Cassius, John, and Derek?"

Malachi cleared his throat. "Yes. Like I said, things have changed. We never planned on being forced to try you with false teaching, along with breaking the Code. Truth be told, we have no idea where that notebook came from, but once it came to light, we had no choice but to change our plans accordingly. Now that you have been convicted of both charges, your rights to have League members train under you, in any capacity, have been revoked. You will need to recruit your *five fingers* outside the city walls. I'm sure there are plenty of cut-throats and brigands to choose from where you are going. As you already noted, this new charge has also forced us to expel you from the city's walls. An idea we were toying with anyway. Fortunately, this exile is not permanent, and we can reinstate your admittance to the city after a five year no admittance period. However, if you re-enter the city before that time, for any reason, your five years are reset. Is this all clear enough to you, Solomon?"

"Oh, yes, quite clear. I'm to build a whole new division of the League with no League assistance and without a single resource the city would provide me. But don't worry your pretty head about it. I'm sure I'll be able to find five suitable men amongst the beggars, thieves, and drunkards that litter the LHC. Also, I have plans to establish an intimidating headquarters inside a disease-riddled tavern. It's going to be a grand adventure. I can barely contain my enthusiasm if you couldn't tell."

Malachi closed his eyes and took a slow breath of air. "Consider it earning your keep, Solomon. We could just as easily have you thrown in the holding cells, or have you demoted or exiled with no chance at redemption. You jest at your situation and mock the opportunity we have gifted you, but I bet you will be singing a different tune once you have lived a few weeks in that shit hole they call a city." Malachi, paused, waiting for Solomon to meet his expectant stare. "Find men worthy of representing the League. Train them and grow your influence. Once you have established yourself in a way that meets our expectations, we will have cause to send you some League assistance. Now enough with this squabbling, there are some essential things we still need to cover."

Solomon gave a mock-filled bow of respect and waited for Malachi to continue. "An envoy from the League will meet you at the Charlatan's Inn on the first of every month for a progress report. He will be wearing a red ribbon around his left wrist. When you see him, sit down at his table but say nothing until drinks are poured. You will report numbers, operation develop-ment, and your current degree of influence in the LHC. You are not to share any information concerning *Aequalitatem* or update the envoy on any recent...questioning. That will be left to other means of communication. Is this all clear to you, Solomon?"

Solomon nodded his head lazily. "Yes, yes. It all seems rather routine. I'm not daft."

"Very well. I will lead you to your living quarters, follow me."

"Well, go on," Solomon barked at Loathe. "Let's go find our new honeymoon suite." Solomon gestured for Loathe to make her way through the make-shift door Malachi had created. After the frail girl made it through unscathed, Solomon followed. The moment after his bulbous body squeezed through the small opening, Malachi began to cinch it shut, slowly building the density of the wall until nobody would have known a hole existed at all.

The odd pair followed Malachi through what seemed like miles of narrow, filth-filled alleyways and corridors. The narrow streets of the LHC faded to a single dirt covered path. A mix of forest and abandoned farmland flanked the lone dusty road on both sides. The group followed a few bends in the path until they came upon a humble structure blending in with the unkept woods. Stones of varying sizes, shapes, and colors were stacked haphazardly together, held in place by a clay-mud composite. The same clay had been used to patch holes in the thatched straw roof, giving the whole place the odor of a musty horse corral. On a positive note, it did give Solomon ample space to work as his new home sat alone in an open field.

"Well... At least it has a decent backyard," said Solomon with a sarcastic bite to his words.

Malachi rolled his eyes. "Would you rather have one of the tents packed around that sad excuse for a city-center? We needed to find you somewhere away from prying eyes. We don't expect you to do any recruiting or interrogating in this small, exposed place. There is an old barn at the back of this property that will do nicely for that." Malachi paused for a moment, looking over Solomon's appearance. "All of our efforts to help you blend in will be of no use if you're going to walk around town wearing those clothes."

Solomon looked down at his polished white leather shoes, matching set of professionally tailored shirt and trousers, and gold-trimmed navy-blue suit. "This old thing? I'll rub some dirt on it. I'm sure it will be fine."

"Enough with this facade, Solomon. Personally, I preferred your egotistical, brutish personality to this overly sarcastic, passive-aggressive one. Is this your small way of showing your defiance? Do you think that slightly annoying me with petty commentary is going to win back a bit of your former respect?

You had better find yourself, Solomon. We need brute force and lust for power in order for this to work—not a fat comedian who has lost his nerve."

Malachi's words rolled through him like a nauseating wave. Normally, he would have turned that sniveling clerk who dissected his house inside out just for walking through his door without permission, and he certainly wouldn't have been so cooperative with Malachi either. Before the trial, most of Solomon's problems could be solved with threats, violence, or his position within the League, but when the Grand Council took all those options away, he had nothing but his sharp tongue. This realization made him feel weak; a feeling he loathed to the core of his being. *Am I nothing more than an over-inflated mass of rage, ego, and power? Is this all it takes to deflate my purpose like a man's member after a session with his personal companion?* Thinking this way made Solomon burn with rage. How had he let those pompous fools get to him to this degree?

Solomon clenched his fists as the rage built up inside of him. An aching desire to peel Malachi's flesh from his bones crept up his arms. His mind danced with images of his fingers wrapping tightly around Malachi's throat, watching his eyes turn cloudy as the last of his breath was pressed from his lungs. The desolate woods flanked his unfocused vision. Memories of his humble beginnings roared to the surface. Solomon pushed the violent fantasy from his head, taking in the sites around him with fresh eyes. The woods swayed in the wind, branches creaking and leaves rustling. He had lived out here once before in the untamed world outside the walls. He had forgotten how limitless...how unrestricted...and how lawless it was. The rage that once filled every fiber of his being quieted to a dull roar. Solomon closed his eyes and coaxed the rage deeper within.

"You're absolutely right Malachi. I have been soft as of late, but please advise the Council not to worry. I have everything under control."

"Good," replied Malachi, taken aback by the eerie shift in Solomon's presence and behavior. He would have preferred Solomon bursting a blood vessel while screaming in his face. This calm and collected Solomon gave him the chills. Without another word, Malachi turned back the way he came, leaving Solomon and Loathe alone. After a few moments of silence, Solomon put his arm around Loathe's shoulder and began walking toward their new home.

"This place has reminded me of something, little one. Something important." Loathe raised her head and looked from Solomon's beaming face to his arm slung over her shoulder. "We are retched little maggots, you and I." The wicked smirk never left his face. Loathe's head snapped back towards Solomon, brows knit together in confusion. "Do you know how maggots survive, my girl?" Loathe shook her head, eyes fixed on her master. "Just like you and I, Maggots are born in shit. They survive by being willing to squirm, scuttle, and tear their way through the decaying carcasses of creatures far more gallant than themselves." Solomon turned his attention to Loathe. "If the world has made us maggots, then maggots we will be, and if the world doesn't give us enough corpses...then I guess we will have to make some ourselves."

CHAPTER 22
THE HOODED FIGURE

Three days had passed since Wren found the note from Oriella on the bottom of her food tray. Last night, as requested, Wren stuck the note under her filled waste bucket with the "yes" option circled in the cranberry juice from yesterday's breakfast. The note had taken her by surprise to say the least. Slipping a note to her in her room felt odd enough, getting a message to her while in a secured unclean room took things to a whole new level.

Despite having no idea how Oriella contacted her, or what she planned to do, Wren decided to trust her. She might be overly perky and a little annoying, but she also showed more loyalty and care than her family seemed to. Wren ran the contents of the note through her head for the hundredth time, trying to make sense of it. *What does she mean, come out and play? Is she offering to aid me in an escape? How could she know I would even contemplate such a thing? Perhaps that's why she used such cryptic language. Coming out to play could mean almost anything. Maybe I'm too quick to fill in meaning where there is none.* Wren let out a frustrated huff. Even if the offer to help her escape existed in her own mind, it still didn't explain how or why Oriella got the note to her.

Despite all of her questions, Wren decided that getting out of her cell to literally play would be okay with her. Over the last three days, Wren kept herself busy by practicing hysteresis. This gave her ample time to think about the two divergent paths her hysteresis had taken in the past few days. She had taken to calling one of them chaotic and the other one tranquil. The chaotic type allowed her to change sand into glass and ignite paper in an instant. She could harness this type of hysteresis by letting her frustrations flow as she focused her mind's eye. The tranquil type required the opposite—a calm and serene state of mine. She harnessed this type by visiting the lake of her childhood. Memories from this time provided moments of pure joy and happiness. Focusing on one of these memories allowed her to do more than filter out the day's distractions. It allowed her to plunge beneath them, accessing a whole new level of calm.

Wren had no idea how or why these two different variations of hysteresis existed, or how they worked, but something about them intrigued her. She began to see these two types of hysteresis as two halves of a whole. The chaos represented her frustration with what life had become and her will to live rather than just exist. When she used this type, she felt a tingling sensation all over her body, almost like each and every speck of her being woke up at once. Her tranquil type represented her hope for the future and the few treasured memories of happiness from the past. When she used this type, she felt an almost eerie stillness. Like the world and all its problems could no longer touch her. Her body and mind felt light as a feather, and if she held it long enough, she would begin to feel as if she had left her body behind.

At first, she thought she had to decide which one of these

forms of hysteresis represented the real Wren Crivelli. Ultimately, she decided that they represented her in equal, yet distinct parts. She could not abandon her hope for the future and the treasured memories of the past. Nor could she forget the anger she felt when reflecting on past and present abuses. She wanted to live free but could not forgive those who had imprisoned her and so many like her. As she continued pondering the usefulness of these two strange phenomena, the guard came by to return her waste bucket.

Wren's heart pounded in her chest as the guard unlocked the small door at the bottom of her cell. Without a word, he slid her emptied waste bucket through the door, followed by a fresh tray of fruit. Despite her rumbling stomach, Wren went straight for the bucket, flipping it over as her mind raced in anticipation of what she might find. Sure enough, she found another note attached to the bottom.

Yippee! I'm so glad you finally want to be friends! Now, get yourself out of that stuffy old room, would ya? Oh yeah, one more thing. I don't expect you to make me any crumpets. You'd probably burn them, anyway. ☺

-XOXO Oriella

I've been waiting three days... for this? What the hell kind of response is that? Why couldn't Oriella speak plainly? Did she always have to be such a weirdo? After her initial reaction, Wren took a deep breath. Maybe something in the note was a clue. Oriella might be an odd-ball, but perhaps there was meaning behind her madness. One thing Wren knew for certain. Oriella expected her to take action for herself. The only other content in the note made mention of crumpets.

That's it! Wren yelled in her head. *The only time I've ever mentioned crumpets in my life came the night I first turned sand into glass. Which is the same day Oriella left me the note on my bed.*

She must be referencing that. What else could it be? Okay, I think I'm on to something here.

Hastily, Wren picked up the note for a second read. "You'd probably burn them anyway..." *Could Oriella possibly know that I burned that note?* It made sense, in an odd Oriella type of way. Wren figured she had nothing to lose. She wanted to get out of this place anyway, so she might as well use this as an opportunity to make her first move. She had three more days in her cell before being deemed clean. If she could get out sooner, it might give her a head start.

With her mind made up, Wren decided to continue analyzing Oriella's odd note. *Okay, so let's say she knows about that night. How does that help me now? Assuming she is overly clever, rather than psychotic, all of her words would be carefully chosen. There isn't much room on these small pieces of paper. So why let me know that she knew about that night?*

Wren's mouth hung open as she realized the only implication this line of thinking could lead to. *Oriella knows about my chaotic style of hysteresis and is urging me to use it to get out of here.* Wren harbored these improbable thoughts in the back of her mind as she contemplated what to do next. Chaos hysteresis appeared to be her only shot of escaping on her own volition. Correctly interpreted or not, Oriella's note gave her the encouragement she needed to try. Determined to take control of her life for the first time since childhood, Wren placed her right hand on the cold metal surface of her cell door and channeled her chaotic side. Her frustration, anger, and resolve flowed through her as naturally as the blood in her veins. All of this melted away in an instant as searing pain engulfed her right palm.

"Ouch!" Wren yelped as she shot a look at the door just quick enough to see the last tinge of orange dissipating from its metallic surface. Anxiety flooded her mind as the smell of seared flesh filled her nose. She looked from the door to the angry red blisters that covered the palm of her hand. The throbbing pain took a back seat to the sudden memory of her mother crying out in pain as the blowback tore through her chest.

Wren's eyes lingered on the angry blisters. She could hear the pop and sizzle of her brother's murderers in the back of her mind. Her breath caught in her throat as she waited for her impure actions to send the blowback through the rest of her body. Seconds leaked by like syrup from a near-empty bottle. More than enough time for Wren's mind to dig deeper in the implication of her actions, to the childhood stories of Esteban Cortez. His body deconstructing and reconstructing itself like the ebb and flow of a river.

Wren fought to control her racing breath. *It's not blowback.* She knew there had to be some other explanation. Her mind might have been wandering in her chaotic state, but she knew her thoughts centered on the door and nothing else. She recounted the various affects her new hysteresis created: *sand into glass, paper into flame, and now, metal into searing hot surface.* She had no idea why the sand turned into glass, but the other two seemed to follow a pattern of things heating up. Blowing cool air on her aching hand, Wren decided to run a test on something a little safer. Scanning the room, her eyes landed on her wooden food tray. It would act as a perfect test subject.

Without further delay, Wren used her good hand to apply her chaos hysteresis to the tray. In an instant, smoke trailed between her fingers. She pulled her hand back and a small flame sprang from the wood in its place. Wren jumped up and down, raising her hands in silent victory. Smoke continued to leak from the flaming tray, cutting her victory off with a slight cough and fits of worry. Wren tore off a strip of her dress and smothered the fire without a second thought, surprising herself at her quick, bold thinking. Seeking out answers and discovering new things had brought her a thrill nothing in her caged life could match. She couldn't stop here.

She needed to think outside her Oriella-created box. Oriella might have known about her ability to burn paper, but there was no way she could have known about the other path of hysteresis Wren had discovered within herself. Ignoring the pulsing pain in her right hand, Wren approached the door a second time. *Breath in... Breath out... Breath in.... Breath out...* She concentrated on wringing the last fragments of chaos and anxiety from her mind. This tranquil style took Wren quite a bit longer to use. She found it easier to embrace the frantic emotions of anger and pain than the elusive emotions of hope and joy. Minutes ticked by as Wren continued to walk her mind into the tranquil state. Despite her best efforts, the door stood unchanged. A solid block of steel laughing at her adorable effort to conquer it.

Wren struck the door with her dominant hand in frustration. One of her recently formed blisters popped upon impact. Her eyes watered as she flung her hand about in the air in silent agony. After the shock of pain wore off, Wren refocused her eyes. Something about the door seemed different. Using her good hand, she traced a finger over the door's perfect surface. Her finger paused as it passed over a slight disturbance in the sea of smooth. The hairline fissure wormed its way two feet above and below the oily smudge mark she had made on the door. A mixture of confusion, fear, and excitement coursed through her.

The cold, hard surface of the thick metal door stared back at her. Wren paced around the small room. Her mind abuzz. She plopped down on her lumpy bed and began recalling her thoughts and emotions; anger, frustration, desperation, pain, regret, loss, loneliness...followed by love, peace, hope, wholeness and longing...and ending with a final burst of frustration. A momentary overlap of the two sides. *That's it!* New idea fuel at the ready, Wren placed her left palm on the door, channeling her tranquil side. At her side, her injured right hand curled into a fist. She allowed the frustration of defeat to flow through her, just enough to sneak past her tranquil state. Drop by drop, she channeled her quiet rage into her tightened fist. The two opposing forces fought to maintain control of Wren's mind, each pushing for more space.

Wren's eyes popped open as she swung her fist at the door. The tranquil surface of the door pushed against the bits of chaos she had channeled into her fist. The echo of knuckles meeting metal rang in Wren's head. A rush of pain shot from her fist all the way up her arm.

Shit! I hope I didn't break my hand! No... I can't think like that... You're making progress.

Wren eyed the spider-webbed door. It looked impressive, but the fractures were barely a fingernail deep. *Just deep enough to be noticed...*

Perhaps she needed to hold both states of mind longer than a fraction of a second. Or, maybe thoughts of frustration were not strong enough. She needed something that evoked both types of emotions in her at once. Something that made her feel love and hope as well as pain and anger. Something that would allow her to channel her chaos and tranquil styles side by side instead of opposed to one another. As much as it pained her, she knew what she had to do.

With the perfect tool for the job, Wren approached the large steel door once again. She closed her eyes, widened her stance, and placed both palms on the door shoulder width apart. Pain shot up her arm as her open blisters made contact with the door. A wheeze of pain escaped her lips, but she held her ground. She took herself back to the house on the lake—to memories of her father encouraging her curiosity and complimenting her on things other than her appearance. She remembered her mother, strong and free, singing her to sleep on her roughest of nights. Then she allowed herself to unbury her memories of Elias, the big brother who spent countless days playing with her in the fields and swimming with her in the lake. In her young mind, he seemed invulnerable. Strong and confident where she felt tentative and unsure. The memories were not perfect, but they were happy. A loving family, dedicated to bettering each other.

Then she allowed herself to recall that fateful night. The night the mountain clans changed everything. She saw her father's face etched with fear, ripping her rabbit from her hands. She pictured her mother, screaming out in pain as she tore her son's murderers apart with her mind. Last of all, she remembered Elias. Eyes wide and cloudy. Head limp and lifeless. Body bloody and broken. Her entire world changed that day. The trauma divided her two selves like an invisible iron curtain. The painful memories of that day brought her mind to the curtain's edge. To her parent's collapsing at her feet in the Hollowlands...and to the hooded figure that had saved them.

"MORE THAN NOTHING, YOU SAY?" The hooded figure eyed the girl with an air of suspicion. "You've managed to keep the Hollowlands at bay by telling yourself that you're more than nothing?"

Wren lifted her chin, doing her best to look upon the figure's shifting face. "It's a magic phrase...I picked it out with my mom and dad..."

"The same Mom and Dad that I see laying at your feet, I

presume?" Wren nodded, ducking down in an attempt to see a smidge more of this strange person's face. "I see... And why, exactly, do you think they are on the ground and you are not?"

Wren shifted her focus back to her parents. They sat a few feet from her, slumped over and drooling on themselves. "I-I don't know... Maybe it's fake Elias."

"Fake Elias?" asked the figure, tilting their head to the side.

"Yes... He's my brother... Er... I mean... Used to be my brother... I know he's dead and all. I helped bury him. Mom wouldn't leave unless we did."

The hooded figure opened their mouth to speak, but couldn't seem to find the right words. Instinct kicked in as they reached a calming hand toward the young girl. Wren burst out in tears, dropping to her knees and burying her head in her hands. The figure jumped back. "I'm sorry, little one. I didn't mean to..."

"They're dead!" Wren screamed as she grabbed the stranger's sleeve in white-knuckled grief. "They're all dead! Elias is a ghost in my head, and soon mom and dad will be too!"

The hooded figure placed a gentle, translucent hand over her small shaking fist. "I hate to be so curt...but time is of the essence here. If you don't find it too...difficult...would you allow me to ask you a few questions that might help?"

Wren's wails shuttered to a raspy stop. "Questions?"

The figure nodded. "Just three," they said, holding up three fingers before noticing their exposed flesh, quickly tucking their hand back into their freed sleeve.

Wren wiped the mess of tears and snot from her face with the back of her hands and nodded. "Okay then," responded the figure. "Question one: how did you and your family find your-self in the Hollowlands?"

Wren's wide glassy eyes fixated on the ground. "We've

always been out here. Well, not out this way. Mother said never to come out this way...but that was before..." Emotions welled up in her throat and closed off her speech.

"I see..." mused the stranger as he surveyed the land around them more closely. "Question two: does anyone in the party possess..." The stranger leaned in close. Wren could almost make out the color of their eyes. "The gift?"

Wren froze. The previous emotions of overwhelming sadness and grief evaporated in an instant. Her body tightened as her eyes darted from her collapsed mother to her collapsed father and back again.

The figure put out a reassuring hand. "Do not fear, child. I am a user myself."

Wren peered at the translucent palm held up before her, noticing the stranger's skin in full for the first time. She could see the gentle outline of several bones beneath the skin. The figure noticed the change in her gaze and quickly tucked their hand away.

Wren looked from the hooded figure to her mother. "You've got it worse than mom. What did you do?"

The stranger paused, taking notice of the newly stitched wound poking out of the top of Harmony's blouse. "Your mother... How did she get such a unique wound?"

Wren bit her lip and wrung her hands. "I'll tell you if you tell me."

The figure paused for a moment. "This power...is called a gift, but it is not always so for those who carry it..." The figure squatted next to the traumatized girl. "That's why we must learn as much about our gift as we can. So we can erase the need for such pain in the future."

Wren mulled the stranger's words around in her addled brain. "She *killed* them. Bubbled their insides and melted their skin. She... They killed Elias!"

The hooded figure squatted down by Wren's mother. "So, she did it to protect those she loves… A much nobler cause than my own… I did it for myself."

"For…yourself?" Wren asked, wiping fresh tears from her face before raising her head. "You mean, like protecting yourself?"

"In a way…I…wasn't who I wanted to be…and I was tired of hiding it…" Wren gave the figure a confused look. "I know… I have trouble wrapping my own mind around it sometimes. Let me put it in a way you might be able to understand." The stranger let out a long sigh, muttering something inaudible. "The way I looked was telling people I was someone I wasn't."

"The way you looked?"

"Yes… Sometimes, people have an idea of what a person must be, or what a person must do, simply becaaaaaaah!" The stranger's jaw bone popped free and slide to the left, followed by a quick shift to the far right. Wren's eyes doubled in size as she watched more and more of the stranger's bones join the dance. "Argh!" the stranger cried as he finally managed some form of air out of his wandering skeleton. *"I am who I am… I am who I am…"*

"I am who I am!" the stranger said as they slid their jaw into its rightful place. The rest of their bones followed like ripples in a pond.

Wren sat in silence as she watched the stranger return to a fully upright position. Her mind wavered between heartache and terror. The stranger shivered a few times before turning toward the horizon.

"Wait!" Wren shouted. "Was that… your magic phrase?" The stranger froze. The sound of his robes flapping in the dusty wind was his only response. "Did the Hollowlands do this to you? I mean… I thought it was blowback…like mom…but if you have a magic phrase…"

"Something like that..." The stranger sighed. "That's only part of my story...but I'm afraid we don't have time for all that right now." The stranger nodded toward Wren's unconscious parents.

"Oh! How could I forget...your questions... You had one more, didn't you?"

Wren swore she saw the stranger wipe a tear from their eye before taking a few steps towards her. "How good is your memory?"

Wren scrunched up her face. "Memory?"

The figure nodded their head. "Yes. Like, when you recall your brother...Elias. Can you see each hair on his head? Recall the smell of his sweat? Hear the cadence and pitch of his voice?"

Wren scrunched up her brow. "Every hair? And what does cadence mean?"

The stranger took a short breath. "My apologies. It's been quite some time since I've interacted with anyone, let alone a young girl... The important thing is, the more you can remember, the better. And not just how things *looked* either. Memory is as much about perception, emotion, and environment as it is aesthetics."

"'ae..stetics?'" repeated Wren.

"Sorry... The unique way that something looks. Its...visual presence."

"Ooooooh," Wren responded, feigning understanding.

The stranger dropped their head and stroked their chin. "Perhaps simple is better for one your age. I assume you have many wonderful memories of your brother... Elias, was it?" Wren nodded. "Search your mind for a memory that you can do more than see with your mind's eye, but one you can smell, hear, and maybe even taste or touch. The more senses you can recall, the better."

Wren shifted her position on the ground. "But...won't that bring out false Elias?"

"Yes... It most definitely will," the stranger replied. Wren took a sharp inhale of air that got stuck in her chest. "Don't worry. I'll do the rest."

Wren steadied her breath, a look of determination etched onto her face. "What's the rest? What do you plan to do?"

The stranger let out a lazy sigh, staring out towards the horizon. "You are young, alone, and a girl at that. And it will help the hysteresis if you are aware of my actions..." the stranger muttered to himself before snapping their attention back to Wren. "I was once part of something grander... Something that stood at the apex of reshaping this ravaged world... That is until I could no longer bare it..." Wren waited in silence as the stranger collected themselves. "I am one of only a handful of individuals trained in a form of hysteresis called Sensory Projection. This is what I will use to lead you and your family out of the Hollowlands."

Wren stood to her feet. "Hysteresis has forms?"

The stranger nodded. "Sensory projection allows the user to cause others to experience things that are not real."

Wren squinted her eyes. "You mean like the Hollowlands does with fake Elias?"

"Not exactly... Tell me, how does it feel when you think about what happened to your brother?"

Wren crossed her arms and shifted from foot to foot. "Like...there's a painful knot in my chest that won't let go."

"That knot, as you say... The Hollowlands feeds off of it, pulling it tighter and tighter until the soul is bound so tight that it cannot bear it any longer... Sensory projection does not search the souls of others, but of the user. It takes vivid memories and projects them onto the consciousness of others."

Wren bit her lip. "I...don't really understand... Sorry."

The stranger placed their translucent hand on Wren's shoulder. "Don't worry... Just find that memory and leave the rest to me."

THE MEMORY HIT her like a bucket of ice-water. She had only been eight years old when she met the hooded figure, and until today, her only memories of them were terrifying snapshots of their shifting bones and translucent skin. She had forgotten what they had taught her about the knot in everyone's soul. The knot the Hollowlands feeds off of...and... *Wait... Sensory Projection!* The realization rushed through her. *That...person. Could they have been?*

Over the decades that Solomon Pipher had been a Sr. Father, he had only taken on a handful of apprentices, and the ones he did never lasted long. Most of them were scared off by the stories of what happened to the only apprentice who made it to League Father...Esteban Cortez.

CHAPTER 23
THE GRAY

The realization rumbled through her mind, tossing all other thoughts aside. *Esteban Cortez.* Half of her always thought of him as just a story. Another way to keep Purity Maidens from exploring knowledge outside of their approved list. In a way, she was right. The stories she heard didn't quite match up to the ones she remembered from her introductory purity lessons, or the rumors she heard floating around the Crystal Pedestal. Those stories would have you believe that Esteban was a monster. A man who broke the most sacred rule of hysteresis. A man who experimented on his own body... *What was it he said about how he had gotten that strange form of blowback? Something about doing it for himself...* *"The way I looked was telling people I was someone I wasn't."*

His words hit so much harder than they did when she was eight, painting a picture beyond Esteban's terrifying physical appearance. In those days, the League was still looking for him. News of his strange blowback was the buzz of New Geneva when she had first arrived, but such news was always accompanied by the relief that he was being imprisoned deep in the

League's holding cells. Did he escape? Was that hooded figure even Esteban? It had to be. Who else would have shifting bones and translucent skin? Him being an apprentice of Solomon Pipher also made quite a bit of sense. Solomon rarely had any students, and his form of hysteresis was always under scrutiny for pushing the bounds of the Hysteresis Code.

Wren shook her mind free of the tangent that Esteban had sent her down. There would be plenty of time to wonder about Esteban's story once she was clear of the League's prison. For now, she had to focus on the hysteresis lesson he had taught her all those years ago. The memory was faint and confusing, but it was all she had left to cling to. Esteban had asked her to find a memory of Elias. One that was vivid and powerful. One that she could smell, taste, hear, and feel. She had chosen the memory of when Elias first trusted her enough to teach her how to plant seeds for next year's crops. The sweet smell of sweat mixed with the earthy aroma of dirt. The feel of the tiny cluster of seeds in her palm and the soil under her nails. The calm and direct tone of her brother's voice and the rush of wind that whispered alongside it. It had been so fresh back then, so full of brightness and color. She could scarcely remember it now, trapped under a sea of false faces held fast by the pit of worthlessness nestled in her chest.

After finding a suitable memory, Esteban had reached out his translucent hand, *"What was your magic phrase again? I am more than nothing?"* Esteban had asked her to keep that phrase in the back of her mind. He said that it would link their hysteresis together like a bridge between minds.

"That's it!" Wren shouted, her words echoing off of the empty stone walls. *If my magic phrase could help link my memory to Esteban's mind, then perhaps it can help me link two different parts of mine.*

Wren approached her metal nemesis with a renewed

determination. The decent into her darkest memories helped her access what she had long buried. The house on the lake had been more than the treasured childhood her mind made it out to be. It was messier than that—full of arguments, yelling, and loneliness... of wondering and mystery and longing for what could be. The house on the lake was not her savior, nor was it her condemner.

Wren closed her eyes and retreated to her mind's eye. She brought herself once more to the day of Elias's death. This time she would not jump from horrid memory to horrid memory; she would remember it all. The heat of the sun, the cool summer breeze, the pride in Elias's eyes, and the smugness in his sideways smile. The smell of kicked up dust, the wide terror in her father's eyes, the tang of blood, the shriek of heartbreak, and the stillness of death. The day played out exactly as it had all those years ago. Smooth, unbroken, raw, and under it all, Wren repeated her magic phrase. "I am more than nothing... I am more than nothing..."

As she chanted, she directed each passing memory to either her chaotic right or her tranquil left, allowing the gray that fit in neither to help her create her bridge. She would not take on what was not hers, or cast blame. She would not hide, wince, or bit her lip. She was an observer. No, a conductor of her memories. And in this moment, she felt something shift within her. Like an invisible hand had reached into her and tugged at one of the strings that made up the knot of her soul.

Wren blinked clarity back to her hazy mind as her eyelids fluttered open. The spider-webbed fracture on the door floated into focus, it's edges mottled and dull. Wren checked herself for fresh injuries before returning her attention to the door. Her mind rushed with wonder and amazement as she traced the mottled area with her index finger. A flake of metal peeled free. Wren's breath caught in her chest as she sank her fingernails into the crumbling metal. Flakes of door crusted off as if it were made of sandstone. Sunlight from the hallway poured in through the small hole, filling her room with its familiar glow. A burning desire to free herself from the dank, lonely cell rushed to the forefront of her mind. Without a moment of hesitation given to her blistered hand, Wren tore at the dull areas of the door. As the weakened sections crumbled away, Wren's heart soared. Before long, she cleared a space big enough to slide her slender frame through.

In this moment of freedom, Wren didn't care how it happened or who might be running to punish her act of impurity. She had buried her memories for so long that she almost forgot they existed. She always knew that she resented Elias for dying, for bringing so much pain on their family, for forcing her to live in this place. Those thoughts crumbled along with her cell door. She would live the way he would have wanted her to. For herself.

Leaving the complex emotions of her family history in the cell, Wren stood alone in the empty hallway. The ecstasy of her escape began to wear off, and reality started creeping its way in. It had been years since she last stood outside the doors of the Crystal Pedestal. Even if she made it that far, she had no supplies, an injured hand, and a ripped dress. Before Wren could worry any more about what would come next, she noticed a figure standing in the doorway down the hall. The morning's light poured in from behind, making them impossible to identify. Frozen in place, Wren made no move to run or hide. She would die before she allowed them to put her back in a cage. Never again. With her mind set, Wren squared her body toward the figure in the doorway, waiting for them to make a move.

"Oh, my, god. You look *so* badass right now." Oriella's perky voice echoed through the hallways as her impossibly light feet carried her towards Wren's doorway. "I never thought you would power up this quickly," Oriella said while holding a hand over her mouth in astonishment. "I mean, I left my note hoping to clue you into my plans. Or at least keep you entertained, burning stuff or whatever until I could make a key. I made one for the entry to the purity rooms months ago, but little miss perfect never gets in trouble." Wren's wide glistening eyes fell to a hard stare. Oriella met them with a smile. "So...I erased your name from the festival prep board to make sure you got your well-behaved ass down here."

Wren struggled to keep up with all the information pouring into her mind. Oriella's nonchalant attitude made it hard enough, let alone her added inability to explain a single fragment of what she said.

In obvious exasperation, Wren blurted out all her questions at once. "Hold up... Were you spying on me? Have you always been spying on me? You seriously erased my name?" Wren crossed her arms. Oriella waited patiently, smiling, and rocking from heel to toe. "What do you mean you were going to make a key?"

Oriella cocked her head to the side and puckered her lips. "I wouldn't call it spying so much as...watching out for you." Wren opened her mouth, but Oriella put up a finger. "Someone's got to! We have a gift, Wren, and what do we do with it, *hmm*? Thicken silk? Remove mustard stains? My daddy raised me better than that!" Oriella planted her hands on her hips, daring Wren to refute her.

"So did mine," Wren muttered to herself. Oriella cupped her hand to her ear. Wren cleared her throat. "You skipped the part about the key."

Oriella pressed her lips into a wry grin. "You're not the only one with tricks up their sleeve," she cooed as she pulled a small rectangular piece of metal out of a make-shift holster strapped to her upper thigh. With metal in hand, Oriella channeled her hysteresis. Wren watched as the small piece of metal shifted, transforming itself into a crudely fashioned key. "It doesn't matter how pretty it is. You just need all these little bumpy things to click into the little slotty things. Like I said before, I memorized the bumpy things of the other doors, but not this one. Otherwise, I would have broken you out on the first night."

"Broken me out?" Suddenly, Wren remembered the situation they found themselves in. "That's amazing, Oriella. It truly is, but don't you think we should be getting out of here?"

"Oh, don't worry your badass self about that. It's too early in the morning for anyone to be up in the Pedestal, and I already took out the guards."

Wren closed her eyes and shook her head. "What now? Oh, I get it. A joke, right? Well, ha-ha, very funny. But seriously, we need to get out of here, or we are in big trouble. All of that scraping metal is bound to raise suspicion." Oriella crossed her arms and jutted out her hip. Wren let out a sharp jet of air. "Yeah, right, like a five-foot, unarmed Purity Maiden could take out a couple of fully armored guards."

"Who said I'm unarmed?" Oriella responded, pulling three metal rectangles from her hidden holster. She danced the metal rectangles between her knuckles with lightning-quick fingers. With a playful wink, the metal morphed into three wickedly sharp throwing knives.

Wren looked at her in shock, stuck between impressed, mortified, and relieved. "Where did you learn to do that? Nobody would dream of teaching a Maiden metal manipulation."

"Well, somebody did, and you'll get to meet him if you come with me."

"Yes, great. Let's do that." Wren was anxious to get out of

the ever-expanding catastrophe she found herself in. "I'm assuming that having no guards around bought us some time to figure out our next move."

"Well...kinda," replied Oriella. "Shift change happens in about an hour, and those guys are going to be *super* pissed."

Wren looked at Oriella with wide eyes. "Then let's get the hell out of here before they show up."

"Calm down, geez. There was no way I was getting you out of here without answering a bunch of questions first. So, if you're all done with those, I've hidden some supplies for us by the cellar doors. The League uses them to bring in raw materials for hysteresis. A very helpful discovery, I might add."

"Yes, please. Let's do that," Wren said with an edge of hysteria mounting in her voice.

"Sure thing, Wrenny," Oriella said while attempting to hide a wry smile. "I think my dad is going to like you."

CHAPTER 24

THE BLACKSMITH'S DAUGHTER

"So, how did the information gathering at the Winter Festival go?" Randle asked in his usual gruff tone.

Nico looked at his friend and co-conspirator with tiredness in his eyes. "You mean on the Purity Maidens? Not well, I'm afraid. Despite being as polite as possible, I managed to scare away the only pair I found far enough away from the prying eyes and ears of the League. It seems Purity Maidens are more skittish than I thought."

Much to Nico's surprise, Randle did something that Nico hadn't seen in years. He smiled. Nico looked at his fellow rebel with an edge of nervousness. "I can only think of two possible reasons to see that weathered old face crack an upward turn. Either you have something truly sinister planned, or you've got good news I am not yet privy to. I'm seriously pulling for the latter."

Randle let out a deep, hearty laugh. "Well, you've got me there, friend. It's not good news; it's the best news." The hardened blacksmith's eye's twinkled as he spoke. "My daughter is finally coming home! All those years in that beautified prison, and she has finally decided to come home!"

Randle's voice bordered on perky. Nico shook his head and cracked a smile. "*Decided* to come home? I don't think Purity Maidens have that luxury Randle, but if what you say is true, then this is great news. She can give us the information we've been looking for on the Purity Maidens, and we will no longer need to hide the identity of our informant from the rest of the inner circle. Did she say how she planned on escaping? If she could have left at any time, why choose now? Sorry, I'm talking a lot, aren't I?"

Randle shrugged eyes and shoulders in unison. "My daughter does as she pleases, when she pleases, and in her own unique way. The League guards the Crystal Pedestal against outsiders, making the assumption that no threat could come from within. This proves how ignorant the League is when it comes to those they perceive as weak. My daughter is one of the most dangerous people you will ever meet, but they probably see her as some harmless little girl."

The old man's face soured like he had been sucker-punched in the gut. "If you're going to have any chance of understanding what kind of person my daughter is, you will first have to understand her mother."

Nico softened his gaze, placing his hand on Randle's arm. "Her loss must have been hard on both of you. Perhaps this is the right time to share her story with a trusted friend. Especially if you think it would help me understand your daughter. She will be our primary source of information on the League, and the last thing I want to do is offend her through ignorance or underestimate her like those fools in the League have done."

Randle let out a deep, sad sigh. "You're right. I've been holding her story for far too long. I guess it feels like it's the only part of her I have left. I know it's stupid, but it kind of feels like sharing it would take that part of her from me as well." Randle paused. His entire body relaxed into a downward slump. "Perhaps you are right, Nico. Maybe it's time to let someone else share the burden. When I'm finished, I hope you can still call me friend."

Nico pressed his lips together and eased his hand up to Randle's slumped shoulder. He had never seen this side of him before. Nico would have handled it better if Randle punched him in the face and walked off without a word. Nico waited in silence for Randle to make the next move. After a few ragged exhales of air, the weathered blacksmith began.

"Her story starts far to the south of New Geneva in a town called Marseille. My wife Collette and I were never the happiest of couples, but we grew to love each other deeply. Her parents died at an early age, and nobody else would take up the burden of a woman with no dowry, land, or family prestige to offer." Randle perked up a bit, making eye contact with Nico. "Don't go getting the idea that I married her due to my gallantry...far from it." Randle's eyes once again found the dirt. "As a blacksmith's apprentice and an orphan, I didn't have much going for me either. No loving father would have allowed their daughter to marry a man of my station. So, the marriage worked out well for both of us.

"Colette was always the strong one. Or maybe it was pride. In either case, her combination of fearless confidence and wounded pride made her a prickly, yet passionate partner. She had a look to match her spirit. Skin the color of desert sand, smooth, sultry, and intoxicating. An adorable button nose and mesmerizing chestnut eyes... Smart as a whip, too. When she spoke, I listened. It worked out better that way. More woman than I ever deserved. I see a lot of my daughter in her..." Randle took a small rectangle of metal from his pocket and began to twirl it between his fingers.

"Over time we grew to love each other, sticking it out through the loss of a son and a complete lack of support from our community. Despite our hardships, we were mostly left alone. Except for one man who wanted nothing more than to see Collette ripped from my arms. Thomas Driskel, the local leader of the Serendipity Guild." An eerie hardness came as he spoke the name. "Thomas knew the hefty price a woman such as Collette would bring in at a companion auction. Without a father, she had no man to protect her rights. That is until I came in and offered to marry her. From that moment on, Thomas saw me as a thief robbing him of his property, and you don't steal from a man like Thomas Driskel. Men like him have no real need for money or power. They are already full of both." The rectangle of metal Randle had been fidgeting with came to a rest in his palm. "Men like him are empty. The only way to fill their wretched souls is through the pain and suffering of others."

Randle stared at the small piece of metal in his hand. His fingers curled around it in a fist. "Knowing that he could no longer legally take my Collette, Thomas set a devious plan in motion..." Randle tucked the metal into his pocket and rubbed his palms on his rough pants before taking a few breaths.

"Thomas knew we lost our firstborn to malnutrition. I made next to nothing as an apprentice, and Collette couldn't find anyone willing to hire her. As the first few months of our son's young life ticked by, Collette lost the ability to produce breast milk..." Randle stopped as his voice cracked at the last few words. He cleared his throat before continuing. "He died in her arms at only three months old..." The old man looked up. His eyes were cloudy and far off. "She always blamed herself for it, cursing her body for failing our son. Thomas knew of this pain and used it to exact his revenge when he heard we were with child again."

Randle took a longer pause to regain his composure. Nico waited in awkward silence with no idea what to say to his normally hard as nails friend. Fortunately, warm silence was the best response to moments like these.

"I had recently taken over for my former teacher at the local blacksmith forge. This didn't stop Collette from losing her mind with worry. Her heart could not bear to lose another child, and the anticipation of the birth left her anxious and terrified. One day, after I left for the forge, Thomas paid my wife a visit." Randle's hands wrung the leather cuff of his apron so hard Nico could hear it squeal under the pressure. "Thomas... He offered her a deal. She would give her body to his guild, and in exchange..." The wetness that had been pooling in Randle's eyes leaked steadily down his cheeks. "He promised to ensure the health and safety of our unborn child."

Nico opened his mouth to respond. To offer some comforting word, or a simple apology, but all he could do was wait.

"In her grief-stricken state, Collette agreed, forging my signature on the contract he had written up. I tried taking the bastard to court, pleading that I never signed his damn paper. Nobody would take the word of a blacksmith over a rich and powerful man like Thomas. To make matters worse, Collette failed to read the document she signed thoroughly. While it did seek the possession of Collette and promise to take care of our unborn child, Thomas failed to mention *how* Serendipity planned on taking care of my unborn's wellbeing. In short, Collette agreed to not only sell herself...but our child as well. The guild had offered to take care of our child by 'providing for the child's needs as the child provided for the needs of their clients.'" Nico ground his teeth to suppress his rage.

Randle's tears flowed. His eyes were glossy, and his tone was flat and even. "I had cause enough to act irrationally when that greedy louse took my wife from me, but offering up my unborn child to the same perversions? I'd die before I let that happen." A hardened stare pulled Randle from his numbness, the tone of his story shifting from sorrow, to disbelief.

"I stormed over to the nearest gambling den and demanded to play a game of Scrive." Nico gulped but nodded for Randle to continue. "I knew the risks of the game. I also knew that a Scrive Master might be crazy enough to defy Thomas. The second I saw the Scrive Master's scarred face twist into a grin, I knew he couldn't resist. He pulled the small six-sided Scrive box out of his robe and began scrawling down the five alternatives to my request. The Lamb: my wife and child would be returned to me, and Thomas Driskel would be assassinated. The Snake: my wife and daughter would be submitted to the Scrive Master's forbidden forms of hysteresis experimentation. The Bird: my wife would be taken for experimentation and my daughter returned to me. The Ox: I would be forced to work the salt mines on the Scrive Master's behalf, while my wife and daughter were left to their fate. The Hawk: my wife would be returned after giving birth, but our daughter would remain at the guild. The Goat: the Scrive Master would do nothing for my family, taking me for his twisted experiments instead.

"Blinded by rage, and the urgency of the situation, I foolishly agreed to the Scrive Master's terms. Taking the cursed box in my hands, I spun it around three times and let it fly across the gaming table, a valid toss. As I watched the box spin this way and that, the various animals scrawled on its surface stared into the depths of my soul. I realized what a mistake I had made, but it didn't matter anymore. Helpless to change my circumstances, I watched and waited, hoping beyond hope that the box would land in my favor.

"After what seemed like an eternity, the box came to a stop.

A crudely etched bird sent shivers down my spine. Upon seeing the wretched little thing, my heart stopped as I grieved the stupidity of my rash decision. While my gamble saved my daughter, it damned my love to a fate worse than being a personal companion. I don't know what that abomination did to my Collette, but a couple days after she gave birth, I found a newborn baby girl on my doorstep. I packed a bag for myself and my baby girl, praying that the guild didn't find us before we could make our escape. As I left town with my daughter strapped to my chest and a single bag of belongings to my name, I could hear Collette's screams echoing from the tavern where the Scrive Master resided. Swallowing my grief, my pride, and my anger, I turned away from the plight my wife found herself in and never looked back. From that moment on, I have never considered myself to be anything more than a coward."

Randle's jaw quivered a few times before he let out a raspy breath of air. "My daughter and I wandered the wastelands for years, learning to survive where many have not. She proved to be extremely resilient, surviving on goat milk and continuing to thrive when most would have perished. Throughout our wanderings, I taught my daughter everything I knew of weapon forging and key making. I even trained her on how to use a blade. She quickly developed a unique affinity for throwing knives, and to this day, I have never met anyone as accurate or quick to the draw as her. Her lethal skill and sharp wit gave me some reprieve, but I could never stop worrying that Thomas would show up and take her from me. Years went by, and she got stronger, passing my own abilities in every way imaginable. All things considered, I got off lucky. I could have lost everything in that game of Scrive, but I got her instead. A hysteresis user born with my penchant for metalwork, her mother's unbreakable will, and her own unique brand of fearless joy. When you meet her, don't let her perky demeanor and quirky way of speaking fool you. She will have you stuck full of knives in the blink of an eye if she deems you a threat.

"The two of us went about our lives on the run until one day she shared her plan to become a Purity Maiden. She argued that it would keep her safe from the clutches of Serendipity and allow me to lead some semblance of a life. I knew the League could keep her safer than I ever could, but that didn't make it any easier to let her become the League's pet. It helped to know she didn't see it that way. In her mind, she would use them, not the other way around.

I had taken to calling her Coll, after her mother, but she asked me to give her a name befitting a Purity Maiden. Something *cutesy,* to use her language. For the first time in years, my mind conjured up the image of the crudely etched bird from my Scrive box, and for the first time ever, I didn't curse my decision. I suggested the name Oriole after Collette's favorite bird. My daughter wrinkled her nose, but she also realized that the name meant something to me. She compromised and suggested the name Oriella. The name has stuck ever since.

"Yesterday, I got word from Oriella, that after three years in service to those bastards at the League, she would be leaving the Crystal Pedestal. In true Oriella form, she left me this note in our designated spot."

Randle handed Nico the small piece of paper he had been holding ever so tightly as he told his tale.

Bringing my bestie

-xoxo Oriella

CHAPTER 25

CONSEQUENCES

Harmony sat with her head cradled in her hands and her elbows planted on the table. Gerolt positioned himself across the table with his normally exaggerated posture, rigid and refined. A look of pure satisfaction smeared across his face.

"Tired, my dear?" offered Gerolt in the best mood Harmony had seen him in since setting foot in New Geneva. Harmony said nothing, lifting her face out of her hands long enough to stifle a yawn. "Well, I guess that's one way to answer the question," replied Gerolt, entertained by his own witty banter. Harmony stared at her husband with cloudy expressionless eyes, leaving him to stew in awkward silence. Gerolt shifted in his chair, attempting to straighten his posture even more. He cleared his throat, even drummed his fingers on the table. Still his wife said nothing. "I hear the League will be approving a new set of books for Purity Maidens soon. I'm privy to that sort of information as the Lead Provider, you know."

Harmony crossed her arms, leaned forward, and locked eyes with her cheery husband. "Well, isn't that nice. I'm glad

263

your hard-earned title has granted us such valuable insights." Gerolt struggled to decipher his wife's statement, squinting his eyes as his mouth searched for the right words. Getting no response from her bewildered husband, Harmony continued. "Tell me, does your new position grant you enough influence to let your only daughter spend the rest of her time of cleansing here with us, or in her own quarters at least? I can't imagine how scared she must be down there all alone."

Gerolt took in a breath to respond...

Bang! Bang! Bang!

The loud banging on the door startled them both out of their less than riveting conversation.

Bang! Bang! Bang! "Open the door, in the name of the Grand Council!"

The couple exchanged nervous glances as Gerolt sprang up from his chair to answer the door before the men on the other side broke it down. A sea of highly polished metal greeted him on the other side. Gerolt put up a hand to block the beam of light their pristine armor bounced his way. The scene took the Crivellis back to the night Harmony planted the box of fake evidence in Robin's locker. Harmony sat up straight, shaking the stagnation from her expressionless face. Gerolt stood by the open door, eyes still in a state of myosis and mouth slightly agape. Once the Crivellis got over the initial shock of the guards, they noticed the presence of a third man standing between them, Charles Krenshaw, the warden of the purity rooms and Father of Conglomeration. Gerolt's attention drifted toward the man in charge of this unscheduled early morning visit.

"Warden, what brings you to my door so early?" asked Gerolt with the smallest hint of reproach in his tone.

"We are here to escort your wife to the purity rooms under the authority of the Grand Council."

Gerolt tilted his head upwards, his eyebrows creasing inward. "And since when does the Grand Council trouble itself with matters of purity?" he said proudly, refusing to move out of the guard's way. "I demand to know what business you have with my wife. This has to be some sort of mistake."

Warden Krenshaw motioned for the antsy guards to stand down. "There is no mistake, Mr. Crivelli. The Grand Council itself has deemed Harmony Crivelli to have *permanently* damaged her purity. We have orders to lock her in the purity rooms until it is decided what her ultimate fate will be. As of this moment, she has been stripped of the title of Sr. Maiden, and her marriage to you has been dissolved."

Gerolt turned red with anger. His stiffened posture shook with boundless rage. "You can't just dissolve my marriage!" he screeched. "I'm the Lead Provider. I should have some say in what happens to my own wife."

The Warden kept an eerie amount of coolness about him despite the tense situation mounting in the Crivellis' doorway. "She isn't your wife anymore, Lead Provider." The Warden waited to see how Gerolt would react.

When his words were met by nothing more than heavy breathing he said, "Your new title has no bearing on this matter, but I will allow you to know the depth of the Council's accusations against her out of respect for the years you spent as husband and wife."

Gerolt fumbled to find the right words to form a response. In the end, he simply glared at the Warden with hatred in his eyes. Warden Krenshaw pulled out a small piece of parchment that bared the seal of the Council.

"Harmony Crivelli is being charged with the following losses in purity; breaking curfew, damaging League property, obstruction of truth, illegal use of hysteresis, and aiding in the escape of a Purity Maiden."

Gerolt scoffed at the list of accusations, somewhat relieved that the issue didn't seem to be stemming from Harmony's actions on the night before Solomon Pipher's trial. "There must be some sort of mistake. What would my wife possibly be willing to risk this much loss in purity over? What Maiden would be willing to risk this level of impurity over *anything?*"

"You make my point for me, Lead Provider. As the early morning guard made his rounds down in the purity rooms, he found one of my *reinforced* steel doors...tampered with. Even more troubling, several of our guards from the previous shift lay dead. Small puncture wounds were found on each of their necks. Finding two fully armored guards sitting in pools of their own blood held plenty of shock, but the audacity of the situation did not stop there. The damage done to the door of the purity room boggled the mind. Damage like that had to have been achieved through some illegal form of hysteresis, and considering that no League Father would have the need to go through such channels, that leaves Purity Maidens as our prime suspects. The room violated by these outrageous illegal activities held a Maiden by the name of Wren Crivelli."

Gerolt's face went limp. His mind played out the memory of his wife turning a pair of mountain raiders into lumps of boiled meat.

HARMONY SAT IN ABSOLUTE SILENCE. The hairs on her arms and neck stood on edge. She dared to hope that upon hearing such a ridiculous accusation Gerolt would defend her, or at least put up a fight on her behalf. But Gerolt did neither. Instead, she saw the anger drain from his face as he shuffled to the side of the doorway, allowing the guards to pass by. His body slumped in defeat. His eyes were distant and devoid of their usual clarity and spark.

"How dare you," Harmony seethed. She turned towards her husband with fire in her eyes. "You have the nerve to abuse your power in our home. Force me to act in ways I would never dream of. Control every aspect of my life like an overbearing father. And now, when I need you most, you cast me aside?" Anger boiled deep within her chest as she continued to speak her deepest secrets aloud. "For years, I thought you were putting on a brave face like the rest of our broken family. That you too were grieving the loss of our children and our love. That it felt like a miracle that we ended up at these accursed gates at all!" Harmony's skin began to flush as the release of her innermost secrets began to shift from enraging to exhilarating. "I might be able to forgive you for being a controlling, power hungry bastard if you continued to have a spine in other matters, but no. When it comes to standing up for those you claim to love, or using your precious power for anything but yourself, you cave like a sniveling boy."

Gerolt glanced up for a second, meeting his wife's intense glare. Her eyes were wide and glistening. Focused yet wild. They bore into him with more force than he could bare. "You are a coward, Gerolt. A spineless, egotistical coward. I'm *relieved* to be released from the bondage you dared to call a marriage." Harmony's glare lingered, finding him no matter where he looked. She gathered her breath for one final farewell. "You know... You always did leave me wondering, 'Is there a difference between living and existing?' I guess with you, I finally know the answer."

～

GEROLT'S JAW dropped open as the blood drained from his face. He wondered where this outburst had come from. How long had his wife harbored such feelings towards him? If she could hide all of that from him, maybe the Grand Council's accusations fit the crime. Even if she proved innocent, her recent outburst provided ample precedent for her to be sent to a considerable amount of purity lessons. Despite all of these logical thoughts, nothing but incoherent grunts escaped Gerolt's lips.

"I guess that settles it then," said the Warden. "Move her out boys, and be careful, she could be dangerous. You both saw the state of that door."

The door clicked closed behind them. Gerolt stood alone, his brain struggling to process everything that just took place. He stumbled over to his favorite wing-backed chair and fell into it. Mere moments ago, his body and mind hummed with energy. Life seemed to finally turn his way. He had achieved the dream, escalated his family's standing in the League. *Family...* Gerolt lingered on the word in his mind... *Can you have a family of one?*

Gerolt shook his head and set his jaw. His wife had never spoken to him with such hatred or violence, not even in their early years living in the wilderness outside the LHC. He found himself wondering if he even knew her anymore. The look in her eyes when she spouted the deepest aches of her heart sent chills up his spine. It held a similar aura to that fateful day when they lost their son. He thought things would be better in New Geneva, where her gift could get some much-needed rules and boundaries. If she really tore open a steel door, leaving her to the Council's judgment might be the smartest thing he could do.

He'd lived by their rule for long enough that this felt like the only path left for him. *Is there a difference between living and existing?* The words crept into his mind... *Coward!* proclaimed her tightly drawn lips. *Worthless!* accused her wide, burning eyes. *Heartache...*called the depths of her soul. She had that same look the moment she saw Elias dead in his arms... No, that wasn't right. Gerolt closed his eyes, trying to see her face from that fateful day.

"Her mouth... It quivered." his own voice shook from the comfort of his cushy chair. "And her eyes..." His mind flashed between his wife's final, judging glare and their glossy, terrified gleam from the past. From extinguished hope to ignited defiance. "How did I not see it?" he muttered. "And Wren? How did she end up a part of all of this?" It didn't matter. Gerolt knew all he needed to know. His wife saw him as a coward, and his daughter hated her life enough to risk it all to escape.

You've got a gift my little songbird. What are you going to do with it? Another voice called to him. Gerolt sat up in his chair, rubbing some of the numbness from his eyes. How had he been so blind to their unhappiness? When had he become more of a Provider than a husband and a father? Gerolt let his body go limp in his chair. For the first time since the passing of his son, he allowed himself to weep. His body convulsed as it broke the seal on years of pent up emotion, dropping him to the floor. He thought he brought his family here to keep them safe. To save them. Where had it all gone wrong? How had his path ended up in these walls? Hadn't he longed to live within them more than anything in the world?

With self-loathing in his heart, Gerolt recalled the past month's events. The clues stared him right in the face. No longer absorbed in his quest for power, he could see the pain and suffering of those he loved. He forced himself to relive the moment he offered his daughter to Solomon Pipher like a common personal companion. It had been the same day that monster beat one of his other Purity Maidens to death. The look of pain, confusion, and betrayal in Wren's eyes peered at him alongside Harmony's fiery judgement. *What kind of man would do such a thing?* Gerolt knew the answer. A man seduced by power, crippled by fear, and blinded by buried grief.

The title, Lead Provider, hung on him like a weighted blanket. It felt like wearing another man's skin. The warm, caring, and concerned father transformed into a cold-hearted Provider. Through his shuddering sobs, Gerolt pulled himself to his feet and stumbled into the kitchen. Visions of his loving wife making his required breakfast to perfection drifted through his mind. Each memory brought more harshness to his voice, turning requests into commands, favors into expectations...a marriage into servitude. The early morning sun glinted off one of Harmony's serrated cooking knives. It called to him. A high-pitched hum he couldn't ignore. Gerolt willed his heavy body towards a particularly large knife. Memories of his years of abused power reflected off the glimmering metal surface and into his fluid filled eyes.

His hand shook as he reached for the blade. A metallic ping cut through the eerie silence as he lifted the blade off the counter and pressed the serrated edge firmly against the side of his throat.

Blood began to ooze out of his neck as an inner voice goaded him to finish the job. Gerolt gritted his teeth as he began to pull the knife across his throat. Sharp pain shot through his entire body. *Do it!* the voice roared. *You know it's the only way to end the twisted thing you have become.* Gerolt bit his lip, mustering his strength for one final pull. Underneath the angry, demanding voice, he heard another. Quiet yet firm. Its calm certainty drew him in. As he strained to hear it over the demands of the first, he heard it whisper his wife's final words to him... *Is there a difference between living and existing?*

The knife clattered to the floor. Gerolt dropped to his knees in agony. He had betrayed them all. The voice knew what he vehemently denied all these years. He led his family to this wretched place out of fear, not a desire to protect. As he held his dying son in his arms, powerless to save him, his wife's rage tore their adversary apart. The stench of boiled flesh. The soul-wrenching cry of agony. The weight of the scar she carried with her... The warm blood of his son pooling in his hands...

He strived so hard for a little power of his own, but his true power had always been them. The privilege of knowing a few mundane pieces of information before everyone else, or the ability to oversee other Providers, paled in comparison. Of all people, a Provider should have known that a father's status would never make up for the life of abject servitude bestowed on a Purity Maiden. No matter how high he climbed, Harmony and Wren would never be more than tools for a job. Treasures in the League's locked vault. Deep down, Gerolt knew this all along. He convinced himself that his selfish actions benefited his family. It took losing them both for him to admit his true motivations.

Disgusted with the man he had become, Gerolt made himself a vow. His family didn't need more power or influence, they needed their loving father back. With all the pain and suffering he caused, he owed it to them to bear the pain of his own actions and live long enough to right his wrongs. From this day forward, he would use every ounce of his ill-gotten power to free his wife, find his daughter, and get them as far away from the grip of the League as possible. The law of the land granted husbands power over their wives and fathers power over their daughters, but both were trumped by the League's power over the Purity Maidens. Gerolt would have to find some other way to free Harmony.

Gerolt clamped his eyes shut. His mind fixated on a pair of

fiery, scornful eyes. They burned his feeble defenses like paper, exposing the trueness of his soul for the first time in ages. In this exposed center a different set of eyes stared back. Eyes that lit up at bringing joy into the world, even if it was one meat pie at a time.

Tears rolled down Gerolt's cheeks. His head tilted up to the sky. "Harmony..." he whispered. "It's finally time for me to live."

CHAPTER 26
A ROLL IN THE HAY

The first night in Solomon's new home came with three humbling revelations. Winter's cold soaked into your bones, the smell of moldy hay went away with enough time, and never underestimate the importance of a well-crafted mattress. As insulting as these new realities were, Solomon would have accepted them with gratitude if it meant he would never dream as he did last night. Something about his new environment triggered some lingering memories of his days before the League. Memories he thought he had mastered long ago.

It took him much longer than he would care to admit to get out of his lumpy bed and into the rags the Council called clothes.

"Fitting in," Solomon huffed to himself. "How droll. At least it gives me the proper motivation. Before long, I'll be the king of the LHC." This last thought made Solomon chuckle to himself. "All Hail the King of Piss and Shit!" cried Solomon as he stretched his aching back.

Solomon had been thinking over his first move as Lead

Father of the Inquisition before his thoughts gave way to his wretched dreams. He sat wide awake now and dreams no longer held any power over him. Solomon's first order of business involved getting some underlings. He could be plenty intimidating on his own, but he needed more sets of eyes if he intended to keep tabs on an entire city. Today he would recruit some of the local talent. The first official members of his Inquisition. Solomon initiated the first step of his plan the night before, allowing Loathe to bathe for the first time since he acquired her as a personal companion. He also provided her with a clean dress, trimmed her hair and nails and taught her how to brush her teeth. An almost normal looking fourteen-year-old girl had been hiding under all that filth. Plain, and a bit big boned by the world's standards, but she would get the job done well enough. Solomon knew that none of the life-hardened cut-throats around here would listen to a word a girl like Loathe had to tell them. Well, not without the proper motivation, at least.

As he waited for Loathe to return from her night out on the town, Solomon explored his new kingdom. He shielded his eyes from the bright morning sun and stretched his aching back. A clear sky and brisk wind met his face, awakening his mind and his stomach. He ventured a guess as to where the nearest marketplace would be and dreaded the thought of what people out here might call a proper breakfast. After walking for several minutes, Solomon stumbled upon a small food cart selling semi-edible leftovers from a nearby inn.

"One copper. One copper for your breakfast!" called a young boy working the pushcart.

Solomon jingled the change in his pockets. Even he could afford one copper. "I'll take three," he declared as he strode up to the crude shop.

The young boy's eyes lit up. "Thank you, sir. Have an extra

on me."

Solomon stared down at the scraps of food the boy offered him. "Oh, you shouldn't have."

After bringing the meager morsels back to his house, Solomon laid out his meal options on a small wooden table. He picked out the items he could stomach and sat down to begin hysteresis. He focused his mind's eye, infusing as much flavor as he could into the sad excuses for food lying before him. Solomon popped a piece of sausage into his mouth and immediately spit it out. "Blah! This tastes like a burnt piece of oak dipped in sugar water! I guess some things remain vile even if you bring out their best qualities. It looks like Loathe is going to learn how to cook." As if summoned, Loathe appeared in the doorway. "Ah! How goes the socializing my fellow maggot?"

"I did as you asked sir," Loathe slurred, barely able to keep her balance.

"And what of it? Speak up, girl."

"Sorry, sir. I mean Solomon...Father, sir."

Solomon gave an annoyed huff and motioned her in. Loathe stumbled through the doorway, leaning up against the nearest wall for support. "Everyone laughed and bought me drinks. So many drinks. But I don't think they really talked very much."

"Of course, they didn't talk to you, you tit. Do you really think the kind of man who would make plans of that sort would let them be known? On a more important note, did you run into any decent taverns in your travels? My mood is going to turn most foul if I do not get a proper breakfast soon."

Loathe swayed lazily back and forth, her mind straining to piece together her fragmented night. "Yes, sir. The best smells came from the Charlatan's Inn, but I'm not sure if I actually made it inside."

Loathe's sway turned into a shuffle as her stomach lurched.

She held her hand up to her mouth as vomit sprayed through her fingers.

"Dear lord, girl," Solomon fumed. "Why don't you go lie down for a while? Sleep off all of the menfolk's generosity. You can clean up your mess when you get up. It's not like this pile of sticks could smell much worse with a little stomach bile in the mix."

"Thank you, sir. I am rather tired," Loathe mumbled as she collapsed on her sad excuse for a bed. Within a few seconds, Solomon could hear the raspy, labored sounds of sleep. Her soured breath pushed a thick string of drool out of the corner of her flaccid mouth.

"Ah, my sleeping beauty," remarked Solomon as he ventured out once again in search of some decent food. This time he brought an extra layer of clothing and took an alternative path leading from his country home. Before long, he found what resembled a quaint town square. No more than a dozen buildings clustered together in a shape resembling a circle. For every one building, stood at least four cart vendors like the one Solomon visited before. Solomon turned up his nose at all the vendors crying out their bargain prices. He learned his lesson on that account.

As he pushed the door open to the Charlatan's Inn, Solomon wondered if the man with the red ribbon sat amongst the sparse morning crowd. He would like to know a little bit more about his future informant before their first meeting. He thought it best to stay a couple steps ahead of the League if at all possible. His mind couldn't contain the rage that would be unleashed from another manhandling courtesy of the Grand Council. Those old bastards couldn't be trusted. If they turned on him again, he would at least have a plan for retaliation. Even if here, the League's contact wouldn't be wearing his red ribbon, so Solomon turned his attention to the barkeep.

"Good morning, my good sir. What can you offer to break my fast this morning?"

The weathered barkeeper wiped down the bar with a filthy rag. He looked up to meet Solomon's gaze. "I've got eggs and some pork shoulder. Comes with our signature breakfast ale. It'll cost ya six coppers."

Solomon dug deep into his pockets. He hadn't prepared well for life outside the walls, only bringing the change in his pockets with him. "I've got a small silver. Can you make change?" "Aye," replied the barkeep, slamming four coppers down in front of Solomon and snatching up the silver. "I'll go get yer food."

Solomon pulled up a stool and sat down at the bar, using the opportunity to observe his future place of correspondence with the League. One visible entrance. A cellar used to store wine and ale. A second-floor currently displaying a closed sign. Twelve to fifteen wooden round tables able to seat eight men each, and a couple crude windows. Overall, a decent enough place. The low level of natural light would allow him to make better use of the shadows, even if the tight layout of the tables made speaking in secret next to impossible. Perhaps once he got some money in his pocket, he would inquire about renting the upper floor.

"Here's yer food." The old barkeep slid a steaming hot plate in Solomon's direction. Despite its mediocre quality, Solomon's mouth watered in anticipation. Not wanting to set off any alarms, Solomon decided to forgo the use of hysteresis. It did little to improve things last time anyway.

With his stomach satisfied, Solomon made his way back to his little hut. Loathe had slept long enough, and they had a lot more preparations to make before tonight.

"Wake up, girl. We only have until nightfall to get everything ready." Startled from her deep sleep, Loathe fell off the bed, nearly breaking her neck in the process. Solomon rose his upper lip and shook his jowls. "I allow you to bath, give you clean cloths, even give you important tasks to do, and this is how you act? You can't even stand up, can you? And here I thought you might be more than a piece of bait."

Loathe did her best to make herself presentable, struggling to her feet and holding her aching head. "I tripped is all. I won't be a burden, sir. I promise. I'll do anything you require of me. Just don't leave me here alone."

Solomon smiled treacherously to himself. Picking Loathe had turned out to be one of his few good decisions after the trial. Desperation to have value made her willing to go along with Solomon's plans. The girl would do anything to avoid being left alone to wallow in her own self-hatred. Grace would have run off by now with all that god-damned self-respect he allowed her to retain.

Solomon's inner smile revealed itself on his portly face. "Come along then. Just don't make me regret it."

The odd pair made their way to the barn at the back of the property. Solomon went over his expectations. Loathe hung on his every word. "As I go through tonight's events, remember that my projections will not be directed at you, yet you might experience a bit of their influence. It's the men who come calling who will get the full treatment. My projections are likely to be sufficient enough, but the more convincing you can be on your end, the better. I will be attempting to maintain multiple fields of projection on multiple targets at once, so the effects might not be as potent as they normally could be. You will make as little noise as possible, and no matter what you hear, see, taste, smell, or feel, do *not* leave the barn. Once the men enter, you will need to aid me in selling the final projec-tion. I will be quite drained by then, and the visual projections are by far the most difficult. Now, let's go over all the projections I will be using so you don't lose your mind upon catching a whiff of one…"

By the time Solomon finished setting the stage, only a sliver of sunlight remained. Loathe sat in the barn as instructed. Solomon waited at the first trigger point to ensure everything went off smoothly. Now, he would wait and see how many fish Loathe could reel in. The first group of men began staggering through the woods about an hour after the sun went down. Solomon counted the shadowy figures. Three in total. Perfect for testing the intensity of Solomon's first projection.

"Shhh! Guys, do you hear that?" said one of the men as they stumbled through the woods in eager anticipation of what awaited them at the end of the path.

"What are you talking about man? You're just drunk."

"So. You are too, ya idiot. Shut up and listen."

The other two men quieted down to appease him. Before long, they heard it too. The sound of a woman's voice, barely more than a whisper. *"I'm over here, boys. Come and get it,"* the voice cooed from the woods flanking the right side of the path. *"You won't be sorry. I promise,"* it echoed from the left before giggling in delight and floating further into the woods. *"Catch me if you can,"* it teased one last time before dissipating into the night.

The men hurried after the voice with curiosity and trepidation. "What the hell? Did it sound like the young one we saw at the tavern last night to you?"

"Maybe," said a second. "If so, how is she moving so goddamn fast?"

"Who cares?" demanded a third. "If this little bitch wants to be a tease, it'll be that much more satisfying when we catch her." The third man hurried his pace along the moonlit path. The other two looked at each other in wonder before offering each other a shrug and making their way down the path in pursuit of their overanxious friend.

The two pursuers emerged from the forest path and into the clearing. A thick, mold-colored fog rolled in front of them. The two men scrambled to seal off their sense of smell by any means necessary.

"What is that god-awful smell?" one of the men managed to muffle through his tightly clasped hand. "It smells like... rotten meat...that's been"—the man stopped to halt a gag— "cooked."

Swirls of the putrid mist came and went with the winter wind. "I can't hear a word you're saying. You might as well uncover your mouth, nothing lessens the smell of this shit, anyway. It's almost like it's..." The man was cut short by an eerie sort of weeping. *Mmmmwwwaaahhhh.* The strange sound froze them both in place. As it grew in clarity, a lumbering shadow parted the mist.

"Help... me..." it managed as it stumbled, dropping to a knee by their feet. It was their overanxious friend. "I'm rotting!" He bellowed as he looked up at them with cloudy eyes. "It's *in* me! Hurry! It'll eat my brain soon!"

"Let's get the hell out of here!" cried one of the remaining men as the two stragglers tore off down the forest path in the opposite direction, leaving their hallucinating friend to fend for himself. Solomon gave a slight chuckle as he snaked through the underbrush to check on the state of his prey. The man's fingernails were bursting with chunks of his own flesh as he tried to tear away a non-existing rot. His pathetic mumbling erupted into vocal cord rupturing screams.

"Perhaps I underestimated how suggestive drunk men can be," Solomon cooed. "I'll have to tone down the second projection for the next group, hold a slightly less putrid memory in my mind's eye. I think I'll leave the screaming maniac though."

Solomon muttered to himself as he held his fingers up to frame the scene. "He adds so much to the ambiance."

By the time Solomon finished adjusting the intensity of his second projection, he heard another group of men wandering down the forest path. *Either Loathe holds more sex appeal than I previously believed, or the men in the LHC are truly desperate,* Solomon thought as he crept closer to the barn in preparation for the final reveal. He could hear the second group of men whispering in the trees. A couple moments later, four men wandered into the clearing, slightly less drunk than the first group.

A particularly alert member blocked his friend's path with both hands. "Wait up... Y'all see that guy over there?" He nodded toward the wandering maniac. Strips of skin hung from the man's face. Blood dripped heavy from his fingertips. His eyes fixated on nothing. A few guttural moans and grunts sputtered out of his shredded larynx. Solomon couldn't have hoped for a better set up. He couldn't resist sneaking closer to their conversation.

"Do you think it's a zombie?"

"Don't be an idiot, Brock. He probably got a bad batch from the Spicers is all. Besides, there's an eager virgin waiting for us in that barn. This one seems dedicated to harming himself anyway, and we've got Deebo if that maniac decides to do anything stupid."

"You're right, Sal. It's just...something about this place is giving me the creeps."

"It's probably that awful smell. What is that anyway? Did someone light their dog on fire?"

"Shut up, the both of you, or I'll smash your gutless teeth in."

"Sorry, Deebo," replied the two men in unison.

Solomon slipped around the back to get in better proximity

for the big reveal. These men showed promise. They were brave enough to push past his broken one, and treacherous enough to keep heading towards the barn in spite of him. The corner of Solomon's mouth twitched in approval. He closed his eyes as a memory of one of his many nights with the young Lust filled his mind. A few moments later, the group began pushing open the barn's sliding door. Loathe waited patiently inside, stretched out seductively on a pile of hay, ready to play her part. As soon as the barn door began to open, Solomon worked his hysteresis.

"What in the... Where *are* we?" Brock asked as the group staggered around a lush jungle filled with long hanging vines and towering trees. Even the large man they called Deebo seemed to be out of his comfort zone. His eyes darted from side to side for any signs of a physical threat.

"I don't like this," said Sal. "I think I know what we're dealing with."

"If you know something, spit it out already!" snapped Deebo, eyes still darting from side to side.

Sal pulled up his collar and slunk down into a defensive stance. "A witch. It's the only thing that makes any sense."

"Pshh. Whatever, coward," Deebo sneered, relaxing considerably. "First zombies, now witches? What do you think this is? A costume party?" The other men chucked at the big man's joke. Sal shrugged it off, doubling down.

"Because zombies aren't real, genius. Brock's just an idiot." Brock clenched his jaw and started towards Sal. Deebo put his huge hand on Brock's head, holding him back like one would a young child. "Think about it," Sal urged as he aggressively pointed to his own head. "A *young* girl we've never seen around before lures *us* into the woods. We hear a creepy yet enticing female voice, but it moves faster than humanly possible." Sal's finger's danced from left to right and back again. "Then, when we follow the voice, we find some sort of...crazed man, probably a familiar tainted by the witch, and now we find ourselves wandering through a jungle housed inside an old-ass barn in the middle of winter. It's a god-damned witch, boys. I'd bet my life on it."

"Sal's got a point," agreed Griff, finally making his presence known. "There is no other way to explain it. Let's hope it's a friendly witch."

"That depends..." came a voice wrapped in velvet. "On what kind of men you are," it finished as the voice materialized before their eyes. A beautiful young woman with flowing blond hair and dangerously alluring curves. She dressed in a flowing gown made entirely of transparent silk. Precious jewels of every size and color wrapped around every slinking joint, clinking together as she writhed seductively towards them.

"She sure is pretty," whispered Brock at a less than subtle volume.

"Shut up, you idiot!" Sal retorted. "For once, just be cool, okay?"

Brock scrunched up his eyebrows. "I'm plenty cool... You're the idiot...idiot."

Deebo rolled his eyes. "Shut up, the both of you," he said before turning to the alluring woman. "Please excuse the intelligence level of my friends here. Did you lead us out here? What do you want with us?"

Loathe did her best impression of Lust, moving her hips side to side as she sauntered up to the four men. "Why, yes I did, young man. But don't worry your big old self about it." Solomon pulled his head back from his peephole and rolled his eyes. *Sexier girl! Don't screw this up!* He projected towards her. His harsh tone sent a shiver down her spine.

Her eyes locked onto Deebo's. "I only wish to find servants

worthy of the many *pleasures* I can offer. Tell me, are you worthy of such a gift?" Loathe traced the big man's jawline with her finger. "If you have the stomach to do as I command, I will reward you in every way imaginable," she hummed as she sucked on her wandering finger.

"Every way, imaginable?" croaked Brock.

"*Every* way. Not only will you get the virgin you were promised but wealth and power as well. Enough to buy a harem of virgins if that is your desire."

Solomon shook his head from his hiding spot outside the barn. *Do not offer them anything we did not discuss. Stick. To. The. Plan.*

Loathe nodded at the voice in her head. The witch made her way within arm's length of the four men. Her breath smelled like freshly ground cinnamon. Her voice was as smooth and sultry as buttercream. Her silken dress hugged every curve with the slightest of grips. Loathe let the projections take over, letting herself fade into the background. The men could feel the warmth of her grow in their chest, hear her subtle moans whisper in their ears, taste her salty skin on their tongue, and feel the press of her breasts onto theirs. Unable to withstand the barrage of sensual stimulations, the four men moaned in awkward unison.

Outside the barn, Solomon struggled to his feet. "Even I am having a hard time watching this." He chuckled to himself as his plan fell into place. "Four men of exceedingly low moral character will soon believe their souls are bound to *Loathe*." A laugh sputtered from his lips. "Not quite the kickoff I'd first imagined, but it will serve to keep me in the shadows." He looked up at the stars, serenaded by moans of pleasure and dread. "Tonight, the Inquisition is born!"

CHAPTER 27

A WALK THROUGH THE WOODS

Oriella gave Wren a quick wink before heading over to a knapsack stashed behind a few stacked boxes. The knapsack contained wool coats, some plain looking but warm wool dresses, and a satchel full of food. The scratchy wool felt foreign on Wren's skin. A sentiment she got over rather quickly as the harsh winter wind flew in the large cellar doors.

"Come on!" Oriella grabbed Wren's wrist and pulled her into the freshly fallen snow outside.

Cold shot up Wren's legs, stealing her breath. She kept her eyes fixed on Oriella's firm grip, stumbling forward despite the numbness growing in her toes. Wren watched as Oriella led her through a side gate she didn't know existed, careful to evade the pair of guard's stationed around the corner at the Crystal Pedestal's entrance. Wren shut her eyes and followed Oriella's pull, unable to think about anything but the growing sense of numbness in her feet. A dozen foot falls later she could no longer contain her anxiety and forced her eyes back open. Oriella's head was on a swivel, eyes dialed into every unnatural movement. Wren pulled her focus from her feet, trying to mimic Oriella's sense of controlled alertness. Soon, all they could hear was the sound of their own breath and the soft crunch of snow.

"Ori...ella..." Wren managed.

"Hmmm?" Oriella turned towards Wren, finally dropping her wrist. "Oh! Are you tired, Wrenny?"

Wren dropped her freed hand to join her other on her knees. She took a few steadying breaths before straightening her back and pointing to a nearby clearing. "There. A house, or something. Think we could stop...see if they have a fire?"

Oriella clicked her tongue. "I wish. People who live this close to the wall tend to be spies." Oriella grabbed Wren's right hand, flipping her palm over. "This right here. A Maiden with a burn like this? Suspicious indeed!" Oriella winked as she reached into her knapsack and pulled out a lump of cheese. "Digesting some food will warm you up," she chirped with a cheery smile spread across her reddened cheeks. Wren stared at the firm white cheese. A bit of discoloration ate at one edge. She bit into it with fervor.

"Come on, we've still got a long way to go!" Oriella moved swiftly and silently in her scratchy, traveling clothes. Almost as if she hadn't spent the last three years of her life in doll outfits like the rest of the Maidens. On top of that, she had an uncanny way of seeming to know exactly where to step to keep her footfalls silent. Her movements were almost hypnotic, their purposefulness the only thing keeping Wren's rising anxiety at bay.

Wren spent the next few hours trying to learn Oriella's dance. A sideways glance across a flanking tree line. A quarter spin to place a foot just so on a nearby root. A shuffled step to keep her shadow hidden in the trees. A closed fist woke her from her observations. Oriella peered from behind a large tree, holding up her arm behind her. Wren assumed this meant she should stop as well, so she waited quietly for Oriella's next move. In the stillness, she could make out the sound of crunching snow. Oriella remained transfixed, her hand raised in a fist until the sound faded entirely.

Oriella turned towards Wren. "It's probably best to find somewhere off the path and wait for it to get dark before we move on. You know, just to be safe."

"Why, what's up there? Where are we going?" Wren asked, peering off into the endless line of snow-covered trees.

"Why, the secret rebel base, of course. I've been feeding them information about the League for years now, but my dad is the only one who has seen my face, and we don't want to risk being mistaken for intruders. That's why we need to wait until dark. Then we can sneak into my dad's tent without setting off alarms."

Wren blinked a few times, digesting all she had heard. "Rebels?" Wren raised a brow. "You mean...people rebelling against the League? You're telling me there are enough of them to have some sort of hidden base?"

Oriella put her finger on her chin. "Well...I might have made it sound cooler than it really is. It's mostly a bunch of dirty tents set up in a big cluster type thing..." Oriella's tone dropped an octave. "But it really is a secret," she whispered as her finger pressed up against her puckered lips.

Wren nodded, pressing her finger to her lips as well. "So, where should we hide until nightfall?" she whispered, looking around at the identical layout of trees and snow.

"Oh, we don't actually need to be whispering now. I've only seen rabbits and mice since we left. I only whispered to add to the *allure* of the secret base."

Wren cleared her throat. "Oh, yeah. Gotcha." *I'm following a lock-picking, knife-throwing, Purity Maiden into a cluster of dirty tents...* "Very alluring."

Oriella ignored Wren's sarcastic tone. "There's a nice cluster of trees a little further into the woods. They will block the cold wind as well as the view of any baddie who might walk by."

Wren took a deep breath before giving Oriella a quick nod. "Well, lead on then."

Wʀᴇɴ's sʜᴏw of confidence glimmered in Oriella's eyes. Despite Wren's typical level of annoyance with her, Oriella sensed something more from her than the other Maidens. Like her, Wren came to the Crystal Pedestal from the outside. She knew what living outside the League's power felt like and that gave her something extra to fight for. She wanted to dig deeper, find out her story, but she knew from experience that those kinds of stories only came without asking.

With this question still lingering in her mind, Oriella pulled off her satchel and plopped down on a nearby stump. "Well, here we are, might as well get comfy. We have quite a bit of time to kill before it gets dark enough for our stealth mission."

Wren found a fallen log next to Oriella, wiped the snow from its surface, and took a seat. A subtle awkwardness sat between them. At the Crystal Pedestal, Maiden's conversations included acknowledging requests, respectful compliments, and the occasional greeting. The few interactions Maidens had with each other could hardly be called conversations. Strangely enough, that kind of made them best friends. *Best purity companion ever,* Oriella thought to herself, a small smile twitching at the corner of her mouth. To her surprise, Wren smiled back.

"I must say, Wrenny. I'm awfully surprised at what a good mood you are in. I thought you would be grumpy for sure."

Wren scrunched up her face like she always did. "What makes you think I would be grumpy?"

"I'm a spy...remember?" Oriella pointed to her eyes and then at Wren. "I've been watching you for a while now, and the only time you smile is when you need to keep up appearances. So, cough it up. I want to know how to cheer you up the next time things get gloomy." Oriella's face took an oddly serious turn. "Never underestimate the power of positive thinking."

Wren relaxed her eyebrows. "I guess there wasn't much to smile about in that place."

"Oh, don't be such a sourpuss. Things could have been much worse."

Wren sat up a bit straighter. "Oh, really? How, exactly? Apart from being locked in the purity rooms with Solomon Pipher."

Oriella raised her eyebrows and crossed her arms. "Your mom and dad are still alive. You're healthy, strong, and beautiful, and you're a badass hysteresis user. Oh, and you have me as your purity companion." She smiled warmly.

Wren gave Oriella a sideways glance. "You're oversimplifying it. You only had to endure that place for three years. My father might be alive, but he is more Provider than Father. I only got to see my Mother three or four times a year at most. I can barely even remember what it's like to make my own choices, to have a life that I can call my own. The Crystal Pedestal took all of that away from me. It made me question being alive." Wren paused and looked at Oriella before continuing. She had dropped her smile but not her attention. Wren lingered on her gaze as if judging its authenticity. "While I appreciate your willingness to count my blessings, flowers still smell like shit when they're covered in it."

Oriella stared at Wren in silence for a couple seconds before sputtering in laughter. "Did you just say something about *shitty flowers*? So, you *do* have a sense of humor."

Wren blushed. She hadn't made someone laugh in quite a long time. "Oh, stop it. I had to do a lot of gardening as a child. It's all I could think of!"

Oriella stopped laughing and put a hand on Wren's shoulder. "Pain is pain. No matter which face it wears..." Her gaze drifted to the horizon. "I would never mock yours... It's just..." Her smile flattened into a tight line. Her mischievous gleam replaced by a distant stare.

Wren scooted closer, placing her hand on Oriella's. Her gentleness startled Oriella out of her traumatic memories, snapping her attention back to Wren. "Ori... Can I call you Ori?"

Oriella clasped her hands together. "Cuuute! A nickname!" Oriella squealed in delight.

"I'll take that as a yes," replied Wren, slightly regretting the question. "Ori, you mentioned your father earlier. Is he one of the rebels or something?"

"Yep!" she chirped. The mischievous gleam returning to her eye. "He is one of the inner circle, whatever that is. Like I said, I've never met any of them but my dad. We would meet up from time to time, and I would pass him any important information I came across concerning the League. A few days ago, they started asking questions about Purity Maidens. I figured this was as good a time as any."

Wren gave Oriella a confused look. "If you could meet up with your father regularly, why did you keep returning to the Crystal Pedestal? And when you did return, why did your dad want to hide you from the rest of the rebels?"

"I know what you're thinking, that my dad used me, controlling my actions and whatnot, but he's not like that. I came up with the idea to become a Purity Maiden, not him. He voted against it, calling it reckless and a waste of talent. I chose to go back to the Crystal Pedestal. He's tried to convince me to stay several times..." Oriella paused in thought. "Although, he did want to keep my identity a secret from the rest of his group. I'm not sure why. I've never really thought about it until just now." Wren scrunched up her eyebrows and clenched her jaw in silence.

"What crawled up your butt?" asked Oriella, breaking Wren's internal dialogue. Wren's eyes went wide "My butt is fine, thank you. I'm just wondering how safe the rebels are if your father didn't even want you to meet any of them, that's all."

Oriella cocked her head to one side. "My daddy has always been a cautious man. Plus there are several former guild members in the group. My family has a dark history with the guilds, so keeping my identity a secret probably had something to do with that."

Wren paused, giving ample time for Oriella to share more. Oriella only starred back. "I see," Wren offered to break the awkward pause.

Oriella smiled. "Besides, even if the rebel base is a teensy bit dangerous, tell me someplace that isn't. At least I have a friend amongst the rebels, and I'll vouch for you, don't you worry."

"Thanks, Oriella. I honestly don't know what I would have done without you."

"Ori, remember?"

Wren smiled. "Yes, of course. Thanks, Ori."

Oriella jumped to her feet. "Well, I don't know about you,

but I'm starving. I'll wrestle up some food from the satchel while you start a fire. Sound good?"

"Sounds great, Ori, but I'm not sure I know how to start a fire."

Oriella gave Wren a disapproving glare, "You blew open a metal door. I think you can handle making a little campfire," she said with a snort. "You don't have to hide your gifts from me, Wrenny. Unlike the baddies back there, I want to see what you're capable of. Besides, you don't want to eat cold fish, do you?"

Wren allowed a sly smile to cross her face. "You know something, you're right. I'm on it."

Wren stood to gather some firewood as Oriella rummaged through the knapsack for a bit of dried fish. Wren's calculating personality and warm yet guarded interior reminded Oriella a lot of her father. They each gave her the same "come on quit messing around" look too. She couldn't show it around Wren but taking her to the rebels scared her. What if the guilds had spies and were waiting for her to let her guard down? She hated to think about the possibility of getting Wren caught up in their schemes. Oriella shook the sobering thought from her mind.

"Where's that fire, Wrenny? I'm starving over here."

"Sorry, Ori. Just lost in thought is all. I'm on it."

"You're *always* lost in thought, Wrenny, but don't worry, it's one of your more endearing qualities."

Wren scrunched up her face. "Thanks, I think..."

A few moments later, Wren had their campfire roaring. "See, I knew you were the right gal for the job," Oriella said with a smile. "Now, let's eat."

After filling her belly, Oriella glanced up at the sky. "We still have a couple of hours before it gets dark. What are a couple of Purity Maidens to do for fun?" Wren shrugged her shoulders. Oriella's mischievous gleam darkened. "Practice their restricted forms of hysteresis, of course." She rubbed her hands together.

"Before our little campfire, I've never actually seen you use yours before. I just smelled the smoke. To tell you the truth, I'm not really sure I understand it. Why would you even learn to heat things up like that? I mean, my dad taught me everything there is to know about blacksmithing, and I haven't the slightest clue how to start a campfire without a match."

Wren furrowed her brow. "I won't pretend to know anything about blacksmithing, but don't you need some sort of heat?"

"Of course you do, silly. But I'm no blacksmith. I'm a hysteresis user. I don't actually *need* a kiln. My dad taught me about all the properties of metal so that I could manipulate specific aspects of it as I saw fit. I focus on the qualities I wish to change one at a time. Otherwise, you could end up with a piece of steel exploding in your hand."

"Ah, that makes sense. I suppose."

"My dad is smart and only taught me what I needed to reshape the metal. When I do my hysteresis, the metal stays cool to the touch." A playful smirk spread across Ori's face. "Wanna see?" Before Wren could answer, Oriella pulled out one of her small metal rectangles. "Do you trust me, Wrenny?"

"It seems pretty silly to stop trusting you now." Wren offered her good palm.

Oriella placed the rectangle in Wren's hand and focused her mind's eye. In a split second, the metal morphed into a small knife.

"Wow, you're right. I didn't feel a thing. In fact, it's quite cold."

Grinning with satisfaction, Oriella turned the knife back into a harmless piece of metal. "I chose this metal for its quickness. It's high in both formability, and cuttability... That basically means it takes fewer steps to shape and can still slice stuff. I've got a lot of other tricks up my sleeve once I get my hands on a full kit of different metals. I can't keep them all in the Pedestal, though, too risky. My dad will have them all ready when I arrive, though."

Wren thought for a second about how to respond. "To be honest, I'm not quite sure how mine works." Oriella gave Wren a disapproving look. "No, really," Wren shuffled on her log, holding her hands up to the fire. She warmed them for a bit in silence. Oriella watched, and waited. "It has something to do with channeling my hysteresis while allowing my mind to focus on all the chaos, frustration, and despair in my heart. I know that sounds cheesy, but it's the best explanation I can come up with."

"Come on, Wren. That's not fair. I told you how I shape my metal. Don't you trust me yet?"

"I do trust you, Ori. I really do..." Wren looked over at Ori's gleaming eyes. Wren let out a calming sigh. "I'll do my best to explain." Oriella clapped her hands and leaned forward. "As you know, to use normal hysteresis we must clear our minds and focus on a specific aspect. If our mind's eye is broken by an outside distraction, then the hysteresis sputters out. We both know all that and have experienced it first-hand. Well...I found a way past it."

"Wait... Is that why you scrunch of your face so much?" Oriella asked.

"What? No!" Wren shook her head and turned towards Oriella."It's a way to keep my mind's eye focused and sharp while allowing my mind to burn with emotion."

Oriella tapped her chin. "So, you're telling me you found a way to use hysteresis with a distracted mind?" Wren gave an uncertain nod. "And here I am, practicing my heart out to get my focus time down. I'm pretty fast if you didn't notice, but being able to stay focused in stressful situations would be extremely helpful." Oriella's eyes lit up. "Do you think you could teach me?" Oriella gave her best puppy dog pout.

Wren sighed. "I'm not a client, Ori. Puppy dog eyes won't work on me."

"Well damn," remarked Oriella snapping her fingers.

"But that's not why I won't teach you. I won't teach you because I have no idea how to describe the state of mind I put myself in. It's almost like I direct my mind into two places at once. One side is hyper-focused, channeling hysteresis, while the other is fueling that hysteresis with various emotions and memories." Wren entangled her fingers in front of Oriella. "Mind and heart as one, you know?" Oriella gave her a sideways smirk. "But it's not that simple either... There's a piece that's hard to nail down, another ingredient in the formula that I'm not sure I can reproduce."

Oriella nodded slowly. "So...that's how you blew open a reinforced steel door? You made it hot enough with your... supercharged emotion bomb?"

Wren gave Oriella's attempt to understand a hearty laugh. "Well, not exactly. I tried it that way, but I only succeeded in burning my hand." Wren turned over her blistered palm.

Oriella grimaced. Yeah... I was wondering how you got those. You're even more confusing than I thought."

"Sorry," replied Wren, wringing her hands.

"Stop that! Why the heck are you apologizing? Being confusing is another one of your endearing qualities."

Wren cracked a smile. "Thanks. I think?"

Anxious to hear the rest of the story, Oriella pushed Wren to continue. "So, if your supercharged emotion bomb didn't work, how did you get out?"

Wren shook her head, eyes distant. "This will sound..." She

blinked and cleared her throat. "I'll just try anyway. Heating things up isn't the only hysteresis alteration I've discovered." Oriella's eyes lit up with excitement. "I also discovered that if I split my mind like before, but center myself on feelings of peace, hope, and my desire to recapture the moments as I last felt them, then a completely different effect occurs. For lack of a better description, it seems to cool things off, or perhaps slow them down?"

"So, you froze the door to pieces? That doesn't make any sense."

Wren shook her head. "When I tried that, it didn't work either, but something prompted me to try using both forms at once."

"So you broke the door with what, mood swing hysteresis?"

Wren stifled another burst of laughter. "It wasn't so much a mood swing as holding both sets of emotions at once."

"And you did that while also splitting a part of your brain off to preserve your mind's eye? What do you have, three brains?"

"Perhaps splitting is the wrong word. It felt more like being whole for the first time, allowing all parts of me to come together at once. When I held this state of mind for long enough, the two forms of hysteresis collided, resulting in the destruction of the door."

"So, could you blow something up right now? Like could you blow up that tree, just for the hell of it?"

"Probably not. It took everything I had to use all three parts at once, and I'm not even sure what exactly triggered things. For all I know, the explosion came from a massive form of blowback. It's quite likely that I altered two aspects of the door at the same time. In that case, I was lucky to walk away unscathed. I think I have a lot to learn before my new forms of hysteresis can be used again."

"That's probably a good idea. Blowback is scary stuff. I just have one more question. Why hot and cold?"

"That, my dear Ori, is the question worth a million silvers."

Oriella beamed, positive energy surging through her. Other than her father, she'd never had a true friend. She guarded this new relationship closely. "You really are the best purity companion ever."

Wren scrunched up her eyebrows. "Don't you think we should ditch the whole purity companion thing?"

Oriella squirmed on her log. "Oh, yeah, sure. Keep it professional. Got it," she said, giving an exaggerated salute.

Wren sighed and shook her head. "I mean, we should ditch the label the League gave us. We aren't purity companions anymore, we're..."

"Battle buddies! War women! Mind Melders! Hysteresis Heroes? No? Too much alliteration?"

Wren fought off a smile. "How about, friends?"

"Friends. Sounds boring. How about League's Bane!" Wren sucked air through her teeth. "Okay, fine. Friends then, but best friends—and you keep calling me Ori."

"Deal."

CHAPTER 28

COMPLETING THE CIRCLE

It's difficult to be discreet when you're the leader of a rebellion, even more so amongst your own people. Today marked a huge milestone in Aequalitatem's fight against the League. If Nico could get his more influential members on board, then the rest of the group would fall in line behind them. Nico had already talked to Randle the day before. Now he needed to find Shanks, Colt, and Dawn.

The sun inched its way over Atlas Hill. Despite the hour, Nico knew where Shanks would be—the Charlatan's Inn. This early in the day, Nico felt fairly confident he could rouse the hung-over Shanks from his ale induced coma without drawing much attention. To his surprise, two rough-looking men sat sprawled out in the corner only a couple tables down for where Shanks had collapsed from his nightly bender. From the looks of things, they were worse off than Shanks. He hoped they were as hungover as they looked. With no other options, Nico crept over and gave Shanks a rough shove in the shoulder.

Shanks jumped upright in his chair, fighting to keep all legs on the ground after the surprise greeting. "Get yer hands off me ya filthy dogs! Oh, it's you, Nico." Shanks quickly went from irate to complacent upon seeing Nico's mischievous grin. Shanks stretched open his mouth and arched his back. The stench of a dozen mugs of marinating ale bellowed out. "What did ya have to go and wake me for? It's too god-damned early for any of your rebel mumbo-jumbo. Come back later. I'm getting my beauty rest."

Nico waved a hand in front of his nose. "You'd be dead before you slept long enough, you old badger," replied Nico. A sarcastic smile stretched across his lips.

"Ha! I'm prettier than you with that trench carved into your face."

"What? This little thing?" Nico motioned towards the six-inch gash drawn from the bridge of his nose to the bottom of his left jawline. "This is what gets me all the ladies."

"I don't know if you can call the things I've seen dangling from your arms *ladies*, boss, but I'll take your word for it." Jesting always ensured Shanks awoke from hibernation in a good mood. Unless he didn't like you, then you might end up losing your head for your trouble. "So tell me, what does the lady slayer of the LHC want with an old drunk like myself on this fine morning?"

"Let's just say we should probably get on the same page about a few things before the next full circle meeting. I need an influential member from the old guilds, such as you, to help me win a few votes."

"So that's how it is, eh? Well, you make a good enough argument, and I'll side with ya on just about anything. It's nothing too crazy this time, is it?"

"Depends on who you're asking. I'm guessing you'll find it crazier than most."

Shanks gave an exasperated moan. He didn't like the sound of that, especially with his head still aching from last night's revelry. "Why in the hell are you calling a circle meeting at the devil's hour anyway? Let me guess, old man Clive is going to propose some half-brained assault on the walls again, and you need me in a particularly cantankerous mood to shut the old goat up quick."

"Although I'm sure Clive will bring up the notion as he does at most of our meetings, this issue involves nothing of that level of insanity, I assure you. This is more of a private gathering, no more than a handful of us from the inner circle will be there. We will meet at the spot where it all began."

"Well, I'm glad I made the cut. I'd jump for joy if I could spare the energy," Shanks said sarcastically. "I'll join you after I've rid myself of the ten gallons of piss I've managed to house in my gut overnight."

"That's what you get for drinking enough ale to drown an ox," Nico called after him.

Shanks responded with a deep scratching of his ass and a fully extended middle finger. Awake and on his feet, Nico felt confident Shanks would make his way to the designated meeting spot in due time, so he left the tavern in search of the next name on his list.

After Nico moved on, one of the two passed out men at the nearby table prodded his friend in an attempt to raise him from his drunken stupor.

"Did ya hear that, Chuck? Nico's calling a special meeting. You reckon it's about dealing with that witch we ran into last night?" Chuck dragged his head to the side of the table and emptied the contents of his stomach all over the tavern floor. "Ah, Come on, Chuck! What did ya have to go and do that for? If the barkeep sees that, he'll have us out of here faster than you'd have been out of that virgin last night."

Half dazed and fighting back a second lurch in his stomach, Chuck snapped to attention at the mention of the word *witch*. "So...its real then?" Chuck wiped his mouth on his sleeve as he struggled to regain consciousness.

"I'm afraid so. I, for one, would rather stay here and get drunk enough to not be so damned sure about it. It's only a matter of time before we run into Butch out there, and I sure as hell don't want to see what's left of him after last night. If there's anything left at all."

"You're right, Tommy. Maybe it's best if we moved over to the Disgruntled Cow. The ale's cheaper over there, anyway."

"That's because it tastes like cow piss, ya drunk bastard, but we don't have much choice left, do we?"

Chuck and Tommy stumbled out of the Charlatan's Inn as Nico made it to his next location, Dawn's tent. Not wanting to holler out a greeting and risk getting noticed, Nico decided to forgo the warning and slid his way through the tent flaps.

"Come for a peak, have ya Nico?" Dawn asked unfazed by the sudden intrusion. Not to mention the fact that she wasn't wearing a stitch of clothing.

"Whoa! Um, sorry about that, Dawn. I didn't think you would be awake yet," Nico cried out in surprise. He hadn't expected to see his compatriot awake, let alone in the nude. Nico attempted to gather himself, searching for the right mixture of words for the awkward situation he now found himself in. "I believe our, um, conversation would be more productive if you were to put some, um, clothes on, Dawn..." When Dawn made no move to respond or get dressed, Nico drifted his gaze upwards. "Got a few holes up there. Probably makes that winter chill even, um... chillier. Especially in the nude and all." Nico chuckled nervously.

Dawn planted her hands on her hips. "Well, not that it's any of your business, but the frigid air makes my skin feel alive.

Like I'm still a sexual being despite not getting my tender bits worked for nearly a month." Nico coughed, lurching forward and getting an eyeful. He swore he saw Dawn smirk as her face whizzed by. "It's not like plenty haven't offered. It just don't feel right when I'm approached like a wall that needs conquering, ya know? What is it with you men and your fear of powerful women anyway?"

Nico paused for a moment, hoping Dawn would stop talking long enough to put her clothes on, but she kept standing there naked, not a care in the world. She wasn't an unattractive woman, that wasn't the problem. Nico saw her as a brother in arms, and one of his most trusted friends.

"Well, did you have something to say, or did you really come in here to get yourself an eyeful?" Dawn asked after an uncomfortably long silence.

Feeling his skin start to flush, Nico rushed to find his voice. "Ah, yes, I did have, um, something to, a, discuss with you." The words sputtered out of his mouth like an adolescent boy on his first date. His flustered state made it all the more difficult to keep the appropriate amount of eye contact. If he looked away too much, he might come off as weak, possibly even discourteous, but try as he might, Nico couldn't keep his eyes locked onto hers, not with all of that skin calling to him from the edges of his vision. "I'm calling a special meeting of some select members of the inner circle. I'm attempting to be discreet, hence sneaking into your tent... We will meet by the old oak tree on top of Atlas Hill in one hour. I trust you will have found your clothes by then?"

Dawn looked at Nico with a twinge of mischief in her eyes. "Relax, Nico. Nobody wants to deal with the chaos that would ensue if I waltzed down the street with my tits flopping in the breeze." Dawn paused for a few more moments, biting her lip and letting her hips wander. "You can expect to see me fully dressed and sexually repressed within the hour, sir."

More than ready to exit, Nico gave Dawn a slight bow and headed for the tent flaps. Dawn couldn't resist one last chance to push her chances. "Feel free to stop by again sometime. I rather enjoy surprises."

Much to her delight, the unsuspecting comment sent a rush of red to Nico's already flustered face. Nico cleared his throat, managing a curt nod to Dawn on his way out. Determined to put all distractions behind him, Nico straightened his loose-fitting duster and started making the long walk to the food stand on the north end of town.

"One copper! One copper for your breakfast!" Nico could hear Colt shouting his discounted prices to the early morning beggars and drunks who littered the dusty streets of the LHC. "I'll take the lot of them," exclaimed Nico as he wrapped his arm around the boy's neck, tussling his hair.

After wresting himself free from Nico's grasp, Colt stood red-faced and smiling. "What are you doing way up here, Nico? I can't imagine you'd venture out of the square this early in the morning to give me a hard time.

"Colt, you are as perceptive as ever. I've come to ask you to attend a small circle meeting. That is if you're able to leave your booming business for a bit."

Colt had half of his cart packed before Nico finished his sentence. "Of course, Nico. I'm glad you came to get me. You know how the others can get without you and me there to straighten them out."

"Indeed I do, Colt. That's why we should leave now. It's quite the walk to Atlas Hill from here, and trust me, we don't want this meeting to be decided without the two of us present."

Randle, Shanks, and Dawn stood alert and ready under the

ancient oak tree that marked their designated meeting spot. Nico and Colt walked up the hill to join them.

"I'm glad you all could make it. You should take your presence here as a compliment as I've only invited the most trusted and influential members of my inner circle to this meeting. I have a lot of information to share with you this morning, and not all of you are going to like it. I only ask that you hear me out. Can we all agree on that?" Each member of the reduced circle nodded silently in turn. "Good, then I won't waste any more of your time. You are all aware that we have been in contact with an individual within the walls of New Geneva, and that this individual is responsible for all the information we have received concerning the Crystal Pedestal and the League. What you don't yet know is who that individual is, but that will change very soon, most likely tonight."

Nico glanced around at his closest companions, trying to gauge their reactions. Randle already knew of the situation, so Nico focused on the other three. Colt stood up straight. His eyes wide, bright, and brimming with hope. Dawn stood with arms folded, leaning slightly to one side and wearing a crooked smirk on her face.

Shanks leaned his back against the huge oak. Face contorted in thought. As usual, he broke the silence. "So what? Is this supposed to be good news? How will this informant continue to be of use to us *outside* the walls? Wasn't the whole point having someone on the *inside*? I say send 'em back."

Dawn looked over at the leather-faced drunk. "I tend to agree with the old scab. Unless this informant has something more valuable than an insider's ear, they are of no use to us out here."

"Now, wait for a second here, guys," Colt blurted. "You two are always so quick to judge, but we don't even know the whole story yet. Let's hear the rest of what Nico has to say before we jump to conclusions about what we should or shouldn't do. There has to be more to the situation to warrant such secrecy."

Nico smiled to himself. He knew bringing Colt would pay off. He might be the youngest member of the inner circle, but he had two things the rest of the group lost long ago. Optimism and compassion. Despite how much Colt's voice helped to balance the scales, Nico worried his next piece of information could send some of his companions over the edge of reason.

"I understand where all of you are coming from, and let me say that I truly believe the informant can be as much use to us outside the walls as she proved to be inside."

"*She?*" Shanks raised one of his eyebrows in concern. "There are plenty called *she* on the inside, but most of them couldn't even give you the names of the Grand Council members, let alone insider information. Please tell me this informant isn't a Maiden. I'll have no part in scheming with one of the League's whores." Shanks spat on the ground to add emphasis to his already bluntly stated point.

Dawn gave Shanks a sour look as his wad of spit landed near her boot. "Oh, unpucker your asshole, would ya Shanks? Maidens won't even talk back to their Providers, let alone break out of the city to join a rebellion. Their precious *purity* won't allow it. Besides, Nico said the informant would be of use to us out here. What's a Maiden going to do? Hem our leathers? Cook us a decent meal? Get the blood out of our clothes?"

"First of all, Madam, my asshole is none of your concern," Shanks said before turning his attention back to Nico. "We don't even know if it is a Maiden. Let's hear all the information before we carry on any further, agreed?" The group nodded in agreement, then sat and waited for Nico to continue.

Nico took a deep breath. No use sugar-coating it at this point. He might as well say it. "The informant who has been aiding us these past three years is indeed a Maiden."

"I fucking *knew* it! My god, son..."

"Not only that!" Nico shouted over his sense of good reason. "But she does not come alone." Shanks waited in agitated stillness, huffing like a pent up bull. "Our informant broke out a second Maiden..."

Shanks doubled over in laughter, slapping his knee as he howled. "Good one, Nico. I guess we had that one coming. Can you imagine it? You had me with the first Maiden, but breaking out a *second?* What's next? A Maiden army?"

Nico didn't laugh or offer a cold rebuke. He fixed his steely gray eyes on the snickering old man, waiting for him to let the seriousness of things set in.

Shank's smile fell into a twisted frown. "You're serious? You would bring not one, but two of those domesticated half-wits into Aequalitatem?"

Nico ground his teeth but kept his resolve. Shanks had no clue what Randle's daughter had gone through, or any of the other Maidens for that matter. The thought of one of his most trusted friends betraying his command at such a crucial time ate at Nico's patience. Another voice spoke up in his stead.

"You dare to call yourself members of Aequalitatem, but you forget the principals that built it." Colt's voice cracked as he found his resolve. "When Nico put a spear into the hands of the decrepit and the lame, posting them as guards in some of our most vulnerable locations, you gave it no voice. But even that pales in comparison to what he did for the abominations that stand on this very hill and call themselves part of Aequalitatem's precious inner circle."

The teen turned toward the sour old man. "Shanks, Nico found you half-dead in an alley without a penny to your name.

You were so drunk when he found you that you couldn't even tell him your name, even though he saved you from drowning in a puddle of your own vomit." Shanks crossed his arms and turned to the side. "You were so blasted drunk your slobbering mouth could only manage to mutter the word shanks over and over. We still don't know if you were trying to tell him your name, or if you were so plastered, you couldn't manage a proper thanks to the man who refused to believe you were anything but the town idiot." Shanks curled his lip, keeping his gaze from the boy.

"And you, Dawn." Colt turned to face her cold hard stare. "You were some rich man's personal companion before Nico came along. Sold by your own family into a life destined for nothing but the pleasure of others. Are you really going to sit there and question the worth of a girl you have yet to meet because she is called Maiden?" Dawn blinked and mouthed a few silent words. "You, of all people, should know that just because someone claims you as property, it doesn't mean they get to decide who you really are." Dawn tensed her jaw. Her eyes watering. "When the rest of the circle looks at you, nobody sees the rich man's slave because that's not who you are, and I would dare to say it's not who you ever were." A tear escaped Dawn's guard as she joined Shanks in diverting her gaze.

"And then there's me. An orphan with no perceivable life skills, no trade to offer the cause, no military or combat training to aid in our defense, and barely a single copper to his name. Yet here we all are, standing toe to toe as equals. Isn't that what Aequalitatem is all about? If we are going to start judging others solely based on what this world has titled them as, then we might as well return to the forsaken alleys, chained beds, and lonely hallways we came from."

Even Shanks failed to know how to fill the silence. The

truth of Colt's words cut them all, but in a way that allowed them to be humbled rather than angered. Nico breathed a sigh of relief. Now he could focus on being a leader rather than a Maiden lobbyist.

"Colt is right. If Aequalitatem is going to have a snowball's chance in hell of beating the Grand Council, it's going to be on the shoulders of the people the League has abandoned and abused. As Colt pointed out, I took a chance on each and every one of the people standing here before me, and look how far such optimism and hope has brought us. So, you can either accept our soon to be members with the respect and dignity they deserve, or you can leave this circle for the glorious lives you left behind."

Nico made eye contact with each of his inner circle before moving on. "I'm glad to see everyone has come to their senses. Now that we all agree to let these two girls be more than Purity Maidens, I will open the floor to Randle, who is the only one amongst us with any legitimate knowledge concerning our new members."

The old blacksmith had stayed uncharacteristically silent up until this point. One by one, he looked deep into the eyes of each person Nico invited, searching for any sliver of lingering disrespect or bitterness in their hearts.

"There is a good reason why I kept all of you in the dark about my informant. Until now, I had no reason to risk the type of prejudiced responses I just heard. While it is true the informant is a Purity Maiden, she is more importantly my daughter." Shanks and Dawn looked at their feet, unable to make eye contact with the old blacksmith.

"Thankfully, she has not carried the burden of being a Purity Maiden for long. Three years ago, she voluntarily placed herself in that vile place, saying it would hone her skills as a hysteresis user, amongst other things. Now I know from your earlier comments that you all must be questioning the use of honing a Maiden's hysteresis. You would even be right in asking it for the most part. Except for the fact that not all Maidens are content with the League's insultingly narrow list of approved uses.

"While it is true that my daughter altered garments and removed stains, she also crept about the bowels of New Geneva—even going so far as to sneak into the League's Proving Grounds to observe our enemy's abilities. We already had a bit of information about the Density style, thanks to Nico, but we had little to no knowledge of other styles. Some we didn't even have a proper name for. With my daughter's help, we have a basic knowledge of three of the four styles used by the Grand Council. This information will help us tremendously in the years to come. She did this at tremendous risk to her own safety, but she didn't stop there. From the moment she stepped foot in that god awful place, she kept her eyes and ears open for others like her. Other Maidens who had a darker past, one that would allow them to push past the gilded boundaries they were born into. She went in hoping to recruit an army, she left with a single girl. Unfortunately, I am in the dark about this girl as much as the rest of you, but if I know my daughter at all, she will be well worth the trouble.

"Once both girls are safely within the confines of our base, we can begin debriefing them about their time within the walls. With any luck, this other girl will be able to provide information to aid us in filling in the gaps that couldn't be filled by my daughter's reconnaissance. Any further information about the Father's hysteresis styles, the chances of a Maiden rebellion, structural layout of the League's gated community, or other vital information will be priceless to us in the days to come."

Shanks opened his mouth, but Randle didn't give him the

chance. "If what I've shared has shocked you, you better hold on tight 'cause I'm just getting started. While I can't speak for the other girl, I can undoubtedly say that despite being labeled a Purity Maiden, my daughter is cautious, as well as ruthless." Randle paused, locking eyes with Shanks. "If she gets so much as a whiff of trouble from one of you, she will not hesitate to take your life. As much as you might want to scoff at the idea of a helpless little Maiden taking down one of our own... I've seen her take out a fully armored guard without batting an eye, so most of us would be child's play. We will not be sending out search parties or patrolling the border looking for the girls to show up. We won't even inform the masses of their arrival. We will simply go about business as usual and let them come to us.

"If you happen to spot the girls, do your best to feign ignorance. Otherwise, you might pay a high price for your observant eyes. My best guess is that my daughter will come looking for me as I am the only person she knows outside the walls. She will most likely do this under the darkness of night, not wanting to risk a skirmish in the light of day. Once she has found me, I will set up a time and place for her to meet the rest of the group in a way that allows her to keep her guard down as much as possible.

"You have been chosen to come to this meeting because you carry a decent amount of influence in groups within the circle. Your job is to lessen reactions similar to those some of you had upon hearing that our newest members happen to be former Purity Maidens. Dawn, you need to convince all the former slaves and other recruits under you that the Maidens were victims of the League like any of them. Shanks, you get the pleasant task of convincing the rest of the old guilders, and Colt, you continue to be the voice of optimism amongst all the shriveled hearts. Are we all clear?"

United and inspired, each member of the group locked eyes with Randle and gave a slow, firm nod of their head.

"Wonderful," exclaimed Randle, almost sarcastically. "Now, all we have to do is wait, and hope we catch Oriella in a good mood."

CHAPTER 29

A CHANCE ENCOUNTER

Gerolt paced back and forth. Sleep had become allusive. His mind tortured him, playing out the countless mistakes he'd made with his wife and daughter. His restless mind presented the least of his problems. Armed guards took his wife away under false pretenses. She was destined to rot away in the League's holding cells. The League dissolved his marriage without his consent, and his only daughter had gone missing. Gerolt had not felt this powerless since he held his dying son in his arms.

Ever since passing under the archway into New Geneva, everything had its place. He thought his hard-earned appointment to Lead Provider would have him sailing on top of the world. For a brief moment, it had, but that feeling quickly turned to despair and regret as his world came crashing down around him. Gerolt grew to hate his new title. A large part of him yearned to renounce his new election and step down as a Provider altogether. That was the coward's way out. He would maintain every inch of his status in the League. It presented his best chance of gaining access to the holding cells or finding information about his daughter's whereabouts.

Being a veteran Provider, familiar with the politics within the League, Gerolt knew he would need to be extremely cautious. He would need to be the loyal Provider he had always been while also observing ways to reach and free his wife. Hence all the pacing. The key was to find a way to do both tasks at the same time. Gerolt planned to use his authority as Lead Provider to get others to do the dirty work for him. Providers tended to be very meticulous individuals and not easily fooled, so he would need to play his cards just right. Being obsessed with detail might be the mark of a competent Provider, but it also made them adept spies. Gerolt needed to come up with a way to convince them to feed him information, without looking suspicious in the process.

This made his next task extremely crucial. How he chose to write up his Lead Provider Manifesto could make or break his chances of success. The previous Lead Provider preferred to spend his days lounging in his living quarters with a few choice Maidens to keep him company. While this same approach might give him ample time to sneak about behind the scenes, one man could only do so much without drawing suspicion. A more scrupulous, micromanaging approach would allow him to divvy out the gathering of information amongst his Providers while taking the spotlight off of himself in the process. This seemed to fit his reputation quite nicely. A Lead Provider's Manifesto could only be written once, and only at the start of a Lead Provider's service, so Gerolt would need to think his out very carefully.

The 5th Lead Provider Manifesto: By Gerolt Crivelli
Greetings fellow Providers,
I am honored to be chosen as your next Lead Provider. Many of

you were displeased with how the previous Lead ran things. I can assure you that I will be taking on a much more involved role as the new Lead Provider.

As you know, this can only come about if accompanied by some big changes. The biggest change will come in the form of mandatory reporting of all Providers. As Lead Provider, I expect to be updated daily on each Maiden's personal progress, their current state of purity, and their client lists and interactions. I will also be restructuring how Purity Maidens are assigned. We will no longer have Maidens tied to a single Provider for all their needs. Instead, I will be assigning each Provider to a specific area, or aspect, within the Crystal Pedestal. Below, you will find a list of each Provider's new assignment. Large areas will have more than one Provider assigned. I also reserve the right to recruit new Providers if any of these areas require additional assistance.

Crystal Pedestal Café: Lance Roundtree, Curtis Blevins, and Harold Taft.

Crystal Pedestal Common Room: Jeremiah Fritz, Jedidiah Prim, Henry Fontaine, Burt Redman, Thomas Little, Constantine Orville, Benjamin Reece, and Lukas Pinkie.

Crystal Pedestal Living Quarters – Wake up, lights out, and room inspections: Evander Robinson and Isaiah Benet.

New Skill Training: Color Alteration – Mathias Young and Sr. Maiden Bethany

New Skill Training: Fabric Alteration – Peter Forte and Sr. Maiden Rose

New Skill Training: Stain Removal – Markus Rasmussen and Sr. Maiden Francine

New Skill Training: Luminescence – Fernando Ortega and Sr. Maiden Ruth

New Skill Training: Smell Infusion/extraction – Johnathan Brinkley and Sr. Maiden Angela

New Maidens introductory courses will continue to be overseen by Sr. Maiden Caroline

Along with managing the other Providers, I will also be in charge of handling all issues in purity not directly addressed by a League Father. I will work directly with Warden Krenshaw in escorting any impure Maidens to their respective cells, as well as setting the duration and structure of each Maiden's lessons that have not already been set by a League Father. Any Provider who steps outside of their boundaries or fails to make an adequate report to the Lead Provider will be disciplined at the League's behest.

Dutifully Signed,

Gerolt Crivelli

Gerolt felt certain that his somewhat radical changes would have no problem being granted League approval. His proposed manifesto altered the Provider's responsibilities greatly, but it did not make a single change to the role of the League Fathers. In his introduction letter to the Council, Gerolt pointed out that his structure built upon the brilliance of how the League set up the Winter Festival preparations that year, giving the League credit for their *superior design*. Gerolt also mentioned the recent decline in the number of Purity Maidens in his care over the past month, and that taking this departmental approach would help prevent any future imbalance of Maiden care from happening. It would also increase the number of Providers keeping an eye on the Maidens' level of purity.

The proposal did not give him everything he needed to obtain his goals, but it made the best use of what little power he had. He wished he could have cut Warden Krenshaw out of the picture, but the League would never allow that. Besides, Gerolt already pushed his luck in requesting that other Providers report all non-League issues in purity to him. Confident that he had given himself enough room to work with, while also not pushing his agenda too far, Gerolt sealed his Manifesto and made his way to the Hall of Weights and Scales.

Even this simple errand held a purpose. It presented a rare opportunity to interact with the League itself and not just the goings-on at the Crystal Pedestal. For his plan to work, Gerolt would need more than his Providers. He would need someone inside the League itself. This aspect of the plan alluded him. Finding a League member disgruntled enough to betray the hand that feeds, or stupid enough not to know they were, would be exceedingly difficult to pull off. If he could somehow find a willing informant, he could have them drop off their reports when they came in to eat at the café or get their clothes altered.

With these thoughts running through his head, Gerolt walked to the Hall of Weights and Scales, eyes open to any and all information that could be of later use to him. How many League Fathers did he pass? Were there guards posted on the walls at this time of day? Main gate open or closed? Such simple observations would be the start of Gerolt's arduous planning process. The League had forced him to hone managerial skills above all else. He would see them put to good use.

"Good morning, Lead Provider. I don't normally see you out of your element." The gruff voice pulled Gerolt from his wandering observations. "What brings you outside of the Crystal Pedestal this fine morning?" Gerolt turned towards the source of the unexpected greeting with a smile. It came from Sr. Father Titus, one of the four members of the Grand Council. Without delay, Gerolt snapped into character.

"What a privilege to be greeted by such an esteemed member of the League," Gerolt said with an exaggerated but authentic bow. "I am truly honored that you even know my face, Father Titus." Gerolt held his bow for a few moments, ensuring Father Titus had nothing to add. "As for my purpose outside of the Crystal Pedestal, I am heading to the Hall of Weights and Scales to deliver my proposed Lead Provider Manifesto."

"Ah. Very good, sir. I can only assume you will have things under better control than your indolent predecessor." Gerolt raised a brow but waited patiently for the Sr. Father to continue. "With all the uncharacteristic follies as of late, we could really use a man of your conviction and caliber at the helm."

This time, Gerolt raised both brows. He hadn't expected to be given such praise from a Council member. He couldn't let this rare opportunity go to waste.

"Whatever do you mean, Father Titus," Gerolt replied with a look of genuine concern in his eyes. "I am well aware of the trouble Solomon Pipher has caused lately, and I must add that I apologize for my role in that dreadful trial. I assumed him to be in the right, with him being a League Father and all, but other than that unfortunate incident, what else afflicts our wonderful city?"

Titus didn't seem to take Gerolt's prodding as anything suspicious. In fact, he seemed more than willing to share. "Don't you go worrying yourself about that trial, Mr. Crivelli. You did what any upstanding citizen should have done and backed up the word of a League Father. The results of the trial rest solely on the shoulders of Solomon Pipher." Titus gave Gerolt a reassuring pat on the shoulder. "As for other ill tidings, I'm afraid you and I are the ones to be most pitied."

Gerolt realized that Titus must have been referring to the incidences involving Harmony and Wren. The news had not gone public yet, but Titus's station granted him access to all sorts of knowledge outside of the public eye.

Gerolt cleared his throat. "You are most certainly right,

Father Titus. I have been keeping my family's recent issues hush-hush, but now that you mention it, I am rather down about the matter." Gerolt swallowed a lump in his throat. *My words are my mask.* "I mean, who else do you know, whose entire family turned traitor?"

Father Titus gave Gerolt a few more hardly claps on the back. "Now, don't you be too hard on yourself, Gerolt. Sometimes the apple falls far from the tree. Besides, with a mother like that, it's no wonder your daughter fell to impurity. Your impure ex-wife probably planted all sorts of false ideas in that poor child's head. You are much better off without her. I'm sure you will find a more suitable wife soon, Lead Provider."

Heat poured from under Gerolt's starched collar. Until this moment, he hadn't realized how much hatred he held for the League. Any other day, he would have been ecstatic about such praise and attention from a member of the Grand Council, but recent events had forever changed his outlook of the League. He couldn't let such raw emotions go to waste. What better situation to practice maintaining his façade.

"It is truly horrible to have had such a young mind tainted so. Please let the rest of the Council know how grateful I am to have been released of my ties to that woman. But enough about me, you said that you and I *both* were to be pitied..." Gerolt scrunched his forehead in thought. "What could possibly ail a great man such as yourself?"

Titus let out a deep sigh. "Truly the most distressing news of all, Gerolt... It's my grandson, Cassius." Titus squeezed Gerolt's shoulder so hard he thought it might pop. "He lost his life during the Caste Exams."

Gerolt heard rumblings that something tragic happened at the Caste Exams, but he had been too consumed by his own Lead Provider ceremony to know much about what happened.

"My most sincere condolences Father Titus." Gerolt felt Titus's grip soften as he spoke. "While I didn't personally know your grandson, I'm sure that his loss will be felt in the heart of this city for years to come."

Titus pulled his hand from Gerolt's shoulder and took on a more serious candor. "You speak the truth, Gerolt. Cassius represented the future of the League, hence him being selected as one of only two apprentices worthy of testing during a Winter Festival. As a result of his early departure, the Council is debating whether or not we need to scale back the intensity of the exams. I hope we don't see a decrease in the quality of our Fathers because of it. The good news is that my grandson died with honor. He used his last remaining scrap of strength to successfully complete his exam; he died a League Father."

Gerolt locked eyes with Titus. "Truly a glorious way to go. An even greater reason for him to be deeply missed." Gerolt allowed his gaze to wander, bringing a hand to his chin. "If I may ask, how is the rest of your family taking the news?"

Titus looked down at his feet. For a moment, Gerolt feared he had overstepped his bounds. "It's been difficult to put it lightly. Some are not able to see the heroism in his efforts, which obviously makes his death less bittersweet and more, well, just bitter. Living through the Holy Wars gifted me with a different perspective on the fragility of life and the importance of a man's intestinal fortitude. While the rest of New Geneva thinks of the League as indestructible, the mountain clans would argue otherwise. While it's true that we killed hundreds of them for every one of us that fell, we lost many over those tragic years. I'm afraid Cassius's brother Simeon is taking it hardest of all... He also participated in the Caste Exams—had a front-row seat to his brother's grizzly end." Titus paused in thought. Gerolt thought better of filling the void.

"He passed his entrance exams and now takes his brother's place as an apprentice in my Friction School."

"Ah, a fine way to continue the great family line," Gerolt said.

"A replacement in number alone," Titus groaned. "Cassius personified bravery, boldness, and heroism. Simeon is anxious, quiet, and tentative. I'm afraid the loss of his brother has forced him to retreat even deeper into himself. He rarely talks to the other apprentices at the school and is quickly becoming a bit of a pariah. If it weren't for the fact that he is my last remaining grandson, he would already be expelled."

Gerolt fought to suppress the burst of excitement surging through him. A League apprentice who kept to himself, but also held privilege as the lone grandson of a Grand Council member. The opportunity for such an informant felt too good to be true, or perhaps a bit of good luck had finally fallen into Gerolt's lap.

"I, too, lost family in my days outside the walls. Killed by the mountain clans while trying to protect our family's crops..." Gerolt choked back his tears. Titus took note. "I would be more than willing to talk to the boy if you think it would help. Perhaps hearing from someone who has experienced a similar loss would give him some...perspective."

Titus considered Gerolt in silence for a moment. "That's very kind of you, Gerolt. Your service to the League knows no bounds." Gerolt managed a meager smile. "To tell you the truth, I'm at my wit's end with the boy, but I am much too busy with the affairs of the Grand Council to guide him back to sanity myself... Your offer won't soon be forgotten, Gerolt." Titus raised a determined finger. "I'll talk to Simeon tonight and have him set up a time to meet with you." Titus gave Gerolt one last pat on the shoulder before moving on to his original destination.

Gerolt couldn't believe his luck, even if Simeon proved a useless endeavor, it couldn't hurt to be in good standing with a member of the Grand Council. *Be strong in there, Harmony... This isn't over."*

CHAPTER 30

BOUND

Winter winds howled through the trees. The frigid air soaked into Wren's bones, along with an ever-present aura of uncertainty. She would be lying is she said she wasn't anxious, even a little bit scared. She watched Oriella, expertly darting in and out of cover. Her feet silent and precise. Despite her obvious comfort traipsing through the snow-covered woods, she didn't make Wren feel awkward or weak as she stumbled after her. Something about her felt different, but Wren couldn't put her finger on it. She still worded things in a somewhat childish way and carried herself like someone dying for attention, but she had no one left to impress. Oriella turned and gave Wren a warm smile before motioning her forward. Perhaps Oriella had not changed after all. What once felt fake and contrite now felt authentic and beautiful. Wren found herself wondering what Oriella's life had been like before coming to the Crystal Pedestal.

From the way she carried herself and the ease with which she draped herself in luxury, Wren had assumed her to have come from privilege. Seeing her now, in her woolen traveling clothes, springing through the woods with ease, Wren knew that couldn't be further from the truth. Oriella possessed a different sort of confidence. The kind that came from facing hardship and coming out better on the other side. Oriella knew her true self. Something Wren buried a long time ago. The idea of Wren's *real* self rising to the surface simultaneously tantalized and terrified her.

"Wren," snapped Oriella in a raspy whisper. She pointed two fingers to her eyes and then to the path ahead of her. Wren woke from her internal fog and directed her attention through the trees. A single sentry stood guard on at the edge of a clearing. A collection of tents and small stone huts littered the horizon as far as they could see. A single cobblestone path snaked its way through the tightly packed collection of homes. Countless dirt paths split from the main stone road, winding their way through the sea of tents and huts. Despite its crude appearance, the LHC housed a significant number of people. One tent towered over the rest. A huge, brown monstrosity at the heart of Aequalitatem's command center.

Wren and Oriella sat amongst the trees. The lone sentry stood motionless on the cobblestone path no more than twenty feet away. Oriella motioned for Wren to follow before creeping through the edge of the woods that encircled the city.

"This is weird," whispered Oriella. She sat with her back against a stone hut that shared a border with the nearby woods.

Wren looked around, trying to see anything other than darkness. "What's weird?" she whispered back.

"Everything," replied Oriella. "Why would they post a single guard, and why stand him on the most obvious path into the city when outsiders can enter from almost anywhere. I mean, it's not like there's a wall or anything. So, either these rebels are a few scoops short of a full bag, or Dad told them we were coming and posted the lone guard to allow me to sneak in with ease. A completely unguarded city looks rather suspicious after all."

"You know all of this from one guard?" asked Wren.

"No, silly. I just know my dad. Follow me." With an attitude boarding on vindictive, Oriella stood up and marched towards the guard with her chin held high. Surprised by the sudden shift in tactics, Wren had little choice but to follow. Wren took a few long, steadying breaths to calm her outrageously loud heartbeat. The two girls approached the guard. One stamping her feet while the other did her best to make herself invisible. The guard made no move to call them out. His eyes fixated forward as if asleep while standing. Kicking it up a notch, Oriella started talking at full volume. "Well, I guess this is the place," she called out to Wren over her shoulder.

Unable to fain ignorance any longer, the guard turned toward the girls. "Halt! Who goes there?"

"Oh, shut it would ya?" snapped Oriella. "It's stupid enough to post one guard for an entire city, but it's another thing to pull your normal watch to make a few harmless little girls feel better about coming to such a *scary* place." Oriella's voice dripped with sarcasm. Her mouth turned down in an exaggerated frown to drive home her already obvious point. After getting the guard's attention, her comical frown snapped into a stern and serious glare.

She continued as if speaking to an incompetent child. "Oh, did you think one big bad guard would scare us off? Or did you think one inept guard enough for a couple of poor defensive women? I guess my basic question is, are you more of the overconfident type or just ignorant? I guess those are sort of the same thing... Let me try again." Oriella cleared her throat with a little added force. "Are you some sort of hysteresis phenom, or something?"

The guard gave Oriella a sheepish grin and shrugged his shoulders. Oriella looked back at Wren to hide the grin sneaking onto her face before planting her hands on her hips and snapping back toward the guard.

"I'm just following orders, milady!" the guard said. "I was told to 'make things appear as normal as possible.' The others saw this as an opportunity to get a good night's sleep. I guess I should have been clearer with them."

The grin returned in its full glory. "Did you call me *milady*?" Oriella pressed her gaze up at the guard. She could scarcely reach his chin on her tip toes. "I've never been called that one before! I'm usually called 'Maiden' or 'girl' or 'you there' but *never milady...* How utterly *adorable*," Oriella squealed as she clasped her hands and held them to her chest. "Maybe you're not so stupid after all. No, you're a breath of fresh air, aren't you? Now," Oriella stated with a clap of her hands, "be a good boy and go tell Randle that his daughter is here."

"Of course," the guard replied with a slight bow.

"Of course, what?" Oriella responded with a playful smirk.

The guard stalled for a second, confused by the whole exchange. "Of course...milady?"

Oriella squealed once again. "That's better, now go on," she demanded, shooing the man with her hands as he stumbled down the cobblestone road.

Wren stifled a giggle. The whole scene felt bizarre, yet invigorating. She wondered what gave Oriella the courage to attempt such an approach. Before long, a small group of people appeared out of the darkness. A man of medium build with long black hair, cool gray eyes, and a very prominent facial scar led the way. "Greetings, my name is Nico. It is my pleasure to welcome you both to the LHC. Let me introduce you to a few more friendly faces: Dawn, Shanks, Colt, and of course, Randle." Each member of the inner-circle gave a slight bow. "I bet you are both tired and hungry. Do the two of you have any questions before we retire for the night?"

Wren looked at Oriella, expecting her to blurt something out the second Nico was done talking, but she just sat there, rocking back and forth on her heels and smiling over at her. Not expecting the silence, or the opportunity to express her own thoughts, Wren stammered a bit before voicing her concerns. "Yes. Um, thank you, kind sirs...and madam." Wren blushed as she glanced over at Dawn, who didn't look the least bit offended by the oversight. "Thank you for your welcome, but what exactly do you plan to do with us? I know little to nothing about you, and frankly, the last thing I want to do is to follow a group of strangers to an unknown location. I'm not going anywhere with you until I know who you are, and why you would harbor two escaped Purity Maidens."

Nico glanced at his circle of companions before responding. "Why don't we let Oriella head to her father's hut and get settled in. The rest of you can return to your homes. I will stay with this one until she is convinced that I mean her no harm. The group exchanged arched eyebrows but turned to obey Nico's request. Nico kept his eyes fixed on Wren's, holding up his hand when he saw the unease in her eyes. "I have one request before you all turn in for the night. Bind my hands and give the girl a knife. A proper combat knife, not some dulled down butter spreader."

"But sir...we have only just met this girl. What if she tries to kill you? What if she is an assassin sent by the League?" Wren's eyes darted back and forth like a cornered animal, her mouth struggling to form words.

Nico set his jaw. "This morning, you referred to the Maidens as 'domesticated half-wits.' Did I get that right?" Red crept up Shank's leathery neck. He gave the slightest of nods. "And now this one is a ruthless killer and a trained assassin? Tsk, tsk. Make up your mind, Shanks, and while you are, do me a favor and follow orders. There is some rope in the guard's tent. Go and fetch it for me."

Shanks's face twisted in anger, but he took his leave regardless. He returned with a length of rope and a wickedly sharp knife. After binding Nico's wrists, a little tighter than necessary, he flipped the knife around in his hands, catching it by the blade and shoving the handle toward Wren. Wren looked at Oriella, who gave her a reassuring nod. Wren nodded back before reaching a shaky hand out to grab the blade. With a curt bow, Shanks excused himself for the night, followed by the rest of the group.

Nico sat down under a nearby tree and crossed his legs. "When you are satisfied with your level of safety, cut me free, and I'll show you to your hut. Now, ask me your questions and I will answer them as openly and honestly as I can."

Wren avoided looking directly at Nico, still unsure what to think about the situation. The League forbade her from talking to men unless spoken to, yet here she stood, knife in hand. Her mind buzzed with questions, but she couldn't get over the idea of a man purposefully sacrificing his own power to make her feel more at ease. It made her feel awkwardly self-aware. She wished they could just talk, but the rope and knife did put her mind at ease a bit. Even if the ugly brute from earlier had tied the ropes so tight that Nico's hands already started to turn a dark shade of red. Refusing to give in to the nagging voice in her head urging her to shy away from her questions and obey, Wren took a seat across from Nico and met his steely gaze.

"Oriella referred to you as rebels. What are you rebelling against?"

"Rebels, huh?" replied Nico in a nonchalant tone. "Well, I

guess that's one way to put it. I would say that we're more idealists than rebels, but if someone is looking at things from the League's perspective, we would certainly come off as such."

"So, you're rebelling against the League?" Wren responded in amazement. "If that's true, then why have they not swooped in to destroy you? It's not like this place is well guarded, or very far from their walls for that matter."

Nico smiled. "You assume we are enough of a threat to get the League's attention. Currently, we are an underground uprising, working in the shadows until the time comes when we can act in the light."

"What do you mean, *working in the shadows*? From what I know of the League, even a whiff of defiance would be enough for them to burn the LHC to the ground."

"If the League believes we crossed a line from minor annoyance to thread-bare threat, the battle would be a short one indeed. At this point, we haven't done much. We've grown our numbers and gathered information about the League through contacts such as your friend Oriella. We have handed out pamphlets with anti-League propaganda and other minor tactics like planting evidence against Solomon Pipher at his recent trial. Evidence which I hear aided in getting him expelled from the city. It might be a small thing, but one less Sr. Father isn't nothing, especially when it's Solomon Pipher. Eventually, we want to do more, but we aren't strong enough to take on the League in any real capacity. Maybe the two of you can help us change that."

Wren suppressed a laugh, which came out as a snort. Despite being embarrassed, it didn't keep her from leaning into Nico's last comment. "Are you serious? If you think that Oriella and I are what's going to tip the balance of power, then your group is in even more trouble than I thought."

Nico offered up a hesitant smile. "You underestimate yourself. I don't even know you, and I can see that." Wren looked to the side. "You're a hysteresis user, aren't you?" Wren nodded her head, but kept her gaze on the ground. "When did your gift first appear? I hear it can surface earlier in women."

Wren had never heard that before. She assumed everyone born with the gift had it since birth. "I've had the gift for as far back as I can remember." Wren's mind drifted to memories. "I used to have this stuffed rabbit I'd practice on as a child, altering its color or material to my current favorites." Wren paused. The memory of the rabbit being torn from her grasp flooded her mind. She did her best to fight it off. Now was not the time.

Nico waited for her to continue. After a while, he broke the awkward silence. "That early, huh? You must have had a rather unique family to have supported your gift as a young girl. I'm assuming these years practicing on your rabbit took place outside the walls? Did you live in the LHC?"

Wren swallowed a lump in her throat, her hands wringing the handle of the knife. "No...we were further out than this... My family tended a farm far away from the rest of civilization." Wren's eyes welled with tears. Saying the words somehow felt more real than keeping them in her head alone. "I don't really want to talk about that time if you don't mind. Tell me more about how hysteresis is different for men."

Nico gave a slight nod and moved on. "Most males don't have their gift surface until mid-to-late adolescence, sometimes even later. Technically speaking, you have as many years of hysteresis use under your belt as a middle-aged League Father."

Wren blew a sharp puff of air out of her lungs. "All those years of experience changing colors and altering clothes... sounds like a force to be reckoned with."

Nico gave her a look that reminded Wren of her father when he thought she underestimated herself. It made her stomach churn. "Oh, come on now. Randle assured me that his daughter had high standards and would never dream of bringing someone along who hadn't sufficiently impressed her. From my short time with Oriella, she seems like a difficult girl to impress. So, what are you not telling me?"

Wren bit her lip. It had been hard enough to try explaining things to Oriella. "It's...complicated."

"Complicated?"

"Yes, complicated. As in, I'm not entirely sure how I do what I do."

Nico paused for a moment. His face twisted up in thought. "I'm assuming you are referring to some form of hysteresis. If that's true, please explain to me how a hysteresis user could ever be unsure of their skill. Hysteresis requires an intimate knowledge of the subject being altered and the method of altering. How would you alter something and then have no idea how you did it?"

"Like I said, it's complicated."

"Humor me with your best shot. I've heard and seen my fair share of the unexplainable. You can do the short version if you don't feel comfortable with the details."

Everything from Wren's past experiences told her not to trust this man. Yet something kept her from turning away. She trusted her father once. Those memories were some of the best she had. She looked at Nico's tied up hands, almost purple at this point. She thought about how respectful he had been towards her, and how easily Oriella dropped her guard around him and his friends. He seemed to value her opinions and expressed genuine concern to answer her questions. He also seemed to see something more than a Purity Maiden when he looked at her. He reinforced the voice in her head. A voice she had tried to bury ever since her father stopped feeding it. Even though she now roamed the land outside the walls, she wasn't entirely free. Maybe listening to her inner voice would prove to be the first step in shedding the League's version of her identity and embracing her true self.

"It first happened out of desperation," she said as Nico settled in. "Somehow, I held my mind's eye without focusing on any one thing. Kind of like splitting my mind in half and then forcing those two halves to exist simultaneously." Nico squinted but kept silent. "Later on, I discovered I could do this same thing with an altered focus and get different results. The biggest surprise came when I tried holding both of these different mindsets at the same time, while still keeping my mind's eye intact, essentially splitting my thoughts in three..." Wren trailed off when she saw the look of confusion on Nico's face.

"I'd scratch my head if I could," he said, holding up his bound hands. Ashamed of how long she left Nico tied up, Wren reached over and cut the ropes. "Thanks, they were really starting to burn. That stubborn fool really did cinch them tight." Nico paused long enough to rub some blood back into his tingling hands. "So, how did this mysterious ability help you escape?"

Wren froze for a second. "I, um, tore an opening in my door."

Nico stopped rubbing his hands and looked up and Wren. "What, like the wooden door to your living quarters? That's pretty impressive!"

"No...I faked my flow...and got sent to the unclean rooms."

Nico's mouth dropped open. "You mean to tell me that you blew a hole in a reinforced steel door big enough for you to step through?" Wren nodded. "If you could cause that kind of destructive force without a full understanding of what you are doing"—Nico brought his hands to his head—"imagine what might happen if we fill in the gaps!"

"Fill in the gaps? Do you even have the slightest clue what I'm talking about?"

Nico shook his head with a thin smile. "No, but I know someone who might."

CHAPTER 31

THE KING OF THE LHC

Solomon's new recruits lacked professionalism, training, and hysteresis ability, but they made up for it with low morals, a penchant for violence, and easily moldable minds. He could no longer depend on the League for support. No matter. He never needed those fools in the first place. He clawed himself free from the shadows of his mother's cabin. Surely he could manage conquering the LHC. The work of the Inquisition would require brains, finesse, a good ear, and a strong stomach.

"Time to figure out what's in our toolbox," Solomon said as he stood from his bed and stretched his aching back.

Faulty tools could be replaced or thrown away, especially in a place like the LHC. Tools that proved themselves useful and loyal to his cause would be rewarded. This included his oddly devoted virgin. "Good morning, little witch," cooed Solomon as he roused Loathe from her slumber. "Tonight, we start the trials. Are you up to the task?"

Loathe rolled over, rubbing her eyes. If Solomon didn't know better, he might think her happy to see him. "Of course, master. Whatever you need," Loathe replied as she popped out of bed.

Solomon looked down his nose at her. His scrupulous eyes calculated her chances of success. "What I need is for you to make yourself look halfway presentable. I'll take care of the rest. Once you're done combing the lice out of your hair, scrubbing the filth from your face, and washing the stink off of your newly pubescent body, come find me. I'll let you know what to do next."

Without another word, Loathe ran off to prepare herself as best as she could. This meant cleaning herself and putting on the one decent dress she owned, but the distraction got her out of Solomon's hair long enough for him to figure how to best use the girl. Truth be told, he didn't really need her. He could project the witch on his own and make it realistic enough. Using a live puppet, like he did in the barn, increased the realism and intensity of his hysteresis, but it came with risks as well. The more the puppet deviated from the projection, the greater the chance that the projection would be seen for what it was. If his new minions witnessed their beautiful witch turn into the homely virgin from the tavern right before their eyes, even morons such as them would become suspicious. To this point, none of them have proven to have a strong enough mind to resist even the simplest projections, and now that they had been bought into the presence of a witch, Solomon's influence on their minds would be even more certain.

For this reason, Solomon thought up a different approach to the trials. One where the exhausting presence of a living witch would not be required. He needed to reserve some mental energy for other tasks, but he also wanted to avoid setting up the virgin trap a second time. Even in the LHC, one could only get away with such a devious undertaking so many times before being found out.

With this in mind, Solomon decided to forgo rigorous, individually crafted tests. League members would have been different. Their minds had more depth. These four did not seem worth the extra effort. One way or the other, it would have to take place in the barn due to the severe lack of working space the League left him with. This also meant he would have to do the tests one at a time, but before any of that, he needed to locate the examinees.

Lucky for him, there was nothing to do in this godforsaken place but drink your sorrows away. Daytime drinking proved to be more about camaraderie and keeping warm than getting shit-faced. The night would prove to be a better time to conduct his trials. Less bonding, more distractions. A sadistic smile stretched across Solomon's plump lips as he thought of his next move. He had just the thing to keep him entertained until tonight, and it would enable him to do a little reconnaissance at the same time.

Now that he had lived in the filth of his small hut for a time, Solomon felt fairly comfortable intermingling with the dirty peasants of the LHC. Not only did he look the part, but news of Solomon's trial had not yet made its way beyond the walls. Nobody from the LHC had laid eyes on Solomon before his arrival either. Few had enough money for a writ of passage into the city, and none possessed the wealth required to rub shoulders with a Sr. Father. Solomon wanted to take advantage of this opportunity to work from the shadows. As much as he wanted to announce the presence of Sr. Father Solomon Pipher, that glorious moment would have to wait. It would be just as satisfying to watch them all squirm.

As Solomon walked down the dirt path that led into the city, his mind hummed with ideas on what he could do with his projection hysteresis in a place where people had no idea such a thing existed. Nobody out here paid for the services of

Purity Maidens or had the slightest clue what wonders the League could conjure up. Their knowledge of hysteresis proved to be simplistic and crude, leaving them much more likely to assume the presence of a witch than some sensory form of hysteresis. Not only did Solomon have all of these advantages at his fingertips, but he no longer had to behave himself for the League's sake. As a Sr. Father, he could get away with disciplining a few uppity clerks or an impure Maiden now and again. If he used his hysteresis as he planned to now, it would have granted him a summons to that pretentiously long hallway in the Hall of Weights and Scales.

With freedom at his disposal, and a bit of time on his hands, Solomon made his way into the first establishment he came across. A foul-smelling place called the Disgruntled Cow. Solomon couldn't think of a better way to propagate rumors of a witch taking root in the LHC than a well-crafted sensory projection amongst drunks. Being careful to make his entrance as inconspicuous as possible, Solomon crept in the front door of the stale smelling tavern. He paused briefly to ensure he had not attracted too many eyes before shuffling his way along the back wall and settling down at a small table in the far corner of the room.

In his dark corner, Solomon made use of a dark nightmare that had roared to the surface since coming to the LHC. His memories had always been the perfect hysteresis fuel, and it seemed he had forgotten how many of them he had locked away. Getting removed from his life of privilege and comfort awoke some of his earlier memories, ones that he'd buried in the weakness of his youth. Solomon cleared the dust off one of these recently retrieved memories, allowing himself to be consumed by it.

...

"Just who do you think you are Solomon Humphrey Pipher? I ought to skin you alive, you rotten, worthless child!" Solomon found his mother in a particularly foul mood whenever she drank the brackish smelling brown liquid she loved so much. Today, Solomon discovered the one thing that put her in an even worse mood, dumping the foul-smelling stuff down the washbasin. Solomon chanced a frantic look over his shoulder. His mother stumbled close behind. Her eyes were frantic and glossy. Spit clung to the corners of her mouth. Her slug of a leg kicked up dust in her wake. Solomon darted from side to side, avoiding his crippled mother's furious grasp like his life depended on it.

"You had best come here, boy!" she spat. "I'll go light on ya if you stop yer running about!" Solomon's mother stopped to catch her breath. Catching a spry child proved difficult, especially when dragging a dead limb around. Her breath steady in her lungs, she set her steely gaze on Solomon. He could feel her hate permeate to the center of his being.

"If you make me drag this stump one...more...inch, you'll wish you were never born... You hear that boy? Come get what's coming to ya!" Solomon's mother unsnapped a loop on her belt, letting a crude knife drop into her palm. "Unless you want to wake up one morning missing a body part or two."

Solomon froze. His eyes locked onto his mother's rusty fillet knife. He knew from experience that she had no issue making her threats reality, and he would rather keep all of his parts. Solomon trudged over to his mother, holding his breath as he approached in an attempt to prevent himself from gagging on the stench that came from her infected leg.

As soon as he came within arm's length of his mother, she reached over and slapped him across the face. "Why would you take away an old woman's only source of comfort in this dreadful world? What are you? Some sort of demon child?"

Solomon didn't say a word. He just stared at his feet, his anemic body swaying in the breeze. His mother held his silence for what seemed like forever. Her enraged mind doing its best to come up with the most horrid punishment imaginable. Her mouth twitched into a half-grin. "I have the mind to whip you raw, boy. Whip you raw and make you sleep in the box."

Solomon's eyes went wide. *The box...* The only gift she ever gave him. It was made from rough pine. Unstained, unsanded, and raw. And the smell—an earthy spice fused with the mold of old sweat and the metallic tinge of dried blood. Solomon's breath caught in his chest as the walls closed in around him.

"Relax, boy. Even though you don't deserve it, I'll keep my word and go easy on you. In fact, I've found some new friends for you to play with. You're always complaining about not having any friends. Aren't you, Solomon?" Solomon lifted his glossy gaze and gave a slight nod of his head. "Well, come with me then. I've got loads of them for you."

Solomon breathed a sigh of relief, mind satiated on the fact that he would be spared from his whipping. Maybe the box wouldn't be so bad without his exposed flesh being ripped open every time he moved. The box sat on the front porch as it always did. His mother motioned towards it with a serious gleam in her eye. Solomon opened the lid and peered inside. His heart pounded in anticipation of what might lay within. Much to his surprise, Solomon found nothing but the blood-stains of previous punishments. Maybe his mother would be merciful after all.

"Well, what are you waiting for? Strip down and get in," ordered Mother as she slid into the cabin to retrieve the box's lock.

Solomon moved to obey, removing his clothes and curling his thin, frail body into the small space within the box. What-ever she planned to do to him, he wished she would get it over with and leave him be. Solomon heard some clattering and cursing come from inside the cabin, followed by the rhythmic scrapping noise of his mother dragging her useless leg through the dirt. The potency of her festering wounds grew as she neared. Solomon held his breath, trying not to gag. Whatever his mother had planned, vomit would not be a welcome addition.

"I brought you some friends to keep you company, just like I promised," huffed Solomon's mother as she hoisted a wooden bucket onto the edge of the box. Solomon slowed his breathing. His nerves sat on a razor's edge. His mother tilted the wooden bucket, spilling its context across Solomon's back. "Now, you sit there and think about what you've done. I'll let you out in the morning if your squealing doesn't keep me awake all night."

Solomon sat still as a statue as he heard the metal lock click in place. The only light in the box came from a small gap in the lid. Given enough time, it would let him see his fingers. Until then, he would entertain himself with a sensory guessing game he called *What's in the box?*

Normally, this would involve hours of categorizing smells —earthy, acidic, floral, spicy, foreign. Analyzing pain—irritant, laceration, burn, itch. As his eyes adjusted to the light, Solomon would work a sample up to his face to confirm his analysis. None of that was necessary today. Today, he felt the contents *move*.

Curled up in the pitch-black left him unable to see, but he could feel them, furiously burrowing their way into the dark corners of the box, scratching and clawing to find a way out. He remained still as glass. His chest moved in and out in a slow, regular pace. Hours ticked by, and most of the scurrying died down. Then it came. A pin prick of an itch rose to the surface of his skin. The first of many. It was up to Solomon how long he could stand it. How long could he hold mind over body. Will over relief. An hour passed. The itch had grown to a thundering roar. A sensation Solomon had grown to appreciate. An unscratched itch could do wonders to distract the mind.

Shit, Solomon thought to himself as a dull ache started in his left knee. *Here comes phase two.* Soon, every joint in Solomon's body would project a similar message. *I need to move.* A cold sweat broke out over Solomon's frail body. *No...not yet... It's too early....* Solomon tried to slow his breathing, to refocus on the itch...

Ahhhh! Solomon screamed as he thrashed around the box, disturbing the collection of friends his mother had collected. A few moments later, he felt the first bite pierce his skin. A sharp, stinging sensation that would have made him jump if he could have moved enough to do so. Biting his lip to stifle his screams, the young Solomon spent the next several hours in the box with his new friends, suffering bite after bite as the spiders scrapped and struggled to free themselves from the tightly enclosed space.

...

Solomon held the wretched memory in his mind's eye, sitting in the dark corner of the Disgruntled Cow tavern. The horrors of his time in the box saturated his mind. Energy swirled within him in waves, begging to be unleashed. When he could hold the terror of the box no longer, Solomon let the memory go. Hysteria spread out from him like a wave. Those closest to him felt the effects first. Itchy skin, phantom legs crawling up their spine, the unease that soaks into your mind when trapped in a tight space. The unrelenting compulsion to *move.*

The effects spread like a disease. Some cried out with their eyes darting around the room in search of the threat. Others dug their fingers through their hair and scraped their backs against the walls. Anything to get the hair raising pin pricks of pain to subside. Then the bites began, and the nervous scratching ignited into all-out panic. The severely hung-over patrons scurried around the tavern like an overactive ant hill, bumping into tables and screaming out in pain. Solomon looked around the room. A sinister smirk spread across his plump lips. He watched the handful of drunks trip all over themselves. Eyes wide in equal parts confusion and horror.

One of the patrons stopped clawing at his arms long enough to register a thought. He stood on a nearby stool and shouted over the crazed crowd.

"Everyone calm yer tits!" he hollered as he twitched in pain. "I know what's going on here, and it ain't real. It's witch-craft, I tell you!"

A few of the other patrons looked his way. Other's soon joined in, eager for any form of logic to step in. "Steady your minds, boys, and maybe we can fight off her dark magic." The man slapped the pain from his skin and bared his teeth. "We rebuke your power witch!" he spewed. A crazed look danced in his eye. "Lord, help us!"

Intrigued by this turn of events, Solomon released the memory of the box from his mind's eye, ending the projection as quickly as it started. A hush came over the tavern as the men sat in the ecstasy of normal. The man who cried witch took this opportunity to catch up with the insane turn of events.

"Well done, my brothers," he shouted from atop the table. "You have witnessed the work of a witch first hand and lived to tell about it."

The relieved patrons rose to their feet and gathered around the table the man had taken up as his soapbox. "Chuck and I encountered the work of this very same witch no more than two nights ago in the woods by the old Jessup farm."

The small crowd of men looked at each other, murmuring various reactions to Tommy's declaration while keeping one eye out for any lingering spiders. Eventually, one of them regained their composure enough to join the conversation. "No offense Tommy, but don't ya think your explanation is a little... crazy? I won't say I have the foggiest idea what the hell happened, but a witch? What proof do you have? We can't go around telling people there's a witch without some sort of reason."

Tommy puffed up his chest and tilted his head upward. "Well, I'll tell you how I know, Harry. You've got to shut yer pie-hole long enough to listen." Harry hung his head in shame while the rest of the men gathered around like a bunch of boy scouts at a campfire. "There we were, just minding our own business, walking through the woods outside of town. Out of nowhere, we heard this ghastly yet sweet voice, beckoning us to venture deeper into the woods." The men shuffled nervously, eyes glued upward. Tommy grinned. "The voice sounded innocent to the untrained ear. I was suspicious, but Chuck convinced me to keep going and check it out." Chuck opened his mouth to respond, but Tommy pressed forward. "That's when we nearly choked to death on the putrid smell of the witch's rotting soul."

Tommy scrunched up his face, pantomiming the whole encounter. The men who gathered around him sat with jaws open, hanging on his every word. "Nothing else could explain the stench that clouded the air that night. If you don't believe me, go find what's left of Butch. He inhaled too much of her stink, and now he's a raving lunatic."

The murmuring amongst the gathering increased. Several of the men mentioned that they had seen Butch wandering around, face scraped to the bone, and muttering nonsense. With several men collaborating Tommy's story, and the lot of them experiencing what felt like a curse first hand, the small group of men bought Tommy's claims of witchcraft hook, line, and sinker.

"Maybe you're right Tommy, or maybe some other evil is lingering around. Either way, we've got to tell Nico about it. He's the only one that might be able to save us from whatever this is." A chorus of "hell yeah!" floated around the room in support.

Solomon chuckled to himself at Tommy's machismo laden version of the story, but that wasn't what caught his attention. *Nico, huh? He must be the top dog in this cesspool. Perhaps I'll join their pathetic little meeting and see if I can coax any more information out of this Tommy fellow.* Solomon exchanged his hard-furrowed brow for the face of a wide-eyed coward. Taking shallow breaths, Solomon stumbled towards the buzzing group. "Um. Excuse me, gentlemen."

"Who're you? And where the hell did you come from? I don't remember seeing your flabby ass screech'n with the rest of us," Tommy remarked with a sharp tone to his voice.

"I beg your pardon brave, sir, but I'm afraid I'm a bit of a coward and only recently able to pull myself out of the corner I hid in during the attack. Do you really think that unspeakable horror could be traced back to a *witch*?"

Tommy exchanged his accusatory tone for his previous bravado. "Oh, I'm damn sure. Like I said, I heard her in the woods over by the Jessup farm, whispering sweet-sounding words, acting all young and innocent, but she didn't fool me. Chuck and I got out of there fast, you know, so we could come to warn y'all."

"Very brave of you sir...Tommy?"

"Damn straight."

"Tell me, Tommy. Why does a brave man, such as you, feel the need to involve this Nico person? What makes you think he would stand any more of a chance than the rest of us against something as powerful as a witch?"

The crowd of men squinted their eyes and curled their lips. Noticing this strange reaction, Solomon continued. "Forgive my ignorance. I have only just arrived in the LHC, and this experience has gotten me all worked up." Solomon's voice escalated to a pleading tone. "Please, help me steady this horrible anxiety and tell me that Nico is more than just the local mayor. We need someone more capable than a mere politician."

Solomon waited for Tommy to respond. The trembling mask of a fat coward plastered over his rotten and bloodthirsty heart. Solomon didn't mind feigning weakness if it came by his own design. Especially if it meant obtaining his first piece of potentially useful information. Coward or torturer, Solomon would get the information he desired.

Tommy motioned for Solomon to come closer, lowering his voice to a gruff whisper. "They say that Nico has *the gift*. Trained by a member of the Grand Council, too"

Solomon did not have to fake his next expression. "A hysteresis user! Here? Are you certain?"

"Yep." Tommy nodded. "He left all the fancy food, all those young girls, and the chance to live in a mansion to come help scum like us out here in the LHC. He's a real saint he is. And I bet he can use his whatchamacallit to teach that witch a thing or two."

Solomon did his best to hide the sneer creeping its way into the corners of his mouth. *So, Nico is a hysteresis user, is he? And he is rumored to be trained by a member of the Grand Council? This day gets more useful by the second.*

Regaining his facade, Solomon responded, "If what you say

is true, then we should fetch him straightaway. Where can we find this, *Nico?*"

"You really are new, aren't ya? Nobody walks up and talks to Nico, not unless they're part of his group, anyway. Most of us have set eyes on him once or twice, if ever. We'll have to ask his informants to report the news. The barkeep at the Charlatan's Inn is one. Come on everyone, let's go."

Solomon took a seat as the Disgruntled Cow cleared out. The quiet gave his mind room to think. A unique name like Nico wouldn't be that common amongst League recruits and apprentices. Solomon ran over the list of deserters and outcasts the League produced over the last few years, searching his memory for anyone who might have been called Nico. It didn't take him long to narrow down the suspects.

"Nicholai Romanski, the king of the LHC? How delightfully ironic."

CHAPTER 32
A BITTERSWEET SYMPHONY

Gerolt sat patiently at his table in the Crystal Pedestal Café. Any second now a young League apprentice would come walking in, unknowingly escorting a mountain of hope along with him. Gerolt knew the importance of staying focused. He couldn't come off as too self-serving, or reveal anything that would be potentially incriminating. He had to make this boy believe his intentions centered around a concern for the loss of his brother, but at the same time get him to reveal his true nature in regards to the League. Gerolt couldn't risk revealing his own distaste for the League first. He needed to create an environment safe enough to get this apprentice to confess his own embroiled feelings. A fine line to be sure. Gerolt needed Simeon to reveal an emotion with some claws in it.

A boy wearing the crimson cloak of the School of Friction sauntered in. Gerolt's heart sank. The apprentice looked down at the floor, hands in his pockets, and face fixed in an expressionless deadpan. Not a good start for a man hoping to find a spitfire ready to stick it to the League.

As the boy walked closer, Gerolt stood to greet him. "Good morning. Titus's grandson, I presume?" The boy gave a barely visible nod. "Wonderful. Please, take a seat, and tell me, do you like coffee?" The apprentice nodded once more. "Great, I take mine black. Sweeteners and cream accomplish nothing but masking the beautifully natural bitterness that coffee holds." Gerolt fixed his eyes on Simeon as he poured him a steaming hot cup. "Not all things are meant to be sweet. Do you agree, young apprentice?"

Simeon looked up, making eye contact with Gerolt for the first time. "Call me Simeon."

"Simeon, of course. I'll keep it black for now. Let me know if the bitterness gets too strong for you."

"Thanks, black is fine," replied Simeon in a less than enthusiastic monotone.

Gerolt didn't blame him for his lackluster attitude. He must be wondering why his grandfather set him up to meet this overly decorous man. Meeting up with a Provider certainly didn't make the boy's list of exciting things to do this morning.

"If I had to guess, I'd say that you're wondering what in the world the two of us have to talk about," Gerolt offered. Simeon said nothing, glancing over his steaming hot coffee while taking a small slurp. "Well, there is no use in beating around the bush. I asked your grandfather if we could meet. It seems that despite our various differences, we have one commonality. Grief." Simeon's gaze locked onto Gerolt's. "You have recently experienced your only brother unjustly ripped from your life, and I have recently experienced the same hardship with my wife and daughter."

Simeon set down the coffee. "Gramps told me you knew what it's like to lose a brother. What's this about your wife and daughter?"

"Ah, yes. You are right. I'm getting ahead of myself. It's just that these losses are so fresh in my mind. The wound has not had time to heal. Forgive me, we can talk about the more distant past."

"No, it's okay. I'd rather not talk about your losses, or mine for that matter. It's like you said, the wound is still too fresh... Unlike you, I'm not as hopeful that time will see it healed."

"Fair enough. I wouldn't want to talk about a loss as final as death. Especially one so fresh...and perhaps a bit bittersweet?"

Simeon shrugged off Gerolt's probing comment. "So, your wife and daughter aren't dead? Then what's the problem?"

Gerolt let out a soft sigh. "One of them has been extradited to the holding cells on suspicion of treason while the other escaped the walls of the city in hopes of a better life. Truth be told, they might as well be dead. There is no escaping the wrath of the League when you defy them as severely as my wife and daughter have."

Simeon sat up straight in his seat, moving his coffee to the side and leaning forward. "Well, at least your family did something to deserve their fate. My brother did nothing but serve the League. Blind service pushed him to the brink of death and beyond!" Simeon pounded the table, spilling coffee and attracting attention. He cleared his throat and reclined back in his seat. "But now I'm getting ahead of myself. Forgive me. My grief forms my words for me, sir."

Gerolt took a sip from his coffee, setting the cup down with gentle precision. "No apology needed my young friend. Like I said earlier, not all things are meant to be sweet. Every now and then, bitterness is the only thing that tastes right." Gerolt took another sip of coffee, letting his words marinate. "Take me, for example. I will not pretend to be pleased by how the League has chosen to deal with my family's circumstance. It's been over a week since they took my wife to the holding cells, and I have yet to receive an update on her status. Guilty or not, it would put me at ease to have some of the mystery surrounding her condition revealed."

Simeon shifted in his chair, squinting at Gerolt from across the table. Gerolt could feel him judging his words. A cold sweat rushed to his palms. Gerolt wrapped them around the hot coffee mug and waited for a response. His mind raced to remember everything he had said, wondering if he pushed things too far too fast.

Simeon swallowed a mouthful from his mug, keeping eye contact with Gerolt. "That's horrible. You don't even know if your wife is alive or dead? At least I have the peace of mind of knowing my brother was needlessly killed."

Gerolt raised his eyebrows and straightened his perfectly symmetrical tie. "Oh, I doubt they have killed her yet, but it's only a matter of time. It's hard to determine how long her body can hold up to their *methods.*" Gerolt paused to collect himself. *You're a coward, Gerolt...* "Tell me, Simeon. What would you do if you thought your brother found himself in a similar situation? Rotting away in the holding cells deep beneath the Hall of Weights and Scales. Tortured for information he may or may not even possess?"

"Hypothetically?" asked Simeon.

"Of course," replied Gerolt.

"Hypothetically, I would do whatever it took to get him out...and make everyone responsible pay dearly along the way." Gerolt pushed his coffee mug aside, folded his arms on the table's surface, and leaned towards Simeon.

"So would I," he whispered before leaning back to his regularly rigid posture.

Simeon studied him carefully. "Well, lucky for me, my

brother isn't being held in the League's holding cells." Simeon took his gaze off of Gerolt, eyes darting around the room. "That doesn't necessarily change my response." Simeon leaned forward, dropping his voice as Gerolt had done. "They deserve to pay for all they have done to us. I don't care who they are or what they do to me. I won't rest until the life my brother carelessly threw away in their name comes back to haunt them."

Simeon sat back in his chair, arms crossed, and lips pursed.

Gerolt looked intently at the boy, studying his features and judging the authenticity of his demeanor. "Perhaps we have more in common than I dared to hope," replied Gerolt, a slight grin teasing the corner of his mouth. Gerolt pulled out a tightly rolled piece of paper from his sleeve and held it under the table between them. "If you truly mean what you say about making the guilty pay for their transgressions, and if you wish to scratch that itch while also helping out an innocent woman... then take the parchment from my hand." Simeon reached out, but Gerolt pulled the parchment back. "Once you open it, there is no turning back."

Gerolt and Simeon locked eyes, each man desperately trying to gauge the authenticity and motive of the other. Gerolt placed the parchment on the table and leaned back in his seat. Simeon snatched it in an instant, tucking it into the sleeve of his blazing red Friction School robes.

"I sure hope your pen is more rebellious than your mouth," offered Simeon, breaking the long silence.

Gerolt smiled. "Oh, you have no idea," he said as he stood up to leave.

"Wait," beckoned Simeon. "How do I contact you again?"

"It's all in the parchment, friend. Best if we keep our face-to-face meetings to a minimum, wouldn't you say?"

∼

SIMEON GAVE a slight nod and then watched as Gerolt strolled out of the café. A full-fledged smile plastered on his face. He sat for a while at his small table alone. He could feel the parchment pressed up against his skin. Its tantalizing contents called out to him, but he knew unfurling the parchment in public would be extremely unwise. He forced himself to wait for as long as he could bear, then took the last dregs of his coffee and headed out the door.

The ten-minute walk from the Crystal Pedestal Café to his quarters within the Friction School felt more like sixty. By the time he passed through the white marble arches emblazoned with the red ax and grinding wheel of the school, his anxiety was churning within him. Simeon didn't expect to be so nervous. He had been planning to take some sort of action against the League since the moment he watched his brother die in vain over a pointless exam, but now that he held incriminating evidence on his person, it felt real for the first time. Even though he didn't know the note's contents, he assumed it contained some sort of plan to aid Gerolt in freeing his wife.

It didn't matter. Simeon had been looking for an opportunity, and a Provider felt like a safer bet than a fellow League member. Perhaps if he helped this man save his wife, it would soften the pain in his own heart. Simeon looked around the white and red marble that filled the school grounds. He didn't see a single thing that he would miss. The League's obsession with itself screamed the loudest in the hysteresis schools. The League's characteristic white marble filled the school grounds. Walkways of it paved the path from building to building and constructed the towering archways that marked each school's entrance. Three large buildings filled the rest of the space, each of which housed a different department of training within the school. Justice Manor drilled the laws of the League and of being a hysteresis user into student's heads. The Skill House sharpened their abilities before moving on to the Proving Grounds. And lastly, the Residence Hall housed apprentices who had not yet earned the right to live in the gated community.

All the buildings on the school grounds looked like over-sized versions of the tall white tombstones they called houses within the League's gated community. The school's insignias added a splash of color to their otherwise bleached appearance. The Residence Hall's held the most school spirit, having almost as much red as white. It encouraged the new students to develop pride for their individual school, but for Simeon, it only deepened his distaste. Visions of his brother, draped in those dreadful school colors, rushed to his mind each time he approached.

If he didn't know better, he would have been bursting with pride waltzing into such a regal looking place. All of the other students enjoyed this ignorant bliss, talking and laughing without a care in the world. Simeon hated the lot of them. The piece of paper burned a hole in the sleeve of his robe. Simeon already held a reputation for keeping to himself, so it drew little suspicion when he walked past groups of his fellow students and into the Residence Hall. He rushed to the stairs and up to the fifth floor. Away from prying eyes, Simeon locked his door and scrambled to unroll Gerolt's note.

Dearest friend,

I can't tell you how grateful I am to have found such a worthy co-conspirator. Now that we are not in public, I can talk openly about my distaste for the League and what I plan to do about it. If you choose to aid me in freeing the prisoner we spoke of, you will be doing so much more than helping out a stranger.

What I couldn't tell you in the café is that this prisoner is being held under the accusations of illegal use of hysteresis and aiding in the escape of a Purity Maiden. If what they claim is true, this prisoner proves to be quite dangerous as the aforementioned Purity Maiden escaped by having the reinforced steel door of her purity room blown apart. There is no guarantee the prisoner had anything to do with this, but the escaped Maiden could tell us for certain. My experience with both parties leads me to believe that there is more afoot here than the two of them. One way or another, the League must pay for their abuses of power. If I haven't convinced you yet, I would kindly ask you to burn this note and not read any further.

If you are still reading, I assume you are the willing confidant within the League I have been searching for, and for that, I am eternally grateful. While I can't lay out my plans in their entirety just yet, I can tell you what I need you to do first.

It is quite serendipitous that you are an apprentice. From what I have gathered, apprentices are a blank slate, not yet assigned to their role within the League. Until recently, I assumed everyone trained themselves in hysteresis, doing little else but walking about the city like a bunch of untouchable bureaucrats. The best of you will work in the Hall of Weights and Scales, protecting the Council and running the legal system. While this assignment would have its benefits, I doubt it's in the realm of possibility given your lack of participation and enthusiasm within your school. I would like you to actively and aggressively seek to be placed in the unglamorous role of purity ward. I know this role is seen as the catch-all for disappointing recruits, but it serves our purpose perfectly. Not only will it give you access to the cells where the prisoner is being kept, but it will have you working under Warden Krenshaw. Other than knowing he is a hysteresis user of some sort, I know virtually nothing about the man. Any information you can gather about the warden will be invaluable as our plan unfolds. Once you have been assigned to the role of purity ward, come to the Crystal Pedestal and tell one of the Providers you have an issue in purity to report. Once you have completed this first task, I will give you phase two of the plan.

Burn this note once you have committed it to memory.

- G

CHAPTER 33
UNBOUND

A gust of cool air blew across Wren's face, stirring her from her restless sleep. A light groan escaped her lips as she moved her lazy eyes around the large tent the rebels had provided as her private quarters. Patches of different shapes and sizes littered its walls, making it hard to determine its original color. Her mattress was stuffed with sheep's wool. The bed's hard wooden base pushed it around as she slept, creating wandering lumps that would spring up in the most uncomfortable places.

By all appearances, her entire life had been downgraded— no more lavish dresses, pristine walls, or fancy mattresses. No more illustrious clients or domineering Providers. A small smile tugged at the corners of her mouth. She would have traded it all for so much less. Wren swung her legs over the side of her bed. The cold ground sent waves of wakefulness through her. She lifted the hem of her filthy traveling dress to her nose. It reeked of body odor, dried sweat, and campfire smoke. A trunk full of musty pants and roughly sewn tops sat at the foot of her bed. Wren's heart sang as she dug through the trunk, selecting her attire from the slight variations of the same bland clothing. She never would have imagined such a trivial thing giving her so much joy, but something about it made her feel normal. Like she had reclaimed a bit of the true self. The one she knew at the house on the lake. The one filled with wonder and curiosity. The one who made her own choices about her life and her gift. The one who did more than just exist.

New clothes in hand, Wren stripped off her soiled dress and slipped a leg into a pair of scratchy brown pants. She wobbled back and forth, trying to line up a raised leg with the proper hole while keeping her balance with the other. Her raised leg caught on the waistband at the same moment her grounded leg stepped on the end of the pants. She thrashed around, waving her arms in a wild attempt to maintain her footing. Aside from feeling like a complete fool, she couldn't help but laugh. Lying in the dirt, wearing nothing but one pant leg around her ankles, Wren smiled. She used to be allowed to fail—to make choices that drove the direction of her life. Something as simple as picking out her own clothes made her feel a little better about yesterday's life-altering choices.

A few moments after she managed to get her clothes on, Oriella poked her head into Wren's tent. "Good morning, Wrenny," she chirped as chipper as ever.

Wren smiled warmly before giving a sarcastic courtesy. "Good morning, Ori. Do you like my stylish attire? I picked it out myself."

"Oh, very nice, indeed. I hear that itchy wool pants really attract a good customer base," Oriella responded, adding in her characteristic giggle. "All kidding aside, Wren. I've never seen you look so beautiful. Your eyes shine in a way I've never seen before."

Wren had been called beautiful countless times. This time, it actually felt like a compliment. "Thank you, Ori. Any idea what the plan is for this morning?"

"Not a clue. I'm not even sure half of these people know how to tell time. They go about their day as if they never heard the word *schedule* before. I sure hope their meetings are a bit more thought out. Otherwise, my dad and I will be having a little chat."

"Good morning, ladies," Dawn interjected as she strode into Wren's tent. "Looks like you're both early risers. It'll be a few more hours before the morning meeting starts. Come with me. I'll find you both some breakfast."

After inhaling some crudely made sausage and day-old bread, Dawn offered to give the girls a small tour of Alice Square, a small area in the southwest corner of the LHC where Aequalitatem set up base camp.

"If you look slightly south and east, you will see Atlas Hill. The meeting tent is located at the base of it. That's also where you will find most of the members of the inner circle housed. Over here on the north side of the square is where we house new recruits. We like to keep them separate from the inner circle until they have proven themselves worthy of our trust. I'm here because I'm in charge of training and assessing all new recruits. That small creek just north of the recruit tents marks the edge of Alice Square. Follow the path on the other side, and you will find yourself in the LHC's marketplace. That's where you can find the best taverns as well as merchant tents of various kinds. It's also where you might run into a different brand of residents. Down here in Alice Square, we have a strict set of heavily enforced rules that keep us from falling into the chaos and debauchery that has infested the rest of the LHC. Our rules are simple: no killing or maiming, no stealing or kidnapping, no raping or molesting, and no spice."

"What's spice?" asked Wren.

"Spice refers to anything sold by the Spicers. A guild that produces and distributes various types of drugs, hallucinogens, and other poisons. Trust me, nothing they sell is worth a single copper. Stick to our rules, and you are free to stay with us as long as you like. If today's meeting goes as planned, you will be joining the rest of the inner circle by Atlas Hill soon enough."

"You intend to make us part of the inner circle?" asked Wren. "I thought you said recruits had to earn your trust first."

"I did, but that rule is to ensure that there are no League sympathizers or spies amongst them. We aren't worried about those things with the two of you. Frankly, I couldn't think of a less likely spy for the League if I had to. Well, enough chit chat for now. The meeting will start as soon as the sunset peaks over Atlas Hill. We wouldn't want the belles of the ball to be late, now would we?"

The three women made their way into the large meeting tent. Dawn pulled up short as they entered. "Wow. I don't think I've ever seen this many show up on time, let alone early." Dawn shot her two walking companions a look of concern. "All of these early birds mean one of two things. Either they are anxious to show you their support, or they're itching to send you both packing."

Wren took a seat between Dawn and Oriella in the innermost circle of the meeting tent and waited for the rest of the members of Aequalitatem to arrive. The more influential members sat in the center circle with veteran members filling in the Outer Ring. Additional attendees stood in the back and filed out the door of the large meeting tent. The crowd's rumbling murmur escalated to a healthy buzz once the three women took their seats.

"Greetings, friends," hollered Nico, signaling the start of the full circle meeting. The many conversations swirling through the crowd died down to a few whispers. "It seems word has spread quickly since our new friends' arrival late last night. It is my sincere hope that each and every one of you has come bearing an open-mind and an embracing heart. For those of you who may not have heard, the purpose of this meeting is to vote in our two newest recruits as full members of the inner circle, granting them instant access to inner circle meetings and all the intel we have collected over the years."

An old, weary voice broke through a sea of quiet musings. "And why should we grant such undeserved privileges to a couple of fresh recruits, and Purity Maidens at that!"

Another voice piped up from the outer circle. "Yeah! I've been here for months, and I've never gotten such a fancy meeting. It all feels a bit fishy to me." Several voices could be heard around the tent, giving their support to the questions.

Nico raised his arms and waited for the crowd to quiet. "We will explain our reasoning in due time, but for now, I ask that you keep your questions and snide remarks to yourself until the inner circle has presented its case in its entirety." The tent responded to Nico's firm and resolute tone. "Good. Now, if we can maintain order, I will open the floor for members of the inner circle to speak their mind on the matter at hand."

After a few more moments of ever quieting chatter, Shanks stood to take center stage. Nico held his breath. "As you all know, I am one of several members who used to belong to one of the three great guilds of old. As guilders, we hold a lot of bitterness in our hearts. Bitterness for the current state of our guilds and for the League's bastardization of their once glorious selves. Guilders save a special place of contempt in their hearts for Purity Maidens such as these. It's their so-called 'gifts' that sucked the power and influence right out of our guilds."

Wren shot Oriella a nervous glance. Oriella kept her eyes locked onto Shanks. Face unusually expressionless and flat. Wren turned her attention back to the weathered old man.

"We watched for years as our most loyal customers melted away one by one, forcing all of us down dark and treacherous paths. All of what I say is true, yet I stand before you today, a former member of the Guild of Spicers, and say"—Shanks paused, meeting Oriella's flat stare—"Let. It. Go." Oriella's face retook it's joyful shape. Shanks stifled a smirk of his own before shaking it off and firming his resolve. "It took me way too long to realize that the true source of my hatred came from my own guild! For allowing itself to fall in line with the League's gutting of society. Purity Maidens such as these are nothing more than young girls who have been forced to use their gifts to further the League's power. It has taken me this long to admit it, but freeing the Maidens of the cage that has been placed on their minds is the best shot we have of taking down the League..." Shank's tough demeanor began to waiver as his tone shifted down an octave. "And it starts with the two ladies you see sitting before you." He bellowed while tears pulled at the corners of his eyes. "Two ladies brave enough and strong enough to get this far. These Maidens have already stood up to the League more than all of our guilds combined. So, I say give them more than your vote, give them your all. The fate of Aequalitatem, of the LHC, and of all of New Geneva rests in their delicate hands!"

Nico swelled with pride as the rough-skinned guilder stood before his fellow members, hollering his support. Shank's humility and boldness set the tone for the rest of the meeting, ending with a near-unanimous decision to embrace the escaped Maidens as full members of Nico's inner circle.

As the meeting tent began to clear, Nico gave the signal for the inner circle to stay. The vote opened the door for the rest of what Nico planned for the Maidens today. "I can't say how proud it makes me to see Aequalitatem live up to its name. Shanks, I'm especially impressed with your ability to put your own bitterness and resentment behind for the greater good. We are all united by a common cause, and that cause is seeing the League fall from power." Everyone around the circle nodded in agreement, eyes fixating intently on their leader. "Before I reveal some of the last pieces of information I have kept hidden from you all, I need to get our two newest members up to speed. This first piece of information might be the hardest for our two newest members to swallow." Nico paused, gathering himself before continuing. He turned to face Wren and Oriella. "If you had known me five years ago, you would have known me as Nicolai Romanski, apprentice of the School of Density, and student of Sr. Father Malachi of the League's Grand Council." Nico held his breath. The few seconds of silence following his announcement hung in the air.

"So, what did you do?" Oriella asked as if she couldn't care less about Nico's past involvement with the League. "To get kicked out, I mean."

Nico's eyes darted around the circle. Nobody had asked him that before. He always told them he deserted the League due to the atrocities he saw on a daily basis. That always seemed good enough for them. While Nico did abandon the League, his reasons for doing so weren't nearly so simple...or honorable. His mind searched for the right words. Words that would allow him to keep his place as leader. Words that wouldn't send his faithful group reaching for his throat.

"He didn't *do* anything. He didn't like what he saw, that's all," Shanks replied, saving Nico from a very difficult conversion. Nico always planned on telling his friends the whole story, but the right moment never seemed to present itself. He already had to tell the Maidens about his previous association with the League. Pushing his luck any further might break their trust.

"Yes. Thank you, Shanks. Quite right. I left the League because I could no longer stand their unjust methodology. I joined to try and make a difference. Instigate change from within, but the system is too broken to fix. It must be destroyed."

"What you once were doesn't matter much to me," responded Wren. "If you can see past the label of Purity Maiden placed on us, then the least I can do is return the favor. With that being said, there is one thing that still bothers me. If you are a Density user, then those ropes you had yourself bound in the other night didn't exactly make you defenseless. You could have disintegrated them in seconds, couldn't you? I never had any *real* control, did I?"

Nico put up his hands in mock defeat. "I won't deny it, but I wouldn't go so far as to say that you had no control. I chose to keep myself bound, placing the power firmly in your hands. Sometimes not using the full extent of your power is merciful, even morally right, but there are other times where the opposite is true. Possessing the power to take control is not the same thing as employing that power. Sometimes keeping the ropes on is the right thing to do. Other times, it's just easier. So, what will it be Wren? Are we going to fight this battle bound, or free?"

Wren searched the other's faces for clues. Nico met her confusion with a slight smile. "It seems I owe you a bit of an explanation. Last night, after the two of us spoke, I went to find Oriella. After she confirmed your claims of using what appears to be an augmented version of hysteresis, we summoned the others. Oriella and I have already filled in the rest of the group about the details of your escape. Once we convinced them of its truth, they did something very rare. They didn't argue. They all agreed our first big step toward balancing the power should be in helping you embrace yours."

Everyone turned to Wren, waiting to hear what she had to say. Wren sat in contemplation for quite some time, struggling with the two voices consistently at war within her head. The first voice spoke of impurity. Of a girl that had lost her way and abandoned her family. It coerced her to stick to the rules she had been given, stop holding onto false hope, and know her place.

The second voice was softer but had grown louder and louder as of late. It spoke of injustices—the death of a brother, the outlawing of freedom, the loss of a loving mother and father, and the crime of a shackled gift. She allowed this second voice a larger place. It confirmed what she already knew. She had always been more than the League's pet. She had so much more to offer the world than altering clothes and serving the privileged.

Impure girl! The first voice snapped. *The purity rooms will help you see!* The two voices raged within her. The time had come for Wren to decide which voice would shape her future, and which voice would get buried in her past.

Wren had not come this far to give in to the League's mind games. She didn't leave her family behind, illegally blow a hole in her prison cell, and entrust her life to a group of rebels she barely knew for nothing. She thought of the house by the lake. A third voice cut through the confusion of the first two. *"It's your gift, Wren. What are you going to do with it?"*

Wren locked eyes with Nico. "I'm in." Oriella squealed in delight as the others exchanged smiles. "Just tell me one thing. How do you plan on helping me unbind this unexplainable form of hysteresis?"

"I'm not," replied Nico. "That will be the job of Esteban Cortez."

The whole group gave a collective gasp. Wren's eyes went wide as she recalled the figure with the shifting bones from the Hollowlands of her childhood. The hooded figure who risked their life for hers, only to disappear without a trace. Wren spoke her mind before the others could catch their breath. "Esteban is alive? Has he been wandering the Hollowlands all this time?" Wren turned to the rest of the group. "Don't tell me you all knew about this too."

Randle spoke up for them all. "After all these years, I thought I knew all of Nico's dirty little secrets. Trust me when I tell you that this is the first any of us has heard of Esteban Cortez for quite some time. We all assumed he'd been tortured to death by Solomon. I mean, can you imagine a monster like Solomon Pipher letting such a disappointing apprentice roam free? Tell us, Nico. Is Esteban really alive, and if he is, how the bloody hell did you go about locating him?"

"That's a long story, friend, and I'm afraid I can't reveal all my cards just yet. For now, rest in the fact that if anyone can help Wren discover the mysterious forms of hysteresis she is harnessing, it's him. There's just one problem."

"What's that?" replied Randle, as the rest of the group leaned forward in ardent anticipation of Nico's response.

"While Esteban might have escaped Solomon's wrath with his life, he did not get out unscathed..." Wren recalled the shrieks of pain as Esteban's bone's wandered under his skin. The pain came off him in waves. Wren could feel it tug at the corners of her heart. She couldn't imagine what such pain would have done to him after all these years. All eyes returned to Nico. "His mind is...hanging on, but he doesn't have much time left."

"So? Let's get moving! What's the hold up? I have more

than a few questions for the bastard anyway!" bellowed Shanks.

Nico held up his hand. "Okay, so, two problems..." The others waited with baited breath. "We'll have to cross the Hollowlands to find him."

NOTES

6. THE CRYSTAL PEDESTAL

1. *The Bible: Authorized King James Version.* Edited by Robert Carroll and Stephen Prickett, Oxford UP, 2008.

15. A BETRAYAL OF BLOOD

1. *The Bible: Authorized King James Version.* Edited by Robert Carroll and Stephen Prickett, Oxford UP, 2008.
2. *The Bible: Authorized King James Version.* Edited by Robert Carroll and Stephen Prickett, Oxford UP, 2008.
3. *The Bible: Authorized King James Version.* Edited by Robert Carroll and Stephen Prickett, Oxford UP, 2008.

www.ingramcontent.com/pod-product-compliance
Lightning Source LLC
Chambersburg PA
CBHW071218300726
48975CB00002B/276